MW01104380

This book was not yet complete or edited when it was mistakenly printed by the publishers. Besides the lack of editing and proofing, it has 80 pages less than the complete and edited version.

However, rather than destroy all these books, they are being made available at no cost to anyone who wishes to have a copy. It is hoped by the author that if the reader enjoys this book, they will at some time wish to buy the complete edited version and/or consider purchasing one of the pending sequels in the future.

Thank you for your consideration.

N.G. Meyers, April 26, 2018

ELYSIUM'S PASSAGE SERIES

Book One: THE SUMMIT

Book Two: SURREAL ADVENTURES
              Spring 2018

Book Three: MYSTICAL ROMANCE
              Fall 2018

Book Four: THE ELIXIR
              Spring 2019

Book Five: THE RETURN
              Fall 2020

ELYSIUM'S
PASSAGE

THE SUMMIT

Book One
in the Elysium Series

A Philosopher's Surreal Trek into the Mysterium of the Unknown Universe

N.G. MEYERS

Come further up, come further in

ⓒiUniverse®

ELYSIUM'S PASSAGE
THE SUMMIT

www.elysiumspassage.com
   Elysium's Passage Book Series
   Elysium's Passage@NGMeyers

iUniverse books may be ordered through booksellers or by contacting:

iUniverse
1663 Liberty Drive
Bloomington, IN 47403
www.iuniverse.com
1-800-Authors (1-800-288-4677)

ISBN: 978-1-5320-2308-8 (sc)
ISBN: 978-1-5320-2309-5 (e)

Library of Congress Control Number: 2017908802

Print information available on the last page.

iUniverse rev. date: 06/13/2017

CONTENTS

Souls of poets dead and gone,
What Elysium have ye known,
Happy field or mossy cavern,
Choicer than the Mermaid Tavern
Have ye tippled drink more fine
Than mine host's Canary wine?
Lines on the Mermaid Tavern

John Keats, 1795 – 1821

PROLOGUE TO THE SERIES

Hi, my name is James. I'm a lecturer in the Department of Philosophy at one of the universities in London, England. Don't let that concern you though, I don't wish to overwhelm you with a lot of philosophical terms, concepts and jargon in order to show you how clever I am. In fact, my girlfriend says I'm not as smart as I think I am. Although I know she's just trying to keep me humble, I think she's probably right. I mean, if we are to be honest, what do any of us understand about ultimate reality; we hardly see anything past our entrenched beliefs and narrow prejudices.

In *The Summit*, my first narrative of the *Elysium's Passage series,* you will witness me receiving my comeuppance as a slightly cocky *know-it-all* instructor. Yes, I was beaten, whipped, broken and laid bare: stripped of all my intellectual pretences. Well, at least it felt that way to my bruised ego. But I now understand how necessary it was for me to learn these important lessons in humility before I could acquire true wisdom. The challenges and events I encountered did much to rid me of the rubbish that had accumulated in my mind over the years. I didn't realize it then, but I had acquired many limiting beliefs that impaired my ability and desire to comprehend an infinitely larger reality, far beyond what could be discerned through the foggy lens of this world.

Not long after arriving in the Andes for a mountain climbing expedition, I was confronted with a totally different ascent than what I had anticipated. As you follow along, you may come to agree that what I experienced was the ultimate life adventure! Having survived this *crash course,* I came to understand all the clever stuff I thought I knew before wasn't so clever after all. In fact much of it was just plain wrong.

Too often in the past, my thoughts were like shape-shifting clouds drifting in whatever direction the winds of professional acceptability blew. What I came to understand during my time on the mountain summit, is that we all have an inherent capacity to access a higher wisdom that informs and transcends the limitations of our reasoning mind. By discovering who we are, we come to understand that truth is accessed from within the centre of our being, metaphorically referred to as the heart.

Sure, the cold calculating intellect may be the processer of information, but its analysis is of limited temporal value if it doesn't join with the heart's wisdom. Pascal said in his *Pensées: the heart has its reasons, which reason cannot know.*[1] What I came to discover was how to discipline my confused mind to hear what my heart had to say first. With my academic orientation, it wasn't an easy lesson to learn.

It was some time after returning home from this prolonged adventure that I decided to compose a narrative of what happened to me, although it was several months before I became aware of the extraordinary events that had transpired. More correctly, I didn't decide to write about my adventure so much as I was compelled to put it out there by some very persistent and militant muses. I trust you will find it just as compelling to read.

Much of what I first discovered came from a long series of discussions I had with a couple of companions I met on this mountain summit. They were far more advanced and wiser than me, and what they communicated was often contrary to what I thought I knew. So not only did I have to become a student all over again, I also had to unlearn many of my old assumptions. I didn't realize it then, but I had been thoroughly inculcated with many unsubstantiated beliefs through years of institutional teaching and conditioning. I recognize, therefore, what I say may not be appreciated or judged favourably by colleagues holding to their fixed views on the meaning of reality.

I also wish to relate what one of my wise friends on the Mountain asked me to communicate to humanity. He said we should discover how to live as spirit when we're not a spirit. By this, I think he meant we should try to become more aware of how we are immortal spirits inhabiting a mortal body on earth for a brief period of time. If we

---

[1] Blaise Pascal (1623–1662), French philosopher and scientist.

understand this, we will live not for only the outward world of form, but primarily in accord with the spiritual essence of what we are, now and forever.

I didn't understand this before, but since returning, I have no doubt he was right: we are spirits utilizing our outward material form to give purpose and dignity to our lives. No matter how many bodily distractions draw us away from this realization, I believe if we take the time to look deeply within it becomes obvious how infinitely expansive the Source of our spirit is.

You may wonder why the name *Elysium* is found throughout this series of books. The word possesses a rich variety of meanings associated with the idea of paradise and the afterlife in classical prose and poetry found first in Homer, then in other works by such poets as Virgil, Plutarch, Shakespeare, Dante and Schiller. It will be shown in the first book how and why this name was chosen.

These five narratives, are not intended to only discuss interesting ideas and concepts, but to take you on a sensational and often enchanting spiritual journey; my journey. I invite you now to join me on my trek through Elysium's Passage as we explore a universe that allows for infinite adventures and inward expansion.

I experienced a surreal free fall into a new consciousness that led me to discover who I am and continue to become. Through these tales, it is my desire that you will be inspired to plunge into a deeper realm of conscious awareness as you find your own surreal portal that leads towards Elysium.

Note: Throughout the narratives, I have italicized words that I wish to emphasize and, in most cases, have used italics in most cases for internal quotes rather than quotes marks. Various recurring words such as 'Mountain', 'Summit' and 'Lowlands,' are capitalized where a metaphorical meaning may be associated with the literal sense. Sometimes when both seem to apply, I've gone with capitalization.

In accordance with British tradition, external quote marks are single and double with internal quotes, which in the latter case, have generally been replaced by Italics.

INTRODUCTION

ELYSIUM'S PASSAGE: THE SUMMIT
Who looks outside, dreams; who looks inside, awakens[1]

This narrative begins with a most unusual allegory that came to me in an intensive dream one night which, as it turned out, would foreshadow the direction of my future life. The symbolic nature of the objects and environments I encountered reminded me of the allegorical meanings I read of in *Pilgrim's Progress*.[2] My dream experience had a similar quality to it: the most provocative interpretative expression of my life up to that point, including various deficiencies not so obvious to me, though they likely were to others.

Also, you will notice that on my title page I included the words, *"come further up, come further in"*. These few words sum up the primary theme of this book and my new life. If you are familiar with C.S Lewis' works, you may recognize this phrase as the one that was cried out as the characters effortlessly went further up and further into the New Narnia, as described in *The Last Battle*; the concluding book in the Chronicles of Narnia series. Only after my adventure, did I come to understand the meaning Lewis meant to convey with this phrase.

As we ascend our Mountains further up and further in, we continue to gain greater clarity and vision in seeing who we are and why we are on earth. Whatever our path may be, we are all on a trek through life. I wish now to share my very strange venture taking me *further in and further up* on a journey far beyond what I could have imagined.

---

[1] Carl Jung (1875-1961), founder of Analytical Psychology.

[2] Likely most famous example of an allegorical story in the English language is John Bunyan's 1678 classic *Pilgrim's Progress*.

CHAPTER 1

A REALLY CRAZY DREAM

It's a dangerous business, Frodo, going out your door. You step onto the road, and if you don't keep your feet, there's no knowing where you might be swept off to.[1]

I t had been a very stressful week for me at university as I lectured to several over-enrolled introductory philosophy classes by day while diligently marking stacks of midterm essay examinations by night. After barely making the submission deadlines this Friday afternoon, I returned to my flat and collapsed on the bed, completely knackered. But there was still too much going on in my mind for my body to rest, so I got up and poured a half glass of rum. Then I poured another and another to settle my anxieties. Feeling much lighter and more relaxed now, I said a prayer to my favourite god on Mount Olympus.

Officially, I would have described myself as an agnostic, as would many of the philosophers in my department who pride themselves on their scepticism. The prayer, if that's what it was, was completely ingenuous. In jest I said, 'Zeus, if you're still hiding somewhere up there, I need you come down for a while to give me a (bleeping) break. Things aren't working out so well here these days.'

---

[1] Bilbo Baggins *The Lord of the Rings*, J.R.R. Tolkien

It was true; I was disenchanted with my life. I wanted to experience more purpose for my life but wasn't sure what that was or where I might find it. I even began to consider dropping out of society for a few years to find what I was looking for by going to Tibet or the Andes. These places had a lot of appeal to me ever since I became an avid mountain climber while completing my Master's programme in Canada. But as I considered doing this, the cynic in me would say if I couldn't find myself in London, I wouldn't find myself anywhere else.

I was becoming increasingly troubled with my fledgling career, which did little to allay my financial instability. Also, my inability to establish even one satisfactory relationship with a woman was beginning to frustrate me. Outwardly, I had a number of things going for me including my academic credentials, physical appearance and roguish charm. Certainly, when it served my purposes, I was able to use my debonair persona to attract many women into my life and bed over the years. Keeping them there was another matter.

This evening, however, I was hoping to put all my cares behind me, having previously arranged to meet a very attractive brunette for a dinner date. I had recently met her during a charity event at the university, and was most impressed with her confident demeanor. Not only was she well-read and articulate, she had recently earned an MBA and was already working as a senior investment analyst for some major corporation in a Canary Wharf office tower.

Unfortunately, things didn't go too well for us that evening. Perhaps I should have imbibed something less toxic while I waiting for her. Anyway, by the time she turned up at our reserved table, over a half hour late, I may add, I already decided I didn't like her very much. It appeared evident that this was a power ploy to let me know who was most important and who had the real job. Obviously, she had better things to do other than mark term papers written by adolescent students. But considering her pretty face and revealing cleavage, I thought I'd make the best of the situation, try to be pleasant, and see where things might lead; hopefully in the direction of my bedroom.

My problem, however, in attempting to make interesting conversation with her, was that we lived in two very different worlds – which is why I found it so difficult to relate to her incessant talk involving international commerce and her stellar career. I guess I should have been impressed, but from my jaundiced perspective, I decided she wasn't authentic. Her upwardly mobile pretences didn't do anything for me except to make me feel inferior, which is not exactly a turn on. In most cases I'm willing to tolerate such affectations if the intent is to impress me, but it seemed she was more interested in impressing herself.

I tried to be civil, but I'm sure she soon became aware of the bored look on my face, except on occasion, when my eyes may have inadvertently drifted below her neckline. After a couple more glasses of wine following dinner, I suggested we take a taxi back to my place to get to know each other better. She wasn't stupid, as she curtly declined my less than subtle suggestion. I was further chagrined when she insisted on paying half of our dining tab, as if to make it very clear I had no claim on her. Most ungracious, I thought; certainly not how I had planned the evening.

As she left to catch a taxi to go home, I muttered something most unflattering, which she probably didn't hear – but if she did, I didn't care. I can be as obnoxious as any pickled bloke *under the influence*; and by then I most certainly was. At the time, I was very upset with how things turned out and how she rebuffed me; cold and dismissive, as though passing on some marginal investment at work. But as I thought about it the next day, I could hardly blame her for how she responded to my uncouth advances.

Things might have turned out better later that evening had I taken my lumps and gone home to bed. But oh no, I needed to recover some of my ego esteem by making my way to a somewhat less dignified establishment to seek out a new acquaintance prepared to ride home with me for the night. No such luck, even though by now I was prepared to significantly compromise my standards for the night. I suppose drunk isn't considered very sexy, unless the other is just as drunk.

Even worse than enduring the rude dismissive rejections and rolled eyes, was the little skirmish I had just after midnight with an oversized Godzilla bouncer standing at the door. I noticed he had been observing my deteriorating condition for some time, and so I decided he should be informed of my professional credentials. I walked over to him, though not so steadily, and informed him who I was. Not surprisingly, he didn't seem interested in hearing about the scholarly papers I would hopefully be presenting at the finest institutions in Britain and on the European continent.

Rather than being impressed, he preferred to treat me as some common drunk. Sure, I told him, maybe I was little drunk, but dammit, I wasn't a drunk. As I staggered to the water closet, he suggested I find a cab to take me home. Likely it didn't help that I had a contrary opinion. Venting some of my more creative expressions I had acquired during my short bout as a sailor probably didn't help. And likely telling him to 'get stuffed, you fuggin ape,' had something to do with my intimate encounter with the cement sidewalk outside after being unceremoniously escorted out the door. I suppose it didn't help that I took an inept swing at him. And so, the only thing I came away with that night was a bloodied face and a badly damaged ego.

I suppose he was only doing his job, but in my stupor it felt like the greatest humiliation of my life. On my way home, I pondered how I would explain my new face art to my students in class, not to mention various colleagues in the faculty lounge. It also occurred to me how thin the veneer of our civil personas can be, particularly when in an altered state of intoxicated consciousness. I was angry with myself in knowing how I would have stood up to him as a sailor in the days of my invincible youth. I survived several late night forays, with a few decisive brawl wins mixed in for fun and variety. Generally, I came out relatively unscathed at these pugilist events while docked at various Mediterranean ports.

Now look at me, I thought, sipping on lattes with the faculty stiffs! What happened to the street fighter? Apparently I had lost my touch after years of becoming outwardly genteel in the refined academic world. Obviously, I was out of my element on both these fronts tonight; not much of a fighter nor particularly genteel.

I thought it rather sad how, in an effort to establish a secure career, my esteemed salty sea life had been eclipsed by all the stifling civility around me. Muddled reflections of my misspent youth swirled around in my mind as I lay slouched, half passed out across the backseat of the cab, with my nose bleeding. Unbeknownst to me while riding home that night, I was being readied for something most extraordinary that would forever alter my life and character.

I recognize that I'm not presenting a very flattering picture of myself, especially with regard to my conduct that evening. Hardly what you would expect from a man of letters! But I wish you to appreciate the low point from where I was to begin my upward spiritual ascent. Though I had to start somewhere, I could never have imagined at the time that I would soon be led towards a new dimension of awareness and reality.

Like most of us, I had my quirks, strengths, weaknesses and a variety of other *charming* idiosyncrasies. And I suppose I always will. But whatever my foibles, let's just say, notwithstanding my philosophy degree, I still had a lot to learn about life and relationships back then. As was evident with my date that night, it would never have occurred to me that what I perceived in her had everything to do with projecting my fears and insecurities upon her. It was an established pattern I wasn't yet aware of.

Then, something very strange occurred to me that night after I collapsed on my bed and *passed out* for the night; my battered body convalescing from self- inflicted wounds and dissipations. What came to me that night was a most explicit dream with exquisite colours and images with a mystical twist. I suppose those qualities are often normal in dreams, but this dream had a disturbing scene at the end; a most dreadful climax without any final resolution.

I had no idea what it meant, but as I awoke in a panic, it seemed I was about to fall through an abyss. I've had dreams of flying before, but this one didn't promise to be a happy flight. Now fully alert, I stumbled across the room to my computer to record my vivid impressions. Detailed scenes remained emblazoned in my psyche, feeling larger than life. Because it was so unusual, I really wanted to capture all I could as quickly as possible, even though I still had a splitting headache. I didn't bother to turn on a light, since the sky was beginning to lighten with dawn. The more I wrote, the more came back to me with images of strange lands and people that eventually led to an excruciating but exhilarating mountain climbing adventure.

It was a most extraordinary experience. In the days and weeks ahead, I thought often of what I dreamt and new impressions would come to me which I would add to the file. Over time, I sensed my life was taking on a whole new trajectory. It was subtle, but something about it felt like an epiphany that would eventually alter the course of my life.

Normally, I'm not one to remember dreams very well. In fact, if I do have one, I tend to ignore it unless it involves some uninhibited young feline springing onto my bed. However, on rare occasions, certain significant dreams that reoccur will stick with me much longer; some even extending back into my troubled childhood.

This time, however, I knew something profound was brewing in the subliminal spheres of my mind. Rather than fading away, it seemed to become more pronounced, to the point the impressions intruded into my thoughts throughout the day, often distracting me while I lectured. Even the common experiences of daily life had an intriguing mystical hue surrounding them; it was as though my mind was beginning to drift into some rarified domain of conscious awareness. And yet, in some ways life began to feel more purposeful than ever before. My thoughts were deeper and more meaningful, often much happier than in the past, as though I knew I was going someplace without really knowing where.

Though I didn't actually recognize the places and objects in the dream, what I saw felt like various symbols and metaphors that at times seemed to represent various struggles in my life. Previously unrecognized aspirations were given form and meaning, along with many sorrows and disappointments; which is what made this experience so unforgettable in the days and weeks ahead. I couldn't shake it, and so I remained puzzled by the curious impact the dream was having on me. There seemed to be so many contradicting images and messages that often made me feel both sad and hopeful at the same time.

While sleeping at times, I would awaken enshrouded in fear, and yet whatever impending doom awaited me, would not reveal itself. On other occasions, particularly when walking along the Thames, I would receive exhilarating flashes of myself ascending a very high and challenging Mountain. Whenever this occurred, I would sit on my favourite bench in a park nearby the river and contemplate whatever was being evoked within me. It felt like a longing to experience something more meaningful than what was being offered in my life now.

Was there some hidden message in the images intended to jar

me out of my mediocre existence? Some of the dreary scenes at the beginning reminded me of being stuck and disempowered, others spoke to me about being liberated from everything that held me back. But before I go further with how the dream proceeded, let me provide a little background to my life that may give better context to what these images may have been telling me.

As an orphan, my earliest years remained rather unhappy while living in various foster homes in the Liverpool area. Mercifully, I was finally taken in by relatives who must have taken pity on me after their children had gone out on their own. Fortunately, my great uncle possessed an appreciation for the classics and advanced learning which served me well, since I was naturally endowed with a sufficient degree of intelligence to assimilate complex ideas of higher understanding. With his influence, my inner world soon opened to exciting books and utopian ideas.

As I later became a young adult, this provided a basis for me to become caught up in several fashionable ideologies and social liberation movements, as envisioned and espoused in the humanist writings of Voltaire, Marx and Huxley. Consequently, I didn't question science's promise of salvation through the pursuit of pure, objective knowledge of all material reality.

Thereafter, whatever religious moorings I had held from my early childhood memories were tossed aside for this utopian idealism; at least for a while. By the time I entered into undergraduate studies, I had already become disillusioned and cynical about life and the direction the world was going. I had hoped philosophy would help me find purpose on earth and what I was doing here. But later, after reading Nietzsche, Freud, and Sartre, I fell into my own existential *Weltschmerz* as I despaired of ever finding meaningful answers to life's questions.[1]

I was finally able to break this sullen spell after enrolling in my Master's graduate programme at the University of Calgary in Canada. The Philosophy department was highly recommended for its excellence,

---

[1] Weltschmerz is a loaded German term often found and elucidated in the works of Herman Hess, Heinrich Hein and several other literary luminaries exploring man's pervasive condition. The word conveys a meaning of world weariness associated with anxiety, pain and existential despair.

with many of its philosophers having strong ties in Britain.[1] My two years there did much to improve my attitude towards life as I began to develop several significant relationships, both academically and socially.

But nothing could have been better for my character development than climbing the highest peaks throughout the majestic Canadian Rockies. And though I was able to advance in my academic achievements, still none of the ultimate answers I hoped to find were forthcoming. By the time I completed my doctorate in Edinburgh, Scotland, I had resigned myself to the fact that whatever deeper meaning I was looking for would likely remain forever unknown, at least to me.

Now in my early thirties, I was growing weary and cynical towards science, religion and even philosophy. They all disappointed me as being tainted with contrivance, distortion and exploitation for power and gain throughout history. For a season, I indulged in wanton promiscuity until I grew bored with all the meaningless relationships I endured. These flings only reinforced the existential angst of being part of the problem. Yet, even in my frustration of finding meaning and purpose, something in me never gave up; not completely. I wanted to believe someday I would find a way to higher ground, beyond the bogs where I remained stuck.

And so it was that infamous night at the pub, when I felt I had hit bottom, both literally and figuratively, the dream came to me as a flicker of light, dimly shining through the cracks of my broken life. A line in Leonard Cohen's lyrics from *Anthem* speaks of how the light enters through the crack.[2] And Rumi, the Persian Sufi poet, made a similar observation centuries ago: *the wound is the place where the Light enters.*

For me, I first became aware of this light when the dream shone upon my soul that night. What I first heard and saw in my dream became indelibly imprinted in my psyche, never to leave me. In fact, it was more than just a dream; it was an extraordinary premonition that

_____

[1] A number of well known philosophers such as Anthony Flew, Kai Nielsen, C.B Martin, Terrence Penelhum were part of the faculty at one time.
[2] You will find the lyrics to Leonard Cohen's copyrighted lines of *Anthem* on the web.

would soon lead me to several more cracks, including some to my body that almost fatally wounded me.

Interestingly, during the beginning stages, there was a commentator guiding me through the images, events and peculiar landscapes I was observing in my sleeping consciousness. I didn't understand it at the time, but still I could feel this was my story. I thought it most peculiar that someone from another dimension would presume to speak to me about me and my life. Mysteriously, the sonorous voice seemed to emanate from far beyond; a place it identified as being on top of a Mountain far above the clouds. Perhaps Zeus had deigned to answer me after all.

Wherever the voice came from, it spoke with uncompromised authority. I was disturbed at first by how imposing it seemed while enjoining me to accept a new calling for my life. Was this some fate to which I was being beckoned? I wasn't sure what to think. At first it seemed a distant echo: *James, prepare to leave your world.* I half awoke, startled by the abrupt words. Was I about to die? Then I fell back, this time into a very deep sleep before the voice returned, becoming clearer and more personal than before.

> "Listen to us James; we speak to you from high above your plane on a Summit where you often unawares, seek, to join us. From our lofty ridge, we view your life in the lands far below. We may appear very far away but we are very near; we dwell here even while we dwell within your mind to which we now speak, for we are all of one Mind.

> "As we survey the wonderful vistas beyond us, we regret those who have no wish to leave the Lowlands below to discover the wonders of what lies beyond. Though you still remain unaware of who you are and where you're going, we can tell you the Lowlands are no longer your home; you belong here with us because you are of us. Yes, the people you're with have influenced you with their perspectives and opinions; believing their forlorn reality is

the only reality. They say you live and then you die, your body's elements return to the muddy ruts out of which you arose, and that's all there is to life. That, however, is not how things are. Perhaps one day you may tell them the story we are about to tell you now. But you can only speak to those who, like you, imagine the existence of a Mountain in the far distance where we wait. Others will neither see nor hear; they have already decided what is real, though what they look upon is not real at all.

"In your sleeping consciousness you have oft heard our faint voice before and questioned whether it came to you from afar or if it was only of your mind. It matters not, the message is one and there is no separation. You sometimes long to join us here on vistas where you discover new mysterious realms on our side. We speak to you now because you are ready to be answered, just as all are answered who are willing to open their eyes to see what others cannot and will not see.

"As we stand high on this Mountain ridge with you in our sights, we ask that you put aside all thoughts of how you think this may be and try to understand what we have to say. When you come to discover the wondrous sights that lie far beyond the Lowlands' foggy images, you will know. You may not understand, for you have never been told, but we are telling you now. Your perceptions were formed in the Lowlands, a chimera you chose to believe and live in.

"Ask yourself why you cannot see this Mountain on which we stand. Is it real? What if it is more real than all you consider to be real? Tell us if you can, what is real? What makes it *real*, and how can you tell if it actually is? You need not answer us, but consider these questions as we invite you to join us for a season to enter into true knowledge and understanding, not as your world understands. No, we have something more significant in mind for you. But this will remain your choice; to join with us or forever remain in the Lowlands.

"We didn't make our dwelling on this ridge overlooking your world when we entered this threshold between the old and new worlds. But it's a special place you can join us for a time to discover new vistas of existence before you return. Since we departed your plane far below, we have only begun our forays into the infinite landscape of wondrous beauty and truth. It will always seem we are only beginning to move *further up, further in*.

"We now understand that there is no end to the ineffable splendour and indescribable dimensions of un-experienced experiences. You have long considering this quest, and so we call out to you now to join us where your soul longs to be; a domain you have long forgotten. Then one day, you too may reveal to your weary world something of the resplendence you have seen, heard and touched.

"Often you unwittingly gazed off into the distance towards the misty and mysterious peaks. There are others who dwell in the Lowland domains who sometimes share your vision, but few wish to give much attention to what lies beyond. But you did. As you gazed longingly in our direction towards heights unseen and unknown, you yearned to know what lies beyond the Lowlands' marshy *plane*. Ever more frequently you began to dream shadowy dreams with strange images, with strange voices saying *'higher up, further in.'* But to where? You didn't know what this was or where it came from, but it felt right. Maybe, you thought, one day you would be shown a way that would lead out, far beyond the stifling Lowlands.

"As your strange dreams and visions continued to ebb and flow over the years, they seemed to drift and meander without any specific meaning. At first the dreams were just impressions, but then they slowly congealed into something more; a curious knowingness, an inner gnosis reminding you of something. Perhaps it was you, or possibly an expression of who you were yet to become!

"Within the deepest recesses of your ancestral memories, something seemed to speak softly to you, saying you have not been abandoned, you belong to a reality much larger than the Lowlands. You hadn't heard this voice since you were a child. After your years of innocence, you forgot who you were and why you came to this world!

But recently you have become aware of something calling you out to you. And so you wonder if you should leave the Lowlands to seek higher ground towards a Mountain you don't know, and yet longingly envision when your mind is quieted.

"At such times you experience intimations of deep mysteries more wonderful and more majestic than you've ever known. But they also confused you. Such hallowed stirrings are contrary to everything you have experienced, just as they are contrary to what the brooding muck-raking inhabitants of the Lowlands understood or wanted to understand! Whatever these inklings may or may not be, you thought it would be best to remain silent. Such frivolous speculation is not well tolerated in the Lowlands, and so you spoke nary a word.

"As time passed, the calling didn't go away and you continued to nourish the hope engendered in your soul until it became an exciting presentiment of what could be. You began to muse that one day you would take the risk and leave the Lowlands, where all was safe and secure, and venture beyond. Whatever was calling you was something much greater than what could be known in the Lowlands.

"And so your discontentment grew as the amorphous fog hovered in the air where no one could get excited about anything other than their own predictable affairs. With no firm convictions, the air stagnated into thick swamp gases of debilitating apathy. In the mist, you found there was no vision or clarity of thought, and so nothing had purpose or meaning because nothing mattered. Perhaps it was the Lowlands' somniferous aether, but it didn't seem necessary or even advisable for one to think their own thoughts, since that may disturb their slumber. And so it was considered best not to stir things up too much.

"Making one's way along the boggy base was soft and easy. The ruts required little effort to meander through and there was never any concern about where one was going. Eventually all came back to where they started. For what purpose they continued to wander they weren't sure, but it didn't seem to matter. It was what everyone did. The deepest ruts were always the shortest and easiest routes to get to wherever they were going. With so many treading the same way, certain ruts kept wearing down deeper and deeper, making it increasingly difficult to climb out. Not that you would want to. What would be the point? So life's path was predetermined; the very notion of exercising free will was a fanciful illusion.

"They liked to be told what to do by those who didn't know of anything else to do except what had always been done. Thinking they had no choice made things seem easier and more secure, greatly preferred to the uncertainties and responsibilities choosing their own path. There wasn't much worth striving for or to be concerned about. But neither was there anything to become inspired over, they already had enough meaningless amusements to occupy themselves throughout their meaningless existences.

"However it was most inconvenient when the rain continued to pour for long periods. The soft ground would soon become very sticky in certain spots, and one could easily perish while caught in a rut. It was especially easy to sink down when the misty drizzle persisted for days on end.

"But you knew all about being stuck, and it wasn't a great feeling. As you reflected on all this, it became increasingly obvious that there had to be more to life than the ennui you experienced in the Lowlands! At some point you could no longer ignore this call from afar, you remained tentative and unsure, since you were unable to discern anything beyond the Lowlands' veil of mist. You had been told that there was nothing beyond the mist that could be seen or known.

"And yet, as you learned to focus your eyes on what may lie beyond the mist, you caught vague images and shifting shapes. You were not yet certain what they might be, but increasingly you gave more attention to it, albeit tentatively. Was there really a higher domain that beckoned you to leave, or was your imagination deceiving you into believing in something that didn't exist? You didn't know for certain when, but it seemed a time came when you realized you must leave.

"And so, late one evening you stole away into the darkness, avoiding the Lowlands' prying eyes. No one would see you leaving behind the mud, sludge and drudge, and all that felt familiar and safe to you. You didn't know what direction you should go, but you trusted that your inward call would lead you to a higher land. This hope, though still vague and undefined, became irresistible, indelibly impressing you with the mysterious images contained in your unconscious longings."

And with that, the otherworldly voice faded into the distance. I heard no more of its enchanting narration and yet my dream continuing to proceed onward, as I saw myself embarking on this epic journey out of a land the voice had called the Lowlands. Lucid images continued to be impressed upon my mind throughout this improbable trek into the unknown.

It felt it was days, or was it years, I saw myself wandering aimlessly through the Lowlands' boggy marshes. Then, finally, much to my amazement, I sensed a slow, gentle rise under my feet as my leg muscles constricting slightly from the incline's strain. This was rather peculiar to me, since flatness was all that I had known in the Lowlands. Yet here I was, being inwardly compelled, ever upward to a region unknown to me.

Though the fog obstructed my vision for a time, I forged on ahead, believing I was on the right path to wherever I needed to go. I remembered thinking how the Lowlands didn't approve of adventures such as this, and so few strayed very far away. As my austere hovel in the Lowlands retreated further into the forgettable past, I sensed a delectable tingle of rebellion within me.

Yes, I was finally becoming my own man! No matter what I might encounter, life or death, I would *live life as a lion for a day rather than a hundred years as a sheep.*[1] I swaggered onward and upward with a touch of disdain towards their smug mediocrity and complacency. Though the Lowlands' inhabitants would forever remain content socialized within

---

[1] An Old Italian proverb.

their insularity, I had left their fold. Look at me I thought, I'm no longer a sheep: I'm a lion. Yes, the lion has left and he's not coming back!

As I continued upward, I noticed how the ground under my feet was becoming increasingly firm and certain on this higher ground I had so long envisioned; far beyond the marshes, towards somewhere I had never been. No longer were my steps uncertain from traversing the mushy bogs where my footing was always uncertain.

I could see how the landscape was changing and the scenery was becoming more interesting the higher I ascended, yet the journey wasn't becoming any easier. My weary lungs began to labour as a result of the ever upward thrusts of the slopes. No, it wasn't easy, but it was exhilarating!

My muscles and organs were not accustomed to these gravitational stresses; this journey was so contrary to the relative ease of the flat, muddy plains. My body, however, was feeling vibrantly alive as my muscles continued to strengthen from the steep resistances. My determination extended to every molecule in my body's cells as I surged forward with sprints of coagulated energy, stoked by whatever challenges awaited me around each corner and over every precipice.

What vision was driving me to ascend *further up and further in*, I really didn't know. I only knew it felt it was coming from somewhere deeper than just my mind, which frequently protested my ascension. Though I still remained unclear where this journey may lead, I was now convinced this was the Mountain I had been envisioning through my hovel's window.

There would be no going back to the soft, purposeless bogs. My footing had become secure on the granite which provided even greater contrast to the marshes below. With each step forward and upward, I seemed to acquire new confidence, certain I could overcome whatever the obstacles might lay ahead. Though the terrain was strange and difficult, confronting fears as I scaled steep vertical escarpments, while balancing precariously on the narrow ridges; even leaping over deep fissures and ice crevices.

I told myself over and over there had to be a Summit at the top where I would experience new vistas beyond the other side. Then, at last, I would know for certain there was more, much more to my life than just languishing in the Lowlands. Although I realized I didn't know what awaited me, I felt in my gut there was something extraordinary for me up there.

But at times it seemed there would be no end, as I continued to plod along, becoming more fatigued. Then one day, I it occurred to me I had emerged far above the clouds with a bright blue sky above me, such as I had never before imagined. I could clearly see the sun's full orb as it shone warmly on my face, unfiltered by the gloomy clouds that perpetually shielded the Lowlands below. I can scarcely express how excited I was in discovering how things were up here.

At first it seemed disorienting to observe the clouds swirling down below, rather than above me. Certainly it was a new way of seeing things, but it was also a vision of how life would hereafter be different for me. As I journeyed on, something inexplicable seemed to be drawing me further upward, while a complementary force seemed to be pushing me from behind. What strange magic this Mountain seemed to possess.

Though I felt a heightened state of awareness in the brightness of the sun, the way upward became more confusing as I continued to encounter sheer vertical rock walls and deep crevices that at times seemed impossible to traverse. Often I was forced to retreat to lower altitudes to find new passages I hoped would open a way to the Summit.

At times my body would grow cold, weak and weary as it shivered through the dark night. I was uncertain if it was the freezing glaciers nearby or my fears that caused me to shiver the most. Sometimes, when I felt the most vulnerable on the side of a cliff, a huge condor would swoop down towards me with a chilling hiss, perhaps like that of a prehistoric archaeopteryx. To make things worse, my provisions were almost depleted, leaving me with little more than the clear Mountain air and splashes of fresh water trickling down the glistening cliffs.

As I continued to claw my way up these near impossible slabs of smooth, eroded rock walls, I would sometimes think about what the Lowlands people would say if they knew of my aspirations to ascend higher. They would likely consider me to be quite insane for not remain where everything remained flat and easy. Since the air always remained stilled below, there were no lashing winds of sleet and rain to brave.

At times, when I seemed to have lost my way, I longed for the security I had left far behind. Indeed it can be disheartening to struggle upward, only to slide backward in the loose scree. At such times I would question why I was putting myself through all this; forever toiling upwards like Prometheus.

In these moments of doubt, I struggled to stay resolute, especially when my mind imagined what everyone in the Lowlands would be saying about my foolish search for an illusionary, make-believe Mountain. I tried to maintain an attitude of *what do they know?* But in actuality, I wasn't so sure what anyone knew about anything, including me.

The more I thought about what they might say, the greater my weariness. The journey was beginning to take its toll on my resolve. I even found myself struggling to justify to myself the decision to answer this call, which at times, seemed more delusional than real. What would I have to show for all my efforts other than scraped, bleeding knuckles, twisted ankles, blistered feet and a sun-scorched body?

In the depths of the dark, despairing nights, I hunkered down into narrow fissures to escape the wicked blasts of frigid winds. Though the odds seemed against me, I tried to find solace in remembering the romance of the Mountain vision that drew me inward and upward. But in these times of fear and adversity, the vision would fade, becoming elusive and even ridiculous at times. Conflicted, I felt the torment of self-doubt picking into my heart like the vultures I imagined hovering nearby.

Sometimes, as the storms rolled in and pelted me with hail, I thought I heard voices mocking and scorning me to return to the Lowland's safe and secure mediocrity. Though life in the Lowlands can be awfully boring when everything is simple and predictable, at least no effort is required to survive. Even when it drizzled in the Lowlands, the slimy mud still has the advantage of keeping everyone very grounded, preventing them from wandering off onto rash adventures.

And yet, I thought how safe things must be in the Lowlands right now, and how unsafe I was. Admittedly, there are a few hazardous patches of quicksand on the periphery where the odd dweller wanders and sinks out of sight. But all in all, if you don't stray too far from the ruts near the safety of your hovel, you will most certainly be secure.

Although security is really important to the Lowlanders, most, if they were to admit it, don't really feel very that safe since there's an underlying fear and vulnerability, especially towards others they consider different. Many suspect there are raiders and predators lurking somewhere in the distant hills, and so it's important they always keep their doors bolted.

The more I reflected on my past life in the Lowlands, even while lonely and disheartened, the more I realized I couldn't go back. For one thing, it would be very difficult for me to lower myself down the precipices without incurring a fatal fall. Just letting yourself down each ridge and trying to find secure footing as you dangle above the next ledge below, should it exist, is a lot harder and more dangerous than pulling your body up the ledges.

And even if I should make it all the way down, I would have to explain where I went and why I left in the first place. I may never be accepted in their fold again after deserting them. The scoffers would never believe me if I told them what I had seen and experienced. I could already hear them: 'something wobbles in that young man's brain; he's not like the rest of us, thinks strange thoughts and imagines things that aren't there; best not to have anything to do with him.'

In spite of these reflections, I continued upwards without trails, guides or companions to show me the way. I only knew it was going to continue to be up the whole way; never soft and never flat. But I knew if I persisted, I would find a Summit somewhere above. And if there was a Summit, there would be a vista for me to view a world I could never have experienced in the Lowlands. I still wanted to believe that when I got to the top, I would find something there that would forever change my life - what I longed for, yet couldn't even imagine.

Having endured my *dark night of the soul,*[1] I felt again the clarion call that had drew me away from the Lowlands. With my doubts and fears mostly below and behind me now, I was ready for whatever fate may await me when I reached the Summit.

At the stroke or dawn, I slung on my backpack and continued to my along the narrow ledge, trying not to pry over steep cliffs. I took one careful step at a time as I clutched the jagged sides, fearing the dark void beneath. After a great deal of exertion, I struggled towards a very

---

[1] *Dark Night of the Soul,* is the title to a poem by Spanish mystic Saint John of the Cross (1542 1591)

steep and difficult crag, where at last I came to a clearing on a wide ridge that had patches of grass and moss. I found a soft area to relax and soak in the sun's warm rejuvenating rays. After all the discomfort and inner turmoil I had endured the previous night, I fell into a deep and peaceful slumber. When I awoke, my mind and body were considerable refreshed, making my way forward seem more promising than ever.

The expansive views impressed me with how clear everything seemed up here when contrasted with the Lowlands. Were the clouds there to veil the Mountain, or were the clouds a projection of the Lowlanders' collective thoughts, casting a dark veil over all the land? Having lived there for so long, I wasn't sure. But as I thought about it more, I began to suspect the Lowlands' inhabitants had consciously, or unconsciously, drawn the dark clouds to themselves, dimming and obscuring their vision of what may exist beyond them.

And yet, whether they were aware of it or not, this Mountain obviously existed, not just for me, but for all who venture to seek it. From now on, what the Lowlanders thought would no long matter to me; I had come too far. Leave the past behind where it belonged, I thought, and look forward to where I was going, not where I had been.

Slowly I got up to my feet and surveyed the vastness of all that was still before me. I felt a strange a new urge pulsating within me, as though being beckoned upwards without any further delay. Was this my destiny calling me? I couldn't be sure, but I didn't question what I felt. In haste I grabbed my backpack, half stumbling towards the escarpment as I slung it over my shoulders.

By the time the sun was high over me, I had scaled most of the way up when the realization suddenly hit me like a boulder catapulting down from the ridge above. I could now see – yes, this was it, just over the next ridge. There wasn't much distance left for me to reach the summit. My long, weary ascent was almost over! As I pulled myself to the top of the ledge, I wanting to jump up in celebration, but my leg muscles were too strained and fatigued from this last frantic scramble. So instead I staggered up to my feet and stood there in awe of my impossible feat. I was almost there now! I raised my right arm in victory, fist clenched.

But then as I looked upward to the summit, I thought I saw something moving –far off, at the pinnacle of the Summit's ridge, towards the eastern end. I dropped my arm. It was hardly discernible at first, but then it appeared to move closer to the edge, becoming clearer, yet still indefinable in shape. I had no idea what it was, but it seemed to be shimmering: a kind of shining orb of light. Curiously, the longer I focused on it, the brighter it seemed to glow. Then next I saw two or three more; it was difficult to tell what was going on, since they above kept shifting about. Then suddenly, they were gone! Most peculiar – and most startling!

I moved forward slowly, with my eyes fixed on the summit ridge. The euphoria I felt minutes ago was now unsettled by whatever was spooking me up there. I felt my heart beating even harder than when I scaled up this ridge. With this came an eerie premonition that something extraordinary was about to happen; perhaps I would have an encounter with something unknown, whatever that could be. How strange that at this moment of triumph, my gut would be twisted into knots. Was this the delirium of high altitude where I would lose my mind by oxygen deprivation? Or were the Mountain gods not pleased with my intrusion into their sacred domain by sending their flaming chariots to hold me at bay?

I knew something was about to happen; I could sense a disturbing presence – seemingly not of this world. And it wants me! Oh God, I'm not only delusional, but paranoid too. Something was out there though, electrifying, much like what I've sensed before a flash of lightning. Was Zeus about to strike me down?

In spite of these unnerving premonitions of doom, I burst forward to meet the adversary, if that's what it was. Perhaps it's was reflexive, but that's how I deal with fear: head on! Or was this more about me being a moth drawn towards the candlelight, only to be consumed by its flame? Lurching now towards the summit with all my might, at times faltering, I clambered up the next crag, as though attacking this final precipice.

I was most of the way up to the top, when I had to stop for a rest; my legs wouldn't carry me any further. As I stood hunched over gasping for air, I sensed I was being watched. Then, as I looked up towards the summit again, I saw the orbs hovering about the time something began to impinge on my brain, as though voices were attempting to communicate with me. But I didn't understand a thing.

21

I told myself it was just me imagining voices in the wind that swept over the summit. And those throbbing lights – likely just the sun's reflection off something. But off what? It couldn't be off the landscape of shrubs and boulders? Certainly, nothing natural could sashay around like that and then just vaporize in the air. The orbs continued to flit about like fireflies at night, except this was in mid-daylight. Whatever it was couldn't be of this world. Aliens perhaps?

At this point, I knew there was no way out if they wanted me. With my body now overwhelmed with exhaustion, I didn't know what to do – stay here, continue upward, or attempt to let my way down the precipice – then run like hell all the way back to Santiago.

But I couldn't just slink away like a coward, I'd rather die. I had to continue forward! Had they mesmerize me like the hapless Eloi, who passively strolled into the caves and clutches of the cannibalistic Morlocks?[1] Perhaps there were subliminal trance inducing waves emanating out of the orbs to achieve some nefarious end?

Whether it was an irrepressible impulse or not, I continued to proceed further until I found I couldn't go any further. I was at an impasse. On the right was a very large chasm, perhaps the result of a giant earthquake or a cataclysmic overthrust. I couldn't proceed upwards to the Summit or go to the left because the vertical rock was too smooth and sheer to grasp.

Bloody hell, I thought! Earlier in the day I wasn't certain how to proceed upward since it appeared there were only two alternatives. Unfortunately, I chose a direct trajectory that brought me to this chasm. Had I taken a route to the right, I may have ended up around on the other side where I could have easily made it to the summit ridge. If I would have spiraled around to the south side, it may have been much easier, though my aerial photo showed evidence of a very steep glacier which may have been very difficult to traverse without specialized equipment. If I now retreated all the way down to the ravine below, in search of a less precarious approach to the right side of the chasm, it could take at least half a day to recover to this altitude.

---

[1] *In reference to H.G. Wells' science fiction novel, 'The Time Machine' (1895) and the 1960 film version of the Eloi falling into sound induced trances that caused them to saunter into the dark tunnels of the brutish Morlocks to meet their fateful demise.*

I found the chasm's walls to be steep and unforgiving, but it appeared there may be enough of a ledge to make it across to the other side. But it would be risky, very risky! Once across, however, I could do a few switchbacks and then scramble to the top. It wouldn't take long. Then I would confront whatever was waiting up there for me.

I looked down the deep abyss. It was dizzying. Attrition over eons of time had created a formidable canyon below that I hadn't anticipated from the angle I approached the summit. No person in their right mind would attempt crossing this without the proper equipment. It would be insane. So I took a few deep breaths, relaxed my muscles, and offered a quick *Hail Mary* in case there was a Mary out there listening.

I took the first few steps by leaning inward to the rock face while using my hands to help secure my balance. It seemed I would be able to make it across – provided the footing held. Then after about a dozen steps across, my knees began to tremble as I realized I had now gone too far and the ledge had become too narrow for me to turn around. You're committed now, James, I thought. You've no choice; it's either do or die.

Though looking down was something I preferred not to do, I couldn't help but gape into the dark chasm below as I continued to carefully positioned my feet one step at a time. I thought of what Nietzsche once said: *when you stare into the abyss the abyss stares back at you*.[1] Indeed it was staring - most terrifyingly so. This would be a very, very nasty drop, a long way down with nothing to break my body's descent until near the bottom. A fall would be fatal.

Oh God, I breathed out frantically, what have I got myself into? With still about another twenty feet to go, things weren't looking good. There was no fissure close enough for me to wedge an anchor if I wanted to rappel out. Even then, my rope wasn't long enough for me to swing far enough off to the chasm's side to find ground. At this point, it was difficult to determine how thick the protruding ledge was and whether it would be sufficiently firm to hold. If only I was able to offset some of my weight by finding something to grasp, even a tuft of grass. But there was nothing to cling to. Again, I tried to turn around,

[1] Friedrich Nietzsche, German philosopher, *Beyond Good and Evil*, 1886

but couldn't. Why didn't I notice how treacherous this would be before I started to cross over?

I wasn't a believer, but out of nowhere in my mind, came the words; *Father into thy hands I commit my spirit.*[1]

I too must commit, I thought, there's no other choice. As I stepped forward and placed my foot down, I thought, careful James, this could be your ...

And so the dream ended.

— but was it just a dream?

---

[1] The words of what Jesus said as he died on the cross, as recorded in the Gospel of Luke; 23:46 (NIV)

CHAPTER 2

WHERE AM I?

I had a dream, which was not at all a dream[1]

I awoke on a patch of dry grass feeling disoriented and dazed, not remembering exactly where I was and yet I felt more rested than I ever remembered. Curiously it felt as though I had been sleeping for days. Most odd, I thought, considering how I had been climbing since early dawn. I must have really been tired since I couldn't even remember lying down. Now wide awake, I remained supine for some time, looking directly up at the scattered clouds in the blue sky, thinking of what that occurred so far on my venture since leaving home.

My flight from London to Santiago via Buenos Aires was lengthy and exhausting, but nothing compared to my extended excursion in a dilapidated bus with wooden seats. For the better part of a day we navigated through the winding and dusty back country roads. But at least we arrived at a remote indigenous village whereupon the next morning, I still had at least a day's trek through the valleys to reach the base of the mountain I intended to climb. Of course, I had to choose it, simple because it appeared to be the most formidable, but from

---

[1] Lord Byron, English Poet, *Darkness,* 1816

the topographical maps I had studied, I knew it would have the best vistas. Since it I couldn't find if it had a name, I thought I'd come up with something creative and inform the Chilean authorities what they should name it. Mount Phillips had a nice ring. But first I would have to conquer it!

I sprang up from the ground with a surprising lightness. It could tell I was only a few hours from the summit now, but it appeared there still remained some major challenges ahead, considering the height of the huge precipices facing me.

As I looked around I thought what a splendid afternoon this had turned out to be, although something seemed wrong. The sun was still in the eastern horizon to my left, indicating it must be early morning not afternoon. But I thought, that can't be, unless I somehow fell asleep for most of yesterday and last night. Was I really that tired?

That was most curious, but for now, it didn't matter; Chile's bright, mid-summer sun was exactly what I needed for a winter break to lift the veil of gloom from London's dreary winter rains. The bright azure contained only a few trailing wisps of haze to the east. Everything seemed so alive, so exhilarating - a perfect backdrop for my summit moment. Amazing what this alpine environment, and a good sleep, can do for one's mind and body!

Not long ago I felt hungry, tired and bruised, but now, near the top, I felt like a new man. It was becoming most apparent there are bigger things in life than marking term papers, dealing with incompetent administrators who jostled for influence and power; embroiled in their interdepartmental politics! Not going to be kissing anyone's scholastic arse up here. But why, I thought, distract myself from this splendid exhilaration by dwelling on that ridiculous twaddle.

Indeed the trip had all been worth the effort, even though I knew I could scarcely afford it. After being in a chronic state of malaise over the last few years, I wished to enter a new world where I would belong, as I faced down the fears that had been holding me back as I struggle towards the summit. Or was it more like a death-wish I subliminally harboured to destroy an unknown fear by destroying myself? In any case, it seemed I had come here to tempt fate. But why?

Going to these extremes of randomly climbing a mountain in this remote area of the world just so I could challenge myself may not have made much sense to the average person. But I didn't consider myself an average person. For reasons I still didn't understand, it seemed I had to prove to myself once again that I was invincible. Though I was no longer eighteen, being battered about by Mediterranean storms on an old rickety merchant ship, still I felt compelled to test the limits of my strength and resourcefulness. That's why I chose to be alone in an isolated mountain where few ventured. As a self-respecting survivalist, I had only minimal equipment.

In my various ventures, I always prided myself in being able to stare down the risks of death! An analyst once suggested this was a form of psychosis, indicating I was compensating for something hidden deeply within. But I wasn't that interested in hearing what he had to say; what did he know about life sitting in his office all day? Sure I may push the limits, but at least I had calculated the threats, anticipating what to expect and what to do.

But this expedition had turned out to be not only the most extreme but also the most challenging so far. Still, the greater fears I had avoided all my life were yet to be revealed. These were the festering fears that kept drive me to create more challenges I knew I could overcome with my wits and brute strength.

As an aside, I now know these compulsions were only a ruse to distract myself from the unresolved fears I had hidden from myself for most of my life. I was about to enter into a strange new zone of awakening where everything was about to change for me; where I would be confronted by what had been lurking within. Since I didn't know myself that well, none of this was understood by me as I now stood in the shadow of the mountain's summit. Yet it was here now, I was about to venture towards a new and indescribable Summit in my life.

As I strapped on my backpack to resume my ascent, I thought again about what possibly could have happened. Not only was the sun in the wrong place, but here I was at the bottom of a deep ravine I had already passed through yesterday, or so it seemed. Was I going in circles around the mountain? Hardly! While scrambling up the screed slope before me, I gave no more thought to these peculiarities.

It now became apparent, with my body's new found strength and agility; it may not be long now before I would be able to reach the summit. I congratulated myself on having made it this far with only a thirty foot rope, a few anchors and no climbing companions.

Feeling giddy, I looked up towards the summit to address Zeus, the mythical god I addressing the night of that unfortunate incident at the pub last October; just before having that weird dream. '*Veni, Vidi, Vici*,'[1] I yelled upwards. 'Time to get your welcoming committee ready, and be sure to bring plenty of champagne —and your goddesses; we're going to celebrate!'

After scaling up an escarpment of considerable height, I thought about the shimmering orb *thingies* I had seen darting around on the summit yesterday. At least, I thought I may have seen something like that. But no, I couldn't have, I wasn't here yesterday. Probably I dreamt it -- sometimes when I'm overly exhausted, I get really weird dreams. But even if there was something shining up there, it would probably be nothing more than the sun reflecting off a satellite receiver/transmitter on top or some other weather installation.

However, I thought I may prefer it be something a bit more interesting – say an assembly of charming green aliens perched on the summit ridge, wagering whether I'd make it to the top or not. Probably their craft was equipped with strobe lights that appeared to me as orbs. Who knows, maybe later they'd give me a joy ride around the sierras.

These thoughts amused me at first, as I continued my final upward thrust. But the more I thought about orbs, gods and aliens, the more difficult it became to dismiss any of these possibilities from my mind, making me feel increasingly uneasy. What if there really was something up there – then what? Was it possible I had been drawn up here for reasons I hadn't been aware; something more than just conquering another mountain?

Suddenly, as I paused on a narrow ridge, flashbacks came to me from that strange dream. Had that been a premonition of what I was now experiencing, I wondered? I could still hear the voice calling to me from somewhere on high, imploring me to join them on a summit. I remembered written down every detail l could recalled, up to where

---

[1] *I came, I saw, I conquered.* Attributed to Julius Caesar, approx. 47 BC

I was stranded on a ledge I couldn't seem to cross. This was becoming queer! Probably, the most logical reason for these flashbacks was the altitude's rarified air that caused peculiar chemicals to be released into my brain that caused me to have these strange visions from that indelible dream.

So I thought, just put these quirky thoughts out of your mind James, and begin to think instead of other climbing escapades you'll make to even higher peaks. I was still a relatively young man, in excellent condition, with plenty of strength and stamina. Maybe I should try K2 next. No, that's probably a bad idea, with one chance in four you won't come down alive – not good odds. Maybe I'll settle for Everest, like everyone else, but in any case, I really should to do this more often.

Damn, I thought, I'm really feeling inspired -- like I can do anything! I've scampering up this slope without even being knackered, as though it were level ground. I couldn't remember being so energized before. How long was it I rested at the bottom? And just look at the view up here; I can hardly wait to get to the summit to find what's on the other side.

As I continued my rapid ascent, I came to a chasm that looked very familiar – too familiar to be a coincidence! Moments ago I was elated, but now I was unsettled. Had someone mixed some peyote in the gruel I bought in the village? I sat down on a ledge for a moment, examining the chasm before me and how I should proceed from here. The longer I sat there, the more I got an impression if someone, or something, watching me. Much like when you sense you're being stared at, and then you look around and find there was someone looking at you.

I wasn't sure what to think, but nevertheless, it felt eerie. And so I got up and continued climbing until I was very near to the top of the chasm. Strangely, I imagined I had been here before. But unless I was clairvoyant, I couldn't have. Or perhaps I had foreseen this in my dream? It's too bad I don't believe in such nonsense; it may be helpful in explaining much of what I was experiencing today.

As I was deciding the best way to across the chasm, I noticed there was something moving about on the summit! Well I'll be damned; I said aloud, it appears there really is someone up there. Not exactly dazzling light orbs, but it seems there may be two or three humanoid figures moving about. Or are they just stunted trees swaying in the wind? Yes, that's probably it. But if it were my choice, I'd prefer they be beautiful mountain nymphs waiting to reward me for my efforts. Why not make it worthwhile? I was beginning to think anything was possible up here. Maybe it's the altitude, but the thought made me giddy as I started to laugh at myself.

Yet I sensed there was possible more happening than just my light headedness. I felt something like an electrical force field wafting about me, very much like the electricity you feel before lightning strikes, raising the hairs on your arms. It seemed I had that same thought yesterday, but I couldn't be sure. Everything felt so muddled up with my dream and all that was occurring here. In fact, there seemed to be a lot of strange déjà vu going on in my mind, ever since I awoke at the bottom of the canyon ravine.

And then, if all this wasn't enough, out of nowhere I heard what sounded like a voice calling out to me. Was it from the summit or the synapses misfiring in my oxygen deprived brain? Lots of people hear voices in their head in abnormal conditions like this. Bloody hell, I thought, now I'm really losing it; I need to get some oxygen before my brain completely decompresses!

Just as I was about to dismiss it as nothing, I heard the voice again. This time it was calling out my name. Now that's really strange, I thought; too strange for words. Is there someone up here who knows me? Some mountain guru I've never me, the kind that sits on top of mountains giving audiences to seekers who climb ten thousand metres to spend a few with them. That's about as likely as the gods waiting up there to celebrate my arrival!

Then I heard it again, this time the voice was so clear it could have been from someone standing directly in front of me. Was it one or many? I couldn't tell. I sat there stunned for a few minutes, waiting to hear if it would call my name once more. And soon it did, but this time it was a different voice. This one was soft, alluring and ah, so feminine! My exotic mountain nymph, or goddess beckoning me to the Summit. Maybe they're the same, why not, anything is possible in the imagination? For the ancient Greeks, the gods and goddesses were supposed to have lived on the mountains along with Zeus. I liked that idea, even if was a myth.

But whatever was calling me, was more than a myth. It was real and peculiar. I sense her voice resonating from within my mind, having nothing to do with what my ears hear from without. Normally I'm sceptical about this sort of thing, and yet there it was, I couldn't deny it. And now, rather than hearing her voice, I saw images imposed on my mind's eye, showing me an alternative route to the summit. Since I didn't have a good feeling about the thin narrow ledge that crossed to the other side of the chasm, I decided to follow the inner prompting I was receiving. Without hesitation, I retreating downward about twenty metres before veering off to the left where I found a narrow indenture into the precipice. By wedging myself between the narrow sides I was able to straddle and maneuver my way up the fissure at least fifty metres towards the summit ridge. It should have been extremely difficult for me to do this, but for some reason it wasn't.

After struggled for the last few days to make it to this summit, I was finally here on top, feeling totally exhilarated. I stood there a while, taking in the full panoramic view of the majestic ranges all around me. Then I remember what I had seen from below, wondering if there really was anyone up here as it had appeared. I surveyed the long ridge, but I saw no one – likely I had just imagined it all, along with the voices.

Or was it possible they had gone into hiding, waiting for an opportunity to pounce on me? I didn't relish the thought! From my earlier observations this was the general area I thought I had seen something, and yet there were no trees here to explain what I saw. I was surprised how broad and flat it was on the summit, especially towards the western end where the ground seemed to slope gently downwards. The landscape was littered with large boulders and huge slabs of granite protruding out of the ground. There were patches of short alpine meadow grass and moss, along with shrubs and a variety of small but hardy mountain flowers. I decided to make my way along the ridge as it narrowed towards its highest elevation.

I wasn't exactly sure where the ridge would end before dropping down its steep precipice. As I continued to walk, I became aware of something standing in the distance, not at all appearing to be trees or shrubs. As I drew closer I had the impression these were two distinct beings with the possibly of another standing further in the distance.

31

At first I thought they must be other climbers who had approached the Summit from the other side. I wanted to believe one of them was my nymph, patiently waiting centuries for me to me to arrive; the one calling to me when I was still below the summit.

Though I've never believed in the folklore of elves and fairies since I was a child, I continued to entertain the fantasy -- had she not called out my name and showed me the way forward. In my rational mind I understood such things can only happen in one's imagination. But as I got closer now, I could see only two figures now. Likely, the third was an illusion from something further in the distance that made the two appear as three.

I continued my advance warily, one slow step at a time, my eyes riveted on them. They remained standing perfectly still at the end of the highest point of the summit ridge – a bit unnerving and intimidating, to say the least! Who were they; why didn't they proceed to meet me half way? What if I too just stood still; then what would happen? Of course, I could walk away in the other direction, but I didn't want to turn my back on them and risk being followed, not knowing who or what they were. After about another thirty yards, I was close enough that I could tell they stood there motionless, staring directly at me. I had an uncomfortable feeling deep in my plexus that they had been waiting for me for some time.

Was I just imagining it, or did I just hear my name spoken, as with someone standing beside me? If so, what other powers might they possess besides their telepathic voodoo? Did they have something to do with those glowing orbs I may have seen, if only in my dreams? It seemed there was some really spooky stuff going on with me up here. Were these two beings in the distance decoys for aliens? But then, where was the ship; hovering invisibly over the summit with their cloaking shields up? Hmm, wonder if they have laser weapons! "Stun lasers set, ready --- take the earthling."

Then for whatever reason, in juxtaposition to this, a vision suddenly flashed before my mind that reminded me of the Biblical *Transfiguration* story.[1] Where did that come from? Had the source of the voices

---

[1] According to the Transfiguration story, both Moses and Elijah stood talking with Jesus whose face and apparel shone in brilliant light. Next a bright cloud overshadowed them. When the light left, only Jesus remained standing. Matthew 17:1–9

projected this image on my consciousness? As befitting any credible philosopher, I'm familiar with most stories and teachings of the major religious traditions, and so as I knew this had to do with Christ being transfigured into a dazzling form of light. The incident is said to have occurred somewhere in Palestine on an unknown mountain that is traditionally referred to as *The Mount of Transfiguration.* So were these two mysterious beings standing before me Moses and Elijah preparing to witness my transfiguration on this *Mount,* if only metaphorically? That would be most extraordinary!

And wasn't there something in the story about a brilliant cloud shining down on them? Maybe that's what those blazing light orbs will be coming in this scene. Trouble is; I'm no Christ. Not even close! Besides, I wasn't sure what any of this was supposed to mean: transfigured --- but from what to what?

For a few more moments I stood there, my oscillating imagination blending popular science fiction with religious mythology. Then, as I drew closer to them, more insane thoughts hit me: I think I know these two! But do I? No I don't. Yet I think I do; but I don't know why I would think that; I've never seen them before. So why do I think I know them when I don't? Obviously I'm confused. None of this makes sense. Yet I can't deny there's something familiar about them, even if I don't know what it is. Just like when you think you know a stranger from somewhere before, perhaps thinking it's from a prior life; except I don't believe in prior lives or any other life than this.

Mixed impressions continued to flood into my mind, though I tried not to allow my fears and imagination to get carried away any further than they already had. I stopped once again to see if they would make a move towards me, but they didn't, remaining stony silent and unmoved, as if to unnerve me. I continued to move forward, keeping my eyes firmly fixed on them with each step I took.

Again, I sensed the older one had an eerie presence of someone I may have known in the distant past but I still couldn't identify who that may be. I felt uncomfortable when my eyes met his. He seemed to have a very serious demeanor, like a Himalayan sage; not that I've ever met any mountain sages before. There was a venerable Moses appearance to him, reminding me of when he came down from the burning bush on

Mount Sinai in the movie,[1] except he was wearing hiking knickers you sometimes see in the Alps. His prophetic image seemed accentuated by his thick white hair, extended just above his shoulders. His penetrating blue eye had a laser focus, commanding my respect, even though I wasn't sure why.

The other man seemed much younger, possibly in his early to mid-twenties, yet equally interesting in his own way. I estimated him to be close to six feet tall with an athletic build. He had long blond/brown hair braided into Rastafarian dreadlocks. This, with his tattered Alpaca sweater, reminded me of a young bohemian drifter. Likely my fear and bewilderment was evident as I approached them. In response, he gave me an assuring smile to allay any lingering concerns I may have towards them in this most unlikely of encounters.

'*Buenos días*,' I said.

'Good afternoon,' said the younger, with a cheerful British accent.

'We've been observing your arduous journey up here' said the elder, in a subtle mix of the Queen's English underlying with a Gaelic inflection. 'We are pleased at long last to have you join us here. Congratulations on completing this stage of your ascent, James, and welcome to the summit.'

'I beg your pardon sir, but how do you know my name?' I said with some alarm. 'There's no one on God's green earth who could know I'm here.'

'You're right,' he said, 'no one knows, at least not on God's green earth, as you say.'

'But obviously you do!'

'Indeed, we do,' he said.

'But how?' I asked, trying to remain composed.

'May we introduce ourselves?'

'If you would, that would be most appreciated,' I said, with a tinge of impertinence in my voice.

'You may call me Eli,' said the younger.

'And if you please, you may call me Mo,' said the other.

What the bloody hell, I thought to myself. They just called

---

[1] I thought of the portrayal of Moses in Cecil B DeMille's classic, *The Ten Commandments,* played by Charlton Heston.

themselves Eli and Mo, short for Moses and Elijah. Those were the two with Jesus on the Mount of Transfiguration. Had I not in my mind just assigned those names to them? I wasn't serious though, the names just somehow came to me. So how could they have known? But then, if they were able to know my name, why wouldn't they know that too. This was just too uncanny to be real. Mind readers? – no such thing! There had to be a more rational explanation. Obviously a coincidence!

'If you care to join us,' Mo said, 'we'd be pleased if you join with us to at our campfire towards the other end of this summit ridge. We have plenty of extra food and drink.'

'Since at the moment I really don't have anything planned up here,' I said, I'd be delighted to accept your invitation.'

As we hiked towards their camp, they seemed genuinely interested in my trip to Chile and the experiences I had while climbing this mountain. My impressions of them were that they were civil, gracious and genteel, perhaps more than should be expect from strangers in such a remote part of the world. Often their eyes remained fixed on me as I spoke; a quality I always consider to be an indication of personal integrity.

Though they were still strangers, I had a good feeling about them. In some ways they still seemed oddly familiar to me; perhaps too much so. I wasn't sure why, but it seemed they already knew me, even if I didn't know them. Yet I kept asking myself, who are they? Was this just a friendly chance encounter or were they sent by someone to meet me for some specific reason? That certainly would be reason for serious concern! Thoughts of orbs and alien abduction still played in the back of my mind. Under normal circumstances I would never allow myself to think in anything so irrational. But fear is never rational.

It still mystified me why they were up here. Obviously, they didn't just stroll up here on some eco sightseeing tour. It had taken me a very long time to make it to the summit, while risking life and limb and I'm sure I must have looked the worse for the wear. Yet here they were; fresh as daisies! Very few climbers Mo's age could have even made it close to this summit. For these reasons and more, I couldn't shake the feeling that something very strange must be going on around me.

And not only that, I began to suspect there was something most peculiar about me too. I should have felt starved and exhausted from these last days of my near vertical ascent. This was likely the most precipitous and dangerous climb I had ever experienced, but surprisingly, my body still felt inexplicable light and spritely, considering what I had recently been through.

My provisions of dehydrated foods were almost depleted, and what berries and herbs I gathered along the way were long gone. Not that that worried me too much, since I understand that most can survive for about forty days without food. In fact, I once fasted for over four weeks with only water. But certainly not while climbing. But where did this surge of energy in my body come from?

As we continued along the ridge, I thought how I'd like to celebrate my ascent with a cool bottle of sparkling champagne. Had I not made this request to the Mountain gods?

As if reading my mind, Eli stopped and pulled out a bottle of Pernod Ricard Perrier Jouet from his battered backpack! He shook it, popped the cork and directed the spray towards my face. Most refreshing! Laughing, he handed the bottle to me to guzzle down what possibly was the most delicious bubbly I ever tasted.[1] We merrily passed it around a few times and just as soon as the bottle was empty, Mo pulled an identical bottle out from the inner pocket of his overcoat. This time glasses appeared as you may expect from a magician on stage. I assumed it was just the libations, but in this strange mix of confusion, conversation and laughter, I was beginning to feel more alive and vibrant than I could remember feeling in a long time. Now that my residual fears were set aside for the moment, I felt in my element. I suppose with enough champagne that may be expected.

But what occurred next was even more surprising. How it all happened as it did, I had no idea. After arriving near the western end of the ridge, we came to an area which was somewhat lower down, recessed among large granite boulders. Evidently this is where they had camped since there were still hot coals smouldering from an earlier. Curiously though, there were no tents or evidence of bedding.

While Mo was stoking up the fire and Eli off somewhere finding

---

[1] I didn't realize it at the time, but later learned that a bottle of this champagne sells for over £30,000. No wonder it was the best I ever tasted.

more wood, I decide to take a stroll further along the ridge to view the northerly sierras. I lingered there for a while, as I took in the spectacular views. Upon returning not long after, the next thing I saw – and I know this may sound unbelievable, was a feast of exotic foods that had somehow appeared, all laid out on a long wooden table.

Where they got all this, I had no idea. Not only were there foods, seemingly imported from all over the world, there were also several bottles of wine displayed for me to choose from. I wondered if they had procured them for just me, since they were all my favorite blends, which, considering the expense, I rarely indulged in.

I commended my hosts on their exquisite tastes, as though I was standing in the tasting room of an elegant winery on the Mediterranean shores, explicating the comparative merits of their finest wines. In the past, I've amused myself at dinner parties by assuming my most affected airs as a wine connoisseur, just to see if anyone would take me seriously. I had learned enough of the vocabulary and clichés to convincingly pull it off in most cases.

'Gentleman,' I said in my most unctuous tone, 'may I recommend this elegant Zinfandel vintage with its robust yet delicate solera bouquet comingled with a subtle European vitis vinifera. Now contrast that with this dry red Bordeaux, obviously most aptly aged in a cured French cask. Don't you agree, unlike this sweet, racy Italian Merlot, it provides a more mature and satisfying oaky char?' Though they humoured my little charade, I'm sure they realized how little I knew what I was talking about. But that didn't matter, the wines were about as good as anything I had ever had tasted.

Over the course of the evening, I found that Eli`s offbeat humour and banter sometimes struck me as being a little too much like mine. The more I got to know him, the more it seemed we were two old shipmates that had been reunited after several years.

Mo too had a sense of humour, which he often expressed with his sharp wit. I noticed during the evening he would sometimes wonder off to gaze into the sky as if he was zoning into his own universe of rarified thoughts. Then he would re-emerge in silent contemplation for a minutes before uttering something sounding exceedingly profound, and yet most peculiar, that I didn't know what to make of it.

In spite of their affable natures, I remained wary of getting too casual with them. Often they would say or do something that was just too bizarre to make any sense. I wondered at times if they did this just to throw me off. Not just that, but besides Mo's stargazing eccentricities, Eli seemed to enjoy answering me just before I would him ask a question, as if to shock and gobsmack me; which he did continually.

But even more disconcerting was how they seemed to know so much about me. It was unsettling. No just my name, that was only the beginning; they also knew what my favourite food and drinks were – even my favourite books. Was it only coincidence they had read many of the same authors and titles as me, from Teilhard de Chardin to Dostoyevsky? Which made me wonder how Eli, appearing at least a decade younger than me, could have possibly have known so much; perhaps even more than me.

And yet they disclose very little about themselves, as if to keep their lives a secret so they could mystify more. Even with probing, all I could get out of them of any significance was that they were very independent beings, having come into great abundance several years ago. They were now free to come and go as they pleased, even to places I could never imagine. And that was about it. How they made their fortunes, they wouldn't say. There was too much intrigue to their story for my comfort. Eli once said something about a great inheritance, but I remained suspicious if there wasn't something more suspect about their story.

After a remarkable evening enjoying all the food, drinks and laughter, they suddenly got up and wandered off in the dark without any explanation, leaving me to sit alone in the glow of the hot coals. What a strange day this had been! Was any of it real or had I gone over the edge into some altered state of reality! What if I was actually still back at my flat on a wild psychedelic trip, higher than this mountain summit? With my body and mind feeling so light, I began to wonder if I had taken leave of my body. And yet I recognized that would only be an illusion; I wouldn't actually *go* anywhere, it would only be my addled mind imagining it.

As I poked away at the coals with a stick, I remembered similar experiences like this in my undergraduate days. I did some interesting *stuff* back then with some of my more experimentally inclined friends. But that was over ten years ago, I hadn't participated in anything like this since. If for some unknown reason, I really was on another of these excursions it would have been one of the better ones. I smiled as I thought this. But at least once I came down, if I did, I wouldn't have to wonder about all this confusion here anymore. It wouldn't matter because none of this would have actually happened. Yet I knew this was happening; my mind was suddenly more lucid than ever.

When Mo and Eli returned from wherever they had gone, I said laughingly, 'you know chaps, I was just thinking, with all that's happened to me today, I don't think I have ever been this high before, even on a Mountain. But I think it's time for me to come down and retire for the night.'

'Indeed,' Eli said, 'truth be known, you are even higher and lighter than you may care to know at this point. But that's okay, you'll get used to it. Here; before you bed down, let me fill you glass with this very smooth Scotch. It's from Edinburgh. You studied there; right?'

'Yes I did, but how did you know? I didn't tell you!'

'Because you seem a man of great erudition;' said Mo, 'deserving of one of the finest institutions in Great Britain. And because you seem to know a thing or two about Scotch, for which they are famous. So before you retire for the night; here's to you Dr Phillips.'

As he and they raised their glasses, Eli said: 'to your arrival and ongoing expedition here. Cheers!'

'Thank you,' I said, 'though I don't understand what's going on or what you mean by "ongoing." But at least I can say you've been most gracious this evening. Cheers to you both!' I said, as I raised my glass of Scotch to them. I'd certainly do more climbing if I knew I could celebrate like this every time I peaked a summit.'

'Well, maybe you can,' Mo said.

Darkness had descended over us hours ago, leaving only the bright red embers to illuminate our surroundings. I thought I should be exceptionally weary by now, having regaling at the sumptuous 'Summit Diner Club', as Eli called it. But I wasn't tired. In fact, I should have passed out from all I had imbibed this evening, especially after all my climbing.

I had surfeited my badly neglected body on the most delightful delicacies I could remember having. Caviar never tasted so good, especially when sprinkled on stuffed deviled eggs. How did they do that? That's awfully finicky work to accomplish here or anywhere else for that matter. So where did they get all this fresh food; who's the chef? Santiago is a very long way off for catering services. As I laid awake in my bedroll, I thought of my fortuitous, yet most unusual encounter with these chaps. And that was the last thought I remembered; once asleep, I didn't awake until dawn.

As I watched the sun rising, I continued to lie there completely relaxed, feeling I had never before slept so peacefully – except perhaps the previous night in the ravine, when it seemed I had slept for days. I stared up at the bright pink clouds as I reflected on strange events of yesterday. Everything came back to me in a big swoosh, as did my curiosity regarding my new friends and where they had gone.

If they were still here today, I would make it my business to learn as much as I could about them. I was more curious now than ever. These were most unusual characters! I remember how last night I was often surprised by their adeptness in everything they did, as if camping was their natural element. These were very harsh environs, and yet nothing seemed to concern them. In some ways they seemed a little too in control of everything -- including me. Still my big question remained, just what were they doing up here on such a remote mountain. And for that matter, how did they get here -- Sherpas? Ah, wrong continent. There's no way they would get this far. Unless …

Yes, of course, that's it! They were dropped in by helicopter; probably with some eco-tour company. Likely they'll spend a few days here, get airlifted to return to wherever they came from. That certainly would explain their large stash of food and drinks. Why didn't I think of that last night? Amazing how much clearer things become after a good night's sleep! The only problem was, there was no outfitter or eco-tour operator doing anything like that in these parts. But then, if they had the resources, they could have hired both the copter and outfitter. That's likely the most probably answer.

And yet for some reason, I wasn't completely buying it; even if it was most probable. That would be too simple and logical when nothing else here was simple or logical. Though my new friends seemed to be reasonable and well-tempered, still there was something about them, so mysterious I couldn't identify what it was. It made me wonder if this chance meeting was more than chance.

Had the gods driven me to climb this remote mountain? My rational mind never believed in fate any more than gods; but if it wasn't these, what else could it be. Divine providence was completely out of the question since I didn't believe in that either. Yet here I was a philosopher, of all people, having these irrational thoughts and experiences.

Once again I recalled that strange dream I had. I wondered, was it insane or was it there to drive me insane? I could still hear the haunting voices that called to me. Was it to this mountain I was called? The more I thought about it, the more the dream seemed to merge with the reality I was experiencing here. Maybe there was a plan or agenda my new friends were complicit in. But why; was there something they wanted from me?

With each new inexplicable phenomenon, it was getting increasingly more difficult to explain things away; beginning with the shimmering orbs I may have seen. And then there were the voices I heard, even from a very long way off. Obviously, no sound waves from that distance could have reached my ears, so something else must be communicating directly to my mind.[1] And how could I deny the soft and sensual voice of the enchanting mountain nymph directing me to find my way up the summit. I could still hear her -- if only I could make real what I imagined!

Still I wanted to believe there was no direct reason for them to be involved in this psychic mischief. I mean, why would they? Perhaps I was in denial, but they appeared no different than me, just two mountaineers on the same mountain as me. I'd wait later to find from them how they were able to know my name and all the other things about me. I'm sure there was a logical explanation; likely they knew of me through someone in London. And so I had nothing to be concerned about. As for everything else that had been happening, I didn't wish to think it.

---

[1] Interestingly, this wasn't the first time I had experienced something like this. I tell of a similar incident while camping in the mountains.

Enough paranoia, I told myself, it's time to get up and start a new day. Hopefully my friends hadn't left yet so we may make our way down together. I needed to find a better less steep route down and find how they got here. Otherwise, it may take a couple more days to get to the base after a lot of difficult traversing in finding a better way down. Unless, of course, there was a copter coming by to airlift them out, in which case I'd ask to catch a ride out with them to Santiago, if that's where they were going.

I noticed there were dark clouds beginning to sweep in from the west. The early morning sun shone brightly in the clear eastern horizon but likely it wouldn't last for long now. I knew how quickly things could turn nasty this high up, especially with the way these clouds were rolling in now. With all my brooding, perhaps my thoughts had attracted a storm. If this was being a little superstitious, at least I didn't take it seriously like many do. I certainly wasn't given to such foolishness that links mind with matter, weather conditions or anything else.

And yet many of my assumptions about what may be possible were being challenged with all the telepathic tricks being played on me when I first approached the summit. Still I believed that none of this wasn't really possible, it only seemed that way.

I sprang to my feet, again amazed at how easily I was able to get up. It seemed I must be in much better shape than I thought: my muscles weren't in the least sore as they often were after a long day of climbing. I stuffed my bed roll into my large backpack, slung it over my shoulder and made my way along the ridge to find shelter, hoping to avoid the rain that would soon be gusting in over the summit ridge. In spite of all the confusion last evening, I was feeling great, ready to take on whatever new surprises and challenges the day may bring.

But as confident as I was feeling then, nothing could have prepared me for what awaited me this day – my life would never be the same.

CHAPTER 3

STORY TIME

From these depths depart towards heaven,
you have escaped from the city full of fear and trembling[1]

E ven before I was able to find shelter, the rain and sleet had already swooped down on the Summit, as I trudged along in search of an overhang to take refuge. But I hadn't gone too far, when I suddenly caught a whiff of smoke that seemed to be wafting up from somewhere below. I scrambled down the ridge a short way, and there I saw what appeared to be like a shelter nestled on a small plateau by a granite slope. As I got closer, I could see it was more like a sizeable log cabin, complete with the rock chimney where the smoke was billowing out. I would never have suspected that there would or could be such structure in this a remote area of the world. How could this have been built here? I had a hard enough time making it up here, so hauling logs up from far below would have been close to impossible without airlift.

The squall passed as quickly as it arrived, which is normal at this altitude of volatility. In the distance below, I could see someone sitting on a deck with their feet propped up on the deck's railing. As I got

[1] Rumi; 'Ode'

closer I noticed Eli strumming on a guitar with a fag hanging out the side of his mouth. With the sun brightly shining on the landscape, the scene reminding me of one of those over-embellished mountain scene paintings, except this was very alive and vibrant. It appeared the cabin lodge was conveniently sheltered far enough down from the Summit ridge to avoid the howling winds arching over the ridge.

'It's about time,' Mo yelled at me from the doorway. 'Eli ate most of the sausages, but I can fry a few more for you if you like. What else would you like?'

'Anything,' I said as I stepped onto the plank deck. 'So, this is where you mountaineers hang out! You didn't tell me about this last night. What a great view overlooking the chasm. Most impressive! How much do your outfitters charge you to stay here per diem?'

They didn't answer my question. 'Glad you like it,' Eli said, finally taking the fag out of his mouth and flicking it over the railing as he surveyed the front gable end. 'It's solid alright, designed it myself. A real gem, wouldn't you say? We built and outfitted everything ourselves, just the way we thought you would like it.'

I just nodded, not taking him too seriously. The cabin had obviously been built here a very long time ago.

'There's a loft and bed if you care to stay,' Mo said.

'How much; I only have a few pesos with me?'

'Nothing, and if you don't have any wild and rowdy parties going on, you may remain here as long as you like.'

'That's rather generous of you. I suppose I could stay an extra day or two, but are you sure you want to do this?'

'Where we come from, we have no need for money;' Eli said with a chuckle, 'yours or anyone else's.' I wasn't sure what he meant by that but I wasn't about to argue with his offer. I had just enough for food, lodging and transportation from the village to make it back to Santiago before catching my flight home.

I looked around inside as Mo cooked breakfast for me on what appeared to be an ancient wood burning stove that reminded me of something similar I had seen somewhere before. Yes, now I remembered, it was the rustic alpine lodge where I stayed for a few days with a girlfriend deep in the Canadian Rockies. This wasn't as big, but it was still spacious and fully furnished, including three well-worn leather chairs by the fireplace. I wasn't sure whether to consider it a large cabin or small lodge. It seemed like both.[1]

The interior was completely open except for a couple of small rooms at the rear. The upstairs' loft had a window on the gable end facing northeast where the sun was shining in. The old hand hewn logs and mud caulking created a warm atmosphere, as though the place had been occupied for over a century. But by whom; no one would even find their way up here. Obviously Eli was spoofing me when saying he designed the cabin for me. Which was typical since it was often difficult to tell if he was being serious or not.

There were a number of woven rugs covering the old wood plank floor, a large bin filled with split wood, and, interestingly, several old books lined up on the mantel over the large fireplace. They all appeared to be hardcover copies from a bygone era, although I didn't examine the titles just then since Mo placed the breakfast he made for me on the old table, including fresh fruit, toast, a few slightly burned sausages and what tasted like a favourite blend of Columbian coffee. Most satisfying! The clouds were completely gone now as I stepped outside to survey the magnificent southeasterly Mountain range. It appeared they may extend well into Argentina. The sun's warm rays on my face evoked fond memories of staying at that isolated lodge years ago.

This lodge, though considerably smaller, had the same warm alpine atmosphere about it. I certainly hadn't anticipated having such good fortune when I planned my expedition. It hardly seemed real. In fact, I was beginning to wonder if it was. As with everything here, not much seemed logical: the food, the drink and certainly not this cabin. Certainly this wasn't a reasonable location for a Mountain retreat; much too remote for anyone to access. In fact, it was improbable to impossible; yet here it was, as were they. What else was I missing?

And what about them; how did I know they weren't on the lam, hiding up here from the law? It made me wonder about the great largess they claimed to have and where that may have come from. I should had good cause to be concerned, I thought, considering how little they had

---

[1] Since I couldn't decide whether to call it a cabin or lodge, I called it both. Sometimes Mo and Eli would refer to it as a chalet.

been forthcoming. But if they didn't want me to know, there wasn't much I could do about it. I thought that if maybe I told them some interesting things about myself, they would reciprocate by becoming a little more transparent about themselves.

Though they didn't ask, I presumed they would be interested knowing more about me. And so I found myself rambling on about who I was and what I had accomplished and all the important people I had met. All I was looking for was some respect and validation for who I thought I was. It seemed, however, I was a lot more impressed with me than they were.

Though they were attentive, there was no visible expression to anything I said. No commentaries, compliments, nods, smiles or request for my autograph. Nothing! The more I put myself out there the more I felt I was just flapping in the wind. This was most uncomfortable, since I normally try to present a confident persona of understated achievement -- except, of course, when I may overplay my hand due to a few too pints while attempting to interest some cute lassie in a public house.

Considering my all my academic scholarships, awards and various achievements, it seemed they didn't give a damn about any of this. Rather than show a little deference to me, they put me in the awkward position of having nothing left to say, as though I was a spend force. Eli continued to stare blankly at me, making me want to get up and throw a pint in his face to get a reaction. And Mo, what can I say? He just sat there staring into the sky again, thinking about God knows what.

It wasn't until later in the day it occurred to me that perhaps they already knew everything I had to say. Maybe that's why they appeared so insouciant; I hadn't thought of that before. But then, how could they have known? And yet it seemed they did. In any case, after I finished what had been an unintentional soliloquy, Eli picked up his guitar, played a few improvised licks, then offered to share a pint of bitter with me.

'Thanks,' I said, 'but I think I'm going to take a short walkabout on the ridge. I'll be back in a short while.'

Midway to the summit ridge, I suddenly changed my mind. I wasn't sure, but I decided instead to go down towards the chasm's mouth, not that far below the cabin. I was still feeling churlish and agitated as I stewed over them shutting me of their world. Though I was open and transparent with them, they gave me little information on themselves. Throughout the day, they evaded my questions, and even when they deigned to give one an enigmatic answer; it generally was about something ridiculous, as though they were from another planet.

Clearly, this was not a level playing field: everything was tilted against me where they got to change the rules to suite themselves as they wished. In particular, I was most annoyed with Eli for not taking me more seriously. Most of my students in his age range regarded me as their intellectual superior; but not him. At times he even acted as though he should be my teacher. Mo was much older and obviously very astute, and so I didn't expect the same deference from him.

Still I had to admire Eli, albeit begrudgingly. Obviously he was very bright, perhaps too bright for his own good – or mine. I associated him as being a mild mannered flower-child from a bygone era; a sixties counter-culture type who had the good fortune of inheriting a large estate. It seemed to me he would be content living as a aimless bohemian, loitered in old second hand bookstores, Turkish hookah lounges and grungy coffee shops where he probably cavorted with muddled young Goth woman wearing black clothing, bright red lipstick and high army boots. All in all, I would say, he probably had a good life.

Likely was caught up with the latest fashionable trends of *social injustice* issues. Or perhaps he was just a free spirit wanting to live out his life as some character in a Kerouac novel. I once knew several students like him who dropped out; often fashioning themselves as savants, reading just enough Marcuse or Sartre to ridicule the values and aspirations of bourgeoisie culture, just as I once did. It's what you do to remain radically respectable.

Not that I actually knew any of this about him; he just seemed to fit this mould based on his appearance. I envied his life, as I vicariously projected my images of idealism and wanderlust on him, wishing to live this life of freedom. In painful contradistinction, I had been spent most of my adulthood struggling to earn the respect of people I didn't even care about. What had I given up to prove something to myself? For all my trouble, all I had to show were a few fancy certificates hanging on my wall, purchased with a student debt higher than this mountain. I'd be indentured to the bank for years to come unless I received tenure to earn what I deserved for all my time, effort and money.

As I dwelt on this, my thoughts continued to spiral downward in self-pity while I descended to the chasm. As I stood overlooking the gaping abyss, I felt both fascinated and eerily troubled. There was something about this place that remained unresolved in my mind. I thought I remembered crossing it; yet I wasn't sure how that would have been possible. Possibly I did, at least in that weird dream I experienced back home.

From where I stood I could hardly see all the way to the bottom. For whatever reason, a strange déjà vu was haunting me here. I didn't know why, I just knew I had made it to the summit by scaling up fissure wedge in a precipice on the other side of the chasm. I still remembered how I had imagined being directed by a sweet enchanting voice that continued to echo in my mind.

I stared up towards the cabin near the summit ridge. Had I not even looked in that direction when I was on the other side of the chasm? The cabin should have been in plain sight, but it wasn't. So what am I supposed to make of that? Like everything else here, it was an enigmas. I sat on top of the chasm's precipice thinking about the growing list of inscrutable mysteries that seemed to mock my rational mind. Finally I made my way back to the cabin, having given up with finding out what was going on here.

I sat down on a chair outside beside Mo, hoping he would tip his hand without me having to ask him about was going on. We chatted for a moment about the topographical challenges in approaching to the summit, as he wondered why I had selected the most difficult route possible. I didn't have an answer, except to say it was an adventure and I always had remained confident I would eventually find a way, from whatever approach I took. I always did.

He looked at me quizzically for a moment but didn't say anything. Perhaps he thought I was crazy; certainly he wouldn't have been the first. Then after a few minutes of silence, he finally said, 'I have an important question for you James.'

'Of course; what would you like to know?'

'I've wondering,' he said, 'do you think it's what people do in life that makes them who they are?'

The question felt like a reproach and so I wasn't sure what to say. I thought it may have something to do with how I had earlier been blathering on about myself and my academic career. Perhaps it seemed to him I was defining myself by what I did rather than what I was. So was this his way of making me feel shallow? I hoped not. As I considered the question, it seemed he may have only intended it to be a rhetorical question, although it still made me feel defensive.

'I think,' I said to him, 'what we do gives us our sense of identity. And yet I'm sure are many things we may have done in the past that don't change the essential character of who we are. I was a sailor for a short time and now am a professor of philosophy. Yet I'm the same person.'

'So how shall we judge you, as a philosopher or sailor?'

'I would hope you wouldn't judge me at all, but rather look beyond the outward appearances of my vocations and see only my inward qualities.'

He nodded, as though in agreement. I then realized his question had been a ploy so I would hear the answer coming from my own mouth. So now he had me in a corner of my own creation, or should I say his. In any case it caused me to ask myself why I always needed to know what others did in life when evaluating them in relation to myself. Was this something I was in the habit of doing to leverage my outward credentials that I may gain some one-up-man-ship with those less educated and accomplished? Inward qualities often seemed incidental to the more obvious reality of appearances.

So is this why I was so determined to have Mo and Eli tell me about themselves – so that I may know where I stood in relationship to them? Based on my initial impressions, I thought I already had Eli figured out, but Mo was still a mystery.

As an aside, I only learned much later that Mo was highly regarded in the world as a scientist, inventor and thinker. He also had a doctorate in psychology with the equivalent of another PhD in physiology. It was most fortunate for me he didn't establish his credentials to re-assign me to a lower place in the pecking order.

Eli stepped outside with a loaf of freshly baked banana bread and placed it on a table. He then cut me a big slice and poured each of us a coffee from a full pot he just brewed. It was hard for me to remain upset for long with them when they were so gracious in their hospitality. So for now I tried to swallow my pride along with the bread and let things go for now. The inexplicable mysteries could wait a little longer. They hadn't said anything to humiliate me, not in the least. I did that to myself and realized my initial umbrage had mostly to do with my inflated ego's need to be recognized and affirmed. I wasn't accustomed to feeling subordinate to less educated people.

I wished to believe that I didn't give a rip what others thought about me since I had no need to impress anyone. Yet that's precisely what I had been trying to do. I was chagrined to realize I hadn't been able to detach my ego from what other's thought about me. I realized for the first time how the fear of being judged adversely could cause me to act irrationally, quite opposite of what I intended Likely that's why I became so reactive when I didn't feel sufficiently affirmed. It was disillusioning to think I was really no different than anyone else.

Strange as this place may be at times, at least I was learning a few things about myself; even things I didn't necessarily want to know. As it turned out, this was only the beginning. There was still much for me to discover before I could begin to know who I was, not just what I did. Finding my identity within was to become a major theme for me while I was here, as I supposed it should be for all of us.

Dark clouds began to billow over the ridge as rain poured all around us. With us remaining comfortably sheltered under the covered pergola, it didn't matter. I had much on in my mind as more questions kept coming to me such as this cabin's sudden appearance on the slope.

Mo went inside and Eli followed a few minutes later, leaving me alone to contemplate my situation and what I should do. I was greatly conflicted; perhaps it was time from me to leave. I would at time swing from placid contentment (or denial) to near panic whenever I considered my bizarre circumstances here. Who were these men? I had no idea what the consequences of staying here may have for me.

As much as I wanted to believe everything here was normal, I knew it wasn't. Worse, they seemed so damned oblivious to my concerns.

There was no interest in giving me with a rational explanation for all the anomalies I continued to encounter here. When I was around them everything was so calm and serene while playing chess by the fireplace. What could be more ordinary? It was only when I stepped back from the situation that I could see how queer things were – perhaps I got snagged into some friggin' warp on the space/time continuum.

Sure, I had rationalized away the voices I imagined hearing yesterday, although at the time I still wasn't completely sure about that. It seemed reasonable to assume it was only the wind's swirling gyrations sweeping over the rocky slopes combined with the exhaustion of my oxygen deprivation brain. As for the vision I had of the fissure route to the summit, it was just a lucky intuition I saw in my mind's eye. It all made sense and so I wasn't going to risk asking more questions for fear of what they might say. Most likely, they would tell me something that would make the question even more perplexing without offering any further explanation. That seemed to be the pattern here.

But the question that really bothered me the most was what the bloody hell they were doing up here in the first place? And, of course, there was the latest mystery of how I could possibly have missed seeing the cabin yesterday. Even putting that aside, the question remained how and why a cabin would be built here. No one lives on top of an inaccessible Mountain in such uninhabitable conditions. Also, it amazed me how they had managed to have every provision here that one could possibly want, including kegs of the finest Czech Pilsner stashed in the cellar. Added to that, Mo showed me several cases of fine European wines he had stored down there in case I felt thirsty at night.

The only answer I could come up with for this, as I suspected earlier, was that they hired a copter to airlift everything up here. But why would they do that? I confronted Eli about this earlier and he just said they didn't need a helicopter. And that's all he would say.

Then, there was also the question of those damned light orbs I thought I saw darting about on the summit, although I no longer was sure about anything up here anymore. Perhaps it was only in that dream. If the orbs were real and not an illusion, Mo and Eli should have known since they were already up here then. The more I thought about these unsolved mysteries, the more determined I was to interrogate them until they gave some straight answers.

But as it turned out, I didn't have to bother. It wasn't long before I would finally have a response, albeit not in a way I could have ever anticipated. Apparently it wasn't so much about what was happening around me, but what was happening to me. Hardly a satisfactory answer! Nevertheless, I was about to discover that by some strange quirk, I was implicated and embroiled in the very questions I was seeking answers, far beyond anything I could have imagined.

'James,' Mo called from inside, 'looks like the rain's not going to let up for a while, so why not come in and join us by the blazing fire Eli had stoked up. We have a few important matters to discuss with you that might help you understand a few things we suspect you've wondered about lately.'

I was completely caught off guard by this; and frankly, a little concerned where things may lead. Just when I was planning my offensive, they had me on the defensive again. Anytime someone says they wish to discuss something with you, you already know it's most likely not going to be good.

'So what's on your mind?' I said somewhat cavalierly as I went inside.

'Please take your favourite lounge seat and make yourself comfortable' Eli said, 'this may take a while. Here, have another slice of Mo's banana bread. It's best when it's fresh.'

'Yes, of course,' I said, 'and I'm sure the bananas in the bread are fresh too, picked off the trees growing in the glaciers on the mountain's south face. So what's this about' I asked somewhat uncomfortably, 'is there a problem?'

'No, no, not at all,' Mo said, 'at least not unless you wish to see it as a problem; but we hope you won't. What we want to discuss with you is something we think is most significant, something that will likely change just about everything in your life and even how you look it. But before we get into all that, if you don't mind, we'd like to review the last several years of your time on earth.'

'That's what this is about, the story of my life?' I said with a mocking laugh. 'No disrespect to either of you, but you don't even know me, even though you think you do. And so now you're going to tell me about me and my life. What kind of game is this? Maybe when you're done, I can have a turn guessing yours too!'

Ignoring this suggestion, Mo got right down to what he had to say. 'James, not long ago you had a dream. Do you remember? It was a very vivid dream about living in a dreadful swamp in the Lowlands before you escaped to climb a very high Mountain to free yourself from the ruts you had become stuck in. Perhaps it was to this Mountain you escaped. The dream was so vivid that upon waking you immediately wrote everything down that you were able to remember. You were fascinated and intrigued with its stark realism and yet it greatly frightened you, feeling more like a nightmare at the very end, although you weren't sure why.'

That's truly exceptional, I thought; as a matter of fact, it's rather shocking. I hadn't told anyone about my dream so how could they know? Indeed I was shaking as I woke up in a sweat but I wasn't going to admit that to them. My first reaction was to deny having any such a dream. But obviously he already knew too much. If I denied it, he would know I was lying; and, if he called me on it, he'd really have me and we both would know it.

'What are you Mo, psychic or something even weirder? I've never told anyone about this dream so how do you know?'

He ignored these comments as he began to slowly recount my dream to the very end, scene by scene, all in sequential order. I'm serious. This wasn't what I was expecting when Mo said they had something to discuss with me. At times Eli would take over certain segments and between them they wove their tale most impressively, describing it even better than what I had remembered.

In fact, they were dead on accurate with details that depicted my life in a phantasm of miasmic swamps, bogs and thistles. Next, they went on to describe how I stole away from my hovel in search of an elusive Mountain far away, which I eventually discovered after drudging and slogging for days through the marshy Lowlands. I remember how it felt I had struggled for years ascending the Mountain.

As I already indicated, I wrote all I could remember immediately after the dream; and even for days thereafter as more scenes appeared to me in greater detail. But as I listened now, many of these images flashed back to me as they described my climbing adventure in amazing precision and vivid detail.

Though I tried to remain outwardly aloof, I could hardly believe what I was hearing. They were even able to conjure impressions I had forgotten about, such as the condors swooping at me like cacodemons out of hell. Which as it turns out really did happen while crossing over the narrowest of ridges when I would wildly swing my rope to keep them at bay.

That's another thing that was amazing to me. While climbing, it never occurred to me I had already experienced this in my dream long before coming here. It was all there, they were just reminding me of these parallel realities, the one portended and the one I just experienced in time and space.

When they both finished with their story, there was a long silence as I continued to stare into the flames. After a minute or two, I got up without saying anything. Although I was careful not to show my reaction, I was feeling stunned! It was also disconcerting to have them intrude into my private inner world, telling me what was happening in my mind while I slept. If they knew this much about me, what else did they know?

I got up and walked to the stove and poured another cup of coffee, then stood by the window vacantly gazing outward. I was in shock, and for the moment, all I was aware of, is that the rain had stopped and the sun was shining brightly again. After a few minutes, I returned to sit in my chair as I stared at them blankly, not knowing what to say. They hadn't said a word since completing their narrative, or, they said, my narrative.

I didn't have a rational answer for any of this except it shouldn't have been possible. It was as astonishing as it was disturbing. Initially I was taken by their story, but when I realized this was my dream they were reflecting back to me, I felt confused, exposed and resentful with them probing the inward sanctum of my mind. Considering everything else I was grappling with up here, this was one more layer of fractious intrigue to complicate my world, which was turning out to be spookier by the minute.

At last I spoke, trying to remain as detached as I could. I may have been a bit rude and dismissive, but then, I hadn't exactly invited them to analyze my dream. 'In a swamp you say? That's most hilarious! Sorry chaps, I'm not Pogo[1] and I don't live anywhere near a swamp; so guess you've got the wrong opossum. Sounds like some wild science fiction parallel universe that writers like to dream up. Besides, I don't get what all the swampy bogs and ruts in the mud are supposed to represent.'

Admittedly my cavalier attitude was not that convincing, but I wasn't going to blithely accept everything they had to say unchallenged. It was my life, not theirs. Just what right did they have to presume they knew everything about me? So rather than admit to the merits of what was said, I became increasingly flippant as I challenged their interpretations.

If I was perhaps being a bit obnoxious at times, likely it was because I feared having all my personal shortcomings being laid bare. I'd prefer to find a certified shrink if I thought I needed to be psycho-analyzed rather than have these amateurs meddling with my mind. I also questioned why they were doing this; what was in it for them? Perhaps to show me how smart they were? The more I thought about it, the more preposterous things felt, which made me even more irate and suspicious of them. I was a rationalist, but nothing here was rational.

However, they weren't about to be deterred as they began to press on with their interpretation of my dream. According to them, its purpose was to allegorically illustrate to me how my life in the Lowlands, because of my disillusionment, eventually led me to pursuing some higher purpose symbolized by the Mountain image.

This wasn't news to me, since I was already aware of how much the dream paralleled many of the real life challenges I had recently experienced over the last few years. In fact, I remember reflecting on this for weeks after the dream. Also, as an educator, I was well aware of both Freudian and Jungian theories of how effective allegories are as literary devices in communicating universal concepts.

---

[1] Pogo was a popular and insightful American comic strip, published several decades ago, full of political satire and allegory with swamp animals in southeastern USA. Pogo, the lead character, was an opossum who often said such astute things as: *"We've met the enemy, and he is us."*

I had to admit, at least to myself, there was something more to this dream that I needed to understand, especially with how it may have prefigured a desire for me to journey to some higher plane in life. Admittedly, hearing this story told by someone else seemed to be awakening something in me, perhaps some hidden message I didn't wish to hear.

If so, I still wasn't sure how to interpret the symbolic significance of fogs, snakes, bogs and ruts that supposedly were part of my life. Perhaps there was much more to my dream episode than I cared to acknowledge with all these representing various suppressed fears and frustrations I wasn't outwardly aware of having.

Yet there was something crucial missing. The dreadful end; what was it supposed to mean? They didn't say. When in the past I reviewed my notes on the dream, I didn't want to think about that part since it had caused me to awaken in trauma – that would hardly presage anything good for my future. Yet it seemed everything prior to the ending was to be understood as a preamble to something that remained enshrouded in mystery.

Not wishing to take things too seriously, especially the ending, I contrived a clever rationalization that seemed intellectually plausible to me. Perhaps they would agree and we could come to an intelligent resolution regarding the meaning of the story. Then, perhaps we could finally move on to the more important questions I wished to have answered.

'You know,' I said, 'I very well may have had a dream something like this, but I think in many ways it's also everyone's archetypal dream. Consider man's universal struggle that often takes him from the depths of despair to the heights of ecstasy; from the Lowland swamps to the Mountain peaks. Or, on another level, it could even be understood as a statement of evolution from the primordial swamps towards man's upward ascent into higher human consciousness.'

That last point, I thought, was rather astute and anthropologically plausible. Who wouldn't agree with that? 'So obviously the Swamp/Mountain allegory isn't just about me; it's about the universal human experience that applies to all of us. Furthermore, I'm sure everyone has a dream like this at one time or another with whatever unique symbols may illustrate the visceral struggles of life. For example, Hesiod dreamt up the Promethean myth as someone continuing to toil and strive pushing a boulder up the Mountain over and over again.[1] Don't we all feel that enervation and fatigue with life from time to time?

'As for me, I've lived comfortably in a number of cosmopolitan centres and I'm not sure I would consider any of them to be swamps, even figuratively. And though the flat I lease isn't particularly elegant, I wouldn't consider it a hovel. In fact it's rather comfortable, conveniently located over a coffee and deli shop on a street not far from near the Thames where I enjoy going for strolls. I have hundreds of books I put to good use lining my walls against damp winter drafts. I have a wonderful career, or I very likely will someday. I have several intellectual friends, many of them eccentric but charming enough in their own way. And of course, there's always a number of flighty women in my life who seem to dig me when I get paid – but let's not discuss that now. Considering my relatively good life I think it's important we don't get too carried away looking for symbols and meanings where they don't exist.'

I suspected I wouldn't be able to bluff either of them about my less than ideal life. But I'd try anyway, if only to show them they didn't know everything. It was becoming increasingly apparent they were both ingenious thinkers, though most unorthodox in their various views about life – which was another reason to be bewildered.

At times I felt I was out of my league, even with Eli. As I said before, he was my junior, appearing to be at least ten years younger, much like the graduate students. He possessed a youthful exuberance with his jokes and pranks. And so it was rather humiliating whenever I found I could match his knowledge and understand. It wasn't just about him being clever, that's common enough with some the students in my more advanced classes. Rather, there was a certain sage quality he evinced with a quiet confidence that I both admired and envied.

And now to make it worse, he had blithely described much of my dream with an air of confident authority, as though it was his dream. Again I asked myself, how could he even begin to know this? As much

---

[1] Hesiod, the Greek poet, wrote about Prometheus as a mythological character in his epic *Theogony* approximately 8th century B.C. Percy Bysshe Shelley popularized this myth in the early 19th century with his poem *Prometheus Unbound.*

as I wanted to dismiss what they described as a joke, I couldn't deny what they said. Their interpretations were compelling, if not troubling. I had no rational 'box' to explain how they managed to know so much. I asked them several times how they could possibly knew so much about me and how they could possibly interpret a dream I hadn't told them about and still I couldn't pry any meaningful information out of them.

Feeling increasingly frustrated and exposed after not getting anywhere, I stood to my feet and raised my voice angrily. 'You know gentleman, I think you realize I've been very forthright about myself, so I think it's time you come clean and reciprocate the favour. So just tell me once and for all, WHO THE HELL DO YOU THINK YOU ARE?'

'Oh, don't let that concern you, James,' Eli said, with a mischievous and disarming smirk on his face, 'we know who we are. We don't even have to think about it. But we think it's more important that you find who you are, and then you'll know who we are too.'

More gibberish, I thought – always turning things around on me to their advantage.

'But we understand why you may feel uncomfortable with how we seem to know so much about you,' he said. 'We sympathize completely; that's really got to be unnerving. So just be patient with us ol' chap, we're coming to that part. For now, let us again assure you we're harmless. As much as we know about you, we're definitely not with INTERPOL, Mi6, CIA, or worse yet, the British Internal Revenue Service. So don't be concerned, we're your friends wishing to help you along your way.'

'But I didn't ask for your help,' I responded churlishly, as I headed towards the door. 'I found my way up here alone, and if you please, I'll soon be finding my way down.'

With that I left the cabin to determine what I should do next as I walked along the summit ridge. With all they had thrown at me, I needed time to reconsider what was going on here. I began to wonder if maybe, just maybe, my companions were from somewhere other than earth. Admittedly, a most irrational thought, but perhaps there was some reason for the *heebie-jeebies* I felt yesterday just before meeting them. That was no ordinary encounter. Now on top of that, I was really bewildered after hearing their story of my dream, wondering if I wasn't participating in some surreal scene in the *Twilight Zone.*[1]

The longer I was with them, the more obvious the quirks were becoming with the odd things they would say and do. Various things would magically appear whenever there was a desire for them; food, drink, firewood and even books. Certainly, from what I could tell, there were no smoke and mirrors. The manifestations had now gone far beyond trickery to something much more serious.

The more I thought about this the more I felt I had to leave this place before it was too late. I didn't want to get caught in something so strange I wouldn't be able get out again. As much as I would have liked to have stayed in this idyllic lodge a little longer under normal circumstances, I determined I would begin my descent tomorrow morning just after sunrise.

For the remainder of the day, I decided to do a bit more exploring along this long Mountain ridge to decide the best route for my descent. I was hoping for clear weather tomorrow; it appeared the current pattern may hold but you can never really tell from day to day, or hour to hour in these mountains.

When I returned by late afternoon, they were still at the cabin preparing something that appeared to be a fine dining production. Indeed, these were really likeable chaps when they weren't being so unpredictable. Even by British norms they were eccentric.

Obviously it was Italian night on the summit with pasta and the finest Sicilian wine in the neighbourhood. I wasn't hungry, at least until I saw the cheese baked penne primavera. Actually, eating on the summit was more like having a ravenous appetite for delicious food without actually having hunger pangs. Funny, I thought, I couldn't recall feeling any hunger since arriving here half starved!

In spite of their levity and good cheer, I began to witness more dubious events going on around me that evening. As an example, we went outside after dinner to sit by a roaring fire which Eli built not far from the cabin. The lingering twilight fading was into darkness as a few

---

[1] *The Twilight Zone* was a weekly television series in the late 1950s and early 1960's that dealt with unexplainable events, often being paranormal encounters with beings outside the Earth's dimensions.

stars began to poke through the indigo sky. After more talk, laughter and whiskey, Mo got up to take a long stick out of the fire that was enflamed on one end.

As he stood there by the flames, he held the stick up towards the sky like it was a staff by which he was about to perform some ancient Celtic ritual. Perhaps it was the leaping flames behind him, but suddenly he appeared to have grown much taller, perhaps seven or eight feet tall, much like Tolkien's Gandalf hovering over the dwarfs, with me being the dwarf. I made some ingenuous remark about him appearing to be a wizard against the glow of the flames.

'Oh really,' he said, 'then this stick I'm holding must be my wand; every wizard must have a magic wand. Then he tossed the fiery stick into the night sky as it began to rapidly twirl like a propeller, shooting through the darkness like a hot flaming star. I never did see it come down again, maybe it went over the chasm, but that would have been a very long way for it to fly. What I witnessed was impossible, unless. ...

Then he turned to me and said, 'I have a much deeper wizardry for you James. It has to do with the alchemy of your soul. It all starts with the question Eli brought up today. The answer, when you find it, will cause you to glow brighter than the flames of a wizard's wand tossed into the night's sky.'

By now I was rather dazed and confounded. 'I'll see if I can find the answer you're looking for,' I said.

'Or more correctly,' he said, 'the answer you're looking for. It's a very simple question with a rather difficult answer. Think about it very deeply tonight and every night; you may find that it takes a considerable amount of time and effort to receive an answer.'

There was a long pause, with nothing more said. Before I could respond, he got up and slowly walked out into the darkness. Eli stared at me for a moment with a curious look I didn't understand. Then after a few moments, he too got up and walked off into the night without saying a word. Suddenly, I began to feel very alone and wondered if I'd ever see them again. If I left at sunrise as planned, likely I never would.

Alone in the cabin, the question continued to haunt me through the night. Who was I? Such a basic question, and yet I hadn't given it a lot of thought, even though I understood in the ancient past such ontological considerations were essential to philosophical enquiry. Am I more than my body; such that my inner awareness makes me, me, rather than being just a function of my biological constitution? If I don't know who I was, how would anyone else?

I struggled to find a meaningful answer, frustrating myself with even more introspective questions. Where did I come from, where am I going, will I ever get there, wherever that is? Will it be another Mountain range that's even higher next before I find contentment? Was I a Prometheus, pushing my boulder further up the Mountain without being able to make it to the top? Or perhaps my challenges were far less dramatic, where I kept getting stuck in the ruts back home on a journey that led to nowhere.

Whatever the case, I asked why life was such a struggle where I always had to be striving for something bigger and more significant in my life? What was I trying to prove? And why am I even bothering to answer these insane questions? Well okay, I admitted to myself, they may not be insane, but they certainly may drive me to insanity if I don't soon get away.

Possibly I needed to reread Viktor Frankel.[1] At least he spoke of the meaning of life even though he wasn't a philosopher per se; probably he was beyond that. I had never asked myself what was the meaning and purpose for which I strove. A philosopher should be able to at least provide some understanding to life's basic questions, not just more questions. And if philosophers no longer ask those kinds of questions, that's not to say they're not important and shouldn't be asked.

As I attempted to think things through, I become increasingly confused, which made me consider whether all the answers I sought were found in my dream and there was really nothing more for me to think, only to know. Was the dream something bigger than me, providing me with the all wisdom I had ignored? And were these men sent here to reveal to me some implicit message within the dream?

But why; and by whom?

---

[1] This is in reference to a famous book I once read several years ago called *Man's Search for Meaning*, by Viktor Frankl M.D, PhD. (1905 – 1997). Frankl was an Auschwitz concentration camp inmate during World War II where he conceived of an existential analysis for the meaning in life he later called Logotherapy.

CHAPTER 4

THE COMPANY YOU KEEP

A person starts to live when he can live outside himself[1]

I remained in bed for some time in the morning, thinking more about who I really was. It weighed upon me that I hadn't come up with a single plausible answer to such a basic question, even though I thought about it through much of the night. It was simple, but the answer was elusive.

As I went down the stairs, I could see my friends hadn't returned, causing me to wonder if there was some other place on the summit where they stayed at night. Perhaps somewhere they didn't wish me to know. No matter, that was their business.

After brewing a coffee, I decided to take a short walk along the ridge to survey the westerly horizon where the storm clouds often swept in from the South Pacific. As I viewed the horizon, my mood began to improve as the rising sun illuminated the glacial slopes with a pink glow. Very beautiful, I thought, like an inspiring omen portending something extraordinary, though I wasn't sure what that may be. Perhaps there would be a tenure contract waiting for me in London when I returned!

---

[1] Albert Einstein

It appeared the weather would be ideal for me to begin my descent into civilization, although I still wasn't sure which route to take. If possible, I'd like to find a way with fewer escarpments, even if it took longer.

But before beginning my descent, I hoped my two friends would soon show up that I may bid them adieu. Notwithstanding the inexplicable incidents I experienced, my time here had been eventful; the food, drinks, accommodation and company – most compelling and charming to say the least.

Also, I had achieved what I set out to accomplish, successfully ascending where few have gone or could have gone! However, it was now time to leave, before being overwhelmed with their orbs, voices, mind reading, wizards, nymphs, fairies and whatever else may be lurking about.

With that thought, I smiled to myself, as I headed back to the cabin to stuff my backpack with my belongings and sufficient food to prepare for the long descent to the Lowlands of supposed hovels, bogs and swamps. With all their stories, I would never again be able to view London in quite the same way.

Thinking about home, I wondered if any of the fine young women I dated would be missing me by now, perhaps wondering where I had gone. After all I had gone through on this expedition; I was beginning to miss them. Likely I wouldn't receive a hero's welcome, but I would be grateful to receive whatever pleasures they wished to offer me.

When l left for the winter semester break I didn't tell anyone about my plans to go to Chile. I didn't want anyone nattering about how dangerous it would be to go this far alone, especially in such a remote region. But was this not a scene out of my dream allegory, the part where I slunk out of the Lowlands into the darkness? An interesting thought!

Likely at this time of year, just after summer solstice, there would be close to sixteen hours of sunlight remaining. I thought if I left now, I could make significant headway before nightfall. It will only take a few days, provided the weather continued to hold. Although I had carefully observed the Mountain's topography while on my ascent, I still had some qualms about the best way to retreat and what unforeseen challenges I may encounter.

Hopefully I would find a better route down than the one I chose for my ascent, which made for an overly circuitous itinerary to the Summit. Occasionally, I become disorientated after making a few unfortunate twists and turns, where I had to go a considerable way down to find a new way up again -- much like we experience in life, I suppose.

Once again I wondered about my friends and where they disappeared. I didn't see any sign of them the trail, no smouldering campfires or anything else indicating they were here. I didn't even know if they would return; they didn't say. If they did, it would be a good idea to get their advice before making my way down. Eli, in particular, seemed to know his way around rather well; at least by the way he talked about the region's topography.

Hopefully he would know where I needed to avoid the dangerous crevices that had thinly veiled layers of melting ice. It would be easy enough to tumble down, and even if I survived the fall, I wouldn't likely be able to claw my way up the glaringly ice fissures. To make it worse, there would be zero chance of rescue in this remote region of the world. Hypothermia would probably overcome me within a few hours and it would soon be over. What a way to go! I didn't even want to think about this. Though a more direct route down may be shorter, it may end up taking longer if I encounter some unforeseen difficulties. Hopefully they would return to the cabin soon before I began to find my way down.

As I came into full view of the cabin from the Summit I was pleased to smell smoke wafting up from the fireplace. I didn't know how I was able to have missed them on the ridge, but somehow I did. At least I hoped it would be them. Nothing was very certain here. Perhaps there may be other aliens taking over, I chuckled to myself. Assuming my friends had postal or email addresses, we could exchange our contact information so we could stay in touch and possible meet again someday.

But that was another thing about them; they never did tell me where they lived. I assumed it was somewhere in Britain, but then, many Englishmen have a tendency to live throughout the world in former colonies. In any case, I planned to do more traveling while attending various academic conferences in Europe. Possibly our paths would cross again.

As I stepped through the door, I was greeted by Eli with a jovial *'buenos días.'* Mo was preparing something on the stove while Eli poured me a dark roast coffee. I thought it wouldn't hurt to have a hearty breakfast before beginning my descent. As we sat having an old fashioned English breakfast, Eli suggested possible routes I may wish to consider, but there was something disingenuous about his perfunctory remarks, as if he didn't believe I would be going anywhere.

They both could be so damned disarming with their good natured charm, yet it always seemed there was some ambiguity attached to everything they said and did, so you could never be certain where you stood. This morning they were going out of their way to be extra pleasant; perhaps because of some ulterior motives for wanting me to remain here. I preferred, however, to believe it was because they were making amends for leaving me alone last night after abruptly disappearing into the night; which still had me both curious and concerned.

'I wasn't sure I'd see you again.' I said. 'So where in the heavens did you disappear last night?'

'Exactly where in the heavens is not easy to explain,' Eli said with a grin.

'So did you stay somewhere further along the ridge?'

'You might say that,' Mo said; 'if not further, certainly beyond. I'm sure you may get to see it someday.'

Yes, of course, I thought; someday, somewhere. More mystery, more intrigue. Can't anything be straightforward here?

'Thanks for the meal,' I said after finishing, 'but I really ought to be on my way. I want to get as far down as possible in the daylight.'

'James,' Mo said, 'before you go, I must ask if you've given any further consideration to what we said about your dream yesterday, and what it may mean?'

'Not really,' I said, although that wasn't really the case. 'As I said before, I normally don't pay too much attention to dreams. There are more important things I have to do with my time than make sense of all the subliminal nonsense that sometimes surfaces at night. I'll admit though, I've never before had a dream like that before. At the time it left an indelible impression on me. In fact, I can still remember standing on some precarious ledge just before awakening in a panic. Guess I'll never know what that was about.'

'A real cliff hanger,' Eli said with a smirk.

'It was, so to speak. Don't get me wrong, your interpretations were most provocative, but I'll still hold to my own thoughts about what this dream may or may not mean.'

'It would be good if you could have a session with Dr. Jung,' Mo said. 'I'm sure you are aware how big he was on archetypes.'

'I'm sure that would be most interesting,' I said, 'the only problem is he died over fifty years ago. So I hope you aren't proposing we arrange to have a séance with the esteemed professor, although nothing would surprise me any more considering everything else that's been going on here. Not even something as ludicrous as trying to talk to the dead.'

'We agree, a séance would be ridiculous,' Eli said. 'In fact, under the circumstances, it would be meaningless.'

'Of course,' I said, 'once you're dead, you're dead! It's obvious! So called psychics who claim to conjure the dead are only playing the same kind of mind games you two chaps seem to enjoy, except they charge a fee.'

'Are you saying our narrative of your dream was only a mind game?' asked Mo.

'If you can give me another rational explanation, I may be less sceptical. Besides, I still have some difficulty in accepting the various interpretations of what you think these symbols are supposed to mean. Yet based on what I recall, and the notes I made, I'll admit your narration of events line up remarkably well. In fact almost too well, considering how you were able to evoke many of the same feelings I remembered having, including the last part on a narrow ridge. So what's the trick?'

'If you wish,' Eli said, 'we could give you a rational explanation that may fit within the limitations of your permitted reality.'

'Most certainly,' I said, 'for once a rational explanation would be most welcome.'

'Well,' he said, 'it's really quite simple and logical – and we know how much you love logic. So when you weren't looking, Mo and I scampered up the stairs of your London flat. It was rather easy for us to pick the door lock find your notes in a drawer. Then we ran down the stairs and made our way as fast as we could to a stationery shop that had copier. As soon as we made a photo copy, we ran back the whole way and returned the notes before you had a chance to notice they were gone.

'We had it planned rather well, wouldn't you say? So when you finally got here -- we were all set to trick you. We literally read your dream -- straight from you notes! Aren't we good? Makes a lot of sense doesn't it, no psychic voodoo going on; all is naturally explained. And so, as all intelligent people know, it must be true because only natural explanations can be true.'

Before I was able to respond to Eli's feigned account with, Mo took over and said in a more conciliatory tone: 'James we also understand why you often seem confused by some of the things we say and what at times may appear to be rather bizarre.'

'Like throwing sticks into the air that don't come down?' I said.

'Oh that – not a big deal,' Mo said. 'Think of it as a shooting star in reverse.'

'But if that impressed you, you should see what Merlin can do,' Eli said with a straight face. 'Now there's a real wizard for you.'

'I'm sure,' I said, 'but let's not bring Merlin into this; things are strange enough here as it is.'

'We realize,' Mo said, 'you're anxious to make your descent down the Mountain, but please indulge us a little longer that we may clear up a few more things for you so you need feel so confused when you return to London. We also understand you're probably tired of hearing us talk about your dream, yet we still need to finish telling you a few things, or nothing we've said so far so far will make any sense.'

'Nothing here makes much sense,' I said, 'however, carry on if you must, if only to confuse me more.'

'Don't be concerned,' Mo said, 'eventually you will find our answers to be most reasonable, but first we want to clear up an important item regarding your dream. We appreciate why you may still have a few reservations about our interpretations. After all, your life seems to have nothing to do with marshes, mosquito infested swamps with slimy snakes slithering around your highly coveted hovels made of *wood, hay and stubble* built on sand.'[1]

'No, nothing like that all,' I said, 'not even figuratively.'

'We recognize why some of the meanings behind these images are not all that apparent,' he said. 'Your perceptions were formulated long ago in accordance with the temporal material world you're most familiar with. Yet you likely wouldn't be here now if these former constructs still served you. Our universe is entirely different than what you or your world can possibly imagine. But one day I'm sure you'll understand.'

How condescending, I thought, as though they knew everything and I knew nothing. The presumption being, that if I come around to see things as they do, then and only then will I know how things really are.

'Sorry, but I'll be the one who decides for myself what is real and what isn't.'

'But of course,' Eli said, 'and yet this time it was different for you, wasn't it? Remember, what happened at the beginning of your dream, the behest of a strange voice portending your pending journey from the Lowlands to the Summit? Within, you know that's the real reason you came here.

'At some level, I'm sure you recognize you didn't risk life and limb just so you may climb this remote mountain for no other reason than to challenge yourself to new extremes of physical achievement and survival. Considering the danger, it would seem ill-advised or even foolhardy for you to have even attempted this expedition if there wasn't something significant thrusting you forward.

'After your dream, you understood there was something more to life than you were experiencing, although you didn't know exactly what that may be. You just knew you couldn't live in the Lowlands' swamp anymore. It had become too low and shallow for your higher

---

[1] This last statement of Mo's made little sense to me until I later discovered that it was in reference to a quote about what has lasting consequence in life: *'Now if any man build upon this foundation gold, silver, precious stones, wood, hay, stubble, every man's work shall be made manifest: for the day shall declare it, because it shall be revealed by fire, and the fire shall try every man's work of what sort it is.'* I Corinthians 3:12 (KJV)

aspirations. In a sense James, you never did wake up from the dream but the dream woke you up and began to change your life. After that, you knew you had to follow where it was calling you; and so you have. This is it, the adventure you're now on.'

'Sounds like you have me figured out, Eli,' I said, with a bite of sarcasm.

'Actually, Eli's right,' Mo said, 'it was the inward call that moved you beyond the mists of the Lowlands towards something you didn't understand and still don't. You soon will though; your world is about to change. This Mountain represents that higher quest, and you will soon find it becomes more than a metaphor but a new emergence.'

'In fact, it will be the foundation on which you build your new reality: much more solid than the bogs on which you attempted to build your life.'

'You don't say?' I said, still incredulous.

'Yes, we say this and a lot more,' Mo said, 'so listen carefully because we're about to give you the secret meaning that's hidden behind this. It's what you've been waiting for, a higher order perspective, even higher than this mountain you find yourself on.'

'Of course,' I said muttering, 'it seems only right I should know about higher perspectives after all I endured getting up here.'

'You are right,' Eli said, 'indeed you've gone to a fair amount of trouble, more than you realize. In fact, it's taken you your whole life to get this far, just as it felt in your dream!'

'Let's not get carried away with the dream allegory, Eli,' I said. 'I think it's been less than a week since I left London.'

'You made it this far up,' Mo said, 'but you still have a lot further to go since you can always transcend into higher realms. And as you go further up, you must go further in.'

'Further in; to where?'

'Further in to higher realms,' Eli said.

'Ah, more metaphorical posers' I said. 'You know; every major philosophy of antiquity has contrived higher realms of truth; so which one are you flogging?'

'Not all philosophies are committed to ascending higher realms,' Mo said. 'Many philosophers, particularly today, are more interested in leading their followers to the lowest and flattest realms where they can impose their beliefs on minds that have become too shallow to notice. We suspect that by now, you've heard enough of their claptrap, so you're ready to advance into higher realms of reality. In fact you're already well on your way, you just haven't figured it out yet. Nevertheless you will – the further in you go.'

As Mo focused his penetrating eyes on me in a way that made me feel uncomfortable. 'What we're going to do now,' he said, 'is take you further in and reveal something to you that may shock you, but it certainly will take you higher. We suspect you will resist believing us until it fully registers in the depths of your soul. And when it does, you will come to understand life through eyes you didn't know could see and hear with ears you didn't know could hear. And though you may not at first be able to fully comprehend the significance of what happened; we'll work with you to help you understand your new reality.'

'New reality,' I said, 'what wrong with the old reality? Reality is reality; it's not the kind of thing you can go around reinventing whenever it suits your fancy.'

'True,' he said, 'but who says you can't experience higher dimensions of reality. Rather than inventing, it's more like discovering what's already there, though it may not always be recognised. It's why we asked you if you knew who you are. You are finding how impossible it is to answer that question within the terms of normal rational enquiry.'

'Not that the answer is irrational,' Eli said, 'it's just that reason can't answer questions that are beyond the scope of its understanding. Reason is of the mind but when it comes to certain things, the mind can only see shadows and distortions. Whether you realize it or not, you are more than mind. Until you realize that, you're going to knock yourself out trying to understand the world. Your old terms of reference are inadequate because they are crafted in the Lowlands.'

'Balderdash,' I said, 'reason is either rational or irrational; there's nothing between.'

'True, there's nothing between,' Mo said, 'but there is something over and above.'

'Such as what?'

'There are various ways to understand what transcends the imitations of the linear plane,' he said, 'which we'll explain later. Obviously, none of this is taught in the Flatlands, or you would already know what we mean. If they did teach it, the Flatlands would be flat no more.'

'Flatlands; so where's that?'

'A place where you've spent much of your life,' Eli said. 'Let's just say it's the lowest regions of the Lowlands. But we'll explain that later too.'

'Fine, but your explanations will have to wait for another time and place; I really must be on my way now.'

'Certainly,' Mo said, 'but when you come to answer the question I asked you last night about who you are, only then you will fully understand what is meant by the term *Flatlands*.[1] Knowing who you are has little meaning to anyone who lives there but if they cared to find out they would very soon leave that place for higher ground. It would feel too constricting to remain on such a plain once they discovered the answer to who they are.'

'Good to know – along with your other riddles and metaphors! Possibly we can discuss these recondite abstractions another time should I ever see you in London.'

'Before you go, have another scone with jam and coffee,' Mo said, 'I still need you to tell me if you've given more thought to that question I put to you.'

'You mean about understanding who I am? I didn't want to get into another big epistemological/ontological debate at this time, so I just shrugged and said, 'sure I thought about it but I didn't get too far. But if you really want to know, I can tell you I'm a male Caucasian of British citizenship, thirty three years of age, six feet one inch, 198 pounds of lean muscle and bone, with enough brain tissue left over to be a Professor of Philosophy in London. And I might add, a connoisseur of fine wine and women, though not necessarily in that order. Sorry to disappoint you, but as far as I can tell, that's about all there's to know about me at this point.'

'I'm not disappointed at all,' Mo said. 'In fact, the point of me asking

---

[1] The first writing I know of that uses the term *flatland*, at least in the context spoke of here, was a science fiction classic simply called *Flatland* (1884) by Edward A. Abbot (1838-1926), a London headmaster, scholar and theologian.

you the question was so you would discover how little you know about who you are and how difficult it is to find a serious answer. But don't despair, there is an answer, and we trust you will know it before you leave.'

'Well okay, then let's have it. I've got a few minutes. What's the big ontological secret that's forever eluded mankind? Just the bottom line please, so I can be on my way!'

'When you are ready to know, you will know,' he said, 'not because we gave you an answer, since no one can do that for you. It can't be learned, it can only be discovered. But not by the mind, only the heart knows. Do you remember what the ancient inscription on the Temple of Apollo at Delphi said?'

'NOSCE TE IPSUM! Pythagoras and Plato, along with many other Greeks, were obsessed with this.'

'And that, James, is why you are here – to KNOW THYSELF!'

'That's most excellent, but I know a much quicker way. It's on my ID tag hanging on the chain around my neck. I had it inscribed on a pendant in case I had an accident or got killed climbing here.'

'Oh really,' Eli said. 'Did you hear that Mo: James has his whole identity hanging on a chain. So let's see it.'

'I felt around my neck. 'Bloody hell -- it's not here! Where could it have gone? Did either of you see it lying around? Damn, I hope it's not lost. I can't believe I didn't notice this earlier.'

'What does it look like,' asked Eli?

'It's on a silver chain with a pendant and gold cross.'

'Really' Eli said, 'a gold cross? I thought you said you weren't religious.'

'I'm not, but that but it has some sentimental value to me. The cross was given to me when I was a just a young child. Recently, I came across it in an old box, and so I put it on the chain with my pendant for good luck.'

'For good luck?' Eli said. 'So then you're not religious, just superstitious.'

'Well, actually, I'm not that either, but you know what I mean.'

'I'm certain it will find its way back to you;' Mo said, 'don't worry about it.'

'It has to be around here someplace;' I said, 'it's not like I've gone anywhere far.'

'No, but your chain, cross and pendant may have,' he said.

'What do you mean by that?' I said, because I really must find them before I leave.'

Mo got up to his feet, stretched, and said; 'why don't we move over to the fireplace so we can relax by the fire. Bring your coffee; there's a few things you need to know before you leave.'

'Okay, but make it quick, I've still got to find my ID before I go.'

'We'll help you find your ID,' Eli said, 'and when you do, it will be time for you to return home. But it may take much longer than you think.'

'What was that supposed to mean? Are we talking about the same thing?'

'You've been curious about so much since you arrived,' said Mo, 'now we're about to tell you everything. Perhaps even more than you wish to know. Understand the more answers we give you the more questions you will have. So take your seat, get comfortable and take ten deep breaths, then relax and center within. This will help you find your identity, but it won't be on a chain.'

'What's this, some freaking yoga class? I just want my pendant and cross so I can be on my way.'

I muttered something obscene, which they may or may not have heard; it didn't matter – I really didn't care. I already had taken enough deep breathing on my way up and now he's telling me to be patient and *center* within. How could I stay composed at a time like this – and why do I let them push me into their whacky make-believe world?

Sometimes I wondered if they may be part of some weird cult. I wanted to ask; so what's next guys, satori or charades; seems like these may be some other fun games we could play. But I kept my sarcasm to myself; trying hard to keep cool and not appear more agitated than I already was. To keep the peace I breathed in and out several times as he suggested since I was interested in what he had to say if it helped me to find my chain.

When I was done, Mo said in a soft, conciliatory tone, 'James, there's something we need to tell you that's very important. It's not just about your identity, but about you. We understand you have waited patiently for an explanation of how things are here. Now's the time; we think you're ready.'

'It sounds you're about to go really weird on me. So what is it?'

'This may shock you,' he said, 'so be prepared. Much has happened that you're not aware of. You will likely find it so utterly unbelievable that it may take a bit of time for you to come to terms with our disclosures. However, after making a few mental adjustments, I'm sure you will soon come to understand what has occurred to you, and not deny anything we have to say.'

'Wait a minute,' I said, 'let's back up a bit. What do you mean: has occurred to me? What's occurred?'

'What happened,' Mo said, 'has to do with the hidden part of your dream you suppressed. This is what we now wish to tell you. Actually you will find it to be the most significant part of the dream, everything else was preamble.'

'Oh please, let's not go back to discussing that damned dream again?' Let's just move on to something real, I've got a bus to catch down in the village which only leaves every few days.

'I think your bus already left the station,' Eli said.

It was beginning to feel like trying to sustain a rational discussion with the Queen of Hearts.[1]

'Can we cut to the chase?' I said, as I slouched deeply into my chair. I was losing my patience, but resolved not to react as I had before. If I didn't play it cool, they may never tell me anything.

'We want to answer all your questions,' Mo said, 'but what you seek to know is based on this dream which, whether you realize it or not, has become your new reality. As soon as you acknowledge what we say, you will have all your questions answered. So are you ready for what we have to say?'

'Of course, but can we hurry this along? Sure, it's possible that my dream has some merits, at least as an interesting allegory. To be honest, after giving it some thought, I probably understand more of it than what I've let on, especially with all the allusions to swamps and snakes.

---

[1] From Alice's Adventures Wonderland by Lewis Carroll, first published in 1865.

75

In fact, the more I think about it, the more it sounds like my work environment, especially the snakes in the grass,' I said with a chuckle.

'And so, if you think it's necessary, we can do some deconstructive analysis as long as you promise to tell me where my chain is. Where do you want to start?'

They didn't answer me but looked at each other as the atmosphere became deadly serious. I now surmised this was not going to be a literary analysis on the composition of my allegory. I began to felt a strange foreboding. Did I really want to hear what he had to say, or should I just bolt for the door. I studied Mo's graven countenance and understood something very important was about to be said.

'What is it?' I said. 'You're making me nervous. Is there a problem?'

'There's no problem,' Eli said, 'but there is something you need to hear regarding the rest of the story.'

'What do you mean, rest of the story?'

'As we were saying, it's the part where we ended,' Mo said. 'But it really hasn't ended; actually it's the beginning! We've been carefully preparing you for this since you arrived here so you will be able to accept what we have to say. It will answer why things with us here seem so, ah, different.'

'But we need not get worked up about my dream and how it may or may not have ended' I said, 'it's probably just a little allegorical lesson from my subconscious mind to teach a few edifying lessons about life, learning, growth and values. Sometimes dreams can do that; right?'

'A while ago,' Eli said, not answering me, 'you seemed rather interested with what happened at the end your dream and why you woke up in a panic.'

'Sure, but I think at times we can overanalyse things; don't you agree?'

'You see James,' Mo said, 'it's like this: that little allegory, as you call it, merges with your space time reality more than you know, having little to do with the way you normally think. This is not about analysis; it's about knowing.

'The story we told you, your dream story, tells of how you've now come into a much different state of existence than what you realize! Trust us; we're not making any of this up. As we've said, and you know, it was all presented to you in a spectacularly vivid dream that portended all that was to come. We only reminded you of your vision and gave you our interpretation so you may know what it was trying to tell you. At some deep unconscious level you understood what was about to happen. And that, my friend, is what brought you here.'

I was both mystified and unsettled with what he was saying!

'That's why it's imperative you begin to realize your dream merged with what all you've experienced before your ascent. You may soon come to consider the dream allegory to be more *real* than anything you consider real in your past.'

'What's that supposed to mean?' I said, 'the more you talk the less sense you make.'

'Again we ask you, do you remember what was happening at the end of the dream? Can you feel the foreboding and fear? This drama at the end of your dream actually took place not far below our cabin, where the chasm opens to a very long drop down! You felt it twice, first in your prescient dream last October and then once again here not long ago.'

'Sorry, I still have no idea what you are talking about.'

'Subliminally I think you do,' he said, 'but you don't wish to hear about it. So to make this easier, let's just tell you straight-up what happened at the chasm before we met on the Summit. But tell us first what you remember what happened before that. Close your eyes, go deeply within, then tell us what you see.'

'Well, I remember it was a rather tough climbing the last leg of the ascent,' I said. 'I felt knackered, so I decided to have a long rest in the ravine before going the distance. Then, as got close to the summit, I saw something that was most extraordinary.

'At first it appeared there were two or three shimmering orbs that I imagined to be space aliens or something, not that I actually believe in any of that, but these lights had me curious. And so I was anxious to pass over to the other side of the chasm to find out what this was about. Since it seemed impassable, I took another route to the Summit. It was like I was having a vision of where to go as I heard a voice telling me how to proceed to find a hidden fissure in the precipice. Likely it was just my intuition, but it seemed most peculiar.'

'But do you not also remember taking another route, Eli said, much shorter across the chasm's ledge?'

'That's interesting you should ask that. I remember attempting to cross a chasm somewhere before, very much like the chasm below.'

'Close your eyes again, James,' Mo said, 'and this time really relax. Tell us what you see. What happened as you were crossing the ledge to the other side?'

'I'm not sure.'

'Take your time, and think. Did you cross over?'

'Well, I must have. Here I am.'

'Indeed, here you are;' he said, 'that much is certain, no doubt about it; you did cross over. But did you actually cross over in the way you think you did?'

'What do you mean cross over in the way I think I did, aren't you listening, of course I crossed over, what other way was there?'

'The route you just mentioned, the one the voice directed you towards. Didn't you just say you came by way of an alternative route other than the chasm?'

Even before Mo said this, my last words caught in my throat because I knew something wasn't quite right. How could I have done both at the same time?

I opened my eyes and got up from my chair and took a few steps to stare out the window towards the glaciers. But I didn't see anything. For the moment, I was lost in deep silence as I continued to concentrate on what may have happened next.

Mo's question triggered something that must have been hidden and suppressed in the depths of my mind. I sat down again and closing my eyes, concentrating on what was stir deeply within me. Whatever was there scared me, not knowing where it may be taking me. Then slowly, very slowly, fragments of strange scenes began to emerge in my mind: first they appeared as still frames, then began to run together in slow motion, soon quickening until the veil of amnesia lifted. There it was, the full horrific scene playing itself out in vivid detail.

In an instant, I felt myself falling through space with a torrent of wind swishing by with the force of a tsunami. My cup fell to the floor as I could feel myself descending into oblivion, as I observed craggy rocks thrusting upwards over and past me. Next, I could see swiftly approaching slopes of scree and snow below me. Then nothing! All had become blank.

I felt overcome as I stood by the window gripping on to its ledge. Finally I shuffled back to my seat and sat there in silence, replaying the reels over and over. The images continued to become more vivid and fearsome each time. I wanted to put the impressions out of my mind, preferring to believe this could not have happened.

And yet I couldn't dismiss any of it, I was too mesmerized by what I saw, unable to look away from the gruesome scene. I thought I saw myself looking down on my body at the bottom of the ravine. How could that be? I was both fascinated and bewildered with what I just relived. How could I not have known about this tragic moment? Mo and Eli must have witnessed it all. Would that have been them standing on top the Summit above, appearing to me as orbs of light?

Finally, I broke my silence and said, 'I think I'm losing my mind. I just had the most horrific phantasm – it was dreadful. I can hardly believe this, but I saw myself hurling down through the chasm into a void of space.'

'Yes James,' Eli said quietly, 'that was you in an almost fatal fall off the chasm's ledge. And yes again, to what you were wondering, we were there to witness the end of your dream – the beginning of your new reality.'

I muttered, 'but how could that have happened? It had to be me reliving a nightmare, you know, the end of the dream, the part I didn't recall.'

'It didn't just happen in you dream, it also occurred in space and time on earth. If you're ready to hear, we can tell you exactly what happened; the part presaged in your dream that jolted you into awakening. That's also why it was not yet appropriate for us to tell you everything we saw; we first needed you to re-live what happened so you would realize this was more than a dream.'

'I would much prefer it to be a dream,' I said, 'rather than the horrendous experience of what I just felt and imagined.'

'Not what you imagined,' Eli said, 'it was what your mind remembered, but had censored because of the trauma it invoked. With our prompting, you are now recalling what has been suppressed by your conscious mind. So let's go back once again and see if we can help you remember what you experienced as you were about to cross the rest of the way – just as your dream ended. Can you recall that last step as the thin ledge gave way?'

'No, I don't believe I can.'

'That's because there was no next step for you as your flailing body fell down the chasm, through the canyon below, twisting and gyrating towards the slopes.'

I shook my head in disbelief, not wanting to accept this, though I knew it was what I had just seen and felt.

'James,' Mo said, 'you need to accept what your mind is telling you to be true, so we can reveal what happened next. Look deeply within and allow yourself to be the flying projectile on its swift trajectory to doom. Can you recall how your whole life flashed before your eyes? Over a hundred yards below this fateful crossing with a few ricochets off the precipices, you continued to tumble through the air. Your legs were broken and bashed after you deflected off an igneous protrusion on the way down, but you felt nothing as you were in shock. Then as your body hit the lower slopes, something snapped. It was your neck, and you remembered no more.'

'That's ridiculous,' I said, 'my neck doesn't even feel sore. In fact, my body has never felt better.'

Mo ignored my comment and said. 'We observed the full impact of your body's fall. Fortunately, it was buffeted on a steep slope near the ravine basin. A thin layer of snow and underlying scree caught your body as it continued to slide further down, all the way down. Had you slid a bit further, it may have fallen over another steep precipice, likely never to be seen again.'

'We observed your body lying there' Eli said. 'It still breathed, barely alive. Not aware of its sorry mangled, bloody state of flesh, your spirit took leave. You left home, as you had known it in its familiar earthbound shell.'

'You are here with us now, James, not your body.'

CHAPTER 5

THE FALL

You don't have a soul. You are a Soul. You have a body[1]
We are not human beings having a spiritual experience.
We are spiritual beings having a human experience.[2]

I sat there for some time silently pondering the horrifying experience I just relived. Finally I got up, and paced across the floor, deep in thought. For the moment I remained calm, composed and even detached. Perhaps I was more dazed than detached, as I attempted to reconcile what had just been enacted in my mind.

Nothing in my higher learning could have prepared me for this. I felt like I was witnessing some macabre accident scene where the ambulances show up with sirens blaring, as I watch from the sidelines, most grateful that none of this involved me. Except this time it did involve me, even though I wanted nothing to do with it. I tried to remain cool and controlled. For the moment no emotional breakers had

---

[1] This quote has been attributed to C.S. Lewis. However, some scholars, however, have disputed this.

[2] Pierre Teilhard de Chardin (1881-1955), French philosopher, Jesuit priest, paleontologist and geologist.

blown, no surges in my switching station to melt my circuits; I could work through this.

Steady now James! I said to myself. There's always a reasonable explanation for everything. Perhaps this was just a flashback of some bad drug trip I had a long time ago. Except everything here, unlike my past 'trips,' felt too substantial and real. I was familiar with that fleeting, ephemeral feeling of altered consciousness, but this wasn't anything like that.

With every fibre of my being, I could feel myself falling as I slumped down in my chair again, as the fire began to crackle from the logs Eli just threw on. Over and over I continued to review these images. At times things didn't flow together too well, as I attempted to recompose the fragments into a linear sequence.

Finally I spoke up in a near whisper. 'Yes, of course; I do remember now --- the last step, mid-way across the chasm. It didn't hold, did it? Forgot about that; must have been repressed.'

'That's right James, it didn't hold,' Eli said, 'but the shock did. And so now you need to come to terms with this, along with all that has happened since. You see, there is still more to the story; much more.'

But I didn't want to hear more. I just wanted everything to go away. I wanted to think, in the words of Shakespeare, *all's well that ends well*, but I still wasn't sure what the end was. I couldn't put it out of my mind; flashes of falling continued to haunt me. The more I tried to dismiss my terrifying descent, more impressions began to impinge upon me, over and over again. And it was true; I now recalled how my life flashed before me. There was no longer any doubt about it, this was very serious.

I wondered what happened just before I made that last step. But hadn't I arrived on the Summit by climbing safely up an escarpment somewhere to the left of the chasm? I thought I had, but if I didn't, how did I manage to arrive here without a single bruise or scratch after surviving the fall? Everything was a muddle as I grappled for answers.

'Okay,' I said at last, 'tell me what this is supposed to mean. You said you saw what happened.'

'Indeed we did,' Mo said, 'we saw it all!'

'Then tell me, how did I get here?'

'What happened,' Eli said, 'is that you, the real you, your spirit you, your soul, your essence being; parted your mortal body. But don't worry; your body is not dead.'

I laughed, mockingly, as I got up to get another coffee. 'So you're saying I left my body. I don't have a mirror with me, but I'm rather certain it's still here, standing before you with me happily residing within. Sorry Eli, but I thought you would know better. Science has proven this can't happen, even though at times it may seem that way when the human brain, under certain conditions, secretes certain chemicals such as endogenous opioid neuropeptides. These may induce so called out of body experiences that appear to be real for some. I'm sure you've heard lots about this.

'Is I've already admitted, I've had a few illusory drug trips in the past, so I think I should know what I'm talking about. And I can tell you firsthand, it's not logical or scientific to tell me my body isn't here. If it's not; neither am I. How could I be? At best, this experience would only be a dream or an altered state of consciousness from wherever location my body would happen to be. But if my body had died from the fall, I wouldn't be here with you now, would I? However, since I am.. ...'

Mo and Eli said nothing as I continued to sputter along trying to find a reasonable explanation for what I experienced. Admittedly, my attempts at rationalizing this weren't the best, but their account was even less convincing. If they couldn't come up with anything better than me being out of my body, I preferred not to listen. When I finished, I stood up in front of them, raising my hands before them. 'See these hands, how can I take anyone seriously who says these aren't real?'

'Oh, they're real alright,' Mo said, 'just not in the way you think.'

A most annoying, evasive answer, I thought. Yet what more could I say, they were the only ones who claimed to have seen what happened.

Without responding further, I sauntered outside, looking blankly into space. I wished I could find some compelling evidence that would help solve this mystery. There was nothing in the sky to inspire me: no epiphanies or writings, not even interesting cloud formations. Still restless, I went back in and poured a glass of something strong; I think from a bottle of Russian vodka, ostensibly distilled in St. Petersburg. But who knows if it really was, nothing here was certain.

I had to get a grip before things got further out of control, yet it seemed there wasn't a damned thing I could do about they were saying – which made me angry. Partly I blamed myself; why was I allowing myself to be drawn into their sham world of illusions? I also thought they should accept some of the blame and responsibility for my fall and getting knocked out unconscious. If they were standing there at the top, couldn't they have at least warned me before I attempted to cross the chasm?

I continued to pace in front of them, glass in hand, as I vented my frustrations. My very bodily existence was being called into question, which wasn't comforting – or rational. But I wasn't entirely rational either, reacting as I did; convinced they were completely mistaken. That's just the way anger is: irrational and often incoherent.

'Not only do you keep evading my questions,' I said, 'but you keep insisting I'm out of my body because of some alleged mishap I had off a ledge. How would you know that? Even if you witnessed something, why did you need to tell me? I was fine until then - in fact, ready to begin my descent. But now you've managed to disrupt everything, even making me question the very state of my ontological existence. And still you can't, or won't, give me any straight answers about anything. Why are you holding out? There's got to be a rational explanation for what happened down the chasm.'

'There is,' said Eli, 'and we already told you what it is, but if you don't seem to like our answer. Whether you think it's rational or not, perhaps you could tell us how you managed to get up here in one piece after such a gruesome fall.'

I didn't care for the manner in which Eli spoke. 'I don't have a bloody clue,' I said angrily, 'except perhaps I bumped my head against something after I slipped and ended up with a serious concussion! Who knows, I may have been catatonic or in a delirium when I passed out, so have no memory of how I ended up down there. I just know I made my way up to the Summit after having a long rest.'

'Do you, by any chance, remember how long you rested?' asked Mo.

'Like a said, I was probably out for some time. In fact, it was probably the best sleep I ever had, or can remember having. It felt like I had been for days. God, I must have really been knocked out. Perhaps

I'm still a bit stunned. If so, that would explain why so many bizarre things seem to have happened to me since then: voices in the air, orbs of light flittering about. Not to mention how it appears you can cause things to appear out of nowhere. That's really weird!

'My brain must have really got scrambled, which is why I so easily became delusional. Obviously, I'm nuts! I need to see a doctor as soon as I get home. But hopefully, this will only be temporary. But even then, I'm not sure how that explains all the really strange, nonsensical things you both keep saying. Hopefully you're not, because I can't make any excuses for you, so you're going to have to take responsibility for what you do and say.'

'Just curious, but do you have any lumps on your head?' Mo asked.

I stroked my scalp, 'must have been quite the whelp to my head,' I said, as I felt around to find a lump. 'That's most peculiar, I don't feel anything. Guess it went away. Wonder how long I was out before I regained consciousness – any idea?'

'Yes, we have a very good idea,' Eli said, 'but are you sure you want to know?'

'Of course I want to know,' I said. 'I suspect it may have been over an hour, although it could have been considerably longer; I remember the sun didn't seem to be in the right place when I woke up.'

'You're right, it was longer, in fact, much longer,' Mo said. 'Sit down for a moment, you're making us both dizzy, pacing back and forth. Get ready now to hear the rest of the story.'

I took my seat, most curious to hear what else he had to say. Maybe we're finally getting somewhere, I thought. Before heading back down, I really wanted to know what happened.

'There's a very good reason why you remain confused with what happened after your fall,' he said. 'As your body was tumbling down the last twenty yards, a Chilean forestry helicopter fortuitously flew by en-route to a small forest fire they were investigating near the Argentine border. As though by providence; the pilot noticed your body strewn on the snow. The odds of it being spotted at that critical moment, before it convulsed to death with hypothermia, was likely less than one in ten million.'

'So I was lucky?'

'I suppose so – if luck had anything to do with it.'

'And so then what happened?'

'Your body was lifted out.'

'Lifted out? So where did they take me?'

'They took your body to a hospital in Santiago for examination.'

'Really; but why would they return me to the ravine when I was still unconscious? That doesn't make sense.'

'No, you're right, it doesn't make sense,' Eli said, 'why would they bring your body back?'

'You tell me, you said you saw it all happen – if in fact, you did.'

'Most assuredly we did,' said Mo. 'Look at me James, and listen very carefully to what I have to say.' He paused for a moment to make sure he had my attention. 'No one brought your body back, James. They took it away; far away. Not you, your body! Do you understand?'

'Okay, jolly, that's good, very good! Have things your way if you must. I'm getting the picture now; you really had me going there a while! Most impressive! So, when you're not interpreting people's dreams, you do comedy; am I right? But how much longer do you plan to carry on with this shtick; violating natural law with supposed materializations, calling my name with your wonderfully crafted telepathic gifts, complete with mind-reading? A little intrusive, but nice work anyway, even if you have the advantage of my slightly deluded and deranged brain to work with!

'But you know something? If I wanted someone to mess with my mind, I would have hired Madame Peyroux, the crazy psychic broad with the studio above the pawn shop! Sometimes for a lark, I amuse myself with her exquisite predictions on my love life – or lack thereof.'

'Lack thereof?' asked Eli, with a disingenuous smirk. 'Would you care to – ah, elaborate on that for us? I think we'd like to hear a bit more about this.'

'I'm certain you would,' I said.

'Yes, do tell James,' Mo said, 'just what do you mean by lack?'

'Never mind,' I said, 'it's more a case of what's adequate than lack.' I wasn't in the mood for jesting, still a bit shaken with these latest disclosures. And so I ranted on, believing I would eventually come up with something that made sense if I talked long and loudly enough.

Finally, after exhausted every rationalization I could think of, I realized nothing I said was any more convincing than their account, except their account wasn't acceptable to me.

To their credit, they listened patiently without interrupting me or getting angry with my biting sarcasm and ridicule. This annoyed me even more, since it made me appear confused; which I most apparently was. Not knowing what more to say, I thought I'd try a different tactic by putting them on the defensive. 'So if you saw all this happening,' I said, 'why didn't you climb down to help me? I'm sure you could have if you wanted to.'

'But why,' Mo said, 'take a moment to examine your perfect body; it's flawless. It may seem biological because that's the only way you've known it, but rather, think of it more as a holographic projection of your soul's light, although it far more than that. So why would a spiritual light being need our help?'

'Spiritual light being,' I said, 'I've been called a lot of things, but I can assure you, never anything like that.'

'Believe it or not, that's what gives your body form,' Eli said, 'a pattern energetically configured to the essence of your being.'

'Again, I'm really not sure what that's supposed to mean.'

'That's okay, you soon will,' Mo said. 'As for your biological body; it was already lifted out not long after the fall, as I already indicated. They couldn't land on the slope but were able to drop one of the crew down to where he was able to bundle it in a sling and lift it into the fuselage. Immediately they rushed it to a hospital in Santiago, and then a few days later, it was dispatched to London by a *medivac Learjet*.

'But don't worry; your university's insurance plan covered your body's flight home where it is now being attended by a competent medical team. But will require intensive care for some time yet, since your neck is fractured and perhaps broken. Your brain is barely functioning, and so you remain in a deep coma.

'But it's not only your physical body in London that's been having a rest; you were in a state of deep soul sleep for some time. That often happens after a trauma such as this. You awoke deep in the ravine, close to where you parted company with your physical body. Your clothes, backpack and its contents, manifested in accordance with your belief expectations. That's how things work on this side. And just in case you were wondering, your accident happened over two weeks ago.'

'Oh really,' I said, 'amazing how body, like time, can fly when you're taking a snooze. In a *Learjet* you say; that's great, I've always wanted to do that. Next time I'll be sure to stay awake for the trip so I can tell everyone all about it.

'But really gents, do you actually expect me to believe any of your stories? It just keeps getting richer all the time. Is there someone from the comedy channel videotaping this from behind a bush? For once, let's get serious. You know, it's not funny to joke about something that could have resulted in death; in this case, my death!'

'You're right James,' Eli said, 'it's not, and we're not. We agree this was serious and believe us, we're not joking about what could have resulted in your body's death. But realize we view things from a much different perspective. Let us assure you there is nothing remotely dead about you or your body. It remains very much alive in its earthly plane of existence, albeit in an altered condition. You'll find it in Room 3017 of the hospital's Critical Care Unit.

'The last we heard,' Mo said, 'though marred and twisted, it remains in stable condition connected to a life support system. Note, we've deliberately said *it*, not *you*. Though its lights have been knocked out, it's most fortunate to still be alive since you'll likely need it again. But believe me, as things stand now; you're much better off to be here with us – much less constricting, wouldn't you say?

'Your brain hardware was badly shaken and will need much time to heal before it can fire up its synapses to activate the neural axons and dendrites. Your neurologist says until your neck's cranial and vagus nervous systems mend, there's not much they can do for you except keep the body alive.

'In fact, it could be a year or more, provided it survives. If at some point they suspect it's not going to recover, it will likely be discharged from the support system. However, from what we have told by our informed sources, your body will most likely recover, although it could take much longer to regain your consciousness in it. In other words, for your soul to re-enter the body you think you are.'

'You two just won't let up, will you? Did you just say re-enter the body I think I am; do you know how weird that sounds? Furthermore, what do you mean "our informed sources"? We're way off grid and a long, long way from any transmitter service so you can't be receiving information any sources -- unless you have a satellite phone you're not telling me about.'

'When you are the grid, you don't need a phone,' Eli said, smiling.

'"When you are the grid", what the hell is that supposed to mean?'

'What I mean,' he said, 'there is nowhere that Source is not -- and since we're all part of Source ...'

'Save the metaphysics for later,' I said, 'I just want to know what's real and certain.'

'There's nothing certain about your fragile mortal body,' Mo said, 'and so it's still possible it may not make it. But we think you may still have a lot of important work to accomplish on the earth plane and so you belong on earth's side, not ours.'

'Oh, so now we're talking about sides, are we? It's obvious there is only one side. Either you're dead or alive. For now I prefer to be alive, and if you please, in the body which I am.'

'And so you are,' he said, 'your mortal body must either be dead or alive. For now it's alive, but when it's not, you'll still remain alive in this spirit body, only you won't be here.'

'To the contrary, I think the evidence is apparent that once your body is dead so is your brain, and with it, your conscious awareness, since it obviously comes from the brain.'

'It's obvious to whom?' asked Mo.

'Anyone with a brain,' I said, most wittingly. 'Perhaps I need to give you a little lesson in philosophy. Ever heard of Descartes' famous pronouncement, "Cogito Ergo Sum: I think therefore I am?" Yes, I'm sure you have. So ask yourself, what is it that's doing the thinking? It's got to be something. So what could it be? Let me think. Ah yes, of course; it's the brain! What else could have had this brilliant thought? Obviously something had to have it.

'In fact, as I speak, my brain formulates these very words I'm now articulating. Otherwise, I couldn't be speaking its thoughts! But if you take away the brain, there would be no thoughts for the mind to think, which shows there can be no difference between the thinking brain and the thinking mind. They are the same; the brain and mind are one. It's all rather simple: the brain thinks, ipso facto, therefore I am.'

'And so you are James,' Mo said, 'at least your "*I am*" is, albeit a tad confused thinking it's only an organ of bodily flesh. So to help you recognize the real nature of your identity, it may be useful if you subordinate your separate ego mind that mistakenly believes it's a material brain, with your "*I AM*" mind that knows it's Self to be one with divine Source.

'If you can do this, then you would come to understand your true identity is infinitely more than just a biological modulating device subject to the laws of mortality. You have a mind because you are of Mind. Thoughts didn't originate in the primordial slime and mud as they believe in your anthropology classrooms, but from divine consciousness from which all thought forms emerge and evolve in variations, including that of body.'

I didn't completely understand what he was getting at, but didn't want to get into his "*I am*" esoterica since I didn't see its relevance.

'You look rather confused,' Eli said. 'To properly understand what Mo is saying, you first need to realize you're now thinking without the aid of your earth body's receiver/transmitter unit that rested up on your shoulders. It's a marvelous mediating device to transduce your conscious experiences to the material plane of earthly existence. For now, however, it's not of much use to you. Systems are down, remaining on standby. But that's not a problem for as long as you're here, since your mind, even in its bewilderment, has never been better off. It just needs you to take the fetters off by accepting that it's not made of material stuff, but has, if I may say, *a mind of its own.*'

Once again, Eli was being clever, but I wasn't amused. What they were saying was increasingly bizarre, if not demented! I didn't need to have my intelligence insulted with this talk of having a mind without a brain.

'Sorry,' I said, 'but I'm not buying any of this twaddle. Possibly you're not saying what I think your saying; perhaps it's just my befuddled brain still recovering from the fall. But in any case, I've had enough of this now. The sun's shining again, so I'm going to take my body -- and brain, if you will, on a short stroll along the summit ridge. I still need to decide whether to begin my descent today planned. Almost half the day has been wasted so far, and not only that, I still haven't found my pendant.'

I won't go into everything that was racing through my mind just then, but I considered grabbing my backpack, then and there, to begin my long descent. If they found my missing chain, perhaps they would mail it to me at the university. So much of what they were saying seemed like utter nonsense, which made it increasingly difficult to remain there while keeping my composure.

But still, I had to ask myself; was it really all nonsense? On the surface, is seemed it was! And yet as I trekked along the ridge I wondered if there wasn't something more to what they were saying than I understood. After all, they were both very intelligent men. Not only that, it still amazed me that my body had no trace of injury after having a life threatening fall. Even my most recent cuts and bruises from a few days ago had healed, as though I hadn't even had them. Perhaps I never did, but whatever the case; I couldn't deny I was in perfect condition now, in fact never better.

Though I didn't understand how this could be, at least I knew I had a physical body, with or without scratches. So what's this tripe about my body being in London? Sure, I may have had a serious fall, but that didn't make me crazy. However, considering everything that happened, maybe I was, but hopefully not as crazy as these two – at least not yet.

I turned around at the high end of the eastern ridge where we I first met my strange companions. Perhaps, I was a bit rude this morning, I thought, maybe I should try to have a rational conversation with them to see if we can work through our misunderstandings with some mutual compromise. Besides; who else is there to talk to? Obviously there were no other witnesses to my fall. Sometimes I evince an overtly choleric personality, which can have its strengths at times, but patience isn't one of them. I determined I would keep my cool next time by being more polite, even though I would vigorously challenge them when necessary.

It was probably over an hour before I finally arrived back at the lodge. Perfect timing! A steaming hot meal awaited me, as if they knew precisely when I would return. We sat down for a pleasant time, and no one brought up anything about our earlier discussions. Later we retired to the fireplace area as Eli filled our glasses with what tasted like Castello Mio Sambuca, a favourite Italian liqueur I occasionally purchased for entertaining guests.

The truce was over now; it was time to get back to business and pick up where we left off. The fate of the universe, or at least my universe, hung in the balance!

'James,' Mo said, 'we understand why you may still have a few lingering doubts over what we've told you regarding your current state of existence. We've said this before, but we want you to understand we don't disagree you have a body; just that it's not the body you think it is. If we didn't have bodies, how would we communicate with each other in this dimension? Obviously, we're not an amorphous fog hovering in the air, but spiritual bodies giving expressions to the essence of what we are within.

'In fact, we can communicate in more ways than you may imagine since our bodies don't have the same limitations as the earth's physical body. What I think we're quibbling about here is not the existence of a body, but the ways in which it may manifest. We're only saying a body is an energetic pattern manifesting on whatever plane it may be.'

'I think you're making this more complicated than need be,' I said. 'Where would I be without this physical body? I'm here because my body is here.'

'And so you are, as we can plainly see and agree,' Mo said. 'Most certainly you are here with us – but not in your physical earth body. Sorry, it's gone! Not to dust, not to Jesus, but to London. If you still find that's hard to believe, we could visit the hospital where it's currently residing, so you can see for yourself.'

'That's a splendid idea!' Eli said. 'We can all go together to check it out. Not *check it out* like a library book since it's not in circulation. But considering all it's been through, it only seems right we pay it a visit.'

'Before we go though,' said Mo, 'there are a number of things you'll need to prepare for. But we still have plenty of time for this reunion, long before your body is ready to readmit you. When it's ready, you'll be able to check your own body out of the hospital, just like a new edition.'

'Thanks, but if I want to see my body, I'll go look in a mirror.

If there were such a thing as a spirit body, I wouldn't want to have anything to do with it; too much like being dead. And besides, I'm sure the women like my body just the way it is. Why wouldn't they? And the more of it they get, the better they like it. So don't try to take that away from them – or me.'

'Don't be too concerned,' Eli said, 'though your physical body back home may not be as active as before, I'm sure they will still be there when you finally slip back into it. Meanwhile, we're here to help you adjust to living in your spirit body that has no biological limitations.'

'Are you now,' I said, 'by expecting me to believe I don't have a physical body? How the hell can you make love without having a physical body? Or, for that matter, even think of how to make love without a brain? Answer that!'

'But then,' Eli said, 'when you think about it, sex really is a *no brainer.*'

'You're hilarious Eli. Okay fine, if you're not able to answer my question; then at least tell me how I'm able to have memories without a brain in which to store them? You can't! And please don't speak about me inhabiting some etheric body of light. That's just nuts! I think one body is enough. Ask any neurosurgeon about this, they are the bright people who poke around into the brain's labyrinth to get all kinds of memory impulses! And so they should know.'

'Is the shadow more real than the reality that casts it?' asked Mo. 'What comes first, the brain or the mind?'

'Obviously, the brain comes first', I said, 'or there could be no mind. I just made that point. To use your analogy, the brain is the solid reality that castes the subsisting shadow of the mind.'

'Can any surgeon, scientist or philosopher explain how an intricately configured organ of about three pounds is able to produce self aware consciousness, while yielding exquisite thoughts of love, beauty and truth?'

I wasn't sure how to respond to his question since I didn't follow his logic. It was evident this conversation wouldn't resolve anything. I had taught enough Philosophy of Mind classes to know there were always more questions than answers. It's a difficult topic. Yet I wanted to call their bluff about my state of existence rather than getting into philosophical abstracts about shadows, minds, love, beauty, truth and ultimate reality. My problem was I didn't know what more to say, not being entirely lucid at the moment. So rather than argue, I threw my out challenge to them.

'Okay, enough of this; I don't wish to argue more about what's so blatantly obvious, that being me and my body. These aren't just epistemic nuances; you're calling into question my physical existence. So if I'm not in my physical body, then prove it!'

'There's no need for us to prove anything James,' Eli said, 'you can prove it for yourself.'

'And how would I do that?'

'We just told you,' he said; 'by visiting your physical body in London. Then you'll be able to prove it yourself and then you will know who is home. I think you will find it's not your body.'

'Oh, that's a most brilliant idea Eli; you really are a genius. So when I arrive back in London, say in about ten days, I'll catch a cab from the airport and go directly to the hospital you say my body resides. When I get there, I'll ask the nurses what room I'm in. They'll say you're not in a room at all; you're standing in the reception area. And I'll say, 'no, I mean my comatose body; the one lying here in one of your rooms? Which one is it? And then they will look at each other, made a call, and politely ask me to come with them to another ward that is special. When I arrive, nice men dressed in white will outfit me in tight fitting garment, and take me to a room and with rubber walls where I won't be able to do myself any harm.'

'Actually that was rather funny,' Eli said; 'don't you think, Mo?'

'Indeed, James can be humorous when he wants to be,' Mo replied.

'But you really need not be concerned,' Eli said. 'When we go to the hospital with you, no one will see you since they're already convinced you're lying on bed in Room 3017. And so that's where we'll find your body, right where they placed it. Remember, we'll be with you the whole time, so you won't feel you have no one else to visit but your body. I'm sure that could get boring after a while, since your body isn't the most entertaining company to be with these days.'

'But before we go anywhere Dorothy,' Eli said, 'you need to realize you're no longer in Kansas. But then, you're not exactly in

Oz either, though at times it may seem you're in a land such as that. Trust us, if you really knew where you are, you wouldn't even think about places like Kansas or London. And if you knew all the exotic adventures you could have in this new realm of infinite possibilities, you would get so excited that we might have to restrain you - not that we could! Then you would finally realize your struggle to raise yourself out of the swampy Lowlands was more than worth your time, effort and money. Your ascent up this Mountain is where the real journey began.'

'What could I possibly get so excited about that you would have to restrain me?'

'Have you ever watched a Miss Universe contest on television?' Eli asked.

'Sure, the swimsuit part; lots of times – so what's that go to do with anything?'

'Just wondering,' he said.

'Come on Eli, what are you getting at -- trying to bait me? It won't work.'

'No, not bait you -- but maybe prepare you. Nevertheless we understand your confusion! It's perfectly understandable; perfectly normal! But then, this isn't normal, nor are you,' he said with a grin, 'at least not anymore.'

'That's correct,' Mo said, 'you aren't normal, but consider that a compliment. That's why you climbed this Mountain to be here with us. How many would be willing to do that based on a call they thought they heard in a dream?'

'Oh please, not that again.'

'Be honest,' Mo said, 'you remember the call don't you?

'Of course,' I said, 'I've already told you that. It was so damned weird; even for a dream. In its own way it seemed very real; a far off voice calling me from afar, and yet reverberating so plainly in my mind that it really didn't seem distant at all. Then, as I said, I thought I heard something like it again as I approached the Summit. This time it wasn't a dream. Though it seemed from somewhere out of this world, it was all happening in my head. I'm not sure what an etheric voice would sound like, but if there was such a thing, I'm sure this would have been it. But more probably, what the voice really means is I should carry an oxygen tank, drink less gin and not fall off precipices.'

'It was no accident; what you voice you heard was from us,' Eli said. 'And not just of us, there were several others calling out to you too as one voice.'

'But of course there were;' I said, 'precisely when I was most vulnerable after having a few too many refreshments that fateful night at the pub. What else? That's when voices often come to me in my dreams, but I'm probably not the only one. And though I'm greatly flattered you're both such big fans of my dream, please do me a favour and try not to get too caught up with the fantasy. It seems you're even wishing to take credit for some of the sound bites at the beginning of the drama. Now that's hilarious!'

'Understand,' Mo said, 'our call to you didn't happen without a reason. It was our response to a vision you had been formulating in your mind. You intuitively knew this Mountain was a place where you could become something more than if you remained in the stifling Lowlands. We answered you by inviting you to come where you had glimpsed us through the mists. However, now that you've ascended here, I'm sure it all seems unreal. That's because you still don't know where you are or how to view it because you've never climbed it before. But when you discover where you are, you will be able to go much further beyond the earth plane. You're here now, not there.'

'Yes, this is a Mountain I've never climbed before. You're right, it really seems to be a new world; just look at the view. It certainly is far beyond any plain I've seen on earth. Indeed, way up there and out of sight.'

'I'm not sure you understood us,' Mo said. 'Likely it's not easy for a modern thinker to concede to transcendence after being conditioned and steeped in the narrow presuppositions of mechanistic theorems and linguistic paralysis; ah sorry, I meant analysis. My apologies to Ludwig Wittgenstein, but even he understood the limitations of what he had posited after grasping the reality of higher spiritual realms in which you now exist.[1] After such an illustrious career, many of his colleagues thought he had gone off the deep end. Perhaps one day they may think the same about you, and in a sense, they would be right, you really did go off the deep end, far beyond what you realize. But that's what life's deep chasms are for, to go down far enough to be able to catapult to the stars.'

God, what a curious brew of claptrap, I thought, and what the bloody hell did Wittgenstein have to do with me and this mountain? Since Mo had once said he had been a scientist, I was surprised he had a handle on philosophy, much more than I would have expected. How many people do you meet on top of mountains that speak of Wittgenstein's writings and other such matters? Although I was vaguely aware of Wittgenstein's esoteric speculations, I wasn't sure what Mo's point was. But In the future I would be more careful not to dismiss what he had to say. If I tried to bluff him with specious arguments, he may challenge me, which might be most embarrassing.

'I think you must realize,' he said, 'much of last century's unfortunate philosophical trends have been getting a bit stale even though their reductionist effects still continue to spread like a bad virus into many of the natural and social sciences in the Flatlands. Perhaps one day brighter minds will emerge, but unless someone tells them about the Mountain, it may take generations to correct the errors of the prevailing falsehoods. One day you'll take on this task to save the world from itself.'

'Of course; right after I save myself from myself,' I said with a laugh.

I then gave him a smug, condescending smile and said, 'really Mo, so you're not only telling me what to believe about the nature of reality, but now you want me to convince the world of what I don't even believe myself! Besides, I'm not so sure the world needs saving.

---

[1] Ludwig Wittgenstein (1889-1951) was considered to be among the most important philosophers of the 20th century. He came to regret much of what he wrote in his 'Tractatus Logico-Philosophicus' (1922), and yet its influence carries on. One of its famous phrases is: *Whereof one cannot speak, thereof one must be silent.* During WW1 he was greatly influenced by the writings of Dostoyevsky and Tolstoy, later becoming a fierce opponent of reductionism and what he considered *Scientism.*

You really don't know me, do you? If you did, you would know I'm an independent thinker – inveterately so!'

'We suspect you are,' he said with a chuckle, 'that's why you're here. But we're first more interested that *you* first come to know you before *we* come to know you. We realize there's considerably more to your Self than you've been able to see or know. That's why we've volunteered to be your mirror, so we can reflect back to you, the real y*ou,* the Self who knows you as you really are.'

'That's a lot of "*you*" in a few one sentences.'

'True, but there will only be one "*you,*" even if you remain uncertain who he is. During this identity crisis you're now passing through, you may become even more uncertain who you are since there's still much in you that you still fear. Outwardly, you weren't expecting this side adventure and so you are feeling a bit spooked, confused and at times angry; but then, after what you've been through, who wouldn't be?

'However, after more time here, you will begin to understand that you are a much different being than what you thought you were when you left London. Only now, after your fall, will this become increasingly evident. Unfortunately, as long you remain uncertain of who you are, you will remain fearful since all fear is based on uncertainty.'

'So what do you expect,' I said, 'after remembering the trauma of my fall, I think I have every right to feel shaken. But you're not exactly helping me by insisting I'm out of my body. Everything now seems so tentative; it's like being told you've been evicted from your flat while you're on vacation.'

'We understand your concern,' Eli said, 'but you haven't been evicted from your home James; in fact, once you accept you are a spirit body, you will never feel more at home. You've just taken the outer bodily shackles off for a while. We're only telling you that you're not a body; rather, you are a soul that has a body form, be it physical or spiritual! By resisting this understanding, you will only prolong your confusion and uncertainty.'

'You may not yet realize it,' Mo said, 'but your world had completely changed since the fall, which not surprisingly, has left you baffled and bewildered. We recognize it may take a while for you to accept that you aren't what you thought yourself to be. That's okay; we're here to help you through this transition. Life may seem different, but your divine essence hasn't changed. When you come to understand who you really are, as an immortal being, you will no longer be uncertain or afraid, but become joyful and confident in your new identity.'

'That's most jolly; but out of curiosity, tell me who you think I am, other than what is obvious.'

'As Eli and I keep saying, that's for you to discover, since no one else can do it for you. We can tell you this much, you are a spirit just like us, regardless of how material you think you are on the outside. Depending in which realm you exist, your body will manifest in accordance to the vibratory essence of that sphere's octave. This is what you still have to realize, you are more than your body, as surely as you are more than the clothes on your back.

'Many of the things you believe about yourself and the universe are wrong. And if you don't like the word "wrong," let's say an inaccurate representation of the truth to which you have assigned meaning. That's why, if you are to gain an authentic understanding of reality, you will first need to unlearn and re-examine much of what you were taught in the Flatlands.

'And not just what you were taught, but the thought patterns you acquired. These new approaches will help you move from separation to union, struggle to response, learning to discovery, and most importantly, from fear to love. It's all offered here at Summit University. That's one of the reasons you came, that you may enroll in these post doctorate studies.'

'I'm not so sure about that,' I said. 'I thought I booked my flight to Chili so I would be able to get as far away from studies as I could during my winter session break. Yet according to you, this is not so. But then, what do I know, I'm just a supposed immortal, who thinks he's mortal?'

'You're not mistaken,' Eli said, 'just unaware the advanced education you would receive here. There's nothing like it anywhere else. But if you don't like it, you can leave anytime, although you may find it rather lonely should you go home now.'

'Should you choose to enroll,' Mo said, 'your lessons will begin tomorrow morning immediately after breakfast. Eli and I shall serve as your instructors, at least initially. The first unit of our programme will focus on deconstructing all you believe to be real, that you may learn the true nature of the universe and your purpose in it. We welcome and encourage you to challenge what we say with your rebuttals, protests and outrage. That might be good therapy for you, but as it's said, to know, *one must learn from him who knows.*'[1]

'Meanwhile, you should spend the rest of the evening coming to terms with what we've told you so far, your fall, and the new realm in which you unknowingly exist.'

Without giving me a chance to reply, they stepped outside and disappeared into the darkness as they did last night. *'Buenas noches hasta mañana mis amigos,'* I muttered as I continued to sit by the fire for a very long time; maybe half the night, while flashes of the fall flashed before me on my mind's screen.

As I sat there, late into the night, I considered their plan to re-programme me after all my years of studious learning. As if I needed this. Most annoying, was their insistence that I was out of my body. More than once, various girlfriends told me I was out of my mind, but never out of my body. After all the shenanigans up here, I was beginning to think I perhaps was out of my mind, or at least becoming so.

I also wondered what Eli was implying when he asked me if I ever watched beauty contests? What kind of whacky question was that? It made no sense: much like the Zen nonsense beatniks used to banter about in a by-gone era.[2] And yet I suspected there was a reason for him asking this and for not telling me why. With that, I drifted off into a slumber, thinking about all the beautiful women I had watched through the years, but never known.

---

[1] G.I. Gurdjieff, see under next chapter title for the full quote.

[2] As sometimes found in the dialogues of Jack Kerouac's novels.

SUMMIT UNIVERSITY

A man can only attain knowledge with the help of those who possess it. This must be understood from the very beginning. One must learn from him who knows.[1]

M o and Eli arrived at the cabin in the morning just as I was stepping down the stairs from my sleeping quarters. As usual, I wasn't hungry but after Eli got a fire blazing in the cooking stove, I couldn't resist Mo's fresh rye bread and Columbian coffee. After yesterday's disclosure about my fall and all the ensuing controversy about my physical identity, I was beginning the day in a surprisingly good mood, as if my temperament had been reset. I won't get into all our usual friendly morning repartee. The atmosphere, however, soon became sombre after we settled into our lounging area.

'So James,' Mo said, 'first order of business; have you decided if you are ready to accept the auspicious scholarship we awarded you?'

'You mean to accept the dubious position of becoming a student again? Why would I? Not a great career move, considering I've more than earned my credentials as a professor. I'm sorry, but going back to school and not getting paid is about the last thing I wish to do; I

---

[1] G.I. Gurdjieff; see Appendix 'C'

already spent over a decade doing that. Perhaps instead, I should be teaching you.'

'And perhaps you will,' he said, 'it's the best way to learn, since it's true, we learn what we teach. In fact, I'm sure there is much we can discover by teaching each other. However, our programme is not just about acquiring more information, per se; you probably have more than enough of that already.

'The way you really learn,' Eli said, 'by opening yourself to the truth of what's waiting to be revealed by what we call the full union of the mind and heart, where you will find the divine portal of your soul's being. Once you access this, I'm sure you will become your own best teacher and you will no longer need our mentorship. At best, we're facilitators to show you the way, but we're not the only ones. Others will come at the appropriate times to teach you what we could never teach and show you what we could never show.'

Such was what?

'Oh, I don't know;' he said, 'I suppose whatever you need to learn. Maybe love; how much do you know about love, James?' he laughed.

'Oh really; now you have me curious. Does that mean some of these instructors may include women?'

'You never know, but I'm sure you will find Summit University to be a much different learning establishment than anything you've ever experienced before, providing many opportunities to apply your learning.'

'Think of being a protégé, Mo said. 'Once you get past the basics, you will learn from a variety of unimaginable experiences, some rather exotic. At first our classes will be held in this sitting area, but later you will be involved in some very engaging field trips. We have a diversified practicum programme that extends off-campus throughout the world and beyond. By the time you graduate, you will have discovered more in this dimension than you could possibly take back to your colleagues and students when you return. And yet I'm sure there's much you will take back with you.'

'I appreciate your laudable offer and intent – most interesting. Except for that tantalizing part you mentioned, which I don't believe, I have no desire for any further accreditation, and so I see no reason to begin again without having qualified instructors to teach post doctorate studies. I've acquired plenty of erudite learning through the years, and so I remain confident I'm capable of continuing under my own cognizance. You sometimes give the impression you know something about philosophy, and maybe you do, but are you philosophers? Evidently not, otherwise you wouldn't be promulgating these fantasies you continue to mistake for reality!'

'So let me ask you James,' he said, 'what's a philosopher? And are you a lover of wisdom? As you know, this is the very meaning of philosophy. If so, then you already understand that wisdom is of far greater importance than raw intelligence. I mean no disrespect to you, particularly in regard to the impressive certificates you have framed on your office wall; indeed, but you really don't know that much, do you? And though you've gained admission into the fellowship of the world's most sophisticated thinkers, they really don't know that much either. And what they are most certain of – is often not that certain.'

'I'm sure my colleagues would take great offence at those remarks,' I said.

'Only those who are from the Flatlands would,' Mo said. 'But don't get us wrong, we're not judging the intellectual integrity of the learned gents you've studied under in your hallowed halls. I'm sure they make significant philosophical contributions in their own way, when analysing parts. They're good at that. In fact, it seems that's most of what they do these days.[1] Since that's how they've been schooled, they aren't aware of the implicit unity of all things because they have no comprehension of what union means.

'However, as you discover what your inner wisdom is saying, you will realize the expansive whole gives definition and context to the part, but the part can't know or have a contextual understanding to anything when it remains separate. The Flatlands is only interested in parts, and so it doesn't understand the whole of its being. It will be very much to

---

[1] I'm not sure if Eli was completely fair with this assessment, yet it is true Wittgenstein's Linguistic Analysis has had a considerable influence on the direction and occupation of philosophical enquiry over the last century. As indicated earlier, Wittgenstein was not entirely happy about this.

your advantage when you become aware of the subtle ontological limits of what's being taught in your halls.

'As we keep saying, their approach is necessary, but it can never be sufficient. It's important that philosophers understand the difference between what is *necessary* and what is *sufficient*. Once you understand what is necessary, and what is sufficient, you will be able to inform your colleagues what they're missing. The parts are necessary, but only the whole is sufficient.'

'Missing?' I said. 'That's quite the proclamation. Our scholars are among the best in the world and our reputation remains as such, even centuries after the Renaissance.'

'Perhaps they are the best -- at what they do,' Mo said, 'but how many of today's intelligentsia are prepared to observe life as deeply as did the ancients? It seems many of your colleagues see only what they want to see through their microscopic lenses. Even when they look through telescopes, they can only interpret what they see as a representation of their material reality. But then, they can only see and discern what they're looking for. The expansive inter-dimensional nature of the *Infiniverse* requires macroscopic lenses to see what lies beyond the earth's material dimension.'

'Prior to coming here,' I said, 'I hadn't heard the term *Infiniverse* before, but I was familiar with the Superstring theory of modern quantum physics. Physicists advocating this theorem have predicted up to eleven dimensions of reality in what is sometimes referred to as the *Multiverse*.[1] Perhaps one day they may find a way to demonstrate these dimensions by some means other than abstract mathematical equations.'

'Possibly,' he said, 'but I'm not sure how science can provide experiential evidence of new planes of reality with anything more than formulas and Petri dishes that are limited to measurement of data of the earth plane. That's what science does and more power to it, but it should never dismiss what it can never know outside their purview. What lies beyond can't be comprehended by science within its empirically defined

---

[1] The word *Infiniverse* is a conjunctive term they sometimes used when speaking of what they called the divine infinity of the universe. This concept, or something like it, is also referred to as the *Mulitverse*.

limitations. The scope of inquiry would have to expand considerably beyond the linear plane.

'What is required, is not just more advanced logarithms, but a comprehensive understanding of the spiritual principles that remain today just as they existed on earth long before recorded history. Ultimately, what lasting benefit has science if it can't be applied to the art of living, both in the material domain and one's destined spiritual domain?

'Many of these ancient writings understood the integration of the spheres, but these teachings are practically incomprehensible to modern man who is more interested in building better cars and trucks than better lives. Did anyone teach you the wisdom contained in the venerable Vedas? Did anyone read the Upanishads or the Chuang Tzu; is there anyone in the Flatlands who has an understanding of the Sufis and Christian mystics. How many spoke of Pythagoras, or was his wisdom too arcane? Is there nothing of value in all this antiquity?'

'I'm sure there is,' I said, 'but not for many in our modern world of technology. These ideas would be regarded as incomprehensible as they are impractical.'

It was obvious Mo felt very passionate about this, as he rose to his feet to speak, gesturing emphatically with his arms and hands. 'You know James, there isn't much of lasting value to see inside the cave, especially when you become mesmerized only by shadows that shift about on the stone walls. Who are the real cavemen; the ones carrying bludgeons, or the ones carrying portfolios? Both dwell in the cave's inner recesses of spiritual ignorance, refusing to be exposed to the sun's illumination, lest the light irritate their eyes.

'As Plato so eloquently stated; *their truth would be literally nothing but the shadows of images.*[1] What could be more flat and linear than minds that don't understand what truths exist beyond than these shadows?'

'So tell me James,' he said, 'since you're the philosopher; why has Western philosophy been so threatened by the East's non-dualist perspectives regarding unity and spiritual wholeness? Is it possible these views of divine union may have compromised colonial ambitions to extract power and wealth from those they considered separate?'

---

[1] *The Republic*, Book VII.

'That's simplistic,' I said. 'At least, Western traditions of strict rationalism have led to a much better world of scientific enquiry and development. Repeating *"Om"* over and over again doesn't count much when inventing more effective vaccines and cancer cures. Doesn't this have something to do with, as you say, the art of living?'

'But of course,' Mo continued, 'more pharmaceuticals, more gadgets, not to mention better war machines. Makes you wonder, how did the ancients get along without them? The world now prides itself in knowing more and more. And I suppose it does, but it seems to be about less and less! Who is out there trying to pull it all together? In fact, many dislike the term *holistic* and so dismiss it, most perfunctorily. Fragmentation is the game today.'

'I admit I may at times overstate what I think is insane in the world, but only to make my point as it relates to your current situation. It must be difficult for you to be caught in such a narrow environment that knows so much about so little, and yet so little about what is much. That's got to be confusing!'

'To the contrary,' I said, 'I have a very broad education and outlook.'

'It may seem that way to you,' he said, 'but once you compare what you think you know with what you will be discovering in this realm, you will understand how limited your education was. Not only is this dimension much broader than the material illusion, but it's deeper and higher than you can imagine. In fact, it has no limits or end. We can only give you a fleeting glance of what's behind the curtain, but it will be enough to convince you how fleeting the shadows are on earth.'

'Now I'm afraid you're moving beyond iconoclasm and cynicism to condescension, I said. So what's your problem?'

'We have no problems, but we know you do because we once lived on the earth plane, and so we remember how dark things can become in the bowels of *the Cave*. But we also know how bright things can be outside the cave in the sunlight. Too bad so few chose to live in the light. Each gives contrast to the other. And that's the world's purpose; to provide an opportunity to look towards the darkness or towards light. Most look somewhere in between; as neither this nor that. But as one looks, one becomes that which he observes.

'As you ascended, James, you rose above the clouds and fog below towards the sunlight. Soon you will be able to see what you couldn't possibly have seen before. When the Lowland's could no longer contain your spirit, you left your dark hovel cave to make your way towards this realm of light. Now that you've ascended to this plane, things may seem a bit unreal until your inward eyes adjust to the light. Then the resplendence of everything will appear in its brilliance: and not just with things, but relationships where divine union can be experienced through one another. Only then you will realize all that you thought to be real was only a temporal shadow of the eternal reality that awaits you.'

'Okay Mo, thanks for the engaging oratory! I'm sure Plato couldn't have said it better, but I'm not so sure I want to be included in his allegory since I seem to have enough metaphors going on already in my dream. Based on your strong opinions, I suspect you must know your way around philosophic concepts and it seems you have developed a very serious Platonic bent, as noted with your allusions to *the Cave*.[1] Still, I think that a greater emphasis on particulars as taught by his student Aristotle would be useful to you in balancing Plato's universals.

'Nevertheless, I won't deny that what you have put forth are interesting perspectives for future discussion, but they are probably a bit too abstract for a world that is increasingly preoccupied with scientific achievement. However, should we meet in London sometime, perhaps we could discuss Plato more thoroughly. We could also examine his conjectures about Atlantis, reincarnation, and other enchanting topics such as his *Cave* allegory. I know a couple of scholars who teach Greek philosophy at Oxford. I'm sure we could have a most fascinating discussion over a few pints of bitter at the *Child and Eagle* in company with the ghosts of Lewis, Tolkien, Barfield and Williams.[2]

'But to be honest, I'm more inclined towards more Aristotelian perspectives, as I've intimated, since I find these considerably more down to earth than Plato's abstract universals. However, I've recently been giving some thought to certain *Neo-Platonic* ideas contained in

---

[1] See in *The Republic*, Allegory of the Cave; written by Plato 380 BC.
[2] The pub where these authors, sometimes referred to as *the Inklings*, once frequented in Oxford for many years last century.

Plotinus' *Enneads.*[1] These insights I find more palatable, although they too are often disregarded as being too mystical within the culture of contemporary Western realism.'

'You're certainly right about that,' Mo said. 'It's not easy to advocate the meaning of spiritual transcendence without being shouted down by the more militant advocates of mechanistic determinism. As I alluded to before, Ludwig Wittgenstein, arguably the primary mastermind of modern rationalism, did not limit his views to naturalism. In fact, he once stated: *the whole modern conception of the world is founded on the illusion that so-called laws of nature are the explanation of all natural phenomena.* Only he could get away speaking this way because he was, well: Wittgenstein. Today, however, if anyone has ambitions of advancing towards high academic ranks, it's best to keep such ideas on lock mode until after tenure is granted.'

'You can say what you will,' Mo, 'but I still think perhaps you're being overly critical about contemporary Western philosophy.'

'Am I?' he said. 'Try and see what happens when you rock their boat. But then, you already did, so you should know. Don't you remember the sidelong glances you received when you submitted your dissertation? Though it may have been scholarly, it was not acceptable to them because by had been spending too much time gazing out your window towards a Mountain which, according to them, didn't exist.

'Back then you were distracted, my friend, and it showed. They could read between the lines, and so they did. Only when you acquiesced by flattening your thesis to their parochial weltanschauung, were you awarded your doctorate.[2] And now you wonder why you keep getting squeezed out of the tenure queue. Perhaps they realize you're no longer one of them.'

'Are you trying to make me paranoid; how do you know all this,

---

[1] Plotinus (204-270 AD) wrote his Six Enneads primarily as a clarification of Plato's philosophy. His writings have influenced Christian, Islamic, Gnostic, Pagan and mystical thought through the centuries.

[2] Weltanschauung is a German word meaning world view/perception. It's often used in philosophy since there doesn't seem to be a suitable equivalent in the English language. It seemed my whole purpose there was to acquire a new weltanschauung.

and whatever else that goes on in my department? I suspect, however, you may be right about what goes on behind committee doors.'

'Of course I am,' Mo said, 'because I remember what that's like. That's why I know you will find it difficult to remain in the Flatlands after you return home, especially when you recall all that is happened here. Few in your department would take you seriously; much less understand you, even if they did listen. And yet you possess too much inward integrity to pretend none of this happened. At first you will likely dismiss whatever glimpses you recall as just part of some dream, but one day, much to your amazement, you will have irrefutable evidence that shows up on your doorstep, convincing you your time here was indeed real.'

'I'm not sure what you're getting at about the doorstep, but when I return home, in say about ten days, I'm not sure I would want to say anything about these discussions we've been having. You're right, few would understand. Hell, I'm not sure I do.'

'The return Mo is referring to is not just to London,' Eli said, 'but rather your return to the physical body in London. When it sufficiently recovers to receive you again, we trust you will tell everyone about your adventure here, whether they believe you or not. It would give us much pleasure to watch you rock their boat again. But do you think you'll have the ballocks for this?'

'When I get back to London, I'm sure I'll find a lot better things to do with my ballocks.'

'I'm sure you will,' Eli said with a laugh. 'But be that as it may, we think that in time you will not only rock their boat, but capsize it into their sea of disapprobation; which in the end may not be so bad. Don't be concerned if this happens. We'll be sailing along-side to pull you out of these waters into our much larger boat that will sail you to unknown galaxies. However, if you continue to cling only to boats laden with dense and heavy beliefs, they could sink your spirit when their ship goes under. Would it not be better to sail with us on our cosmic voyage?'

'So what weed are you smoking today, Eli? Nevertheless, to use your nautical metaphor, I doubt my ship will be going down anytime soon. In fact, once the winds begin to blow in my direction again, I'm sure I'll have smooth sailing. The system may not be perfect, but I'll accommodate myself once I know my career is secure.'

'If it seems we challenge Western philosophy too harshly,' Mo said, 'it's because we want you to see the contrast of where you've been to where you're going. Like everyone caught up in the current zeitgeist, you may have assumed that if you acquired enough information from those around you, you would have acquired an understanding about life.

I didn't respond, but it made me wonder if much of what I had been taught was based on nothing more than unquestioned presuppositions of beliefs that had accumulated over centuries. On the other hand, I found many of today's fixations had little substance since they are often based on simplistic over-reactions towards more traditional belief systems.

'Whatever beliefs one may choose,' Mo said, 'be they from the past or the nouveau, too few examine the merits of the inherent assumptions, preferring to accept whatever their friends, leaders or media tell them. It's easier and safer that way. It's really not much different than when religions used whatever means it had available to impose its dogmas on society. Perhaps even more pernicious today, are the false beliefs totalitarian governments continue to propagate and impose.

'This is why one's beliefs, and their proximity to truth, have such significant consequences. Likewise for you, James; what you come to belief about your current state of existence here will have profound consequences for you now, and when you return. And not just for you, but everyone who comes to find out about your experiences on this side. Trust us; as you move further in and higher up, you will be lifted towards people, places and events you would never before have dreamed.'

'Speaking of being lifted towards people and places; if I may, I think I'd like to be lifted off this Mountain to catch a ride back to Santiago when your helicopter returns. Perhaps we could party the night before I have to head off to the airport. I understand they know how to celebrate there.'

'You've already had your helicopter ride,' Eli said, 'at least your body did when it left the Mountain. However, we now have a much better mode of transportation we'd like to show you. But you're going to have to first open you mind to its reality. When you're mind becomes *tabula rasa*, and you have forgotten everything you thought you knew, you will be able to go wherever you wish. And I don't mean just down the Mountain.'[1]

'Eli, why must you always speak in riddles? Do you have any idea of how ridiculous you sound? So where's this new transportation device, if not a helicopter. Excuse me for asking, but is there some UFO craft that you aliens have hidden here to joy ride around in?'

'Something much more efficient,' he said, 'with far less clang, bang and bulk. In fact, there's nothing to it at all. Please understand, James, if it seems like we speak in riddles, it's because we're trying to provoke and prod you into making your own discoveries, which, by their very nature, are beyond learning. Only you can make them because only you can create the reality you experience.'

'This is bloody outrageous!' I said, 'even your reply to my nonsensical question about spaceships is nonsense.'

'Think about it,' Mo said, 'only when you comprehend the meaning of your questions will you understand the answers. We don't think it is nonsense at all for you to ask about spaceships. So why not go further and ask us why we don't need one. You will never understand what you don't know if you don't first ask. Otherwise you may never discover what you seek to understanding. If you don't first ask, you don't receive, since you'll never be ready to receive until you first ask.'

'But isn't that what philosophy is supposed to be about: asking constructive questions to find constructive answers. However, expecting me to ask you why you don't need a spaceship seems rather ridiculous and not all that constructive, since we already know a helicopter would do just fine.'

'Perhaps it would do,' Eli said, 'but since you didn't ask us the question, you still don't know how we're able to get around. You only assume you know.'

'The only meaningful answers you ever receive,' Mo said, 'is a result of the questions you choose to ask. Eli is right, your questions could lead to bigger realities than just helicopters, UFOs and other modes of transportation. The problem is, too few philosophers bother to ask the

---

[1] *Tabula rasa* is Latin, for erased tablet, meaning to keep the mind focused in a blank state so that it may receive new impressions.

important questions that lead to what's beyond; especially since the days of the Vienna Circle.'[1]

'Pardon me; helicopters, UFOs and the Vienna Circle; that's a rather odd mix. What correlation in hell could there possibly be, if any?'

'It's subtle,' he said, 'except that helicopters achieve liftoff and actually go somewhere. But I'm not sure that's the case with linguistic analysis and syllogisms that keep things grounded. One can never transcend to higher planes if it's assumed they don't exist. Of course, these logical constructs can be useful in certain philosophical debate about the limitations of what can be understood on the earth plane. But these tools don't get you very far when you ask questions about the nature and source of consciousness, life after biological death and the meaning of life. And so no one bothers to ask.'

'Possible James, someday you will be the one to ask,' Eli said. 'And not only ask, but answer.'

'I think a lot of people already ask these questions.'

'Often they do,' he said, 'but who is there to answer them; certainly not many in your circles. That's because philosophy put a lid on itself when it stopped enquiring about anything that wasn't related to earth's dimension. Many philosophers now regard any religious or metaphysical language to be empirically nonsensical, that is, without sense. Therefore, as they will tell you, it's nonsense. Consequently, any mention of God, Source, or any other name denoting deity is not deemed acceptable in their discourse. Nor are UFOs for that matter.'

'That may be true among certain the positivists,' I said, 'but not necessarily for everyone in philosophical circles.'

'Nevertheless,' Mo continued, 'these prejudices are the intellectual moorings of the Flatlands, beginning as far back as the 18th century. In fact that's how the Flatlands got its name, by imposing its flat, mechanistic interpretation to everything. It's because of this levelling that you still find it difficult to acknowledge what we tell you about

[1] The Vienna Circle of logical empiricism was a movement in 1920s to 1930s comprised of philosophers who were dedicated to sifting out metaphysical elements in philosophy to achieve what they considered would be a *purified* logic of science. It's interesting to note this movement was being formulated about the time the *spooky* discoveries of subatomic physics were first being observed.

the vertical dimension of reality, even though your heart understands what your mind resists. It knows the flat and narrow approaches can't possible satisfy your soul's deeper longings. Your problem is that you are not yet fully aware of your own inward journey; the one that drew you further in, further up and beyond.'

'Beyond what; my sanity?'

'Beyond the limits of what you consider sanity and the modes of currently acceptable rational enquiry. You'll expand your understanding to new realms of infinite possibilities when you become interested in asking the important questions. Then, perhaps when you return, you will be able to return to your classroom to challenge the assumptions what no one wishes to question.'

'Such as what?'

'Any question that already has the answer's premises rigged into the question,' he said. 'These can't help but yield answers that have already been assumed. There's plenty of this sleight of hand that occurs these days, especially when special interest groups provide funding to legitimize their agenda. Even the universally accepted Scientific Method would be one such example where it's universally assumed only that which can be empirically investigated is worth investigating.

'In fact our very spiritual presence on this plane of existence couldn't be investigated because it has already decided this state doesn't exist. That's an assumption. That's scientism; the kind Wittgenstein had no use for even though his methodology may have been conscripted in its service.

'Actually, I used to ask these sorts of annoying questions when I was an undergraduate student; not that anyone particularly cared. For example, I used to wonder about the various assumptions that are foundational to empirical science. Finally I stopped asking when I began to think everyone must already know what I didn't.'

'Indeed you did ask many inconvenient and difficult questions,' Eli said, 'and that's partly what drew you up here, since you weren't getting any satisfactory answers down there. Mainstream science and philosophy don't wish to go anywhere near metaphysical questions such as life after death, in spite of the vast amount of research that has been conducted over the last number of decades. That's why you will need to remember what dimension you've fallen and what you've learned in your Summit crash course.'

'*Crash course?* – most clever, Eli.'

'Well, think about it,' he said, 'you literally crashed down the chasm to wake up into a new dimension many would deny as existing, even though it's the spiritual substratum that undergirds the apparent world of surface appearances. Once you realize you're no longer confined to the earth plane, you will discover what hitherto has remained difficult to accept. Be assured we'll work with you until you realize that the little box of reality you've been carrying around doesn't have enough room to contain what you are experiencing here.'

I thought his comments were rather presumptuous, if not supercilious, as though he and Mo were ancient sages sitting on this Mountain, thinking they knew more than anyone else on earth. As amateur philosophers, with their peculiar epistemologies, they seemed much too sure of themselves.

'Though you may not realize it,' Mo said, 'the old constraints of your empirical training will become evident when you learn to reconcile your heart with your mind. As we've said, and will keep saying, the heart is the spirit's divine portal to higher consciousness.

'Therefore it is necessary the mind becomes subordinate to the heart's inner wisdom, if you are ever to come into the fullness of understanding. The ego mind remains externally focused, separating itself from the heart's centre of being, and so can't see the implicit unity of the universe. Few on the earth plane realize this, and fewer yet care.

'And that's why much of humanity hears only the meaningless clatter of what intrudes upon them: never acting intentionally, yet reacting to whatever circumstances may direct their lives. It's why the mind must remain united with the heart's wisdom or it loses itself to worthless things and events of the ego.'

'Why do you both keep talking of the heart as being something it's not?' I said. 'Science shows that the heart is essentially a pump that circulates blood and nothing more.'

'We would define the physical heart pump as a metaphor for the centre of being; which is the soul,' Eli said. 'Therefore, we may say the heart, in essence, is the spiritual receptacle of divine wisdom, love and light. Much like the brain is a metaphor for the mind, although few see it that way.'

'When you understand,' Mo said, 'that all physical appearances, including the heart, are vibratory interpretations of Source Energy, then you'll perceive spiritual essence and unity in all that is. Furthermore, every spiritual essence has a corresponding form in which it may manifest across the full spectrum of dimensions.[1] All appearances proceed from the thought patterns we co-create.'

'I have no idea what that means,' I said, '"vibratory interpretations." Really now, you sound like some Eastern guru with an English accent. Mysticism is hardly my orientation, so I'm not sure how well I would have fit in for this *crash course* of yours. I hate to be the first drop out at Summit U, but I have a job to get back to.'

'You may go whenever you wish,' Eli said, 'no one is holding you back, but as we already suggested, it may be rather lonely wandering the halls of your university by day and the streets of London by night, virtually lost and unknown to everyone. Maybe on a bad day you've felt that way, particularly after getting jilted, but that's nothing compared to how alone you would feel now.'

'Really? So you're telling me I'm lucky to be here with you.'

'More than you know,' Mo said. 'We've already told you several times and in various ways, why you are lucky to be here with us, but let me summarize this for you once more.

'Whether you choose to recognize it or not, a few years ago you began to wish for something more than what the Lowlands had to offer. At some unconscious level you wanted to find a vast new reality where you could dwell. Although you didn't know where or what that may be, you realized you weren't going to find whatever you were seeking by remaining stuck in the bogs. All those unconnected parts of your reality weren't adding up to anything close to the sum of what you thought life should be.

'And so you embarked on your journey towards the Mountain, albeit with a few wistful glances back to the Lowlands when things

---

[1] I found this statement to be most intriguing, so was interested to learn that the doctrine of correspondences was very foundation to the writings of Emanuel Swedenborg. (See Appendix B)

got challenging while scaling up the more difficult precipices. Such apprehensions are to be expected; the journey can be very steep, and so the temptation to turn back remained, at least until you were able to see the clouds below. Then you realized why you had never before seen the direct sunlight. And that's why you're here; that you may see a new reality, even beyond your wildest dream.'

'Maybe we could talk about something other than that damned dream of mine for once. I think it's ridiculous to expect me to believe that I'm somehow living out a strange dream drama. No, I didn't ask for any of this: whatever it is that you say I'm experiencing here. And to top it all, you expect me to believe that my brain and I parted company weeks ago and I exist separately and simultaneously on two different continents.'

'Let me to give you more clarity on your situation here,' Mo said. 'Eli, pour James a stiff Scotch, he doesn't need it, but he probably thinks he does – so I guess he does. It may do him some good since he believes it helps when he's agitated.'

'I'm not agitated,' I said, raising my voice, 'just a bit irritated after having my intelligence constantly affronted by … oh, I must say, that's very good Scotch. With enough shots, you may convince me of most anything. Hell, I may even join in this fantasy of yours, at least until the morning.'

'In reality, libations don't work that way here; at least not unless you want by imagining you're getting a buzz for old time's sake. But we prefer that you remain lucid for the moment,' Eli said, smiling as he refilled my glass.'

'So now James,' Mo said, 'I want you take a few deep breaths and relax. This subtle body of yours is well adapted to imbibe the ubiquitous *prana*, much more effective than in your physical body. It is of the divine life force essence which you may think of, by way of analogy, as divine oxygen, or spiritual energy that is absorbed into your form. Be it here or the earth plane, it sustains and vivifies the frequencies of your manifested body.'

I considered this to be more schlock, but after a few swigs, I became compliant as I happily performed a series of deep breathing exercises as I was directed.

'You know,' I said, 'this isn't all new to me, I've had Hatha Yoga lessons in the past, in fact, with some really exotic moves, the kind they do in ashrams.

'Just curious,' Eli said, 'but how did you get involved in yoga?'

'I think it may have had something to do with how the instructor demonstrated her contortion skill. In fact, once we got to know each other, we had plenty to opportunity after class to practise these deep breathing exercises.'

'So with all that,' Mo said, 'and climbing this mountain, you should have no problem taking another twenty breaths. This time slower and deeper, it's all about the cadence.'

'That's what she used to say too.'

'Focus, James – be present and focus on your breath.'

'Are you trying to convince me I'm out of my body by getting me to hyperventilate so I fall into some wild Sufi trance? If that doesn't do it, what's next, a little Dervish whirling? Scotch, breathing and whirling; something's got to work. Maybe in no time I'll be looking down on myself from the ceiling.'

After completing the deep breaths, I threw back the last of my Scotch.

'Now how does that feel?' Mo asked.

'Excellent! Most exceptional -- tastes authentically Scottish.'

'No James, not the drink, the breathing. How do you feel now after the last few deep breaths?'

'It feels as though I'm in my body, not out of it.'

And so you are in a body. So try doing a few more breathes and I'm sure you'll feel much lighter, with or without the Scotch. And yes, this brand is one of the best we serve here, a virtual version patterned after the old Dimple Pinch brand from Edinburgh.'

"Virtual version;" what's that; some knock-off like this virtual reality you're trying to make me believe?'

In any case, the Pinch, being my favourite, went down very smoothly, more luscious each time. A real treat! I seldom buy it since it's so damned expensive.

'Cheers!' Eli said, as we downed another shot.

'I don't know whether it's my imagination or not, I said, but I feel considerably lighter after all these breathing and elbow tipping exercises, and yet I don't feel my awareness compromised. It all feels natural.'

'Most excellent, that's what we wished you would to find,' Mo said. 'But it's really your beliefs that have made it so. Now I want you to continue to relax in your chair, and listen carefully to what else I'm about to tell you. We realize at times you may still feel a bit disoriented here, but try to keep an open mind and you will soon understand why. I know you're getting tired of hearing us refer to your dream, but let me make a few more important observations since I hadn't yet finished.'

I slouched back into my seat, glass in hand, put my feet up on the table and closed my eyes, feeling very relaxed. 'Sure, whatever you have to say, as you can see, I'm listening most intently. Eli, how much Pinch is left in the bottle?'

'As I was saying,' Mo said, 'the dream represents what you were unconsciously asking for long before you set out to find the Mountain. At some deep subliminal level you desired to know what lies beyond the shadows of your Lowlands. You wanted to see beyond the ruts, bogs, fog, thorns, thistles and gnarly shrubs of your daily routine.'

'Yes, no doubt about it; ruts, bogs, thorns and thistles – that's me. It's especially easy to get bogged down in bad relationships. I've had a few,' I chuckled. 'Not a great place to be when they have you sunk, wanting out, yet still wanting more!'

'But now that you've departed the Lowlands,' he said, 'and ascended this Mountain, you will soon see an expanded view of reality up here that reveals new dimensions of understanding you could never have imagined before. In fact the view is larger than what you can possible take in, ever.'

'But we're going to show you just a little at a time so don't become overwhelmed. Though you may not be aware of it, this higher reality is all around you, even while you remain on earth. Once you are able to discern it, believe us, nothing again is going to be the same for you. It can't be.'

'So what if I don't believe you - or see things as you see; don't I get a choice in what I wish to believe?'

'Of course you do,' Eli said, 'this is a liberal arts university. You get to speak your mind just as they did on campuses in the Western world when there was more than one acceptable way to think before the new *Groupthink* swept in.[1] Of course, you may choose to believe you don't have a choice. Many prefer to believe that in the Flatlands.'

'Being a freethinker of sorts,' I said, 'I can't imagine why anyone would want to remain in bondage to the masses.'

'Which is a large part of human history, is it not?' Mo said. 'If you don't see yourself as free and having a choice, then in effect you aren't. You have no choice if that's what you think, while mindlessly allowing the authorities to decide your life for you. In extreme cases, these are the *useful idiots* Lenin would contemptuously refer to, since he had no respect for his pawns. But when you become aware of what you are, and what you truly want, you will always choose to dignity over slavery, just as you choose light over darkness.

'As you ascend higher, you will be able to observe how much there is to your existence, as you become attuned to your new reality. You will soon find you are able to manifest anything that aligns with your new vibratory state. The further in and higher you go, more will become accessible to you.'

'So then, how about the perfect woman,' I said, 'how do I get to be accessible her?'

'When you become attuned to what you really want, she will find you. For now though, you are wedged in a passage between the earth and what's beyond. A day will come however, when you will launch out through your own *Stargate* to discover the infinity of things you may do and places you may go. Though you may continue to have some attachments with the earth plane, they may manifest a bit differently.'

'I'm not sure what you're talking about, but why would things appear differently; isn't a pretty young woman still pretty?'

'Of course,' Mo said, 'in fact, they may seem even prettier when you are prettier too,' he chuckled. 'You will perceive reality differently, based on who and what you have become within. Everything will be

---

[1] An Orwellian term from George Orwell's novel '*1984*', published in 1949, meaning excessive independent thought. Any individualist thought that is perceived to threaten the conformist/collectivist trends were regarded as criminal thoughts. He caricaturized this political phenomena with terms such as *Newspeak*, *Doublethink* and *Groupthink*.

more vibrant and loving the further you proceed inwardly. Whatever you choose to experience, I can assure you it will be far more engaging than anything you have experienced on the earth plane. All is custom designed to manifest as a vibratory match to your special desires and affections.

'Not that you are special; no one possesses a more divine essence than anyone else and yet we are all unique expressions of divinity according to what we have chosen. We become what we are with every decision we make and with every relationship we enter. You are very unique, having inwardly desired to ascend to this plane of being, going where few would go. Few are prepared to leave the Lowlands and so few are chosen. In that sense, you are chosen.'

'One of the chosen, eh; by whom – the Almighty? I'm not even religious; or for that matter, Jewish.'

'Because you have chosen, you are chosen!' Mo said, 'that's the criterion for being on the Mountain, not because you're special. As you know, the Lowlanders prefer to remain stuck in their boggy swamps rather than ascend to higher elevations. That's because most have chosen not to choose, which is a choice unto itself. But not you! You wanted more and so went on to make the most important decision of your life.

'That's why you are entering a new world far beyond the thorns, thistles and mire that had you stuck. It may not seem it, but you've been seeking truth for most of your life. It can be said, you've been trekking towards this Mountain for a very long time – longer than you may realize. Like gravity, the resistances of your ego mind slowed you down and held you back, but you never gave up.

'All the crevices and valleys were part of your journey; there were no wrong people or places, it only seemed that way at times. They all played a part in your conscious evolution, giving you the contrast you needed to know what you didn't want, so you would know what you did want.'

'I suspect these dream interpretations of yours are more poetry than fact, I said. As far as I know I came here to climb a Mountain. It's that simple! It seems you're trying to make my dream into some big cosmological drama.'

'James,' Mo said; 'try not to spurn the gift you gave yourself. This dream was your special revelation to yourself and therefore it's all yours; your poetry, your reward and your future. You earned it my friend. That was no ordinary dream, it was a lucid dream; probably the first one you've ever had.[1] Through it, you received the vision and inward guidance to find your way here. The directions didn't come from your mind, but from your heart.'

'Perhaps in a metaphorical sense,' I said, 'I can agree with some of what you're saying. Just being able to make it all the way up here was like a dream, and so I guess you could say it was my big reward. There are always risks with such an expedition, and in that sense, making it to the top of any Mountain is its own reward. And I suppose it could also be said there's a poetic cadence to the upward rhythm.

'Speaking of which I'd love to climb Mount Aconcagua sometime, though I'm not sure how poetic it would feel trying to climb the highest mountain in the Western Hemisphere. I think it's about forty or fifty miles east of here on the Argentine side.'

'Definitely we should do that,' Eli said; 'you may be surprised that it's not as challenging to climb as you think. Though it's not as steep as Everest, still the altitude has killed a lot of climbers. But coming back to what Mo was saying, your reward isn't specifically about your literal ascent up this or any other mountain such as Aconcagua, but rather your spiritual ascent that leads towards your new reality.'

'I'm not sure I want my life to be understood as figurative rather than literal, unless it's being recited as part of a Faustian poem.'

'The longer you're here,' Mo said; 'the more you will come to realize the literal is inextricably linked to the interior figurative sense. Be it Logos or mythos, this inward dynamic exist throughout life. As you often hear us say, *as within, so without*, meaning, whatever you outwardly manifest derives from the thoughts you have created within. That's why your outward ascent is only as difficult and rewarding as your inward ascent.

'Unlike Prometheus, who struggled to roll his heavy boulder up the Mountain, there will be less toil the higher you ascend until there

---

[1] Lucid dreams are understood to be conscious participation in one's dreams while the body remains asleep. This phenomena, and how it is achieved, is discussed in Book Four.

121

is only the lightness of your being. Have you ever noticed how light, as brightness, and light as in weight, are the same word in the English language?' Eli said. 'When illuminated by the Light of the Spirit, your burdens become so light that, at some point, they cease to exist.'

'I suppose,' I said, 'it's always easier to *lighten up* when you see some light at the end of the tunnel. Or on top of a mountain – except if it happens to be an orb,' I laughed.

'Indeed it is easier,' Mo said, 'that's why I think you will find this Summit is only a base camp for even more spectacular Summits to come, should you wish to ascend further up. While you are with us, you will experience Summits you would never have known of in a million years while occupying your dense earth body!

'Though you may feel you are in an unfamiliar dimension of reality, you aren't, since it has always remained a hidden in your soul. Whenever a person sheds their physical body, the immortal body is able to manifest in the higher vibratory form of the soul. As it is written, *this mortal shall have put on immortality.*[1] That's because the immortal body is an expression of the soul's immortal essence. But the version of your body in London is far from being immortal; in fact, it's barely hanging on to its mortality. What you're experiencing now is for keeps, formed and sustained by divine light. It's always there with or without the mortal shell.'

'Really? All metaphors aside, do I appear to be a ghost?'

'Do we appear to be ghosts?' Eli said, 'whatever you conceive of that state to be. Rather, what you're experiencing now is your glorious body sheath, that's why you don't seem disembodied because in actuality you're not, anymore then when you're occupying your biological body. It's more a case of your biological body being dispirited or vacated by your soul. Time and space are not the same limiting factors in this dimension, and so there is no obstruction to your spirit body's agility when teleporting or engaging in other modes of spiritual experience.'

'I want you to know I'm not taking any of this seriously, but just out of curiously, would you consider sex to be part of these, as you say, other modes of spiritual experience?'

'Please be sure to tell us when you find out James,' he said, 'we'd

[1] 1 Corinthians 15:54

love to hear your story. Perhaps you can do some research on this on one of your upcoming field trips.'

'Ah, if only,' I said laughingly.

'Remember, your immortal body is not of the earth plane,' Mo said, 'not to say it has less desire or fewer aptitudes. In any case, it's the bodily expression you are currently experiencing in what we simply call the spirit body. However, there are several more exotic names that have emerged in various cultures across the continents over the centuries.'

'Such as *spook*?' I said, with a tinge of sarcasm, still not buying what they were saying in all its esotery.

'No matter how you manifest, or what zone you're in,' Mo said, 'you are a divinely created soul; that much doesn't change. And you will always remain individuated as part of Source essence, externally manifested in form, just as goodness is sheathed within the form of truth. Understand, form and essence are not separate, anymore than cause and effect; they are one. If there were no bodily form and therefore no appearance of locality, how would we be able to give any expression when communicating our essence to other conscious souls? Only Source can be pure disembodied consciousness from which all individuated manifestations emerge.

'Only in this sense, does Source have form. In fact, several forms; more than can be imagined! You would be one such manifestation and that's why you may consider yourself an extension of Source essence as a *god* or as a son of God, as affirmed in both Jewish and Christian scriptures.[1] And so you may rest assured you have a body, but it bears no relation to an amorphous spook.'

'However,' said Eli, 'should someone ask a chap about you, even while you were standing beside him on a street in London, he may have a different opinion of how you appear. Even if you were able to speak to him, he'd say you have *no body*, then turn and run in the other direction. You shouldn't be offended though, because you actually are a *some body*,

---

[1] In my research I noted the text Mo was referring to: '*Jesus replied, is it not written in your Law: 'I have said you are gods'*? John 10:34, (NIV). Here Jesus was quoting Psalms 82:6. The subject of *gods* came up a number of times as you will find in these narratives. Also, the term "*sons of God*" is often employed.

just not in the way he thinks. Still, whenever *some body* jilts you, you probably feel like a *no body* because you don't have *any body* to love you.'

'More word plays, Eli?'

'As lame as some of his may be,' Mo said, 'English terms such as somebody, nobody, anybody; well illustrate how humans identify themselves as bodies rather than souls. Although, I'm sure your clairvoyant girlfriend would see more of you than this man on the street. Next time you're in London, you should drop by for a visit. If she sees your spirit body, then at least you'll know she's authentic and that you've been getting your money's worth.'

'Even if I had spirit body, my guess is she would prefer my carnal body,' I said with a chuckle, 'although she claims to also see what she claims to be my astral body.'

'Some call it an astral body,' he said, 'some call it a lot of other things, it doesn't matter, call it whatever you wish. You no longer need a clairvoyant to tell you that your spirit body exists as an ethereal composition of divine light. Names aren't important, except they make some people think they know what they're talking about. You only need to know it's the extended form of your soul's light that manifests according to the appearance you've associated yourself with.'

'Let me add,' Eli said, 'this may be understood as an external spiritual read-out of a higher frequency, compared to the lower frequency of your other body residing in London. Because you are dwelling in a vessel of a higher light frequency, your vibratory spirit form is able to re-enter your earthly vessel, but your earthly vessel with its lower frequencies, can never enter your spirit vessel. And so it just ends up as being no more when it *gives up the ghost*, as they say.

'Even your physical eyes, as incredible as they may be, can only provide a crude read-out of the electro-magnetic configurations contained in the third dimension. When you get down to it, the physicality of the atom is reduced to a schedule of probability pointer readings on a chart.[1]

'You may say that behind the scenes all physicality is illusory and

---

[1] Physicist Sir Arthur Eddington (1882–1944) stated it this way: *Science has nothing to say as to the intrinsic nature of the atom. The physical atom is, like everything else in physics, a schedule of pointer readings.*

so things aren't always as they appear. Everything we think we see, from the smallest microtubule to the body, is actually in a state of shifting energy patterns without any underlying solidity. Only the divine Source is constant, though never static, as the Source extends its divine essence through creation's eternal expansion.'[1]

'What you seem to be saying sounds similar to Alford North Whitehead's *Process Philosophy*. Although I don't understand much of his abstruse esoterica, and I'm not sure many do, I remember once attending a lecture series on this topic by an eminent Whitehead scholar.[2] The concepts are very difficult to understand, even for professional philosophers.'

'Indeed they are,' Mo said, 'but I'll see what I can do to scrounge up a couple of his books should you wish to brush up on his unique cosmological blend of theology and philosophy. In simplistic terms, what Whitehead attempts to express is how God's thoughts are continually in the process of evolving into an infinite manifestation of forms through co-creation. That would include all the individuated consciousness that manifest in the Infiniverse, or as we say earlier, the Multiverse. That's why there can be no other reality or substance other than divine essence, even with what we may call inert matter, which may, at best, be described as crystallized energy.'

'What I learned at the Whitehead lectures,' I said, 'is that there was much support for such concepts from certain physicists such as David Bohm.[3] He considered matter to be the manifestation of the *explicate* reality, a virtual kaleidoscope of variegated energy forms enfolded in what he described as the *implicate order*.'

---

[1] In traditional religion, it would more likely be said: *the Father extents His divine essence...* However, neither Mo nor Eli used overtly religious terms very often. Perhaps out of deference to me, or possibly they weren't comfortable with certain words and expression they considered archaic or misleading.

[2] While attending university as an undergraduate, I once attended a lecture by preeminent Whitehead scholar, John B Cobb who is a philosopher/theologian and founder of the Centre for Process Studies in California. After the lecture, I thought that someday I may delve into Whitehead's barely comprehensible *Process and Reality*. But to this point, I never had.

[3] British Physicist 1917 – 1992, Fellow of the Royal Society. (See Appendix 'A' for various quotes.)

'I believe, Bohm was on to something,' Eli said, 'in suggesting there's an inward implicate universe that's reflected in some of the explicate universe we experience. Again, as we say, ad infinitum: *as within, so without,* it's really the same thing. Though that may be a good place to start, physics can only go so far in comprehending the true nature of the universe.'

'But do we really want to reduce our understanding of infinite Source to just the concept of energy,' Mo said, 'such as we generate from wind turbines or pump out of the ground as fossil fuel? Or as many like to say: *The Universe.* To me, that sounds like one massive accumulation of objects. Depending on what you intend that term to mean, it may lead to a regrettable pantheistic reduction, as if God is a composite of the sum of created parts that somehow came to be. Where's the love in that?'

'I agree,' I said, 'even from an agnostic's perspective, the term *universe* seems rather facile, although many seem to prefer it when speaking of the Ultimate.'

'This is where,' Mo said, 'the concept of the *Ray of Creation* can be of assistance to, so to speak, shed a ray of light. Provided, however, it's understood that the *Ray* is a metaphor of how the effluence of divinity proceeds outward from the Source. Of course, there are no words that can begin to adequately describe the indescribable. But at least Whitehead gave it an admirable shot.

'In a sense we are all swathed in progressively subtler bodies of energy that exist outside the base frequency of the earth's physical body. Since the soul isn't inextricably tied to the biological body, it's free to leave at any time, which it often does during periods of deep sleep. Or in your case; a very deep sleep! That's how your soul managed to be released, although in some way it still attached.[1] Think of your bodies as octaves of advanced vibratory realities emanating from the *Ray of Creation* as divine thought forms.'

---

[1] From what I understood, consciousness, being non local, still remains infused in the biological body for as long as it lives, ensuring each cell remains animated with life. Perhaps this is where the concept of the *silver cord* originates.

'Divine thought forms, eh? Such as what?'

'Such as Eli, such as me and of course – such as you.'

'Oh really;' I said, 'and how about this divine Scotch I'm holding?'

'That Scotch' he said, 'didn't actually come from Scotland. Only the thought did. But a most divine thought it is, wouldn't you say?'

CHAPTER 7

GETTING HIGH

Oh I get high with a little help from my friends[1]

There was a lot for me to think about after these recent fireside chats. It seemed they were wearing me down, but I still wasn't convinced about not being in my body as they insisted. In any case, I looked forward to a sound sleep that I may subliminally re-evaluate and, if necessary, reposition certain beliefs. Especially after having many of my rationalist moorings attacked and uprooted mercilessly by my friendly adversaries. Perhaps a good sleep would help sort things out by the time I woke up. It was late, and the fire had burned down to hot coals. After we finished our drinks, both got up and bid me '*buenas noches*'.

As they were walking towards the door to leave, God knows where, I asked if they didn't wish to stay for the night.'

'Sorry, James, but we think you need some time alone. But don't worry, you'll be safe,' Mo said with a laugh. 'Remember, no one can harm you except your thoughts.'

---

[1] A line from *A Little Help from my Friends* in The Beatles' *Sergeant Pepper's Lonely Hearts Club Band*.

'We'll see you in the morning as the sun rises,' Eli said, as he gestured on his way out with a causal salute.

I couldn't understand why they wandered off each night; it didn't make sense. But then it didn't have to since nothing else did – at least that much was predictable! I was tempted to trail behind to see where they went, then decided against it in case they caught me and asked why I was skulking about. For now, this would have to remain one more enigma in my assortment of un-reconciled mysteries!

With images of my fall emblazoned in my brain, I slowly climbed the stairs to the loft, still sensing some of the vertigo I felt earlier. But were these images any more real than the dream I remembered? I did my best to dismiss what I thought I had seen on the screen of my mind, even wondering if they hadn't for some reason put something hallucinogenic in my drink. How else could I explain a near fatal fall with my body remaining completely unscathed? Possibly I hadn't fallen at all, but only imagined it.

Adding to my confusion were their outrageous explanations for everything that was happen here; I hadn't heard or read anything so peculiar before, not even in fantasy literature. However, if what they said proved to be true, it would mean I was wrong about most everything I believed and nothing could ever remain the same; forever altered in ways I could hardly imagine. And what would become of my career?

As I took off my clothes, I examined my body again. It still amazed me I had no bruises, cuts or injuries. I remember I had a few gashes on my legs and arms from climbing the precipices, but now my body was about as unblemished as I could remember. Mo said it was because there were no wounds there to heal, not even the scrapes and cuts I incurred reaching the summit. But this wasn't very reassuring; now even my body, in all its supposed splendor and perfection, wasn't normal.

For now though, I didn't want to vex myself with more of these impossible questions; my mind already was too frazzled to process more mysteries. Had I fallen into some hole of an alternate dimension in space? Or what if this Mountain was really an inverted vortex? I wasn't sure that made a lot of sense either, but then it didn't have to. With the way things were going, I wouldn't be surprised if I'd soon bump into Alice.

Though my body didn't feel tired like my mind did, still I slipped between the covers of my bed, not sure if I would be able to sleep. And yet sleep I did, most soundly in fact, until awakening with the morning sun rising over the easterly mountain range.

Next morning, as I stepped down the stairs, I could see Mo and Eli were already by the stove cooking breakfast. Eli greeted me as usual, saying: *buenos días amigo.* So did you sleep?' I found it interesting he didn't ask how I slept or if I slept well, but did I sleep, as if sleep was just an option.

'Yes, certainly did,' I said; 'as though in a deep hibernation. I don't remember anything, from the moment my head hit the pillow until the sun's rays woke me just now.'

'You may not realize it,' Mo said, 'but there's much more going on beneath the surface of your consciousness than you're aware. That's why you require much sleep for your mind; that you may get out of its own way so your real Self may sort things out. Perhaps we overloaded your circuits yesterday, but you have an inordinate appetite for understanding our reality, even while you resist it.'

'Speaking of appetite,' Eli said, 'I hope you're ready for breakfast.'

'I'm not actually hungry, but everything tastes so extraordinary in this alpine environment. You know, it would be great to stay another few nights to find out what was going on here.'

'Don't worry,' he said, 'you soon will, and then you won't want to leave.'

'It is a great spot,' I agreed. 'I don't know how you two mountaineers came across an alpine cabin with such character. I can hardly imagine a more inspiring place to stay. In fact, it would be a pleasure to remain here much longer if I didn't have a plane to catch and a job to return to.

I walked around once more, closely examined the antiquity of the charming interior. The log walls appeared to be well seasoned with decades of smoke from the fireplace and possibly with pipe tobacco mixed in for effect. There was something mysterious about this place, even possessing a familiar *genius loci* as Mo described it.[1]

---

[1] This was an unfamiliar term to me until I heard Mo use it, meaning a place that feels replete with spiritual *presence,* sometimes evoking awe and even mystical resonance.

It was hard not to get attached. It had the perfect alpine atmosphere, complete with a comfortable bed, lounge seating and great views looking towards both the westerly and easterly Mountain ranges. It brought back some unforgettable memories I had from my time in the Canadian Rockies when I once stayed at a lodge very similar to this, only much larger.

Though isolated in such a remote mountain region, I had everything I needed, including a charming cellar where there was a large cache of fine wines, whiskey along with bottles of lager and other assorted libations. Oddly though, there was no loo or outhouse. Where did everyone go when they needed to go? But then, I hadn't required such facilities since I arrived here. Considering the amount of food and drink I had consumed during my time here; that was most peculiar.

I also wondered where the water in the urns came from. I had no idea how they would have accessed it, since I didn't see any springs or streams up here. Perhaps they melted the ice from a glacier on the south side, although I didn't see evidence of them carrying ice! Possibly there was a well I hadn't noticed. The only thing I could be certain of is that I would get an uncertain answer. And so after a while I didn't bother. For now though, it really didn't matter; this was the kind of place I always dreamed of owning. One day, I determined, I would build a chalet much like this for my dream retreat in the Swiss Alps.

But it still bothered me how it could have been built here so long ago, considering how far it was above the tree line below. There was no rational explanation I could think of; judging from all appearances it must have been built at least a hundred years ago.

I sat down with Mo and Eli outside and asked, 'how in Jove's name could these logs have been hauled up here when this lodge was constructed? It would have been impossible for horses or mules to scale these steep escarpments; even an experienced climber such as I, was barely able to make it up here.'

'I'm sure there must have been a way,' Mo said, as he turned the sizzling bacon over with the old spatula. 'Perhaps this cabin doesn't even exist within the perceptive range of the earth plane. Did you think about that?'

'No,' I said, 'what's there to think, unless were talking more science fiction.'

'But James,' Eli said, 'wasn't it you who said no cabin existed here when you approached the Summit? If there had been; you would have had to be blind not to notice it, unless you were incapable of seeing it in your physical body.'

'My eyes are fine, thank you,' I said. 'I don't require glasses and I generally see most of what there is to see.'

'Which must really make you wonder why you didn't notice this fine edifice, considering you wouldn't have been more than a fifty yards away. It would have been rather difficult to miss, wouldn't you say?'

'So are you suggesting this cabin just popped into existence from out of nowhere? -- And with whose magician's wand? Though it's true I hadn't see it when I first climbed up this way; but don't forget I was distracted by what I thought were orbs of light on the summit. Still, I admit, it seems strange how I could have missed it; but then, it's not the only mystery up here.'

'Yet it need not be a mystery. As Mo already suggested, it's only because you're now in a different dimension that you are able to perceive what you couldn't perceive before. Very simple! But still, we understand, it's hard for you to let go of your old beliefs.

'It's only been a few days since you were released from the limitations of the third dimension. It may still take a while for your mind to expand beyond the former thought patterns of what it believes to be possible and what it assumes is not possible. The former parameters of perception don't apply in this sphere of existence. For you to realize this though, you will first have to shift away from the prejudices of your entrenched paradigms so you can see with eyes you didn't know you had.'

'Oh my,' I said; 'we're back to the magical pixie dust again, where everything and anything becomes possible at once. I think I'm going to need a few extra strong cups of coffee to make it through another day of impossible possibilities.'

'It will take more than coffee to shut out this new reality you're experiencing,' Mo said, grinning as he poured me a full mug. 'It would be like a fish shutting its gills from the water in the sea. Where you are now, my friend; is not the old norm. But then, you never were all that normal were you? And even less so now that you are beyond the old grid. Without your mortal body holding you back, your spirit body is functioning within a higher vibratory octave than normal.'

I looked at both of him blankly and said, 'that's really cool, Mo. But your right, it's hardly what you would call normal; perhaps it's paranormal.' Not wishing to get to delve further into this, I got a plate and sat down to eat.

'Here, dig in,' Mo said; 'help yourself to this hot stack of pancakes; at least they're normal,' Mo said with a smile, 'depending on what you consider normal.'

'They are fabulous,' I said, 'you're not a bad chef! You should teach Eli.'

'What? So you don't think I'm a good cook,' Eli said. 'Next time I'll show you; but then, in all honesty, anyone can be a five star chef here – there's really not much to it.'

'Then perhaps you will teach me so I can get an honest job. Most likely, it would make more money than me working as a part time instructor.'

'Maybe you could do both,' Eli said, 'prepare food for the body and food for the soul, all in the same day.'

While we were having breakfast at the old wooden table, I discussed with them the various routes I had been considering for my descent. After eating, I pulled my topographical map out of my backpack to show them the contours of the route I took while coming up and where I made a couple of unfortunate turns that necessitated me to go around in other ways.

As though reading my mind, Mo said; 'perhaps you should stay a little longer, James. If you do, I think we may be able to help you find a way down that will have you back in *no time*.' Eli chuckled when Mo said *no-time*, but I didn't understand why. I still had a lot to learn about the nature of time, space and they mystery of non-locality.

I thought this day would be ideal to begin my return, considering the favourable weather. The sun's rays were streaming through our window, and from what I could see, there were not many clouds except a few wisps lingering on the horizon. Yet I remained hesitant about leaving when there were still so many questions unresolved about all I had witnessed here. It would later drive me bonkers, if I didn't at least find a few rational answers to these bizarre events.

'Perhaps your right, Mo,' I said, 'a little more time to properly plan a proper route down may prove to helpful in getting down quicker, or as you say, in no time. I can probably afford another day before leaving and still have plenty of time to catch my flight out of Santiago.'

'If you give us the opportunity,' Eli said, 'we could show you a short cut that will amaze you.'

'That would be splendid' I said, 'provided you're certain I'm not overstaying my welcome in your paradisiacal retreat.'

'Actually it's your retreat too – anytime you wish to bring a friend here, it's yours to use for as long as you like.'

'That's most generous of you,' I said, as I got up from the table to have another pancake stacked in a pan on the old cast iron stove.

I wondered what it would be like to remain isolated in such a primitive old cabin as this. The idea appealed to me as the perfect place to take a break from my daily routine. Perhaps I could give civilization a pass for another day, maybe two, while soaking in this ambience. This would be an ideal venue someday to hold a retreat for intriguing offbeat philosophical discussions. Or better yet, bring a girlfriend along that's not afraid of a little adventure. A little out of the way though, even with a helicopter.

For much of the day we talked at length about everything of interest. I'm not sure how acceptable our discussions would have been considered by my university department and its empirical standards of interlocution. But then, my new friends didn't seem to care about following the established rules of scholarship, or having regard for the conventions of modern philosophical discourse. Not that they were being irrational, it's just that they reasoned with rules I didn't understand, or perhaps it was with no rules. I wondered what undergirded their thought processes. Perhaps trans-rational or supra-rational; I didn't know what, since these weren't very satisfactory descriptions either.

Though I had no specific term for their reasoning, I remembered coming across a book called *Tertium Organum,* by a Russian mathematician and esoteric philosopher name P.D Ouspensky.[1] I believe he wrote it while in Moscow, not too long before the Bolshevik Revolution when he met Georges Gurdjieff, another Russian esoteric philosopher. I was an undergraduate student at the time; busy doing other things, so didn't read much of the book. Besides, it didn't interest me that much since I didn't have a sufficient understanding of esoteric concepts to understand what he was trying to say. But with what little I got, seemed to relate to how Mo and Eli would think; very broad and yet very precise, as if there was a more inclusive way to reason than what modern syllogisms permitted.

From what I understand now, this was considered to be a higher *third logic* within esoteric circles. Within its parametric scope, it transcends the ordinary thought conventions of orthodox philosophy. Mo later described *Tertium Organum* as a system of reasoning that flows from unity of body, mind and soul, whereby the isolated, fact orientated mind learns to reason with a broad spiritual comprehension by its acquiescence to the greater wisdom of the soul's heart.

'Unfortunately,' he said, 'no one learns this in earth's Flatland centres of supposed higher learning, and so it was no wonder I was having difficulty understanding their spiritual paradigms. It was a much more expansive thought system than I was accustomed, since it required an appreciation of not just the exoteric world of outward materiality, but also the esoteric world of inward spirituality.'

It would be some time before I was able to grasp this *novel exemplar*, but as I did, it was with varying degrees of egoic resistance and protest. In fact, It wasn't until I later experienced what I call my magical mystery tour of the *Flatlands*, that I recognise how flat and narrow my understanding of reality was as a result of the limited criteria for rational discourse, whereby there was little acknowledgment of vertical (spiritual) reality.[2]

---

[1] Peter D. Ouspensky (1878-1947) Russian esoteric philosopher writes in this book, *'I have called this system of higher logic Tertium Organum because for us it is the third canon - third instrument - of thought after those of Aristotle and Bacon. The first was the Organon, the second, Novum Organum. But the third existed earlier than the first.'*

[2] This is elaborated on in Book Two, Chapter 13, *First Stop, The Flatland Plains*

Later in the day when we took I break, I stood on the deck, coffee mug in hand, viewing the Mountain range to the north and then looked down towards the chasm's opening that they said swallowed me whole. I wondered where I took my final step before plunging into the void below. Brutal! It didn't seem possible I could have survived such a fall; and as with everything else around here, I had no answer.

Furthermore, they were right; the cabin isn't far from where I may have fallen. I really should have noticed it since it would have been along the trajectory of my vision as I looked up towards the Summit. So why didn't I see it? Was it because I was distracted, or was it because there was nothing there I was able to see? A most preposterous notion! But in this place, where time seemed to have little meaning, where things such as wine and food magically materialize out of nowhere, why not a cabin too? Preposterous, yes! But not impossible if you believed everything else they were saying.

Slowly, it seemed they were wearing me down, to the point where I hardly bothered to argue with them anymore. It was easier to just nod my head and smile. Besides that, I was beginning to notice that time and space felt different, as thought I was now in a new dimension, which made me wonder how long ago it had been since my fall; was it a few days ago or was it, as Mo suggested, weeks ago? It was as though someone was playing with the hour glass, or perhaps they were playing with my mind.

Yet it was reasonable to assume the fall could do something like this to my brain, where time may seem to take on a strange new elasticity. That was an unsettling thought; if it had been out cold for weeks, then I would have missed my flight home and classes would have already begun. To say the least, that would not be good for my record, unless I could convince the authorities to believe my story. But I'm not sure they would, in fact, I'm not sure I would. Surviving a concussion while on a cold mountain slope over a couple of weeks would be stretching the limits of credulity.

As I was thinking about this, Mo stepped onto the deck to chat. From his serious demeanor, it seemed he may have something important on his mind he wished to speak to me about. It felt like things had

137

been building up to where we needed to come to a consensus about the nature of reality up here, on what seemed to be a *Magic Mountain*.[1]

Eli hadn't returned with the firewood yet, so Mo suggested we take a short hike along the Summit. While we climbed up to the ridge, Mo said, 'Eli and I were wondering if you still have questions about the nature of the life you're experiencing here with us!' Had he been reading my mind?'

'Of course,' I said, most emphatically. 'I've asked about a lot of things the last couple of days without getting satisfactory answers from either of you.'

'So what would you like to know,' he said; 'aren't things rather obvious to you by now? We've been telling you constantly that you now exist here as an immortal spirit body, even while your mortal physical earth body remains convalescing in London. Once you accept your current state of existence, everything else will make sense to you. So why do you still find this so hard to believe?'

'Because it makes no sense,' I said, almost shouting. 'It's not possible for anyone to exist outside their biological body. As I've said before, one may have hallucinations of being out of body, but such experiences are only mental distortions of what's occurring within the mind; nothing more; nothing real. You don't go anywhere, it's only the illusion is what's happening in your brain. Whatever paranormal experiences I seem to be having up here, are most likely a result to my brain being knocked around during my fall.'

'I see,' Mo said, 'it would appears then, you really don't have any questions, since you already have it all figured out. Or is it simply a matter of beliefs; what's believed to be possible and what's not? If so, then let me tell you how important it is that you don't cling too tightly to your beliefs because they may blind you from seeing the truth of what's out there.

'Contrary to what some say, reality isn't based on what we wish to believe; it just is. Though perceptions may vary, truth is truth. Even though it's possibly to create an illusion of reality, which is what the ego does, the truth is often much different than what many are willing

---

[1] In reference to Thomas Mann's book of this same name which we discussed later in Chapter 11, *The Magic Mountain* of Book Two.

to accept. Spiritual reality, from which all temporal experiences are derived, is more expansive than can possibly be imagined, which is why it scares so many into living their small insular lives.

'With that said, let me reaffirm your current state of existence here, since you still seem to have some confusion. Though your physical earth body continues to function on the earth plane, albeit marginally; you are here with us in an imperishable, non-temporal form. Let me state once again, most emphatically, this is not a dream or hallucinatory state of existence you are experiencing with us. This will later become obvious when we visit your earth bound body in London.

'In the future, after you awake in your physical body, you will become aware of all your lessons here, including all the higher dimensional experiences, assuming you return to your biological body.'

'But then,' I said, 'what is it that's having all these experiences here? You seem to have forgotten the question of individuation. Obviously it would not be possible to have an identity without a body.'

'That's correct,' Mo said, 'and that's why we keep telling you that you will always have a body, even after the death of your mortal body. But it never was who you were; no matter how impressive you thought you looked on the outside, it never was your identity, but the means by which you express your identity and whatever beauty lies within. As we say, what appears outwardly in the spirit body is what already exists within; form follows content.

'It may be said, therefore, inward consciousness is what characterizes the soul no matter what suit you may be wearing. Yet it's difficult for you to accept you're not currently in your biological form, even though your current experiences and past memories will always remain accessible through this spirit body.'

'Let's back up a moment' I said. 'You still didn't answer how it would be possible for me to have memories if I didn't have a brain?'

'It's possible because your memories aren't stored there, although they can be stimulated from the imprinted adaptations for your life on the material plane. But these are but recorded effects of your memories like grove imprints on a CD or vinyl record. They are not the music; the music belongs to the spirit, therefore the music remains when soul departs the body'

'But then where are they? If the memories are imprints, they have to be stored somewhere.'

'And so they are,' Mo said, 'like a radiant wave, they dwell in the amorphous field of universal consciousness because they are not composed of brain meat or sourced by the brain. By the way, materialists don't appreciate this straight talk about meat when such stark talk threatens their reverence for the brain.'

'It does seem disrespectful,' I said, 'to not acknowledge what it's able to do.'

'The wonderment isn't what it does,' Mo said, 'but how it does.'

'Consciousness may create brain patterns, as the science of neo-plasticity shows, but the brain can't create consciousness, no more than it can create memories. However, the brains ability to access memories may be affected by biological limitations, which is often evident with aging or brain injury. But regardless of loss of memory access or decomposition of the brain itself after death, memories forever remain in the universal conscious field, which may also be understood as ultimately existing within the Mind of God, the Source is all there is or can be.'

'That may be fine for you to believe. Obviously you're a religious man, but I'm an agnostic.'

'The same goes for agnostics, atheists and mud wrestlers; no exceptions,' he said. 'Reality is reality whether you acknowledge it or not.'

'Well, in my reality I would say that one body is plenty enough. And most obviously that body is me!'

'But what you don't realize,' Mo said, 'is that in order for you to be here with us, you had to leave that body behind, since it's limitations obstructed your view of us in this domain, and for that matter, the view of our chalet.'

'I know of no respectable philosophical discipline which accepts such a notion of leaving the body behind.'

'No?' Mo said. 'Well you may be surprised how many traditions do accept these beliefs, whether you consider them respectable or not. Even in the New Testament scriptures of the Christian religion, upon which much of Western civilization was founded, the Apostle Paul relates a mysterious trip to *the third heaven*.[1] Although he seems a bit confused what to make of his *in the body - out of the body* experience since it was a foreign concept without precedence within his traditional Jewish order of Pharisees. They didn't teach about that in their synagogues, any more than in your synagogues of higher learning where you work.

'Many religions, particularly in the West, prefer not to acknowledge terms such as *astral body, astral travel, soul travel*, even *near death/out of body experiences*. Because of their orientation towards materialist expressions such as mass, liturgy, sacraments, literalism, eschatology, etc.; many religious types to be dismissive or hostile towards such mysticism or exotic spiritual experiences. I find that to be most ironic, but not too surprising considering the world's state of conscious evolution.

'In fact, some fundamentalists believe any non-physical expression must have something to do with the devil. As I'm sure you're aware, in the past, they would burn alive anyone who held such contrary beliefs that they may rid themselves of the evil they feared, which happened to be anything they didn't understand. Not surprisingly, they still do something like that in the Flatland universities. Thought they don't burn bodies, they will not hesitate to burn their adversaries reputation's in order to purge themselves of all who would oppose and defy their sacrosanct beliefs.

'It's almost amusing how closely religious and atheist fundamentalists tend to align, when defending their materialist prejudices. But then they reason from the same concrete level of cognitive development.[2] Both camps seem to prefer to employ words such as *hallucination, psychosis* or no words at all, since there are no words available when dismissing metaphysical manifestations of consciousness. If they only knew, how often they engage in these nocturnal adventures, as their bodies remain sleeping, perhaps they would change their attitudes and beliefs about the soul. Most likely though, they wouldn't.

---

[1] I believe Mo was making reference to this passage: *'I know a man in Christ who fourteen years ago-whether in the body I do not know, or out of the body I do not know, God knows-such a man was caught up to the third heaven -- and heard inexpressible words, which a man is not permitted to speak.'* 2 Cor. 12:2-4, (NIV)

[2] I refer here to both Jean Piaget's Theory of Cognitive Development in conjunction with the theorems contained in James *Fowler's Stages of Faith* (1981).

'As for you James, you are more awake now than you ever have been before in this transcendent state of existence, it's just that your mind hasn't yet caught up with what your heart knows. It's always the last to know about these things, but once you're prepared to acknowledge to having a spirit body, you will feel even lighter, knowing gravity is just an earth plane construct.'

By now Eli had returned after gathering firewood from below the tree line and joined us now as we continued our walk further along the ridge. How he was able to do all this in a fraction of the time it should have required, I wasn't sure, but then, as I've said before, I couldn't be sure of anything here. What was abnormal, wasn't considered abnormal, but normal.

'You both keep saying *"earth plane"* at a lot. Just what are you trying to say? I'm walking around in my body on a round plain called earth, and so what are you referring to?'

'Indeed, you are walking around on the earth here with us,' Eli said, 'be it a plain, mountain or valley. The difference is you are not at this time walking on earth with your earth plane body. We mean plane as a dimension of existence, not the geography in which you exist. As we've been saying, that poor body of yours remains lying in a hospital in London. But you, qua you, the essential James, are not there; you're here – with us in this spiritual dimension. And as this becomes obvious, you will be able to do more interesting things than when limited to the density of earth's lower plane where the physical body remains and always shall remain.'

'More interesting things like what? I don't see there's a lot to do here; not that I'm complaining.'

'Well then,' he said, 'why not tell us what kind of things you'd like to do and where would like to do them. Get creative James, you can now fly anywhere you want, just like Peter Pan.'

'Fly? What do you mean fly? I've already had quite enough flying down the chasm, and so have no intention of flying anywhere until I get on the airliner in Santiago.'

'I don't blame you; that really had to hurt, getting all smashed up on the way down. Not you, but your body. Anyway, there's no longer need for you to fall off chasms and cliffs, there are other ways we can teach you. We only ask that you work with us that you may realize what unbridled opportunities exist for you in this sphere – all at no cost! You know, very few get to experience anything like this. A once in a life, *after-life*, experience! Think of this as a sneak preview, even while your biological body remains alive on earth.'

'What in the hell are you smoking, Eli? Whatever is, I'd like a toke.'

'Probably a knock-off from Turkey,' Mo said, 'he still enjoys the pungent taste. Regardless of what you smoke, though, it won't get you as high as this Mountain. So appreciate your time here James, before you know it, this immortal body of yours will be slammed back into your physical form as though it was being thrown back into prison. At least it may seem that way at first, after becoming accustomed to this liberated body. Yet your physical body shouldn't be considered a prison; it's a wonderful learning device once you understand what you're on earth for. It's much more than a vessel for the soul -- however, let's not worry about this now. First we need to get you up and flying.'

'Yes of course, I'll soon be flying back home. Perhaps I should leave the summit tomorrow before I completely lose track of time. It seems so elusive here.'

'Should you ever go mountain climbing after you return home,' said Eli, 'it will be important for you to remember which body you're in, especially when crossing over crevices. There may be serious consequences if you don't. But for now, I'd like you to try jumping that chasm again. Maybe you'll have better luck. Dare you!'

'That's madness,' I said. 'I'm neither a bird nor Peter Pan!'

'You don't have to be either,' Mo said, 'since you are more agile than either. Go ahead and try it. Compared to your biological body which remains constricted to what it can do, (your flight down the chasm being one such example), you can now have freedom to move about as you wish. While it lasts, earth's body serves several purposes; but flying isn't one of them.'

He then paused and said, 'many choose to be born in the earth plane, since it provides humanity with many significant encounters that could only be experienced with the body's physicality. As we've said, these events are often challenging, so we may discover what we want by experiencing what we don't want; lessons that could never be learned if we remained comfortable in the spirit domain.'

'That's why we suspect you're not nearly done with earth yet,' Eli said. 'When you return to your body in the frequency of the earth's plane, you will have plenty opportunities to learn many other important lessons for your ongoing spiritual development. Yet it's not just about learning; there's much for you to contribute to the earth's consciousness in the years ahead once you've become more enlightened.

'When you answer the call, you will view life much differently, and most certainly you won't want go back to the Flatlands, the Hill Country or the Lowlands, even when you're there. Though you may be among them, you won't be of them; only those who wish to see what you see will ascend their Mountain. And in this contrast lies the perfect opportunity for you to advance forward, not alone, but in relationship with those of common vision.'

'So tell me Eli, where, in your fertile imagination, do these imaginary lands exist? You keep talking about the Lowlands and the Flatlands, now you speak of the Hill Country too, as if it's another locale on my itinerary.'

'You already know about the Lowlands,' he said, 'but when you return to the earth plane, you will understand it much better. When that happens, you will forever say good bye to the swamps, bogs, ruts, flat deserts and thorny hills, because the Mountain will be your only dwelling no matter where you lay your head on God's green earth.'

'You really are intent on taking this about as far as you can, aren't you?'

'But that's probably not as far as where you will be going.'

'What's that supposed to mean; another one of your riddles, Eli?'

'If you knew who you were,' he said, 'you would realize where you're going is no riddle.'

'Wonderful, now you're answering with even more riddles. I really think you make this stuff up as you go along.'

Eli just laughed, saying, 'but don't we all? Is that not how our universe, as we experience it, comes into being?'

I would have to think about that, but not right now. Before returning to the cabin, we stopped where we first got to know each.

Or did I make that up too? I sat down on a rock, still trying to make sense of what they were saying, which seemed to be about existing in some alternate body form in alternative dimension.'

'After brooding for a while in silence, Mo asked me, 'what are thinking about, James?

I didn't say anything at first, but finally got up to my feet and pronounced most emphatically: 'You know something chaps; you're both wrong. No matter how much you try to convince me otherwise, sure as hell, I'm still in my body!'

'It only feels that way,' Mo said, 'because you sure as hell are,' Mo said with a smile, 'But as a butterfly, not the caterpillar. Though you shed your exterior form, your essence remains the same as an indestructible butterfly, which can never die or be harmed, since this body is formed of spirit, and therefore immortal.'

'As we've said, there are many names that have accumulated over the centuries for the body's more subtle forms among various traditions and cultures. We simply call it your spiritual body because that's what it is: a divine thought of Spirit. In whatever dimension you exist, this immortal body derivates from your spiritual essence, which is one with the qualitative pattern of your form. Therefore, it has no *best-before* date and never becomes *stale-dated*.'

'Take our word for it,' Eli said, 'your new body just keeps getting lighter and brighter as you continue in this plane of existence. Quite the opposite of how the earth's plane of entropy debilitates the physical body over time, making it feel dark and heavy until it finally expires, often in pain.'

They continued to talk about these and other related matters as we returned to the cabin. I was listening but didn't say much since I was outnumbered. As we relaxed by the fireplace with a fresh pot of tea I said, 'I'm still not sure what to make of these notions you so glibly speaking about. Perhaps you actually believe in paranormal phenomena; in fact I'm sure you do since it's all you seem to talk about. But to me it's a most ridiculous joke; in fact, an insult to my intelligence, especially when you tell me I exist in a body without a brain. If you're saying it comes equipped with a spirit brain, I'm not sure that makes much sense either.'

'No, you're right,' said Mo, it doesn't. So allow us to prove what we're saying is no joke.'

'Are you saying flying like Dumbo is no joke?' Obviously, I wasn't in a credulous mood and wasn't about to be taken for a fool with more of their chicanery. 'I'm trained to be a sceptic, and so I seldom sacrifice rational beliefs for fantasy; in fact I never do, except around woman for whom I have fantasies.'

Still grinning from my last comment, Mo said, 'all we ask is that you open your mind and keep it open long enough for us to teach you a few basic manoeuvres that will prove you are in a body that's not subject to the limitations of the earth plane. A sceptic can't learn anything by remaining closed to new experiences and possibilities. That's as foolish as it is arrogant. Is that the kind of sceptic you pride yourself in being?'

That question seemed to hit me below the belt! Now I was really angry. I got up to my feet and said, 'sorry chaps, but I think I've about had enough of your metaphysics. I'm from London, not Tibet. We think differently. Truth be known, such esoteric musings really don't interest me that much. But don't let me stop you, by all means, please carry on – only without me.'

I didn't wish to participate in these games anymore. Over the last few days, I had taken in enough of their bunkum. My intellectual sensibilities had been amply taxed; it was now time for me to move on. As a professional philosopher, I didn't need anyone to tell me whether my mind was open or not. At least I was being rational and that's all that mattered, which was a lot more than I could say for them!

I walked to the window, without saying anything, and stared blankly past the chasm, towards the west from where I came and to where I was going. After a few moments, I turned around and said, 'I really should be going now! It's already past the time I planned to leave. Provided the old bus makes it all the way, I still hope to see a few historic sites in Santiago before my flight leaves.'

With that, I went up the loft, stuffed my belongings in my backpack then slung it over my shoulders as I came down to head for the door. 'Thanks for everything, gentleman. If you're ever in London, give me a call and I'll show you around. I know a great pub where I'd be delighted to buy you a couple of rounds of bitter: the least I can do after your kind and generous hospitality towards me here.'

'That would be most jolly;' Eli said. 'I'm sure we'll see you soon; perhaps sooner than you think.'

'Here,' said Mo, 'take a few provisions for your way down. You don't need them, but since you still think you do, here they are. In as often as you partake of this banana bread, remember me,' he laughed.[1]

'Thanks,' I said, as I walked out the door. *'Adios amigos.'*

I made my way along the trail towards the westerly ridge, taking another quick glance at my topographical map as I walked. This was a different routed down but I was confident I'd be able to save at least half a day by taking advantage of the northwesterly slope where I'd be able to *surf* down at least a 1,200 metres of scree before things dropped off.

It was already mid-afternoon when I started, and so after a few hours of navigating my way down, I was satisfied I was still on course to make it in time to a plateau where I hoped to spend the night. It wouldn't be too big a challenge, I thought, provided I was able to find the right footing to the next major ridge below. As I carefully lowered myself down the jagged rocks, I had a few flashbacks of being in a similar situation not that long ago when crossing the chasm. Funny how I had put those dreadful scenes behind me, as though nothing had happened. And maybe it didn't – though it probably did. I didn't know; it could have all been a dream. Obviously, I was in great shape now; there was nothing to be concerned about. If I could survive that last fall without a scratch, I should be able to survive anything. I was right about that, only for reasons I didn't yet understand.

When I was most of the way down the first major drop, it occurred to me that I may be in trouble. Possibly a lot of trouble! In my haste, I became a bit careless while lowering my body down several ledges where it might become difficult to retreat, if need be. That last escarpment I slid down part of the way may put me in a position where I might have no way to go back up to find another approach. If I needed it, my rope wouldn't be nearly long enough. And with the rock being so sheer, I wasn't sure what I'd be able to anchor on to if I had to climb back up.

---

[1] This may have been an indirect reference to a statement in the Eucharist.

I tried not to be concerned though, since I felt reasonably confident I'd be able to find a way below that was less precipitous.

But as it turned out, I was wrong. There was no way down from there, short of a parachute. Bloody hell, I thought, what am I supposed to do now? This is a very difficult position in which to be caught. I needed to retreat about thirty yards back up to try another way down. With some struggle, I was able to scramble part way up towards the ridge to where I had lowered myself, but it wasn't possible for me to climb all the way up, the sides where too smooth and too steep.

Damn! And to make things worse, the skies were beginning to darken with thick clouds moving in from the Pacific. It appeared it may rain and within an hour or less I wouldn't be able to see anything. This is not exactly where I had planned to camp tonight. There wasn't much I could do, but wait for the morning and try to figure something out.

In my miserable solitude that night in the rain, I attempted to distract myself by recounting all the strange things I had seen and experienced on this summit. Yet I couldn't seem to focus on anything before my fears overwhelmed me with despair. Would I remain stranded here until I died a pitiless death; condors picking away at my rotting flesh? The only hope I could cling to was that I'd find some footing that I hadn't noticed before. This wasn't the first time I was in a tight spot, and yet I've always found a way out.

By noon the next day I had exhausted every possibility I could think of: up, down and across the precipice, I was hooped! I really should have planned this better, but my impulsive departure caused me to be careless. I should have gone down the way I came up, or at least studied this side of the mountain's topography more carefully before choosing this route. This wasn't the route Eli had suggested. But I didn't find him to be that helpful with what alternative route may be best, as if he didn't seem care that much. Possibly he didn't know as much as he let on.

I was beginning to think that I should have listened to them, rather than flying off the handle as I did. Perhaps there was some truth to what they said in the broader context of what they considered reality. But the implications of what they were saying made me feel extremely uncomfortable, causing my mind to override and dismiss much of what they said regarding their strange cosmology. I'm sure a less educated person, unskilled in critical thinking, may have accepted everything they said – but not me, I knew too much.

Maybe it was my pride, but I wasn't prepared to concede I wasn't in my biological body. But then, how could I ever bring myself to believe there was even such a thing as a spirit body. Not even for Jesus: likely the resurrection was just another myth perpetrated by Constantine's newly instituted Latin church.

After attempting every possibly approach again, I sat there at last, feeling broken as I watched the sun once again lower towards the western horizon. The realization that I may be doomed became very real as the thought of death became terrifying. I didn't want to die quite yet, since there still was much more I wanted to do with my life. I was never one to pray, except in jest to Zeus, just as I did before my infamous dream.

I tried a technique to relax my mind rather than obsequiously supplicate the gods, wherever they may be. But I wasn't especially good at meditation, especially now in this dilemma. I reasoned that even if there was a God out there, likely He'd have better things to do than conduct *Search and Rescue* missions for stranded philosophers in the Andes: especially the kind that remained sketchy on His existence. From what pictures I had seen transmitted from the Hubble Telescope, the infinite cosmos out there seemed to a rather large area for a deity to manage.

It was another fitful night, and by sunrise, I had resigned all hope of ever finding a way out alive. I decided to pray my agnostic prayer, just in case someone up there was listening. The prayer was rather simple: "HELP!" Not surprisingly, the heavens were brass; no one up there was listening.

No one -- except Eli!

'Get yourself into a fix down there, matey?'

I looked to see where the voice was coming from. Oh yes, someone was up there alright, but not as far away as the heavens. Sitting about ten yards above me was Eli, calmly taking a drag on a fag he held between his finger and thumb, legs dangling casually over the ledge. 'At this rate you're going to miss your flight,' he said with an impish grin. 'And if you lounge here a few more days, you're going to miss us too, if you don't already.'

'Eli, what the hell are you doing here?'

'Watching you; obviously! Mo and I noticed the route you took down and weren't sure it was such a good idea. So I thought I'd check in case something happened. If I'm not mistaken, you seem rather stranded, or did you decide camp here for a while?'

'God; am I ever glad to see you!'

'I'm Eli, but I'm sure He's glad to see you too,'

'I hope you brought a rope,' I yelled, 'we're going to need a long one. If you didn't bring a belay anchor, you're going to have to tie it around you so I can pull myself up.'

'Sorry, James, I didn't think to bring anything along except my pack of fags – you want one?'

'That's just great! So now what are we supposed to do?'

'Why not try jumping back up? You must have slid or jumped down; so jump back up here. I can hardly believe you didn't think of that by now.'

'You're right, Eli. Jump straight up in the air to the next ledge! Of course! Why didn't I think of that? Are you crazy?'

'Why not, don't you think you're up to it?'

'Eli, this is no time for your inane word games. Can't you get serious and go back to the cabin and find a rope – quickly; I don't want to have to spend another night here.'

'You know, I'm not sure we even have a rope, and certainly no anchors. But don't worry about it; I'll give you a hand instead.'

The next thing I knew, Eli was standing behind me. I didn't see him jump, but there he was, fag still hanging out the side of his mouth.

'Oh jolly -- that was clever! Now we're both doomed, you scallywag! What were you thinking?'

'What was I thinking? I was thinking maybe I'd give you a hand as I offered, provided you're interested. Here, take your backpack and hold on as we jump back up.' I took his outstretched hand as I looked at him with disbelief. He laughed, obviously enjoying my bewilderment.

'Okay James, now I need you to focus on where I was sitting, because that's exactly where we're going. Right up there! So if you're ready; here we go!'

And go we did. Sure enough, straight up to where he had been sitting. Instantly! I was in shock. 'Jesus Christ,' I exclaimed, 'who are you?'

'Well, that's a question you might ask him next time you meet. But for now don't confuse us; I'm not your saviour, just your helper. So next time you need to leap, just do it; it's effortless.'

'Sure, of course, whatever you say; but you know, what you just did was completely impossible,' I said, feeling confused, yet relieved.

'James, it's what you did. Is it not becoming rather apparent everything Mo and I have been saying about you being in spirit form is true? Most would have twigged on by now. Think about it, or maybe not. That's your problem, you think too much without believing what should be obvious. There was no trick to what we just did. We can talk more about it when we get back to the cabin. Mo promised he'd have dinner ready for us when we got back.'

'That would be most thoughtful, I said, but how could he possibly know I was returning to the lodge?'

'I told him; what else? You like baked Yorkshire pudding with beef and gravy, don't you?'

'Yes, of course!' I didn't know what to say; what more could be said? After being rescued from such a frightening ordeal, I wasn't about to argue about the dinner menu. I would have preferred to continue my descent, but obviously I wasn't able to continue down this way. In any case I'd have to go up again so that I may find a more feasible route down. By now I should have been all the way to the base.

I was humbled, yet not wishing to come to terms with what had just occurred on the ledge. The physics of natural law had been violated, along with my rational sensibilities!

As we commenced our long arduous climb back up to the summit, I could hardly believe how effortlessly Eli scampered up the slopes and precipices. It hardly seemed possible. After waiting for me to catch up, I remarked that he must participate in a lot of Ironman Triathlon competitions to be in such excellent shape.

'James, I know you are a very bright man and I greatly respect your cognitive prowess. But notwithstanding that, when are you finally going to get it? I just transported you up the ledge and now you're surprised to watch me glide up the precipices. It's always the clever ones that have difficulty in accepting what's obvious, since they're too full of their intellectual clutter to see things as they are or could be.

'And yes, most certainly, I'm in very good shape. I can't be anything other. You don't need to train to be an Ironman when that's what you are. And you know something else? So are you! So why keep pretending you're not by making this a lot more difficult than it needs to be. There's no reason to be lagging behind. We should have made it back at the cabin long ago; hopefully our dinner won't be cold.'

But I couldn't do it! My beliefs about gravity determined that I must claw my way back up the familiar way, even though Eli seemed to have no need for clawing. And yet, what if I had these same abilities, just like he said? Not possible! I didn't know how he did it, but at least I knew I wasn't some comic book hero who went around pretending to defy the laws of gravity.

After several hours of struggling back up the Mountain, we finally returned to the cabin; a most welcomed sight after all I had been through. As I stepped through the door, feeling a bit sheepish, Mo greeted me most graciously, considering how indecorously I had exited. In fact, I couldn't remember shaking his hand when I had left.

'Too bad you had to go through all that trouble the last couple of days,' he said as we sat down at the table. 'We were just about to give you a little demonstration in astral kinesiology that could have saved you a lot of trouble.'

'Perhaps we can still do that in the morning,' Eli said. 'Meanwhile, dig in James.'

Later that night, after I retired to my loft, I reflected on being so overly reactive. I thought how we, as humans, resist what would be obvious if it weren't for our preconceived ideas on how things must be. This seems especially true whenever someone tries to convince us of something that's contrary to our established beliefs. And multiply that triple for anyone like me who prides being a sceptic.

Even after all that had occurred to me the last couple of days, and my rescue, still all I could think of was what trick Eli used to get me up and off the ledge. I sought a rational explanation, but my old cherished belief systems were not of much help. Though there didn't seem to be a natural explanation, my entrenched belief of being a material body would not permit me to consider the possibility of an alternate explanation to natural law. Or, was it possibly these laws were not the last word, but subject to laws that transcended, rather than negating what we call natural law? If so, my little universe hadn't yet expanded into this spaciousness.

After breakfast the next morning, Mo and Eli led me along the eastern portion of the Summit ridge to where we first met; most likely where they would try to demonstrate their voodoo to me. I was in no mood for whatever they may be contriving, still feeling defensive about not being able to come up with any explanation for what was going on. But considering how Eli had just saved my life, what else could I do but go along with their scheme.

'To make this easier for you to visualize,' Eli said, 'let's start from the basics. Picture yourself already sitting on that stump by the big rock near the shrub. It's a solid tree stump, right? It's not going anywhere, in fact, nothing is going anywhere except you. Now imagine for a moment that your body is free to reposition itself to wherever you wish to be, since it's not limited to the same earth plane frequency.

'So with that in mind,' Mo said, 'we will now instruct you how to transition, just like you did yesterday. Except this time you're going to do it yourself. There's nothing strange or difficult about teleporting yourself in space. It's like being transported, except no transition involved since there's in-between, moving stage getting from here to there. There is no *getting*; you're just there. Instantly! Electrons do it all the time. In fact, that's all they do. If you are up on your physics, you will know you are nothing but these units of energy, regardless of what body you're in. As a philosopher, you should know that.'

'I'm not sure exactly what you have in mind, but it sounds like just another mental game of becoming susceptible to suggestions. If you insist, however, after what you did for me yesterday, I'm willing this once to go along with this charade. So what do you want me to do?'

'First of all, James, just relax. That's the most important part. If you take a few deep breaths, it may help to let go of whatever apprehensions may arise from your doubts. Next, I want you to imagine your body being in another location. Envision where you wish to relocate. Don't think about making the transition of getting up and walking over there. Such notions of physicality would only get in the way.'

'So you want me to go to that stump over there without any in-between? That's rather amusing.'

'Was it amusing when we relocated off the ledge yesterday?' Eli said. 'Do you remember any in-between there?'

'Okay,' I said, trying to ignore his comment, 'but what if I wish to go somewhere else?'

'Go anywhere you intend,' he said, 'but let's begin with the stump by the big rock?'

'Are you kidding me? That's a long way!'

'It's less than thirty yards across, and it's not even straight up like you did yesterday. So go ahead! What are you afraid of?'

'Maybe I'll hit my head on that rock just like I did when going down the chasm,' I said, somewhat caustically. Though it was becoming increasingly obvious the rules of my reality were rapidly shifting, I wasn't about to be taken in. Notwithstanding what Mo said, I again began to wonder if this was some drug trip I was on. At least that would be more palatable than having to accept that I was in the company of two dead spooks, even though everything pointed to it. Worse yet, if that was true, what would that make me? I didn't even want to think of it.

Mo's stood by, his stern gaze fixed on me. It felt as though he was taunting me to make my move. 'It's not like we're asking you to jump the chasm,' he said, unless you want to! Remember you tried that once before, not so successfully however. But if you want to make another attempt, we're certain the landing will be much lighter this time.'

'I'd rather not consider that right now,' I said.

I didn't like being pressured to participate in an exercise that was, ostensibly, attempting to prove Newton wrong; a most foolish reproach to what was impossible. As I thought about it, I became even more uncomfortable for having allowed myself to get involved in this little diversion.

'I have an idea, Eli, 'why don't you try it instead? From what I could see yesterday, you're rather agile! If there's something to this, then maybe I'll give it a try too.'

'Actually it would be better if you go first,' Mo said. 'Eli is already more than adept as such feats and doesn't need any more practise. It's much better that you experience this directly. How else are you going to learn?'

Having exhausted my attempts to evade this exercise, I had no choice left other than be a coward if I didn't go along with this. These blokes had me and weren't about to give me an honourable way out.

'Okay, sure, I'll go along with your sport, I said cavalierly, and then maybe later we can take turns playing the child's game *Make Believe*. So tell me again, what is it you want me to do?'

'Just what we said,' Eli said. 'Stop thinking so much and see yourself standing by the stump. It's all you have to do, there's really nothing to it.'

I closed my eyes and was about to mutter some contrived *shaman* incantation in mockery. But I didn't have the chance. As I envisioned myself standing by the big rock as they instructed, it happened, just like that! I was there -- instantly! I was shocked, even more than yesterday when I was with Eli. This time I did it all by myself. I had just performed my first impossible trick. But it was no trick.

'Holy (bleep)! I did that?' I exclaimed from the rock where I was now standing.

'Cool eh?' Eli said.

'Bloody hell – this is madness,' I said. 'How could I? I just broke Newton's most fundamental laws. This is not supposed to be possible.'

'Why not,' Mo said, 'Newton doesn't have a whole lot of sway in these parts. But Heisenberg sure does!'[1]

'Okay, now try to make your way back to where you were here,' Eli said. 'Guess it's never been so true, *wherever you go, there you are.*'

'Sure, no problem,' I said laughing, completely caught up in my new hop-skip game, fascinated with the lightness of my new found agility. I did it! I had to set my pride aside for now, along with the impact this would have on my ontological beliefs. But I didn't care; the philosophical implications and reconciliations could wait until later.

'So let's step things up now, really up, and get you levitating,' Eli said. 'Yogis do it all the time. You've never been on a *high* like this

---

[1] In reference to physicist Werner Heisenberg's *Uncertainty Principle* which was very central to the development of quantum theory in the early 20th century.

before,' he chuckled, 'so don't overdo it. We wouldn't want you to fall and send your astral body into the Critical Care Unit too; one body at a time is enough.'

I was beginning to feel like Luke Skywalker being instructed by Yoda with his gravity defying exercises. The movie scene came to mind as I imagined floating up somewhere from where I was standing. 'Okay, here goes -- WHOA-HO! Look at me!' I yelled, 'up here over the tree!' (One of the few stunted trees on the Summit). 'So how am I supposed to get down now?'

'You could climb down the tree,' Eli said, 'or how about coming down the same way you got up -- just intend it; it's as easy as that. The will is of the spirit and so the body must respond because they are one.'

'Ah, yes, coming down now! Oh, that was fast and this time I didn't even smash my head against anything! *Houston, the Eagle has landed!* Good ol' terra firma. That was bizarre: kind of like being a bird.'

'Or Peter Pan,' Mo said.

'Really nothing to it – I didn't even have to flap my wings to get from here to there. That technique could really come in handy in not getting caught in some situations.'

'Not a technique James, more like a natural state of your being,' Mo said, 'in fact, perfectly normal for a spiritual body.'

'Never thought of myself as being particularly spiritual,' I said.

'It's hard not to be spiritual when that's what you are,' Eli said. 'We agree, you're not exactly a saint, but at least you now have something in common with a saint. Ever hear of Saint Theresa of Ávila?'[1]

'Yes, I remember; the Spanish mystic back in the medieval era. I haven't read her works, but I understand she had some rather profound things of say, at least for the devout.'

'Indeed she did,' Mo said, 'but what you just did, took her years to achieve. Not that she intentionally worked at levitating: likely it came naturally as a result of her sublime devotion and openness to God's Spirit. Many witnesses over the years purported this occurred several times while at mass: quite the accomplishment at that time in history

---

[1] Saint Teresa of Ávila, the Spanish mystic of the 16th century, was observed to have levitated during mass on certain occasions while in a mystical state of consciousness.

considering it was her earth body, not spirit body that rose off the floor. But she wasn't the only one. It happens occasionally to various mystics, albeit rarely, although I once witnessed it for myself when I was in Rome.'[1]

'So James,' said Eli, 'I'd like to see you try that when you're back into your physical body. Perhaps you could give a little demonstration to your colleagues one day during a faculty meeting. Just think, you would be able to literally talk down to them, just by perching yourself a few feet up in the air. That would jolt them into finally looking up to you,' he grinned.

'I'm not sure it would; that may have been alright for Theresa, but I'm not sure I would want to become a curio or perceived as some circus freak down the hall. I'm already considered by many as a bit of an oddity. Which I certainly will be now, but it may be best if we keep such phenomena private. It may be rather embarrassing if word got out.'

'Don't worry, what happens on this side; stays on this side,' Eli said with a smile, 'unless you wish tell everyone someday, though probably not at first. Just wait for the right moment; I'm sure it will come to you. But till then, you will likely be your own greatest sceptic even when you begin to recall what was going on here with us.'

'It may seem more like a dream of a dream at first,' Mo said. 'I suspect your sceptical mind will likely keep you entrapped in its intricate web of clever rationalizations. But I doubt, once you come into full realization, if you'll wish to levitate as you just did here,' said Mo, 'unless your students get bored while you're teaching Kant's Transcendental Dialectics.[2] Such an uplifting may be too transcendental!'

'By then,' I said, 'I'll probably be in trouble anyway with all your bad influence.'

'That's quite possible,' he said; once you come into full awareness of what you did here and what you may be capable of doing on earth. But we don't suggest you to go around suspending your body mid air after you return – unless, of course, you want to. However, you would first have to suspend your old doubts and fears to do what you just did.'

---

[1] Mo later told me about this incident, which I will relay in the next chapter.

[2] A section contained in Immanuel Kant's *Critique of Pure Reason* (1855).

'That was wild,' I said, 'so tell me, how were you able to get me to do that?'

'It had nothing to do with us,' Eli said, 'since we can't convince you of anything you don't wish to believe. Sure, we gave you a little prodding, but in the end, it was about you creating a small wedge of belief, allowing you to take this leap of faith. Had it not been for yesterday's rescue, I'm not sure if you would have been able to do this because your total lack of belief.'

'Yes, I guess I did make the leap, both literally and figuratively. You blokes win; looks like I'm as out of my body as much as out of my mind. So whatever became of gravity?'

'As you just witnessed,' said Mo, 'you don't need to experience gravity here at all if you don't wish to since it is part of the earth plane's frequency. The force called gravity is an expectation you have and therefore you continue to experience, as do we. Yet there's nothing about the spiritual body that requires earth's gravity to claw us back. No one even knows what gravity is, just that there's a magnetic force on earth that keeps things from floating away. And so, it's these beliefs that keep everyone grounded on the earth plane.'

'But there for a moment, with a little coaching, you were able to allow this energetic alteration into your life experience, unshackling you from gravity's attraction. The fact is, gravity is more about what it does than what it is. Did you know electromagnetism is 10^{37} more powerful than what is described as gravity? Because of this, gravity is thought to be a transduced form of electromagnetism required to sustain life on earth. Talk to the physicists about this if you wish, but even for them it gets complicated.

'Had you insisted that you remained in your material body, teleporting would not have been possible. But your soul knew more than your mind would admit. That's why, once you allowed yourself, you were able to accomplish this with relative ease. It's also why we didn't try to make you to do this earlier. Your beliefs would have caused to you to fail and you would never have tried again. We needed to soften you up first. Yesterday's lift from off the ledge with Eli's assistance helped to open your mind, albeit with some resistance.

'For this reason, you should understand hereafter, for as long as you remain here, your subtle conscious body, or soul body, if you prefer, is free of the earth's forces and there are no limits to where you may go. You always have been free; it's just that you didn't know it. Very few in the world today have sufficient skills to transport themselves out of their physical bodies. But it can be done, and still is being done by a few advanced souls. Some can even bi-locate.'

'Bi-locate, what's that?'

'Never mind,' Eli said, 'we'll get into that another time. You're probably not yet ready to attempt these strange exotic feats related to those who have learned to control their spirit bodies to manifest their souls anywhere they wish, sometimes at once in more than one location. But that's because they have learned how to split part of their consciousness from their flesh while still remaining in the flesh. And even without having to fall off a cliff, I may add.'

'So you're saying there are better ways to accomplish what I did.'

'Yes, but probably not for you,' he said. 'Your crude method was how you were able to arrive in our dimension. A bit dramatic perhaps, or should I say *traumatic*, but at least you got here.'

I had to face it; these revelations about my body would change everything in my world. I wouldn't have been able to do what I just did with my biological body, so obviously it was true, I must be in an alternative state of existence. Hard to believe, but apparently Newton's rules weren't the only game in town, or at least on this summit. It was apparent that I would have no choice but to accept this strange new reality now. A reality I hadn't asked for. Or had I?

CHAPTER 8

THE SCEPTIC'S DILEMA

There is enough light for those who desire only to see,
and enough darkness for those of a contrary disposition.[1]

That evening, while celebrating the most improbable bodily achievement of my life, Eli held up his mug of bitter to toast me. 'Congratulations,' he said, 'you did it ol' chap, welcome to Summit U. You passed your initiation rite; you now have passage to enter our esteemed halls of learning - if you can find them; they're all over the place. Just wait until you see the really Great Hall. You may be rewarded with much more than a pat on the back and another certificate.'

When I asked him what might that be, he just smiled and winked.

Holding up his glass, Mo said, 'You may stay as long as you wish or until your physical body calls you back to its domain. We suspect there are several other locations you will want to visit in the future, but consider this your base for your studies and, if you wish, for entertaining.'

'Entertaining? Who would I be entertaining?'

'I suppose that will be up to you,' he said.

---

[1] Blaise Pascal (1623-1662), French philosopher and scientist.

With the recent revelations about my existence, I suspected by now that my winter holiday would be extended further into Chile's late summer, and perhaps much longer if need be. But I wasn't complaining. Except for female company, or the lack thereof, I had everything I needed in this Mountain paradise.

Such fun to be in this body! The next day I went down to the chasm to hop across; as if to say, 'look at me, there's nothing to it; nothing to fear.' In fact, I was beginning to realize there never is anything to fear when you know life is immortal and you can never be lost or harmed. This was a new to me, since I always believed that when the body dies, it's over.

And yet, still unrecognized, there remained much fear hidden deeply within which I would have to come to terms with in the future. But for now, I felt free and happy to be in this dimension with what I had become.

I lightly skipped down to the ravine bottom, to where my body had tumbled after its fall. Yes, this is it, I thought, right here where I woke up after my long soul sleep. Good God; that really was a long, long ways down, I said aloud, as I looked up to where I had fallen off the narrow ridge near the cabin. I couldn't help but feel sorry for my unfortunate body, still laid up in a London hospital room. Hard to believe it could have survived such a plunge, but at least I didn't experience the pain my body would have felt. But I wondered, if I wasn't conscious of the pain, could it be there was pain? I wasn't sure; perhaps it's like the tree falling in the forest.

My new skills as an aerial gymnast were exhilarating and most amazing. I bounded around on every Mountains peak I could see, feeling a little like *Superman*, except there was no journey required between ports. More like flashing about, rather than flying to an intended destination. At first I didn't want to go too far, and so I teleported to positions or objects I was able to clearly see. With Eli and Mo being the only fixed tethers I had in this reality, I didn't wish to venture too far in case something went wrong. At least, then, I could climb back up to the summit.

What a strange place this was turning out to be! Not only had my travel plans to and from the Andes substantially changed, but body too had substantially changed. Now that I was able to admit it to myself, I became aware of how limited I had kept myself, even though I had the capacity before to do all I was doing now. There probably was a lesson there for me to remember when I returned home.

Still, I didn't understand this teleporting process. How was it possible, I asked by friends, I could retain continuity between two spatial points with my body and not be temporarily annihilated when leaving one location, and then be reconstituted somewhere else. At the time I didn't understand their enigmatic answer, and I'm not sure I do now.

'Try to appreciate,' Mo said, 'the time-space continuum is a mental construct, and not a fixed reality. And so in effect, you're not dragging your body's electrons through the aether, one place to another. They exist, don't exist, and then exist again, here and there as you will – instantly. Electrons continually jump from one orbit to another, without traveling through an intervening space while bi-locating in two different locations at the same time.

'Though this is regularly demonstrated in your physics labs; no one seems to understand how this could be possible, other than acknowledge reality is much more expansive than what anyone thought was possible. Since all subatomic particles are inextricably entangled with conscious intent, your spirit body is able to respond immediately in this more rarified dimension. Like the electron, you just show up wherever you willfully intend, without any need to transition through space.'

'But I would never have thought my conscious intent could be that effective,' I said. 'It's one thing to say that happens to an electron, but never to a person. And yet, how can you argue when it happens to you. That really is rather shocking to think about.'

'It often is,' Mo said, 'even by those on the earth plane who understand the body is just an aggregate of electrons. As Niels Bohr once said, *if quantum mechanics hasn't profoundly shocked you, you haven't understood it yet.*[1]

'As I'm sure you realize, theoretical physicists are able to demonstrate what conscious observation has upon the outcome of quantum phenomena. The implications of what that means for the world will

---

[1] Niels Bohr (1885 – 1962), Nobel Prize in Physics

be vast when it finally sinks in. That is why limiting beliefs, upon which the world's perceptions are based, simply don't apply here, since nothing can limit the broad parameters of the rarified spirit domain. It's evident that earth's continuum of time and space, can only provide an appearance of objective reality, rather than being the essence of that reality, which is beyond knowing. Yet this reality is not beyond experiencing, since all souls are derived in it from Source essence.'

'To the contrary, I was taught we are derived from a primordial state of existence, and so that's our source.'

'You mean,' he said, 'from the primordial soup fermenting in the primordial mud? And so how to you feel about that now?'

'To be honest, at the moment, I'm feeling rather confused on the question of origins. Was it bottoms up, from deep down or down, as you say, above from Source essence? But with it now becoming most evident that the true nature of my body is spiritual and not material as I believed, I'm probably going to require some time to sort this out with what we know about evolution of the species.'

'When you're ready,' he said, 'we can discuss this question at length since there are many nuances that need to be considered to properly appreciate how design and evolutionary principles are entangled within the ongoing process of conscious creation. For now, just remember your guiding precepts upon which all creation is based: *as above, so below; as within, so without.*'

'Also remember,' Eli said, 'what is known in the higher spiritual domain is beyond understanding on the earth plane until it is spiritually discerned. Since truth is truth, and nothing else, it can't be distorted and obstructed by narrow spectrums of what is considered possible. When the limitations of these old beliefs are suspended, you'll find what you assumed to be impossible, to be possible, just as you did this morning. This is how miracles seem to occur on earth.'

'Like turning water into wine,' I said.

'Most certainly,' Eli said. 'Since Jesus knew who he was, he had a broad spectrum to know what was possible: by going beyond the patterns of what was considered natural. Yet it wasn't necessary for him to violate the laws of physics in superseding the world's understanding of what was possible by accessing a higher octave of reality. In doing this,

his most significant miracle was able to open the minds to the spiritual dimension of reality.'

I found this response to be rather unsatisfying, raising far more questions than it answered. But in fairness, the longer I dwelt here as a spirit, the more I understood their peculiar cosmology. It may also have helped that I already had a rudimentary understanding of how modern physicists has eclipsed many of the Newtonian rigid limitations, even though I found the broad spectrum of possibilities difficult to accept at first, as with teleporting.

After taking this all into consideration, I took some comfort knowing it wasn't only here things seem irrational and mysterious: the quantum world can seem just as spooky. But then, they aren't different realities, only perceptions of multiply realities dependent on our receptive capacities, which, at times, certainly can make things appear most irregular, if not bizarre.

I had to wonder how all my embedded assumptions and beliefs in the past had held me back from understanding the deeper spiritual meaning of life. Even though I was a philosopher; my mind seemed less than adequate to discern spiritual meanings. But then, based on my experience, few philosophers these days give serious consider to such matters, perhaps finding little meaning there.

I realized how unprepared I was, and how much there still was for me to learn about the inner workings of this dimension. Though I was eager to discover all I could before going back home, I knew it wouldn't be easy. My mind found it difficult to process what they had to say about spiritual concepts. And yet, what we call physical and spiritual, appeared seamless to them. I was accustomed to silos. You have one bin for philosophy and one for theology, but you don't mix them, because if you did, no one would know what you were talking about. Descartes saw to that.

Mo and Eli told me to be patient; there was no need to understand everything at once, since that would be impossible. Also, they said, much of what I needed to understand couldn't be learned, only discovered, which would turn into the really interesting part of my stay. Until then, they would always be available to provide assistance I required before moving on towards new heights. I later wondered what they meant by that; what new heights?

Realizing I was no longer in a biological body, but a spirit body, I found it unsettling to know I was hanging out with two dead guys; which caused some discomfort of what this could mean for my own state of existence. Furthermore, as I continued to lay alone there in the middle of the night, I began to question whether I'd ever make love to a woman again.

And yet it appeared I was no different than Mo and Eli, living in the same environment, eating and drinking the same food, engaging in the some profound discussions along with the same joking and banter. The only difference was I still had a biological body, still on standby. After being hauled in for repairs, it would be waiting for me once again -- or would I be waiting for it? Hard to say, maybe we were waiting for each other.

The next morning, we discussed my concerns and our mutual state of spiritual existence, until I finally came to the obviously conclusion: they weren't dead any more than I was. If anything, they were more alive. Evidently, there is no such thing as death and they were *living* proof. That was a bit of revelation to me, completely contrary to what I believed most of my life until yesterday. Or I should say, what my mind did; but my heart knew better.

As our discussions continued in the weeks and months ahead, the spiritual concepts were beginning to make more sense to me, helping me understand more about how to participate in this new version of reality. Mo often said to me, 'we're not here to teach you anything, we're here to help you to rediscover what you are in the fullness of your being.' That was just another enigmatic statement I didn't understand, since at that point, I still had no idea what would have to happen to me before I could come into the fullness of my being.

In the evenings after they left, there was little to do but sit by the fireplace and read. Often I would select certain books that continued to appear on the mantle, which were almost always germane to what we had been discussing.[1] I also spent a fair amount of time reflecting on

---

[1] One of my special interest to me was Gurdjieff's enigmatic tome, *Beelzebub's Tales to his Grandson*. Also referred to as, *An Objectively Impartial Criticism of the Life of Man*. Not surprisingly, Mo recommended it as one of his favourites; often referring to it for its extraordinary cosmological depth. (See Appendix 'C' for more information on Gurdjieff).

what we had discussed during the day which I could to be a welcome change to my restless life back home.

I remembered many years ago, I enrolled in a Transcendental Meditation course. Unfortunately, it didn't work too well for me, being too distracted with whatever stirred in my mind those days, having mostly to do with all the beautiful young women in my life. But now in this seclusion, there was nothing to divert me. My mind remained calm, no longer worried about the frivolous concerns that once intruded into my life. Who hasn't wanted this?

I was finally learning how to exert more control over my emotions, and less reactive when my beliefs were challenged. At first this wasn't easy to learn when my old thoughts still remained, along with the old doubts and fears that plagued me all my life.

However, over time these disturbances began to diminish as a new, unfamiliar presence of serenity enveloped me. I could not embrace this presence, but I could allow myself to be embraced by surrendering to it. There was something more to than just a feeling. Though I didn't realize it at the time, I was having my first encounter with the divine agape, something I had never before known or, for that matter, believed in.

During such moments of divine intimacy, I caught, or thought I caught, an image of myself reflected to me, as when peering in a clear, settled pond. It wasn't actually visible; more of an impression of something much larger than me, and yet it was me. Or I was it? I didn't know what to make of this mystical encounter, if that's what this was. This was a fleeting glimpse, or vision, of what I could soon come to know as my divine Self, the Christ within.

These rare, but lucid moments, came to me when I was most at peace after putting my residual fears aside for the moment. This was the first time in many tumultuous years I felt so splendidly serene. I suspected it may not last; sooner or later my mind would default to its old habits. As it turned out, I would be right about that.

While dwelling in my (semblance of) *nirvana*, I continued to participate in our discussions, but had less to say as I listened to what was being said. Though Mo and Eli were present with me for much of the day, they seldom stayed for very long after our evening dinner.

They were well aware of my progress and what was going on within me. That's why, they said, they wanted me to have plenty of solitude to develop this relationship; the presence within.

Various traditions call this many things: the Atman, the Buddha, the Christ, or perhaps, among the less religious: the Self, being understood as the transcendent divine *I AM* within. Terms and labels were of no concern to me, since I realized how more often than not, these confuse and divide people. Especially so, when it's claimed only certain names are capable of conjuring authentic spiritual experiences.

These meditative times seemed a new approach to the gate I had turned away from years ago when I dismissed religion from my life. (This was a place Mo and Eli often called the Hill Country, for reasons I'll explain late). Not that I knew much about religious practice, but whatever I was experiencing, seemed centered within the core of my being, and yet it was also connected to something infinitely larger than me.[1]

After these periods of deep, meaningful contemplation at night, we would begin the next day discussing the large array of topics on my mind. My mentors always seemed to know how well I was coming to understand the expanded reality where I found myself, and as I continued to gain more insight, they would nudge me towards ever higher states of conscious awareness. It seemed the more my vision expanded within, the more the universe without expanded; there were no limitations.

I also came to appreciate that consciousness was not only about what comes from the mind's awareness, but the qualitative spiritual awareness that comes from the heart. A discernment of what's true and what's false, what is of light and what is of darkness!

Some discussions were painfully personal, but they helped me understand more about myself and how to reach beyond the confines of my ego self's illusions towards the divine reality within.

---

[1] Once in an undergraduate course on the Philosophy of Religion I was required to read William James's classic: *Varieties of Religious Experience: A Study in Human Nature*, based on his Gifford Lectures at the University of Edinburgh, Scotland in 1901-1902. By now I had forgotten much of what I read, not that I understood it that well, since much of it beyond my comprehension at the time.

At times I would revert to some of my old agitations, prejudices and defenses. Perhaps this was inevitable at this stage of my development, since old egoic thought patterns seldom go away by their own accord, much less their ego source. And so they constantly challenged me to become aware what intellectual clutter I needed to clear out of mind.

Once Mo said to me, 'James, you're a most fascinating, and yet complex creature; a man of contradictions and extremes. You are capable of understanding some of the deepest books in the world, just as you're capable of climbing the steepest precipices in the world. You are an urbane professor even while remaining a crude sailor; you are both wise and foolish. And at times, some may say a saint but probably more often a sinner,' he smiled teasingly. 'You've learned how to charm and you've learned how to brawl, though not that well when you're blotto.

'But now you're moving towards a new extreme, from being a prisoner to the fears of the Lowlands, to become a conqueror standing on the Summit. But to conquer, he said, you still have a very formidable foe to face. Always remember, James: *Vincit Qui Se Vincit; he conquers who conquers himself.*' Yet it is not you that you conquer, but your fears. But don't just conquer this dragon, slay it.

'There's really only one way to do that,' he said, 'and best of all, it means you need do nothing; you only allow. In the words of Virgil: *Omnia Vincit Amor; love conquers all.*[1] Let the heart slay the ego, the ego dies each time the mind allows the heart to love. Fear cannot exist in love any more than darkness can in the light.'

Later that day, as we were smoking a couple of freshly rolled cigars outside in the cool Mountain air, Eli surprised me by suddenly proposing we jet off to London. 'Whenever you're ready, James' he said, 'we can book an instant trip to London to visit you and see how he's getting along. Not because it's lonesome, but we think it would be good for you to reassure yourself it's still alive.'

'Kind of mixing your pronouns aren't you?' I said

'Only to make a point; how do you see your body – as you, as him or as it?'

'I don't know. I guess any will do – perhaps we should think up with a name for my body. What do you think?'

---

[1] Virgil, Roman poet (70 BC – 19 BC), *Ecolgue X*

'Good idea; it may be less confusing. But since *you, he* or *it* belongs to you, I think you should decide what you wish to call your earthly vessel.'

'Okay, I'll give it some thought, but I prefer not to call it a zombie.'

'It only seems right we show some respect,' Mo said, 'considering how well he's served you – which is another reason we need to pay him a visit sometime soon.'

'And then one day,' I said, 'I'll be able to tell everyone how I came of find myself without a shrink.'

'You did, but not in the hospital – rather, up here on this Mountain,' Eli said.

'Along with some rather eccentric gurus,' I said, 'but I'm still not sure if I'm ready to meet the doppelgänger.[1] It may be rather, you know … creepy.'

'But for whom?' asked Eli, 'who do you think the real doppelgänger would be when you meet; you or your physical body?'

'Hmm, interesting – never thought of myself in those terms. I guess from the physical perspective, I would be the ethereal one. Kind of amusing when you think about it!'

'I'm sure as an agnostic you would never have dreamt of being confronted with this.'

'Not during my undergraduate days, back when I still thought I had all the answers. But later, after I enrolled in my Master's graduate studies programme in Canada, I became much more open to what may be out there, particularly after meeting a couple of scholars who greatly influenced me. After that, I began to consider whether there was more to life than what I had assumed.

'As if by coincidence, I came across the writings of Emanuel Swedenborg, the 18th century Swedish seer.[2] It happened when I was rummaging through a stack of books at a used bookstore one rainy Saturday afternoon when an old hardbound copy practically fell into my hands from the shelf above me.

'After glancing at its title, *Heaven and Hell,* I opened it and was intrigued by the Table of Contents. I bought it immediately for only

---

[1] Doppelgänger, from German folklore, literally means *double goers.*

[2] See Appendix 'B' for a brief outline of Swedenborg's life and teachings

a few pounds, took it back to my flat and couldn't stop reading it. I didn't know what to think, but its authoritative quality fascinated me, as if the author actually knew what he was writing about. I wondered how anyone could be so certain of a reality no one else seemed to know anything about.

'It was enough to cause me to consider whether there may be more to life than what I assumed; living out a mediocre existence, waiting for the end while perhaps snagging a few pleasures along the way. The sound of a clock can drive you insane when you remember how each tick brings you closer to your impending doom – not a delightful thought!

My existential angst was exacerbated after recently breaking my relationship with a young woman I really loved. I was really feeling empty. But as I continued to read the book late into the night, I received a glimmer of hope that perhaps life may have a greater purpose and end than annihilation.[1]

'It seemed astonishing how this writer and nobleman could be among the world's most respected scientists, and get away writing about his visitations into the celestial realms over the last few decades of this earthly life. I found him to be a curious mix of both scientist and sage. I went on to read a few more of his books and found the writings, though rather pedantic in style, to be most fascinating with its descriptions, exemplary in its wisdom, and generally *out of this world*.

'Perhaps I may not have taken these writings so seriously, had I not read what a huge impact he had on some of the world's greatest thinkers and literary luminaries through the years. These include Emerson, Carlyle, Jung, Kant, Balzac, W.B Yeats, D.T. Suzuki, William Blake, Helen Keller and even legendary Johnny *Appleseed* Chapman, to name

---

[1] Henry James Sr. (1811-1882), writer, theologian, father of philosopher William James, (as well as author Henry James), was severely incapacitated by a lengthy depression until being inspired by Swedenborg's writings. Thereafter he recovered, and went on to enthusiastically advocate Swedenborgian philosophy in his writings. My disillusionment with life wasn't as severe as his, but as with him, the writings helped lift me out of my funk.

a few. For me, the writings helped shine a light through the *crack in the bell*, as written in Lenard Cohen's song.[1]

'And then, to top it all, a most extraordinary event occurred to me shortly thereafter, something I will never forget. It was in the early autumn when I was camping in a tranquil alpine meadow, deep in the majestic Rocky Mountains of Canada. In the middle of the night, as I was sleeping soundly under the stars, a voice in the air awoke me as it said just one word: "*Nothingness*". Then again over a period of a few minutes, I heard this same word repeated two more times, clear as a bell. By the last time, I was fully awake and very startled. 'Who is this?' I asked. 'And what does this mean?'

'I didn't receive any answers then, nor have I since. It was some time before I was able to fall asleep again, as I wondered what that was and why was it speaking to me. This was very strange; I'm not even psychic. I continued to think about this encounter for some time, until I gradually put the memory out of my mind. Since my profession trained me to be sceptical of whatever phenomena can't be explained, I sought to find a logical explanation for my paranormal experience. But I wasn't able to explain it, other than it being some neurological quirk in my brain – or perhaps a Rocky Mountain *high*.'

'And so now,' Mo said, 'after all that, to make things even more interesting, you just hit the mother-load of paranormal. Look at you James, no physical body. *No-thingness* to it! Nothing to dismiss since there's *nothing* to you. You don't even need to look for the paranormal – you are the paranormal! The old *irrational* has become the new *rational,* as it now turns out to be the higher template for understanding reality. So here we are again: what a surprise!'

'Yes, a big surprise, but even before Swedenborg's writings or the voice came to me in the air, I sensed I was being prepared for something more in life than what my mind was prepared to accept. At times as young boy, I would sense a warm and loving feminine presence drawing close to my side while sleeping at night. I remember after waking, it seemed it had been more than just a dream. This happened most often to me when I had been feeling sad and alone in my early years of

---

[1] I'd like to quote the full lines, but copyright law doesn't permit this. As I stated in the Introduction, you may read Cohen's copyrighted *'Anthem'* song online.

childhood. I had no idea what to make of it, except it always made me feel as though I belonged, though I wasn't sure to whom or to what.

'These nocturnal visitations came to an end as I grew older. But then one night, I felt the presence return during a difficult time in my life. I was attempting to complete my doctoral thesis at the time, and awoke one night with tears flowing down my face. I sat up, while still sobbing uncontrollably like a baby, though I wasn't sure why. I just assumed this was an emotional release to the stress I was feeling those days since I'm not one to cry, and so I was greatly surprised when this happened.

Over the next year, the *presence* returned to me periodically when I was falling asleep. Even though I liked to fashion myself as a hard-nosed sceptic, I felt myself melt on those rare occasions when I opened myself to this strange phantasm of love. However, there was a price to pay. For weeks and sometimes months after these encounters, I would feel unstable and confused by the inner conflict of my beliefs. My mind's rational sensibilities clashed with the deep yearning I had to be embraced by this love. I'm not certain what these encounters were about. But back when I was a young boy, I was sure. You see, I lost my mother when I was five.'

Though he didn't saying anything when I finished with my story, I could tell Eli was moved by what I had said. After a few minutes of silence he got up, put his hand on my shoulder briefly as he quietly walked out the door saying nothing more. Mo left shortly thereafter, softly whispering, 'good night James,' as he stepped out.

Early next morning, as usual, we reconvened for more dialogue. However, my story from last night didn't come up again; perhaps because they thought it was too personal to analyze. Rather, they brought up the subject of scepticism. Sitting by the fireplace after breakfast, Mo asked, 'so James, what does it mean to you when you say you're a sceptic, especially now?'

'First of all, it means I'm not gullible; I always look for a sound, rational explanation for whatever happens, particularly when there's anything dubious about the account. For the sake of truth, reason must always be prepared to challenge whatever assumptions are made in support of a belief that may be based on nothing more than superstition or religious indoctrination.'

'And if that's all scepticism was about it would be commendable,' Mo said. 'Most interestingly I've often noticed when strange inexplicable things happen to sceptics, or at least are witnessed by them; they find it very difficult to deal with such encounters. It's a dilemma to have to believe nothing is happening even when it is. Eli helping you off the ridge would be one such example of being conflicted between a belief and what should have been obvious.

'I remember an experience I once had while living in Rome many years ago. I had a few guests staying with me from back home. One of them was a highly qualified professor who taught Civil Engineering at Leeds that was particularly brilliant with numbers, priding himself as a hard core sceptic about anything that couldn't be reduced to measurement.

'As fate would have it, the four of us were walking across a square that led to the Pantheon, when suddenly, right before our eyes, something most peculiar appeared. An aged, white haired East Indian yogi type, was sitting in the middle of the square in a lotus position with a long cane in his hand. What was unusual about this was not him sitting there, but that he was doing this suspended about four feet above the ground with nothing between him and the ground.

'Naturally we were astonished to witness this strange rout over nature -- except for my engineering friend, who seemed to be more agitated than anything at not being able to determine what the trick was. After consider examination from every angle, he refused to discuss the incident further, perhaps because he wasn't able to come up with a plausible explanation.

'What was also interesting, is that my guest had no recollection of this incident when I mentioned it to him about a year later when I was back in England. In fact, he just laughed when I brought it up, as if anything so preposterous could possibly have occurred. He didn't dismiss seeing the yogi; it's just that he was oblivious as to how he saw him. The way he remembered it, the yogi was sitting on a mirrored box giving the illusion of space under him. He also thought he remembered seeing a pan for donations on the ground. If there had been, I and the others, must have missed it, along with the mirrored box.

'Evidently he was having difficulty processing that strange spectacle that went so contrary to his beliefs. In his mind, this didn't happen because it couldn't have happened. Such is the nature of preconceived beliefs.

'Fortunately for you James, you never have been such a sceptic. At least not the type that is closed to whatever evidence is outside your belief system. That's why you were able to hear that voice in the air when you were camping in the Mountains. You were open to this *visitation*, even though the voice came as quite the surprise.'

'Most certainly it did,' I said. 'The combined beauty and silence in the mountain meadows somehow felt magical, if not sacred – even to an agnostic. Everything felt so vibrantly alive. I think just before falling asleep under the bright stars and moon, I spoke a word of gratitude to the tranquility of nature I was enveloped in.'

'Talk about when the object meets subject and subject meets object!' exclaimed Eli. 'You were at once both the subject and object of your scepticism. So what did you, as a philosopher in training, do with that one?'

'Since I couldn't come up with an explanation, I didn't know what to do with this experience. It's not the kind of thing you mention to your colleagues while you're trying to earn your graduate degree. This was one of those inexplicable encounters you simply bracket out of your belief files because there is no file for something that doesn't make sense. "Nothingness;" what kind of message is that?'

'But this voice must have been rather hard for you to dismiss, was it not?'

'Had I been doing some very good peyote, it would have explained everything. But that night, the only thing I was high on was nature. Over the years I occasionally thought about the message, but never came to any resolution on what meaning to give it. So I told myself it all had to be in my head, after all, I was a sceptic.'

'And so you were,' Mo said, 'but now you need to help build a much larger box for your scepticism so you won't bracket out all the inexplicable mysteries that are happening to you now. It's not possible for you to fit everything in your old tattered and worn box of stale beliefs. You may find even more exotic occurrences coming your way that will require a much larger container to fit everything into.

'And so that's why the first thing we're going to need to do is kick out all the walls – clear out of sight! You're going to need lots and lots of space to contain everything. Yet, in essence, that's not really a good illustration since infinity is too big to be about things: it's more about *no-thing-ness*, just as the voice was telling you that night. Things don't just manifest from things, but emanate from a thought form that was prior, which ultimately, we would describe as the Source.' Jesus knew this, and so quite appropriately called the Source *our Father in heaven*.'[1]

'There's much more to no-thing-ness than you can imagine, Eli said. Infinity is a rather large zone to expand your mind into; if fact it's impossible, but it's good to try. We'll do all we can to help you clear your mind of some of the limitations of *things* that keep you from understanding the true *no-thing* nature of the Infiniverse.'

'Since you put it that way, I think maybe I'm getting the drift of what the voice was saying.'

'Ironic, eh?' Eli said; 'at once, no-thing and yet every-thing.'

'Which means,' Mo said, 'after all your years of struggling in the halls of linear scholarship, you will require a lot of deprogramming. To know what's real; it will be necessary for you to clear out all the intellectual clutter that's been obstructing your understanding. But we recognize it's not all clutter; in fact, much of what you acquired were the intellectual skills necessary to sharpen your mind's acuity to sort through what's true and what's bogus. This will serve you well in the future.

'But even with your sharp mind, there is still much to discover, not just here but when you return back home! If I may, let me use the computer as a metaphor to illustrate this, though you are far more than a computer, since a computer can't be a spirit, any more than your brain. And so your systems will need to be upgraded to handle the new programmes here.

'Crudely stated, your hard drive has been corrupted with conceptual viruses you assimilated from some very bad assumptions that entered into your belief system after years of faulty programming. With your willingness however, it can be cleaned, defragged and repaired. In fairness, it must acknowledge, Newton's laws and precepts helped

[1] Matthew 6:9 (NIV)

humanity understand the laws of physical existence on earth. Good bridges depend on it.

'However, when his programmes are applied to other facets of reality beyond their scope, such as subatomic physics, consciousness and the spiritual essence of life, great distortions of mechanistic interpretations appear in the system. This physical overlay does not represent the truth of higher orders, any more than gravity represents your limitations.'

Mo paused, and then went on. 'Many of these old programmes that factored out the spirit, still remain popular and widely applied in academic circles even though many carry a lot of nasty viral assumptions that have crashed many systems through the years. Some of these weren't just obsolete, but plain wrong. How many countries were devastated last century by programmers programming humans to be little more than drones that served their lies. Today other such utopian programmes continue to mutate with new viruses.

'That's why we'll need to reload you with advanced software paradigms that will enable you to navigate through this new dimension. Once you are rebooted, you will find it much easier to operate here. But we can't do much to upgrade your battered material brain in London since our programmes aren't compatible with it. Your new mainframe, being spiritual, operates on a completely different system.

'When you return to your old hard drive, it will be upgraded and reconfigured to accept the new programmes you're been learning here. Once this is done, they will be able to operate beyond well beyond the old 3D series your familiar with. It may not happen right away, but eventually you will come to assimilate the more advanced software that operates outside your brain's hardware.

In fact, just knowing this will create a huge paradigm shift for you because it will open you to new possibilities of what you will be able to do on earth. The good news is that the neo-plasticity of your brain back home will naturally adapt to your new programmes here since material form always mimics essence.

'I'm not sure I completely agree with your metaphor in reference to the old Cartesian software,' I said. 'I think Descartes had a lot of profound things to say, just as Newtonian physics are as legitimate now as when he came out with his theories.'

'Full marks to them both,' Mo said, 'even though you may find their dualistic interpretations on longer serve you as long you're in this Passage. You are well aware, I'm sure, how Descartes' teachings had the effect of dividing man into mind and matter, or, it may be said, spirit and body. It didn't take long, maybe a couple of hundred years or so, to find how that turned out, especially after the *"if I can't see it, it doesn't exist"* crowd took over.

'Dualistic reasoning is completely entrenched in mainstream thinking now, permeating much of the western world. What this generally means for most scientists, is that if I can't see spirit, it must not exist. In fact the very concept of spirit is now considered redundant because, as they say, the brain accounts for all processes that were once considered spiritual. In other words, the mind is just a mechanical brain event like sound from a radio speaker, except we don't know where the sound originated. That's where they're wrong; mental events don't originate in the brain any more than music is composed and performed inside the radio.'

'Well perhaps I'm still one of Descartes children,' I said, 'since it seems to me that all we are able to perceive is physical in nature and what is internal is intuited as spiritual. The question is how you wish to define reality and what the relationship is between spirit and matter. You say these are spirit bodies, and I'm sure they are, yet I can see you both just physically as I would if you were walking down a street on earth.'

'No doubt about it,' Eli said, 'we do appear physical – to each other. In fact, about as substantial as anything on the earth plane, maybe even more so! And yet the truth is there is nothing *solid* about anything, whether on earth or any higher celestial realm. Mountains, lakes, galaxies, books, angels and pretty girls that look like angels - all are just electromagnetic patterns that our minds interpret into perceptions of solid form. All sentient beings are interpreters of vibration. Matter, at best, is an energetic derivative from these wave patterns. But this doesn't make us waves of energy; we only manifest our soul's essence in these patterns of form. So in that sense, your spiritual body is as physical as your material body; the difference being a higher vibratory form.'

'Further to that,' Mo said, 'I may add these objects and bodies you perceive, exist for you as being physically substantive, because you exist on the same vibratory plane where you perceive them. Let me recite what John Archibald Wheeler had to say on this: *No phenomenon is a physical phenomenon until it is an observed phenomenon ---- the universe does not exist 'out there,' independent of us. We are inescapably involved in bringing about that which appears to be happening. We are not only observers. We are participators. In some strange sense, this is a participatory universe ...* [1]'

'Well stated!' Eli said. 'The way I look at it, if a rock makes contact with your head it can break your skull, just like a woman can break your heart, except as you well know, hearts don't always heal as quickly as skulls. Our encounters with solidity may seem very real, as did yours in the way down the chasm, yet these experiences are actually encounters with energy *events*. Which is to say: non-substantial, subatomic energy waves of no-things, yet appearing to our senses as material forms which we know and experience through non-material mental processes.'

'What you keep saying sounds much like what may be found in the ancient Vedantic writings, not that I've actually studied them.'

'You are correct, what we say sounds much like them,' Mo said. 'I ought to know, since I studied the Vedas for years while still in my mortal body. In fact, most of your ancient sacred texts uncovered in Egypt, Tibet and other areas of the world, speak of the non-material void, just as the voice you heard spoke the word *nothingness* out of the nothingness.

'Much of this literature implies that when you begin to understand the concept of emptiness, you will understand the inverse nature of everything that remains implicit within infinity's un-manifested dream. Not so much a contradiction as something irreconcilable on a linear level, since it must be intuited on a higher level, as with the ancient Zen koan.'[2]

---

[1] Physicist John Wheeler, Physicist (1911-2008), collaborated with Einstein, Bohr and several other luminaries. He is credited with popularizing terms such as 'black hole,' wormhole, 'mass without mass,' etc. He believed that reality is created by observers in the universe, yet asked *"how does something arise from nothing,"* while questioning the existence of time and space. I should mention; Mo kept a thick notebook of quotes by physicists that he suggested I familiarize myself with. Some of these I have recorded in Appendix 'A'.

[2] The Merriam-Webster definition of a koan is: *a paradox to be meditated upon that is used to train Zen Buddhist monks to abandon ultimate dependence on reason and to force them into gaining sudden intuitive enlightenment.*

'So what you're saying; is that out of the Infinite Void of nothing comes all thought that leads to the manifestation of everything that is, everything that will be and everything that can be.'

'That sums it up very well,' he said, 'for nothing exists outwardly that doesn't ultimately come from within the Source's divine vortex. As I mentioned, this cosmology is not limited to just ancient Eastern traditions; some of the earliest Middle East Jewish literature inferred the same thing in the Genesis creation myth: *In the beginning God created the heaven and the earth. And the earth was without form, and void, and darkness was upon the face of the deep – and God said let there be light …* '[1]

'And so,' Eli said, 'it is out of the void, out of the nothingness, that the light of our perception emerges to experience existence as we do. If taken literally, it appears as an actual historic event in time when everything was created in seven days. In reality, creation out of nothingness is an ongoing state of essence being outwardly manifested from within. *As within, so without!* That's why the existential philosophers of our day, who insist existence proceeds essence, have it backwards.'

'From what you seem to be saying, "Nothingness," is just a black hole! Out of the void from which all emerges, *ex nihilo.* Just as the voice spoke to me that night: *Nothingness – Nothingness – Nothingness.*'

'That should have been your first clue,' Elis said, 'so it's no wonder you found yourself attracted to Berkeley's writings shortly after your mountain meadow experience. Something or someone out there was tipping you off that life wasn't about things, but the infinite un-manifest void that brings universes into being. And perhaps, after serving their various purposes; each collapse again, to be reformulated by a new Thought of God, the Source. So maybe this was just one more nudge to encourage you to get your head out of the fog and move your arse out of the Lowland's swamp to where you would be able to see things more clearly up here.'

'So did this something or someone, have a new thought to reformulate me by nudging me off the chasm ledge?'

'I'm sure you didn't need any help with that,' said Mo. 'What's important now is that you understand the Mind's essence provides infinite manifestations of which you are one such expression, whether

---

[1] Genesis 1:1-3 (KJV)

on the ledge or off it, in your current sprit body. You went down into the void to re-emerge, reformulated just as you are. Do you think it is possible that your divine Christ spoke a Thought that led you, of your own higher volition, from the Lowlands into this spiritual realm?'

'Are you suggesting that I brought this current reality upon myself, not just by being reckless, but by design when I attempted to cross the chasm?'

'In a sense, you spoke it into being did you not? In fact, whenever you gazed at the Mountain in your dreams, you were speaking your reality into being. Just as I quoted from Genesis, God spoke out of the void, and so it was. However you may wish to understand this quote, be it metaphoric or not, the idea of speaking is still a declaration of a willful thought called into form, however it may come about. And so, in that sense, we may say all of creation is contained in a *Thought* manifesting into something we earlier called the *Infiniverse.*'

'As we've discussed before,' Eli said, 'the sons of God, being created vessels of Source essence, are able to create because we're created of one eternal Thought. It all begins in the Mind, because that's all there is, and so by our thoughts we co-create the reality that is perceived. Wheeler was absolutely right about this.'

'And not only him, 'Eli said. 'Some of the more astute philosophers of antiquity understood that reality proceeds outwardly from the dimension of Mind/Thought. And, as you well know, Plato had his teachings based on the concepts of *Idea* and *Form*. Predating him, Pythagoras expressed this as the *Logos*, a broad concept related to the universal principle of in-forming, later incorporated into the Gospel of John as the *Word*.

'More recently,' Mo said, 'certain physicists in the 20th century expressed this idea of the *Thought* in much the same way. I like the way Sir James Jeans put it: *Mind no longer appears as an accidental intruder into the realm of matter. We are beginning to suspect that we ought rather to hail it as the creator and governor of this realm.*[1]

'We realize you already understand enough about the amorphous nature of subatomic physics to comprehend the nature of matter and

---

[1] Sir James Jeans, (1877-1946); English quantum physicists, knighted in 1924 and author of *The Mysterious Universe* (1930)

solidity. However, we still need to expand that concept further as we go along, especially as it relates to this plane in which you now find yourself. First we need to review more of what you think you know, and then integrate it with some mind–matter foundational work involving not just physics but other disciplines that draw upon certain ancient religious perspectives.

'As I'm sure you are also aware Aristotelian metaphysics was called *First Philosophy* or the *Principles of Being* integrating all purported knowledge both within and without. For millennia it was a respectable academic discipline, but now metaphysics is largely dismissed and sometimes despised by both science and religion. Perhaps they fear their separate orthodoxies will be compromised by being admixed into other's dogma.

'They have very different and disparate containers for their separate and mutually exclusive cosmologies which will often cause them to war against each other in determining who's right, rather than find how their perspectives may fit and balance each other. Metaphysics, being interdisciplinary by nature, could facilitate this integration. If fact, that's what *meta* does when a prefix to the word physics.[1] But unfortunately, in this era of separation and alienation, neither camp will have any of this.'

'That's another fascinating subject for discussion,' I said. 'But let's first go back and clarify things: my body, my clothing and this unlit cigar; are you saying they're nothing more than spiritual substance? How can spirit have substance? I'm not so sure many scientists would agree with that.'

'I'm sure many don't,' Mo said, 'but most of the really smart ones do. They're the ones who understood the word substance means much more than what is considered material. So let's briefly go over this again to help you understand.

'As we've said, all that is experienced, whether in Elysium, on earth or somewhere else, originates as a conscious thought. Only spirit knows itself, because that's all there is even when it manifests as a *crystallized* perception of matter in unlimited ways. Or, as David Bohm referred

---

[1] *Meta* may be defined at the abstraction between the thing and the event, or the physical (thing) with the spirit (event). When used as a prefix from its Greek origins, it has the meaning of beside, among, with or after.

to this crystallization; *frozen light*, in reference to the enfolded implicate domain, expressing itself in and through the explicate order.'

A rather interesting description I would say, considering how we earlier referred to your spirit body as a light form, rather than a biological adaptation for the earth plane. So where Genesis states; *let there be light,* in as much as it is understood to give form to the void, we could, with Bohm, call all form *frozen light.*'

'This reminds me,' I said, 'of something I read when I was working on my thesis. I think it was about Berkeley saying something about a choir and furniture in heaven, as I recall. According to him, they are objects that are only thoughts existing in God's mind.'

'In a roundabout way, that's what we've been saying all along,' Eli said, 'or at least something like it. Anything that is considered to be physically solid, be it choirs or furniture, anything that has discernible qualities to the senses, is but a temporal electromagnetic pattern. The problem with objects is that their patterns don't hold forever, be it a chocolate bar, an iceberg, the scent of perfume, your planet, or even your body. They don't last. But Mind, as the universal perceiver; now that's different.'

Trying to inject some wit into the conversation, I said, 'you mean to say: *Mind;* now that's a different matter.'

'Provided it is understood, mind is not matter but what makes matter seem to happen, or what may be regarded as matter manifesting through the interpretation of quantum wave patterns. Mind is of Source, and therefore, unlike matter, is non- substantial, unconditional, ineffable and indefinable. We experience it as consciousness. It is through the mind's thoughts that we become aware of our existence.'

'No matter what,' I said.

'That's correct, no matter what,' Mo said, smiling. 'The point here being, there's nothing more real than that which gives form to all outward existence, or should I say, what creates outward appearances. What sensation is possible without a thought first communicating it?'

'So what you're still saying; is that when you come right down to it, thought is the only thing that is real.'

'And your biological body,' Mo replied, 'is that real? If so, for how long is it seemingly real? And when it dies, how real is it after it decomposes? So can you say it ever was *real* while it remained in form?

Perhaps, at best, we should say it's a pattern of temporal mind stuff. Forms are patterns that are constantly changing, due to entropy, where ultimately the pattern no longer holds.[1] In that sense we may say forms don't exist, they're only an accommodation of energetic essence patterns that reconfigure as they come and go.

'Even planets cease to exist in their form, but their energetic essence always exists, as does your spirit essence since it's a thought form of the divine Spirit. And what Source has thought, however that's to be understood, can never be un-thought or forgotten. Forever you remain an evolving expression of Source contained within various dimensions such as in this spirit body in which you exist, at least until you return once again to the physical expression of your soul on the earth plane.'

'So you're saying that most of what is believed about physical existence is basically wrong?'

'It depends on what you mean by physical, Eli said. Most of the world believes the physicality is limited to material expressions, which is why the world's understanding of reality remains upside down, inside out and backwards. It sees matter, not spirit; it sees effects, not causes; it sees the temporal, never the eternal; it sees the plain, never the Mountain; it sees with the eyes, but never with vision. In short, the "it" we speak of is the ego.'[2]

'You will come to understand,' Mo said, 'there's a relatively simple

---

[1] Entropy is the second law of thermodynamics, also defined as the tendency for things to deteriorate from a state of ordered complexity to simplicity, fragmentation and demise.

[2] The word "ego" is the Latin word for I first know to be used in 1787. Though it is used throughout these narratives, it's an inadequate term, re-contextualized from the psychological applications Freud used as an analytical device. But the term is the only modern word that comes closest to describing what was expressed about the human condition. In religious terms, we may say it's the *fallen* or *sinful* nature of humanity. Mo and Eli meant the condition of the mind when identifying itself as the separated "*I*" of self-existence, thereby willfully enthralled with the state of illusions it creates. It was said that the only alternative to that sad state of spiritual existence, is for the mind to perceive reality through the heart's divine enablement, because only that can be real. To my knowledge, only *A Course in Miracles* and its sequel, *A Course of Love*, clearly and thoroughly articulate this unique interpretation.

answer for everything because it all comes back to Mind/Consciousness, which we denote as Source/God because they are not separate, only words expressing the *One* of all that is. When you finally come to understand this, you will understand what your world is and what it's for. It's both a lot more and a lot less than what you may think. But again, that's another topic for another time.'

'I think we should discuss it now,' I said, 'unless you need more time to think it through further before we go on.'

'Before we can go much further,' he said, 'you will need to think things through in a new way. First we'll start by helping you clear the decks of what remains laden in your mind with old earth bound assumptions.'

'Never thought of my mind as being laden,' I said.

'But it is, more than you know, take our word for it! It will be necessary for you to lighten its load so you are able to make headway even when you encounter turbulence. The problem, James, isn't so much with what you don't know as with what you think you know. It tends to blow you off course. Whatever remains burdensome will need to be jettisoned; otherwise the load will sink to the bottom. Up until now, we've haven't said too much about this, but we certainly will as you become more open to what we have to say without storming down the mountain. So try to make more room, we have lots to say.'

'I'll see what I can do.'

'I'm sure there will be more for you to take on board than you may imagine,' Eli said, 'now that you are coming to know what you are.'

'Though you may know *what you are*,' Mo said, 'you still need to find *who you are*. We expect there are some very important experiences coming your way that will help you find your Self when you are ready.'

'With you having been here so far,' Eli said, 'let me ask you what you feel and observe that's different now in your current embodiment?'

'Obviously, there's been much I've had to adjust to. When I became aware I was no longer subject to the confines of the physical plane, I immediately began to notice the lightness my body. I still find this difficult to comprehend or describe.

'After I realized gravity wasn't an issue anymore, I wondered what was preventing me from floating away. And yet I understood I could float if I so desired, such as I did for you with my levitation performance. That was rather interesting; I'd like to see some magician do what I did without smoke, mirrors or curtains.'

'But even if they seemed to perform something like that,' Mo said, 'it would still be an illusion based on distraction and they would be the first to admit it. But not so with you; that was no mind trick. So what else are you noticing, other than your body being different?'

'I must admit I'm now beginning to sense an incremental change in my conscious awareness that at times I find a bit disorientating. Then I wonder if I'm living in a different ontological zone, which is a bit scary when I consider the implications of what this may mean when I go back to my earthly body.[1] If I recall any of my life here, it would hardly be business as usual. Likely I'd remain confused, not knowing which rules to play by.

'On the other hand, I feel very content and alive here. My mind and emotions seem to have the same lightness as my body. And most auspiciously, there is no outward pressure. No term papers to mark, no deadlines, no tormenting staff meetings to attend and no administrative compliance reports to contend with. On the whole, life is very good on the Summit; and in fact, I'm even catching on to Eli's twisted humour.'

'Perhaps you're happier now,' Mo said, 'because you no longer feel such a need to defend your ego's old beliefs and judgments.'

'I admit when I first arrived here I wasn't sure what to think about either of you, especially while you were performing your stunts and talking your strange talk. However, things are beginning to seem a bit more normal now, even though I'm no longer sure what normal is supposed to mean. But at least it's becoming easier for me to accept that I don't always need to understand what's going on, since I realize I'm in a very different reality, occupying a very different body – which is about all I have left to show for myself these days.'

'Or so it seems,' Eli said. 'In truth, this body is your real form, the immortal pattern rather than the biological adaptation for the earth's mode of existence. So you see; you haven't lost anything. Though it may seem less substantial than what you are accustomed to with its light and

---

[1] Ontology is the philosophical discipline that examines the knowledge of *being*, *beingness* or *to be*.

subtle form; it is indestructible, while sufficiently malleable to express the quality of your unique character. We already see this clearly, as will others you encounter on this side. Being of divine essence, your body is energetically configured to adapt to all planes of experience. This however, will require new depths of understanding, as we prepare you for what's next on your itinerary.'

'Itinerary,' I asked; 'where am I supposed to be going?'

'I'm not sure where it will take you,' he said, 'it could be many places, depending on where you want to go when the time comes, including the earth plane. As we said before, think of your body as being the free and happy butterfly that was contained in the groveling earth bound caterpillar. Now that you have been released into a much greater freedom; you can even flutter off to the mountains peaks.

'But when you return to the earth plane, as we anticipate, you will have to stuff your wings back into your caterpillar body, so that you may complete your important journey on earth. Not that you will always have to crawl on your belly, nevertheless you will be subject to your body's physical limitations. That may take some getting used to. In fact, you may not at first realize that your true identity was that of an immortal butterfly that had briefly metamorphosed into a higher state of existence.'

'Fortunately,' said Mo, 'your awareness of all that happened here will follow you back into your earthly body, even if at first you don't recall what happened. But when you do, you will never again feel alone as you often have during your life on earth. That's what I mean by not crawling on your belly anymore. Your spirit will still want to fly, and if you let it, it just may.

'But you won't the only one. There are tens of thousands of others who have short glimpses into the beyond, he said. 'After departing their physical bodies they return again in what is now often commonly referred to as near death experiences (NDEs). Most report traveling through a tunnel of light that takes them to new dimensions and exquisite experiences they are at a loss to explain after returning. Many wish to soar high into the heavens, but few do until the appointed time of final departure from earth.

'Of course, all naysayers believe biochemical explanations debunk all such accounts. Yet they don't. Whatever biochemical activity is evidenced is a natural response to the experiences, not to be mistaken for the experiences as such. I'm sure you'll receive lots of bogus rationalizations when you go back should you say anything about your felicitous time here with us.'

'In past years,' Eli said, 'it was often a lonely time for these survivors, since what they experienced on our side was not regarded as an appropriate topic for polite discussion. Even today, any serious talk of being outside the body scares a lot of people, since they assume the body is all they are. Which is why, many would rather withdraw into willful denial. Such avoidance may be one of the reasons fearful images such as the grim reaper prevails in their minds. Not many wish to speak about what happens when the body dies.

'The exceptions, of course, are the religious movements seeking to proselytize others into their folds by assuring everyone that their soul will remain safe if they join their fold. But then, what would you expect, if it's not guilt, its fear. Both are very effective in corralling the masses into their kingdoms.

'Things are changing though,' Mo said. 'We are pleased how many on earth are now less fearful of death than even a generation ago. It is no longer the taboo topic it once was as more now are seeking to understand what lies beyond their material world. In fact, there are now many excellent first-hand accounts being written by credible witnesses. You may wish to meet some of these someday when you return, although most of their experiences in the spiritual domain are much shorter and exotic than what you have experiences here with us.

'One such person we know of was a neurosurgeon and medical professor, whose beliefs as an atheist were turned upside down, after leaving his body.[1] He later felt compelled to write and speak about his NDE experiences. Of course, he was attacked for this disclosure by certain professional sceptics. Another survivor now telling her story was

---

[1] Dr. Eban Alexander, author of *Proof of Heaven*.

a terminally ill cancer patient, who made a full and speedy recovery shortly after returning from her NDE.'[1]

'That's most interesting,' I said, 'I never heard of them before. If you give me their contact information, I'll try to look them up when I return so we can compare notes. Maybe we'll even form our own support group so we won't think we're nuts, even if everyone else does.'

Shortly after these discussions, they took their leave as usual, just after the sun had gone down. As the weeks went by, my days fell into a predictable routine. Generally, after breakfast, and a morning of informal discussions at Summit U, I would take a hike along the Mountain ridge while contemplating what I was discovering about life on this side. Later as I became more confident of my new abilities, I would often teleport to Mountains further away, taking in other spectacular views of ranges far beyond what I would normally be able to see, including the South Pacific Ocean.

It still amazed me how this new body of mine could feel so natural and yet be so incomprehensibly agile in accomplishing supposedly impossible feats simply by invoking my will. Should I recall anything after returning to my physical body in London, I'd likely miss being a superhero performing these extraordinary human escapades. Indeed, this was just too good; how could I not tell everyone about this? Even getting caught in rush hour traffic would make it difficult for me to remain patient after being so accustomed to spontaneously go wherever I wanted to go. By now, any lingering scepticism I had of this reality had completely lifted by the new agility I found myself possessing.

Yet there still remained much for me to learn, as I struggled to reconcile my old belief systems with this new order of existence. How was I to contextualize these experiences with all I had been taught about life? These were challenging times, but they were among the best days of my life – especially the one I had been living before I got here!

---

[1] This is a very interesting story as told by Anita Moojani in her book, *Dying to be Me*. It's about how she, as a terminally ill cancer patient, came over to the spirit side to be healed, which occurred in just a matter of weeks of returning to her body. Even back in the 4th century BC, Plato discusses what may be regarded as a near death experience in the 'Myth of Er,' contained in *The Republic*.

CHAPTER 9

THE TRUTH OF THE MATTER

You shall know the truth, and the truth shall set you free[1]

This morning, as usual, we settled into our chairs with a full pot of tea, ready to begin our morning session. With me being the student and they the mentors, I had no idea what subjects would be on their agenda, yet I always looked forward to the classes, as I called them.

As Mo settled down in his chair, the first thing he did was confront me with a question: James, you've been here with us for a while now, at least in your waking consciousness. Are there any doubts remaining in your mind about the state of existence you are now experiencing?'

That was a rather direct question that rather caught me off guard. 'No, of course not, I said, 'but that still doesn't mean I'm going to accept everything you say about that state without first questioning what I'm being told. What kind of philosopher does that? As we were discussing yesterday, it's my nature and professional responsibility to be sceptical, and so if I'm to remain true to myself, I'm not necessarily going to agree

---

[1] John 8:32 (KJV)

with everything just because you say I should. I first need to prove it to myself.'

'That wasn't my question James; I know you are trained to be a sceptic and that's as it should remain. However, I asked whether you still have any doubts in your mind about your state of existence here.'

"Then let me restate my position,' I said. 'Though I pride myself in being a professional sceptic, I try to remain open to what I don't always understand, such teleporting across the mountain range. And yet I need to interpret such phenomenon in a way that doesn't clash with what I believe to be logically true.'

'Don't worry about it,' Eli said, 'we're delighted to help you resolve whatever ambiguities and inconsistencies that remain in your mind. We can appreciate how you've been overwhelmed with a lot of extraordinary surprises during this transition, although we've tried to buffer these jolts as best we could. You can be sure there will still be plenty more excitement when you move beyond this Passage towards new Summits of rarified existence.'

'Are you sure I can handle more excitement?' I said, laughing. 'I'm still reeling from what you both say about the nature of immortality, illusions and the shadowy world of spirit bodies, not to mention, materializing, dematerializing, teleporting, hearing voices in the air, orbs of light, mind reading, etcetera. These phenomena may be fascinating subjects, but it's rather unsettling when you find, unwittingly, it's suddenly happening to you, and now you're part of the weirdness.'

'And all this just for the price of airfare to Chile,' Eli said. 'Not bad, I would say!'

'I can hardly wait to tell of these paranormal stories to my medium friend; I said, 'she would have nothing on me.'

'If it was her choice, I'm sure she wouldn't.' El said, chuckling. 'Better not tell her I said that, she may not be amused.'

Ignoring Eli's comment, Mo said, 'things may appear strange on the surface, James, but perhaps not as odd as they seem once you reconcile you've experienced with what you understand now. You may not realize it, but your soul has subliminally been preparing for this adventure for several years now. That voice of *"nothingness"* in the air didn't just happen; it came because you were listening for it. And even that bloody night at the pub was instrumental in creating the dream that ultimately drew you here. Everything happens for a reason.'

'Speaking once again of your dream allegory,' Mo said, 'the sun broke through the mists of the Lowlands so you could ascend here to see what you couldn't see before. But one day soon, that will be eclipsed by even greater mysteries and adventures, drawing you further inward and further upward. You've already been teleporting to all the peaks in our neighbourhood, something that not long ago would have been unthinkable. But before long, you will be transported to even higher highs of the soul.'

'To which new highs are you referring?' I asked.

'You will know when you're there,' Mo said. 'But as Eli suggested, you will first need to achieve a certain state of being. That's the purpose of your enrollment at Summit U. Old thought patterns and Swampland habits will retreat further from your mind as you continue to adjust to this plane by remaining open to all it has to offer.

'Let the old illusions and resistances that held you down, fade back into the mists that hover below. They never did serve you well, and certainly you won't have need of them now. I'm sure you will agree being stuck in the ruts of the ego mind gets to be tiresome.'

'Yes, very tiresome indeed,' I said.

'However,' Mo continued, 'you will increasingly find your life becoming increasingly exciting as you learn to extricate yourself from all that once had you stuck. As the old fetters continue to fall away, you will experience new horizons of freedom and receive new visions from higher and higher vistas. Of course, you could go back to the Lowlands, but then, you never would have come this far if that is where your heart was. As it is written, *old things have passed away, all things have become new.*[1]

'Be assured, we're here to encourage you to go as far as you are able, no matter how much of a sceptic you still fashioned yourself to be. Question us all you want and we'll see you through this transition. It will be at your own pace, so the more willing you are to learn, the more quickly you will progress.'

'That's because learning here has nothing to do with your old approach,' Eli said. 'In fact, it won't seem like learning at all. Our main

---

[1] 2 Corinthians 5:17 (KJV)

task is to deconstruct much of the *information* you acquired along with the underlying assumptions. You may find that in truth, we are the real sceptics. As Mo recently affirmed, scepticism is never a bad thing, provided honest enquiries are made to discern truth from falsehood. That's why, when you return, we want you to become even more of sceptic than you were before, except your scepticism will be directed towards the old order of beliefs you once defended.

'Be assured, we're not going to leave you in a vacuum as we probe into your mind; rather, we're going to teach you to do your own learning. More specifically, your future learning will not always come from what we have to say, but what you have to say, as you discover true understanding comes from within, and nowhere else. Then you will own your beliefs, because they will be yours, and not what we or someone else told you. Wisdom is of your divine Self, as it is ours, all emanating from the mutual Source of our being.

'Our goal for you is to go beyond your old belief systems, and to discover living truth rather than the stale information of what others have thought. Consider us your facilitators in dialogue, rather than teachers in monologue. And who knows, perhaps you can teach us a thing or two, just as you suggested a while ago – things we may not have understood or appreciated while we were living on the earth plane.'

'I hope so; that would help even things out a bit,' I said with a smile.

'But what's most important now,' Mo said, 'is that you continue to move forward, even beyond this Summit's plane of existence and magnificent views. Though one may dwell in a certain place, stage or state for as long as they wish, no one wants to remain stuck at any single destination since we are all called to eternal expansion. But when we move on, we still take its joys with us. And so you too will move towards new expansive vistas and transcendent experiences that will bring you great joy, though your stay here may remain short.

'Trust us; it's not going to be like anything you've experienced on the earth plane. But later, when you go back to your former existence, if you do, as we anticipate, Eli and I will still be there with you, at least in spirit. Our presence may not seem so obvious at first, but after a while, you may come looking for us, if only in your dreams.'

'That's most interesting,' I said; 'but how am I supposed to readjust to my former life after embarking on this mystical journey with you? Should I make the grade at Summit U, I rather doubt the authorities back home will recognize my postdoctoral credentials from these rarified environs. If I return with my mind too out of alignment with the world's thinking, I may need to be reprogrammed to fit in, considering how contrary your curriculum is to theirs.'

'Yes of course,' Mo said with a chuckle, 'I'm afraid your considerably *higher* education on the Summit may be out of reach for them. The content of your philosophical syllabus won't have a lot in common with what they have to offer, since we don't do reductionism; in fact, just the opposite. But then, you've had misgivings about that for some time. Isn't that why you left the Flatlands?'

'Wait a minute; I thought our metaphor for my home was the Lowlands?'

'It is; but the Flatland campuses are spread throughout the lowest and flattest parts of the Lowlands throughout the world. That's why none of their prevailing misinformation was very satisfying to you when you began to receive your Mountain visions several years ago. And so, it will be even less satisfying for you now when you return. You may even question how you could have been so naïve as to believe what you were taught before.'

'Which would suggest, should I return to my Flatland classroom someday; I'd likely be very confused trying to sort things out again.'

'You wouldn't be the first philosopher,' Eli said.

'Who else are you suggesting?'

'They are legion, but we can give you one well known example of one who struggled with his conscience. A.J. Ayer had a near death experience near the end of his long career, and so had an important decision to make regarding what to say to the public about this incident.[1] I suppose he could have said nothing, but for whatever reason, he chose to comment on the incident.

---

[1] A.J. Ayer was an eminent British philosopher (1910-1989), and leading proponent of *Logical Positivism*, a reductionist interpretation of reality and denial of what doesn't have sensible properties. Therefore, he would say, whatever is referred to as *spiritual* (e.g. God), cannot be part of meaningful discourse. At first he called himself a non-theist and then later an atheist.

'And so, not long after the incident, in front of an audience of fawning scholars, he explained how his supposed out-of-his-body adventure was actually just a four minute hallucination resulting from oxygen deprivation to the brain. It's amazing how, for many, a little oxygen deprivation can explain away everything they don't wish to acknowledge. Although he said he clearly remembered being confronted by some rather gruff galactic military personnel, he discounted this as an illusion, although he admitted, that at the time it seemed very real.'

'I remember hearing something about this important talk,' I said, 'as I recall, they gave him a big ovation for his honesty, and perhaps also for not compromising his philosophical position.'

Or more likely, Eli said, the positions of his audience.'

'And yet, Ayer confided quite a different story to his physician in private, just after what he said was a divine encounter. Perhaps he was too proud to confess this experience to public, and so he didn't come clean. For the record though, the testimony from his personal physician, Dr. George, was: *Very discreetly, I asked him, as a philosopher, what was it like to have had a near-death experience? He suddenly looked rather sheepish. Then he said, 'I saw a Divine Being. I'm afraid I'm going to have to revise all my various books and opinions.'*[1]

'Perhaps,' Mo said, 'there was too much of his professional reputation at stake to disclose the truth. His inflated ego was legendary, and so he wasn't prepared to climb this Mountain you climbed. In fact, the ego hates Mountains, preferring flat planes to vertical transcendence. That's why Ayer preferred the adulation he received from assorted like-minded humanists, rather than making an ascent to the more rarified domains of his soul.

'I had a brief acquaintance with him while I still dwelt on earth. And so, not long after I arrived on this side, I chatted with him about his error in judgement. He still regrets how badly he blew it, especially after having such a unique opportunity to tell his kindred atheists the truth about the spirit world he briefly witnessed.

'He realized how angrily many would have reacted had he told them there was more to life than the parochial reductionism upon

---

[1] Dr. George's account may be verified through various references readily available.

which he had built his career. After a lifetime of being a world class humanist guru, he said he didn't relish having to swallow all he had been wrong about because of not being able to swallow a stupid piece of salmon that got caught in his throat. How ironic; that word swallow!'

'Guess that's understandable,' I said, 'when you're too clever for your own good – and everybody else's too.'

'So James,' Eli said, 'how about you? Are you going to do any better when you go back and get another kick at living on the earth plane? Or are you going to crater like him by remaining to clever for your own good?'

I wasn't sure if I should take Eli's comments as an affront or a challenge: maybe both.

Before I could reply, he added, 'you understand from experience how the intellectual establishment can be less than open minded when their materialist prejudices are challenged. But don't forget, you still have Plato and the good Bishop on your side, more or less, along with some of the finest minds from antiquity. Also, there are also several contemporary philosophers and physicists, who have a very broad perspective. In fact, you may wish to do a little research and contact some of them before you tell your story to the world.'

'You mean you want me to form an alliance against the dark forces of Mordor?' I said sarcastically.[1] I was becoming a little uncomfortable with them continually prodding me to bear their spiritual torch should I returned. A tad presumptuous, I thought; since I wasn't sure I wanted to become persona non grata, cast out of the fraternity of acceptable thoughts and correct beliefs.

Besides, how the hell was I supposed to know what to do after returning to my biological body? But then, Eli always seemed to enjoy challenging me, especially when I didn't wish to be challenged. So when he brought up Berkeley's name again, I took the conversation in that direction.

'It's interesting,' I said, 'that you should mention Berkeley again. As I'm sure I said before, he was among my favourite philosophers when I was completing my doctorate degree. My dissertation required

---

[1] As a young man I was an enthusiastic reader of J.R.R. Tolkien's *Lord of the Rings*, so I made this reference to *Mordor*, the dark land.

a comparative analysis of the British Empiricists; Locke, Hume and Berkeley, which involved the respective meanings they gave to the concept of *substance*. Berkeley figured prominently in my research: perhaps too prominently since his musings on the nature of God, substance and reality were in stark contrast to those of Hume, who was most obviously the examiners' preference.[1] (I think I once used the word *bias*, which probably didn't endear me much to the committee).'

'It seems that after centuries,' Mo said, 'Hume has come out on top of the debate, perhaps for no other reason that he had the last word among the classical empiricists. For a long time now, there haven't been many philosophers keen to accept the Bishop's *immaterialism, or, as it is called, subjective idealism*, any more than Plato's elusive concept of Forms.'[2]

'I think it's true,' I replied, 'both he and God seemed to have fallen out of favour among the ardent rationalists that have now taken over during the last couple of centuries. After Hume's tenure, Berkeley was shown the door about the same time God was also being shoved out of the room by many of the world's intelligentsia.'

'Or maybe,' Eli added, 'it was more the other way; perhaps it was the philosophers who left the room, slamming the door behind. Interestingly, there have been more than a few who have crept back with their ears cupped to the door to hear what's being said within. Today there are many noteworthy philosophers who are conversant with the latest research that links consciousness with quantum theory. I think the implications of what is being demonstrated are causing some scholars to reconsider various notions espoused by Berkeley.'

'So James,' Mo said, 'since you're the philosopher and an expert on Berkeley, I'd like to hear more on how you interpret his ontology. I think this could lead to other important concepts we may wish to discuss about reality from our perspective.'

'Well it's quite simple,' I said, 'at least the summation is. Essentially I

---

[1] George Berkeley, (1685-1753), mathematician, philosopher and bishop

[2] Plato's *Forms* presents the idea of an all-prevailing non-material higher reality whereby we can only perceive shadows of this hidden reality. From these, we ascribe meaning to what things are in essence. For example, the 'Form' of 'dog' applies to all dogs without regard to species or breed.

think what he was saying is that all the objects we think we experience out there, don't actually exist outside perception.'

'Be they: *All the choir in heaven or furniture on earth,* as I recall the quote,' he said.[1]

'Ah yes, that's the quote I was trying to remember. It's most impressive you should know that. As I was saying, for Berkeley all objects, be they objective or subjective, exist first as a thought in the Mind of God rather than existing separately. Therefore, by virtue of divine thought, everything that exists is a manifestation we participate in as an empirical experience of the senses.'

'I'll admit his brand of philosophy seems closer to the truth with what I'm presently experiencing in this rather fluid dimension of existence. This may suggest that the intention of the mind is, in some fashion, the basis for what manifests as reality. Who knows, maybe he was on the right track, even after all the bad press. Not to say many consider Berkeley to have the answers, but at least he had an intriguing perspective, which is why I entertained the logical viability of his ideas in my thesis. So there you have it chaps; Berkeley in a nutshell. Now you can give me your enlightened perspective; what do you think, did he get it right?'

'Like you,' Mo said, 'I think Berkeley was headed in the right direction, if not on the right track, although his Western perception of God as being external to us may have compromised his understanding of what Oneness means. It may have helped had he spoken with an enlightened seer to show how we are all of the same Source essence that creates in union with the divine. Possibly there weren't enough good mystics around back then to provide him a broader perspective.'

'Many would disagree,' Eli said, 'but I think he came within rather close proximity to the ancient traditions of the East, which often represent reality as an emanation and extension of the one Source. However, in the West, the external *out there* belief assumption is still

---

[1] Berkeley's full quote regarding mind and substance is: *All the choir of heaven and the furniture of earth, in a word all those bodies which compose the mighty frame of the world, have not any subsistence without the mind … so long as they are not actually perceived by me, or do not exist in my mind, or that of another created spirit, they must either have no existence at all, or else subsist in the mind of some Eternal Spirit...*

implicitly held by almost everyone in the West. It may be argued this is the basis for the great leaps in science and technology, especially since the time of Newton.'

'Yes, I think that may be true,' I said. 'In counter distinction to Newton, Berkley at least understood what we perceive is in and of the mind since the divine Mind is what creates our reality.'

'Which implies,' said Eli, 'there is no basis for knowing anything other than what is processed by consciousness, since there is no evidence of anything out there without it first being perceived by the mind. What we assume to be without; is what's first within. That's why Mo and I continue to repeat our mantra: *as within, so without.*'

'Unfortunately,' Mo said, 'this remains a most unorthodox notion to the West, though hardly novel to the traditions arising from the ancient Vedas! In my opinion, no philosopher or scientist on earth has credibly refuted this concept. Even Kant seemed to indicate agreement with this.[1] And as you now know, this inward reality becomes even more obvious when existing in this spiritual dimension.'

'I wonder,' I said, 'if A.J. Ayer twigged on to Berkeley's ideas after he passed on, considering there's no longer a fan club there for his logical positivism.'

'I'm not sure,' Mo said, 'but I can check. At least Sir James Jeans, who at the time, was as wise a philosopher as he was scientist, seemed to understand Berkley when he concluded, *If the universe is a universe of thought, then its creation must have been an act of thought.* Too bad he didn't have a word with Ayer back then, but I'm not sure if Ayer would have listened anyway.'

'Maybe not,' I said, 'but I think it's great that Berkeley's empiricism finally got a little help from certain visionary philosopher scientists such as Jeans – and most obviously from the publication of my thesis,' I laughed.

'Well,' Mo said, 'whatever renewed interest you may be able to stoke in the mental/idealist approach to reality, is probably a result of how static things have become in the reductionist, *logical positivist* movement.

---

[1] *What objects are in themselves, apart from all the receptivity of our sensibility, remains completely unknown to us. We know nothing but our mode of perceiving them.* Immanuel Kant (1724-1804)

There's really nowhere to go with it, since it doesn't point beyond itself. At best, it's *a dead cat bounce*, as they say. It's an utterly unsatisfying philosophy to the human heart, which subliminally, understands its oneness and implicit unity within the Infiniverse.

'Many of the Vienna Circle's stripped down variations have lost credibility over the last decades, except, most obviously, in certain disciplines of the scientific community, who don't realize how unstable their old empirical foundations have become in the world of subatomic physics.

'There are some very well-known philosophers who are very interested in exploring the entanglement of mind and substance. Especially so, after what has been researched and espoused by various cutting edge theoretical physicists, such as Wolfgang Pauli who once said: *It would be most satisfactory if physics and psyche could be seen as complementary aspects of the same reality.*[1]

'These thoughts are sometimes reflected in certain modern theories, such as the controversial Superstring Theory, which, for some scientists, is considered to be too offbeat and queer to take seriously.[2] The truth is; the quantum universe is stranger and more offbeat than they can imagine!'[3]

'When examining the wacky world of subatomic quantum physics,' Eli said, 'many are perplexed how interrelated mind is with matter. This entanglement was first demonstrated in the double slit particle/wave experiment, where it was shown how electrons respond to the mind's conscious observation.'[4]

'Kind of makes you wonder if the Irish Bishop somehow anticipated

---

[1] Wolfgang Pauli was the winner of the Nobel Prize in Physics in 1945. He also contributed to researching and writing the book *Synchronicity* with Carl Jung.

[2] *The Elegant Universe* is an informative book (1999) and Emmy Award television presentation (2003) by Physicist Brian Green of Columbia University. It graphically and entertainingly illustrates the Superstring Theory and its implications towards our perception of reality.

[3] This reminded me of a famous quote by geneticist J.B.S. Haldane, often misattributed to Eddington: *The Universe is not only queerer than we suppose, but queerer than we can suppose.*

[4] The double slit experiment is discussed in more detail in Chapter 8, *Virtual Science*, of Book Two.

this,' I said, 'or if he just got lucky with some of his propositions. At least in this regard, I think he was closest to the truth among the Empiricists, the only one who, at least in this regard, got things more right than wrong. Not surprisingly, my examining committee won't have seen it that way, preferring more conventional paradigms.

'And not just modern philosophers,' Mo said, 'many scientists still hope to capture the elusive little round billiard balls they persist in calling particles. Most obviously, this is based on their materialist presuppositions, and therefore, determination to find something solid there. Perhaps they don't wish to face what's *not* staring them in the face.

'As I'm sure you're aware, the massive CERN Collider in Switzerland keeps splitting these *particles* of energy into halves of halves of halves while getting – you guessed it, another half of nothingness. Splitting energy into smaller units of energy and then calling these units *particles*; seems peculiar, unless it's used as a metaphor for an energy unit. But I don't think that's the intent, since the word "particle," generally denotes matter.'

'But apart from that,' I said, 'these experiments, though staggeringly costly, may eventually pay big dividends in developing new theories about the nature of the universe and its origins.'

'Perhaps,' said Mo, 'if nothing else, the experiments will teach the world more about reality's underlying subatomic stratum. What they are verifying is that mass and energy are interchangeable, just as Einstein indicated, and so what is considered mass should be considered virtual rather than substantial. With quarks, glucons, and protons disappearing and reappearing within a trillionth of a nanosecond, it's obvious there's a lot going on in the universe that's all about energy with has no lasting substance. As Niels Bohr once stated; *everything we call real is made of things that cannot be regarded as real.*[1]

'If the intent was to find evidence for solid material reality, this has failed. There is nothing out there so far that can legitimately be called particles of subsisting matter. And so, any time physicists believe they've *found* evidence for a new particle, it ought not to be implied it's an indivisible substance. The question will always linger; why should this energy mass not also be divisible? With there being no credible rebuttal

---

[1] Niels Bohr 1885 – 1962, Nobel Prize in Physics 1922

to this: it's an impolite question to ask believers in materialism's faith based community, even though several millennia ago, Zeno identified this very conundrum!'[1]

Eli added, saying, 'is it any wonder Einstein, in acknowledging the illusive nature of material reality, once made the shocking statement, *Reality is merely an illusion, albeit a very persistent one.* Or consider a statement made by Max Planck: *mind is the matrix of all matter -- I regard matter as derivative from consciousness -- There is no matter as such.*[2] Even Aldous Huxley is reported to have said, *the world is an illusion, but it is an illusion we must take seriously because it is real as far as it goes.*'[3]

'Now there are a few zingers you won't often hear in our halls of science!' I said; 'at least not where I work. But are you sure that's what they said? I've never heard these quotes before; perhaps they're being taken out of context.'

'Indeed they did make these statements,' Eli said, 'and no, the quotes are not being taken out of context; they meant exactly what they said. Throughout the last few decades, provocative statements continue to be made about the nature of subatomic reality.[4] I find it rather interesting to watch when new evidence comes along to undermine the materialist interpretation of the world, especially after so many have undermined and dismissed the universe's spiritual reality for so long. Not to say energy and spirit are to be understood as being the same thing. Obviously, love is more than energy even though it may

---

[1] Zeno was a Greek philosopher (490–430 BC) who posed various perplexing philosophical and mathematical paradoxes, often related to time and motions. Mo's comment referred to what is called the *Dichotomy Paradox,* which I won't go into.

[2] Max Planck developed what came to be known as the *Planck Constant,* an equation he revealed in 1905 that gave a basis for understanding the new physics of quantum mechanics which continued to develop throughout the 20th century and into the present. He made this startling statement about reality in 1944, almost forty years after developing his famous equation. (See full quote in Appendix 'A')

[3] Aldous Huxley (1894-1963) was a British philosopher and writer.

[4] Physicist Frank Wilczek; professor at the Institute for Advanced Study at Princeton and participant in developing an important quantum theory (QCD) in 1973), stated: *If you really study the equations, it gets almost mystical.*

energize us. And yet, all that exists; both implicate and explicate, have the same divine Source.'

'I'm sure things could get even more interesting if you should disclose to the world all you witnessed and learned. But you find yourself to be in good company with certain esteemed scientists, even though you come at it from a different angle.'

'Perhaps,' I said, 'but I'm not sure anything I would have to say to the world would make much difference from what it wishes to believe.'

'Don't underestimate yourself,' Mo said, 'just being here has already prepared you more than you realize. There is nothing to hypothesize about when you're already here, living in this reality. It shouldn't be necessary for you to convince your intellect when you already have all the evidence before you.

'In fact, why do we need to teach you anything about this dimension of reality? You did your own little demo when you performed your little *Ávila* aerial maneuver above the treetop.[1] And ever since, you've been touring the surrounding Mountain Summits with great agility. What more do you need?'

'Seemingly I'm able to do that. But to be truthful, at times I wonder if this isn't just mind over matter.'

'But of course it is,' Eli said, 'that's the nature of reality. Did you not just hear what we had to say about energy and matter being of the same interchangeable essence?'

'Yes, but I'm still having some difficulty squaring these peculiar experiences here with my past understanding. As much as I recognize I'm able to do what should be impossible, I still need to reconcile these abilities with my understanding. It's all so damned counter-intuitive.

'I remember a few drug trips in the past where I imagined flying and performing strange feats such these here. There comes a point, however, one realizes the whole trip was just an illusion of the mind. But if you persist in believing your illusion, there are places they put you for your own good, which is what may happen to me if I don't get myself off this surreal mountaintop before it's too late,' I laughed.

'It's probably already too late,' Mo said. 'I suspect you will always remain here, even when you return to the Lowlands. Not because you

---

[1] See the previous reference to Theresa of Ávila in Chapter 7.

will be in an illusion, but because you will see the illusory world all around you.'

'That's an interesting comment,' I said, 'which is all the more reason I need to look at all the angles to prepare myself for what my sceptical colleagues would say to explain these experiences away. First off, they'd probably say I was crazy, which is exactly what I would be if I told them everything. And how would I argue with that? So we may as well put everything on the table now. You know they are going to nail my arse to the faculty wall should this story ever come out about me bounding among the mountain peaks.'

'That's true,' said Eli. 'Neither Superman nor Spiderman can come close to doing what you do up here almost every day.'

'I think that's why it behoves me to be completely satisfied I've exhausted all possible other explanations for what I'm experiencing here. If you don't mind, please allow me to do a little debunking on their behalf to see how I should handle things. This may help me later on.'

'Certainly,' Eli said, 'carry on with what they may throw at you – other than a red cape for you to fly with.'

'Don't laugh,' I said, 'that could happen! So let's start with the standard medical explanation of various chemicals that, under extreme conditions of trauma, discharge into the brain's neocortex, causing one to fall into a coma. I'm not sure I got that right, but it's probably something like that.

'There are plenty of studies investigating alternative states of consciousness that purport to explain how such paranormal encounters are simply the result of chemicals activated in the pituitary gland, giving an illusion of an OBE, out-of-body experience. At least that's what some of the research indicates with the well documented, state sponsored DMT experiments at the University of New Mexico.[1] And so some may say I'm only imagining this crazy trip.'

'And maybe you are,' Mo said, 'if you want to call what you're experiencing a perception. Remember what we just discussed about

---

[1] Much of this is summarized in *DMT: The Spirit Molecule* by Richard Strassman. Dimethyltryptamine (DMT) is a psychedelic drug similarly structured to the body's serotonin neurotransmitter hormone.

that. And yet your biological body remains comatose while you are on this most splendid, extended vacation here with us. Still, all is experienced as a perception in your mind. Perception is perception; however, the point of departure is when it's believed your experiences are merely a result of your brain's release of reality altering chemicals, rather than the release of your soul into an altered spiritual reality.'

'And of course,' said Eli, 'that's exactly what they're going to say; it's always about the chemicals. As a matter of fact, that's all they can say given their materialist presuppositions about reality. The conclusions will be derived entirely from what they've predetermined about the brain's mechanisms. No other propositions are even considered. You will never hear a hypothesis being posited for the existence of a spirit body, since there's no way of determining, much less measuring that.'

'As for the activation of the brain's pituitary gland,' Mo said, 'is that a cause or an effect? If you say cause, you are in league with the epiphenomenal crowd which would exclude the possibility of spirit, since such references are already excluded from the realm of possibility. After all, if it's not in the narrow sphere of their scientism, how can it exist?

'Therefore, when it comes to what is experienced in the coma state, the only plausible explanation can be a chemically induced psychosis. And so *the fix is in.* It's rather difficult to win when all spiritual explanations have been excluded from the realm of possibility. Science can only talk about the soul in terms of being a metaphor, but never a reality.'

'But I really can't really blame them, not completely,' I said. 'They are partly right; the pituitary gland is involved in modulating induced states of drug experiences. The question is, if there's such a thing as a spirit body that leaves the physical earth body, or is it just an epiphenomenal event playing funny virtual reality games in the brain.'

'And if the latter is the case,' Eli smiled, 'we must compliment your brain's creative chemicals that brought into being this superb reality by which we exist here. It is to be commended for how well it created us! Good job, James! Who needs God? Your brain is an innovative genius and creator!'

'But then, my brain always has been,' I said, in amusement.

'I don't know about you Mo,' Eli said, 'but I would never have guessed my existence was nothing more than an illusory phantom in James' fertile mind. However, being relegated to a mental figment of his does little to affirm my existential dignity. But if that's the case, so be it. Still, I think it would be rather sad if all the fun we've had here together was all for naught, or rather, was naught. So when your body awakens in London, James, I hope you won't make us all go pop in the air like a soap bubble. It would leave me with such an empty feeling.'

'Yes, it would be a shame to see you both disappear so indecorously,' I said in mock sympathy. 'But I wouldn't worry about it too much, everything here in my present condition feels more authentic that what I experienced there my natural body. And so, at least from my perspective on this side, the brain chemistry explanation seems rather unconvincing, even if it's possible to experience a temporary drug induced altered state of consciousness for a short while.'

'Not to mention,' Mo said, 'the EEG charts show very little activity in your brain, barely reflecting your body's maintenance processes. You may want to verify this when we pay your body a visit, since there's little evidence of much happening in your brain at this time. Not even a record of you doing five mountain peaks before breakfast this morning.'

'Fine,' I said, 'now that we have that one settled, more or less, let's move onto the next debunking argument. It may go something like this; you are both stage hypnotists, right? Of course you are, don't deny it, I can tell. Just look at you both as you perform your mind games, like when you called my name without even vocalizing it: great shtick, I must say. But really, you were only conning me into believing it was real by your clever hypnotic suggestions. Very good, but you're not the only ones who can do this. Lots of others can do this too if you pay them.'

'You're right,' Eli said, 'we are hypnotists that must have taken a wrong turn and lost our way to our next performance. And so here we are on top of a mountain in the Andes! I suppose without a proper GPS system, you can end up almost anywhere.'

'Or perhaps you just hypnotised me to believe that we're on a mountain. I've seen some hypnotists manipulate the subconscious mind where it wasn't able to differentiate what was real from what was pure fantasy. If you can induce the mind at this level, I'm sure you can make people believe almost anything. Much like some politicians do when working up a crowd with their oratorical skills.

'Once you get some participants up on stage, you simply convince them they are whoever you want them to be, or perhaps who they want to be, including Elvis. I've seen this done and it's rather amazing how some are able improvise, even very young girls who are told they are Brittney Spears; many nailing it with their songs and dance gyrations. I suppose the more impressionable you are, the easier it is to do this.'

'So are you saying you're impressionable?' asked Eli.

'With my sceptical bent,' I said, 'I hope not. I doubt if I'd be doing Elvis on stage, or Brittney, for that matter. In fact, I'm not sure if hypnotism would even work on me, but I suppose anything's possible. I mean, just look at me here.

'Admittedly, if anyone offers hypnotism as a rational explanation for my experiences here, it sounds rather ridiculous while my body remains unconscious at the hospital. I'm sure in that state, I wouldn't be too impressionable. But I wouldn't be surprised if someone suggests subliminal hypnotism as way to explain things away.

'Okay, so here's another one. Everything I'm experienced here is just a dream. Sounds reasonable; with all that time spent in a coma, my bored subconscious mind had plenty of time to come up with plenty of creative fantasies, even though I claim they were real time-space events. So what do I say to that?'

'How well do you remember your dreams,' asked Mo?

'Hardly at all, but maybe things will be different if and when I come out of my coma.'

'A sustained, coherent dream,' he said, 'with a sequential story line that lasts for months, might be difficult to accept, don't you think?'

'Okay, maybe, but what do I say to those who still want to believe this rationalization? Perhaps they will say I'm just lying about the dream.'

'Then tell them whatever they want to hear,' Mo said. 'But make it good.'

'But what if what they want to hear isn't true?' I said.

'It doesn't matter, debunker's rationalizations are often more unbelievable than the reality of what happened. Anyone who remains open to the truth will soon understand which explanation is more probable. I'm sure you've heard of Occam's razor[1]'

'Yes of course,' I said. 'I get your point; give them whatever they want to hear because it's not going to make any difference anyway.

'Well I wouldn't be quite so cynical,' Eli said. 'Some will believe you and some won't, no matter what you say. But you can show how ridiculous these rationalizations are by taking them to their absurd conclusion. That's better than trying to convince someone against their will. In the end, it doesn't matter what others think if they don't want to believe you. It's not your problem.'

'And yet it's indicative,' Mo said, 'how so many contemporary philosophers and scientists can be so intellectually clever and daunting, yet fall for such shallow reasoning, particularly in their discernment of spiritual matters. Too often their learning involves only the contrivances of the mind without engaging the wisdom of the heart. They're very good at creating advanced modems of logical analysis but there's little concern for spirit other than as a metaphor for emotions.'

'I'm not sure that's entirely correct,' I said.

'When was the last time your department offered a class on the teachings of mystics such as Meister Eckhart?'[2]

'I don't think it's ever occurred, or likely to occur any time soon.'

'Of course not,' he said. 'Not so much because Eckhart was religious, since most contemporary philosophers understand philosophers of the past often had various religious views. Rather, it was because he went beyond the intellectual constructs of the mind, to speak more deeply about the heart's engagement with God, emphasizing man's mystical oneness with God. He said such things as: *The knower and the known are one*.[3] Such non-dual belief of intimate union with divine essence is the ultimate secular heresy for the hard core materialist, which explains why

---

[1] Occam's Razor is a principle of determining what truth is most probable, that being the argument with the fewest assumptions.

[2] Meister (Master) Eckhart von Hochheim (1260-1327) German theologian, philosopher and mystic.

[3] The full quote from Eckhart is: *The knower and the known are one. Simple people imagine that they should see God as if he stood there and they here. This is not so. God and I, we are one in knowledge.*

so few scientists know anything of Eckhart. But if they do, they would consider him a quaint footnote in the history of mystical thought.'

'Contrary to the current trends in philosophy and science,' Mo continued, 'there was a common understanding about the spiritual nature of man among certain luminaries such as Eckhart, William James and Carl Jung to give just a few examples. They understood man to be more than material and the mind more than the brain, or any other part of man's anatomy.'

'It would be difficult for me to argue with that,' I said, 'considering the present circumstances of my brain's whereabouts. Most neuroscientists, however, assume the mind is merely a function of the brain and nothing more.

And if you ask them,' Mo said, 'they will tell you they've done lots of brain probing and prodding to prove this, at least on the surface where causality is often ignored. Only effects are deemed relevant, since only they allow for measurement. And what can't be measured, they say, can't be scientific, and therefore can't exist.

'But from our non-linear perspective of reality, we understand what exists in form is a manifest expression of thought. That's why the question everyone needs to be asked is, what are we thinking?[1] If our thoughts create our reality, then what kind of world are we creating for ourselves? In realizing this, would we not need to take much greater responsibility for what we choose to think?'

If this proposition is true,' I said, 'obviously what you think about would have important consequences, since it would contribute to the world's collective reality. Throughout the ages, I think it can be said much of culture and civilization has been determined by the thoughts of philosophers and theologians and how they understand reality. At least that's what we philosophers like to believe, I smiled.

And so, Eli said, as a philosopher it will be in your power to help sculpt what is to become of civilization on earth. With this being the case, what thoughts dominate your mind, James?

---

[1] This has often been suggested by various 20th century physicists such Planck, Einstein, Jeans and other prominent thinkers. See Appendix 'A' for more quotes by various physicists on this topic.

'I think about woman a lot; does that count? I said with a grin. But what if I choose not to think anything?'

'I'm not sure that's an option, at least not for long,' Mo said. 'If Descartes' Latin phrase, *Cogito ergo sum,* is valid as you were affirming a while back, then, *I think therefore I am,* means you must exist. At least from what we can see, you certainly are *I am.*'

'Indeed, *I am that I am,*' I said. 'From what I remember, isn't that what God said to Moses.'

'It is,' said Mo. 'Trust me, I should know since Mo is short for Moses. That's why, at least according to Descartes, God must always be thinking and why creation is eternal. Creation comes from thought forms we create with our thoughts that are conceived within the divine though form that gave rise to our existence from Source. After all, we exist in the image of the divine.'

'But considering what I created for myself here, I must be thinking rather bizarre thoughts. Just look at where I am and who I'm with!'

'And I might add, you even did it a coma. You're good!' Eli said. 'At some level, be it conscious, subconscious, unconscious or even super-conscious, in our out of a coma, our soul is always thinking, processing and analysing even when you aren't aware of it.'

'In light of all this,' Mo said, 'I will repeat the question. What is it we are thinking? Because what we think, is what we bring into the world. What we think brings heaven or hell, peace or war, misery or happiness. That's why everyone needs to guard their thoughts. Whatever thoughts we invite and affirm, will eventually be projected outwardly. It's always up to us, and ultimately we reap what we've collectively sown in our minds.

'That's why countries vary so much, even though they may be located next to each other. East Germany, West Germany in the past, North Korea, South Korea in the present. Same people and heritage; yet some are free and prosperous, the others in bondage and penury. For whatever tyranny may, or may not, have been imposed on them, each possesses their own collective consciousness that determines their state of existence.'

'To take this one step further,' Eli said, 'what one willfully chooses to think leads one to become happy or unhappy, loving or fearful. As the old Proverb says, *as a man thinketh in his heart, so is he.*[1]

'And I would add by inference,' Mo said, 'so is the reality he has chosen for himself – for better or worse. That's why the proverb doesn't say thinketh in his brain, but rather, *thinketh in his heart.*[2]

'For example, it was because you longed to see the Mountain, your affections drew you away from the Lowlands to your new reality. It may not have appeared that way to you back then, but it's what happened because it's what your heart desired. It was the spiritual quest of your heart to find a new dimension of meaning that, in your case, expressed itself as a Mountain, causing you to look upwards. The Mountain was a symbol of transcendence where you could discover your Self, the Christ within; and thereby become one with it.'

'At the time, you didn't specifically understand what you were seeking, and so you had no way of knowing where to find it. You just knew, whatever it was, it must be up there somewhere beyond. This subliminal longing burned deeply within your soul, eventually causing you to abandon the Lowlands. You may not have always been sure where you were going, but still you followed your heart's leading to what was further up and further in. And so here you are.'

'And so I am,' I said. 'But if I return home, as you say is likely the case, it may seem that this was just an extended Timothy Leary psychedelic tour.[3] And then the big downer hits, like coming home to a snow blizzard in northern Siberia after being on a tropical holiday.'

'You need not worry,' Eli said, 'it may take some time after you return home before you realize you were here with us on this extended holiday.'

'But why won't I remember being here when I return?'

'You may imagine some things at first, as with a dream,' he said, 'but aren't able to recall after the feelings fade away. It may be awhile before you are accessing your memories since your brain, as a three dimensional receiver/transmitter mechanism will require some time

---

[1] Proverbs 23:7 (KVJ)

[2] *As a man thinketh in his heart, so is he.* Proverbs 23:7 (KJV)

[3] Timothy Leary was a psychologist, professor and writer that helped popularize LSD in the 1960s.

to heal, although we have no idea how long this may take. Further to that, it has no record of what happened since it wasn't here with you, and so it will obstruct what your soul knows.

'The good news is that nothing is ever lost since all your memories remain imprinted in the universal field of consciousness and not in the brain. In other words, your brain will have to find a way to access your memories from the field so it may imprint them into its hardware, or I should say; tissue. Once it does this, you may later integrate your experiences here into your earth plane life. This download could take some time though, since you will have to relive all the memories you've had here.'

'However,' Mo said, 'there may be some problems in the interpretation of the data since we have a much broader band to receive and transmit than what's available on the earth plane. The three dimensional filter of the brain often gets in the way of these operations. However, some mystics, and a few genuine psychics, are able to override the brain's filter when picking up higher octave signals. Perhaps one day you will learn to do this. If you do, then things may become much clearer.

'To use a crude analogy, think of the brain as being equipped and programmed to accept only low frequency radio signals, but your spirit body is also equipped to receive and transmit high vibratory signals from a higher plane of existence. You now have the same antennae as us to transmit and receive signals that are attuned to the universal field, though you haven't yet learned how to tune in because you don't know it's on your dial.'

'I wonder if my psychic friend can tune into this higher frequency or if she just says she can.'

'You mean the one you talked about who has a studio above the pawn shop?' Eli asked.

'That's her; she wanted to help me with my love life. A real character, she even offered to provide me with a few private introductory tantric lessons at no cost.'

'You didn't tell us this important sidebar information;' he said, 'perhaps you should have taken her up on her samplers. Perhaps she could help you become a better lover for someone someday.'

Of course they had a laugh over this, but then so did I. Eli was right;

it was rather ironic how I, a philosopher, purporting to be rational at all times, would resort to her gypsy advice on my love life. Perhaps that shows how desperate I was to find true love, even if I told myself the consultations were just a lark!

'Don't mind us,' Mo said, with a teasing smile, 'but it is kind of funny. But who knows, one day she could be of some assistance to us should we wish to get through to you when you return home. For all her props and paraphernalia, she does have some genuine psychic skills, but I won't trust her in matters of love; likely she wants you all for herself.'

'Well, to be honest, I'm aware she may at times have tried to throw the game in her direction, but that is part of her feminine charm. In a way, she possesses a strange gypsy mystique that at times enchants me, even if she is a few years and pounds over what I consider optimal.'

'You know,' Mo said, 'life on earth can be rather amusing, even when it doesn't always feel that way, especially during times of adversity. Yet through it all, one is able to enhance the quality of their character by facing the challenges of life with the right attitude.

'These types of opportunities don't exist in the higher spheres where existence is progressively effortless; what's why it takes much longer to advance. There are many obstructions that are encountered on Earth, analogous to lifting weights to develop one's muscles. And so, resistances of adversity are almost always required to raise one's consciousness to an optimal level for what's highest and best.'

'The benefits of exercising your free will,' Mo continued, 'extends past earthly existence. Your soul, being the spirit substance, is adaptable to experiencing new dimensions of infinite possibilities. And so when the time comes for you to return to the earth plane, remember that everything in life has purpose as you continue to learn from all you encounter there. Your physical body is a device by which you may learn, and if used wisely, it will make you a better man within. Having said that, the Madame probably isn't your type, even if she thinks she thinks she knows how to make you feel like a real man,' he chuckled.

'I suppose not, but I don't know who is able to make me feel like a real man, at least for more than a night or two. There's got to be much more to relationships than what I've been experiencing. If there's someone out there for me, I haven't met her yet. It's rather unfortunate I won't be able to meet her here either.'

Mo looked at me and smiled, as Eli said, 'oh, and why not?'

CHAPTER 10

NEW GIRLFRIEND

She's beautiful, and therefore to be wooed; She is woman, and therefore to be won[1]

I asked Eli what he meant when he said, 'why not?' This was an interesting response leading to a much larger question. Was there someone out there they had in mind for me, if only for a night? The question begged to be answered. But rather than answer me, he smiled, got up and walked out the door into the moonlight with Mo.

The suspense still lingered in my mind until they arrived the next morning. But before I had a chance to bring the matter up, Eli said, 'picking up on where we left off yesterday, I think it's time we have a little discussion with you about your love life. We sense this is something you've been wishing to discuss with us.'

'Maybe; I suppose – guess it depends on what you have to say. But I'm not sure I need counselling as much as I need a little female company, which I've noticed, seems to be notably absent on this Summit.'

'That's true,' Eli said, 'not many at all. Perhaps you need some consoling instead of counselling.'

'I think he does,' Mo said; 'just look at him; such an eligible

---

[1] William Shakespeare, *Henry V1*, Act 5, Scene 2

bachelor; debonair, good looking, smart – though probably not as smart as he thinks. It must be frustrating for him not to have yet found what he's looking for, be it here, there or anywhere. Perhaps you should talk to him, Eli, and try to give him a little help, provided if he will accept it.'

'Yes, I think that would be a good idea,' Eli said, as he turned towards me. 'So James; Mo and I were talking and we think we can help. Perhaps you can start by telling us why things haven't been such a romp in the playpen lately? We're very understanding.'

'I'm sure you are, but I'd much prefer if you didn't get too involved in my private affairs – even if it amuses you.'

Though I displayed some feigned indignation, I knew Eli was only provoking me good naturedly, since he understood how I could sometimes be a bit arrogant about some of my past exploits, particularly when I was younger. Most of the time, however, I took his jesting as an indication of some jealousy.

'Sure, I'll admit I've had a few set-backs with woman walking out on me recently, but that's nothing compared to their loss. But then, there wasn't that much for me to lose, considering how seldom they pitched in for food and rent; although, I must say, they did their part in providing extra heat at night.'

'So what else,' Eli said. 'Remember, we're your friends so you can tell us anything; we really do care,' he grinned disingenuously.

'Very touching' I said, 'but why do you think you need to know everything about my secrets to, as you say, *console* me?'

'I think you should know there's quite the file on you! But I wouldn't worry about it; we don't have keys to the cabinet. Much of what we know is inferred from what you have already told us, so don't hesitate to tell us more and we promise not to be scandalized.'

'Actually, you already seem to know a lot more than you should know,' I said.

'In the infinite field of consciousness,' Mo said, 'there can be no secrets in the higher spheres, since there is nothing to hide. The past is the past, only now has meaning.'

'So are you saying there's someone out there in these higher realms out there that has access to all my secrets?'

'Secrets are just an attempt to avoid guilt and judgement,' he said. 'Our domain knows nothing of these since whatever is of fear can't exist in higher planes, no more than darkness can exist in the light. In fact, when you think about it, darkness on its own has no reality; it's only the absence of light. There are no secrets where there is no guilt, sin or shame; the qualities that fester and flourish in the world's domain. And so there's no one to judge you but yourself. Not even God.'

'Only light and truth exist where unconditional love prevails. Whenever you fear, you already sense how much it contrasts with feelings of love. This should tell you how much you don't want to dwell with these dark feelings. They really are toxic, that's evident, but few on earth seem to make the connection. Through all dimensions, Source emanates its living effluence as it flows outwardly, just as we spoke of regarding the *Ray of Creation*, from the highest celestial realms, to angels, humans, ameoba, rocks and all that is.'

'That's fine,' I said, 'but can we defer our discussions on this until a little later? I'd first prefer to resolve the significantly more esoteric subject of understanding female relationships, provided you don't wound my wounded pride with more of your laughs'

'No, we wouldn't do that,' Eli said, 'unless it gives you a lighter and higher perspective so you don't take yourself so seriously. With some relations, it's easy to get stuck in the bogs; that's why laughing at one's self is good therapy. Although, I'm sure this is more difficult when everyone is also laughing at you, rather than with you. So if we laugh, it's only because there are many humorous things in your life we wish to point out so that you need not feel defensive when we all laugh together.'

'Of course,' I said, 'and maybe that's why the Buddha always has such a big goofy grin on his face.'

'And with you now being in your spirit body, things will continue to feel much lighter, which means it should be easier for you to laugh about your own *comedy of errors*.[1] Are you aware how women enjoy being with men who have humour? You are often known more for your wit,

---

[1] In reference to *The Comedy of Errors*, one of Shakespeare's first plays; also the shortest and most farcical.

but that goes only so far in relationships, since it doesn't provide the same warmth as humour.'

'I think you're on to something here,' I said. 'Perhaps I'm too serious for women to enjoy me – other than in bed.'

'We sense there's been a great heaviness to your life for some time now,' Eli said, 'often blocking the peace you've long desired to feel light and happy.'

'Yes, that's probably true, but since I've been with you two comedians, we've had plenty of good laughs. Philosophers aren't particularly known for their levity of spirit. When was the last time you saw one of us do stand-up comedy? I fear that when I return to my old routine back home and settle back into my intellectual life, I may lose much of the joviality I've enjoying here.'

'You're right, why would we ever want to come down from this high, unless you had a really good reason to go back to the old life.'

'So give me a good reason,' I said, 'I'm listening.'

'What if we could find you a beautiful young woman who would keep you so cheerful that you may need to medicate yourself each morning you woke up? Okay, that may be an exaggeration, since I know you're not a morning person, but at least the world's weariness would never again overwhelm you.'

'So how are you going to find someone like that, especially while we're on this plane, when I haven't been able to do that, even with all my years on earth?'

'Don't worry about that, Mo and I already have someone on the short list that we thought may be perfect for you. We didn't say anything, since we assumed you wouldn't want to be distracted from all our brilliant discussions.'

'No, of course not,' I said, 'why would I be interested in finding the perfect woman when I get to sulk in loneliness and despair back home.'

Mo was busy preparing something at the stove so didn't appear to be paying much attention to us.

'Say Mo,' Eli shouted across the room, 'do you remember anything about that woman we were talking about? Miss Lonely Heart's here wants to know.'[1]

---

[1] *Miss Lonely Hearts* was a novel published in 1933 by Nathanael West

'About what?'

'You know, the young woman we were talking about the other day – the one we thought would be a good match for James after he gets home? Her name seems to have escaped me.'

This was vintage Eli; obviously another one of his set ups. At times, such as now, Mo would be complicit in the mischief.

'Okay Eli,' I said, 'if there's something to this, just spit it out. Who is she?'

'Oh yes,' Mo said, 'now that you mention it, I remember us talking about this awhile back. Do you remember which side of the border she resides?'

'If I'm not mistaken,' Eli said, 'I think this one was from the earth side.'

'Oh, that's too bad. Perhaps we should try to find him someone here?' Eli said. 'I'm not so sure he can wait till he gets back home -- maybe some cute mountain nymph. I'm not sure, but I think there may be one who comes by at night to check him out.'

'Most humorous,' I said. 'Carry on if you like, but this time I'm not going to be taken in by your baiting!'

'No, no, not her,' Mo said, 'he's not nearly ready for that one. They're not even on the same frequency – she's way too advanced.'

'You're right,' said Eli, 'he probably wouldn't even know what to do with her if she showed up in his loft. He probably needs someone more down to earth, so to speak. Maybe we should arrange for him to meet the one in London when we go there sometime in the future. But damn, I can't remember her name.'

'Oh now I think I remember the one we were talking about,' said Mo, 'isn't she the charming young lassie who lives close by to James' flat, probably less than a mile away? He might have even seen her in the deli coffee shop below.'

'Yes, of course,' Eli said, 'now I remember – the really cute one. But don't you think maybe too cute for James? It would be a shame if he made her unhappy; she always has such a lovely smile and disposition.'

'Glad you two are finally getting things worked out in your little charade,' I said. 'Even if I were to believe you, I'm not sure any woman, cute or not, would pay any attention to me under the present circumstances. What if I meet her there, what would I say: *Boo?*'

'You could,' Eli said with a laugh, 'likely she wouldn't be the first one you scared off. But if you like, we can set things up for you to meet her'

'You should know all about set ups,' I said.

'No, really James,' Eli said, 'we're serious, even if it seems we aren't. You know, if things worked out for you,' he said a bit over sincerely, 'this could turn out to be a long term set up, at least for what's left of your time on earth. She could be very good for you, considering how badly your body got bashed around and how long it may take to heal.'

'I suspect,' Mo said, 'things might be rather dismal for you back home until you've had sufficient physiotherapy to get back on your feet and into the groove again. Perhaps some extra tender consolation would be of benefit to your body.'

'It's worth considering, but I'm not sure that would be covered by my current medical plan.'

'By consolation, Eli said, I think Mo meant you may require some assistance in helping your body to recover.'

'Wonderful,' I said, 'that's what I thought I heard him say. I'm most grateful you wish to find me someone who's willing to give my body consolation after all the suffering it endured while I was away. I really enjoy massages, provided it's with the right masseuse. But where do you think you're going to find me a prize like that?'

'Yes, that's it; let's call this your consolation prize.' Eli said. 'I mean the young woman, not the massage. I think you would be delighted to win such prize, at least you should. Don't you think Mo?'

'Oh most certainly, I would say so. Yes, most definitely she'd be a jolly prize for any man – most splendid, indeed.'

'Okay,' I said, 'I'm not sure how serious you are about this, or if you are making it all up; it's hard to tell. But if you really mean it; just tell me who she is, or quit making it up. It's already gone on far enough.'

'Should we tell him Mo, or should we make him wait?'

'Probably he should wait,' Mo said, 'it may be best so he can appreciate her more when he's ready for a more meaningful relationship than what he thinks he needs from a woman.'

'You're right, Eli said, 'I'm sure it would be good for him to wait a bit longer for his consolation prize. Besides, if we told him everything about her, he'd never graduate from Summit U or focus on anything else he needs to learn.'

'No, likely not,' Mo said, 'so I think it's more appropriate he wait longer to meet this very lovely woman of his dreams.'

Obviously they were having some fun at my expense, milking their story for all it was worth. I grew even more suspicious now that this was just a fabrication of Eli's.

'Women of my dreams you say? Right about now I think I would settle for any decent woman, in or out of my dreams. So let's dispense with bull; if you're serious, just tell me. I'm never sure what to believe around here.'

'Oh, she real alright,' Eli said, 'and I'm certain it would be especially consoling for you to wake up to her each morning while you're in recovery. Much better than a bouquet of freshly cut flowers by your bedside, although she may bring you that too.'

'But it's up to you whether you want to meet her or not; we don't wish to force anything or anyone on you. Love can't be love if there's not a choice.'

"Let me suggest,' Mo said, 'for James' sake, we have a wee discussion on the topic of love and what it means. Most people don't know, and I'm not sure how well James understands it either.

'Yes, that's a good idea,' Eli said, 'I think its most apropos for him to understand what love means before getting too involved with anyone again. He may think he knows, but he really doesn't. I think many of his past endeavours indicate this.'

Yes, it seems they do, Mo, said concurringly.

'If you will; please stop speaking past me,' I said; 'it's most impolite, especially when I'm sitting across from you. But if you wish, we may discuss this, provided it has something to do with this young woman.

'Remember what we just said, James, if you can't laugh at yourself,' Eli said, 'then others will. So you may as well laugh with us since you're not nearly as bad as we make you out to be,' he laughed.

'So if we're ready now,' Mo said, 'let me make a few points in understanding what love is. Firstly, there's nothing in the universe greater or more mysterious than love. It emanates directly from this infinite Source; the fount of all that is. It can't be taught or known, only recognized by its effects. It is found in relationships, never contained in forms, but containing all forms. As I often say, it's the glue of the universe, the purpose for which we all live. Furthermore it is the …'

'That's wonderful Mo; thanks for the homily, but let's discuss that topic another time. I just want to know more about this young woman you're attempting to tantalize me with, as you continue to dangle her before me.'

'I get the impression,' Eli said, 'he really wants to know. Should we tell him?'

'I suppose,' Mo said; 'he's likely not going to give up until we do.'

'You're right,' Eli said, 'patience doesn't seem to be one James' greatest attributes, does it?'

'If you're both done carrying on,' I said, 'can you just come clean and tell me who the hell she is, once and for all?'

'Oh, did Mo forget to tell you? Her name is Julianne, isn't it Mo?'

'I believe it is,' he said, 'although I think most of her friends call her Julie.'

'Most charming, I like that name; like Julie Christie. I hope she looks a good as her in the old movies. But that really doesn't tell me a lot does it? So just who is this bird?'

'She's the prize we've been discussing,' Eli said. 'There's a catch though. You know that, right? There's always a catch.'

'With women, it seems there always is; so what is it this time?'

'The catch is you first need to catch her. Provided you are able, then you need to hold on to her rather than playing your normal *catch and release* game. This is about more than just fishing.'

'Yes, I'm sure it is. Or perhaps more like cat and mouse, where I get to be the mouse, but never finding out until it's too late.'

'Well,' said Mo, 'this may be a rather different type of game for you this time. It all depends what you want and what she wants from life – and what you both want from each other. Perhaps she'll turn out to be exactly what you need when you return to your life back home.'

'But before I get too excited, you say I need to catch her first. So tell me, what makes this consolation prize such a great catch? Are you running an escort service or something? Possibly you don't think I can hunt my own rabbits – or birds in this case. They're everywhere! Besides, I'm rather selective, with very high standards!'

'And how's that been working out for you?' Eli said.

I winced. 'Okay, maybe I'm not so good at this. But I still need to get a file on this Julie or Julianne for the selection process. So what else can you tell me; do you have any stats on her? That's always a good place to start in determining if she could make the short list.'

Mo seemed amused by my new enthusiasm. 'I'm not sure that is the best place to start; but before we talk stats, let me ask you if you like challenges.'

'Depends, what kind of challenges? I'm not interested in acquiring more high maintenance risks, if that is what you're getting at. I've already had plenty of them.'

'In all sincerity,' Eli said, 'we can say Julianne is a most delightful twenty six year old woman, 126 pounds, five foot, seven inches. And since we know what's important to you, she's particularly well sculpted for your viewing pleasure. She would more than meet your aesthetic criteria, while making you feel proud to have her accompany you at faculty functions and parties.'

'Besides the merits of her outward appearance, she possesses various talents such drama and singing. In fact, she has even performed a couple of operatic scores in the past with a choral group when she was in university. It helped that her mother was once a singing instructor. She also used to enjoy writing poetry in the past.

'However, she is also skilled in less delicate arts which should be of great concern to you, he said, with a very grave expression.

'Oh my – sounds serious; so what may that be?'

'Let's just say be sure to look out for her wicked jiu-jitsu moves; he said laughingly, they could be lethal. But at least they will keep you on your toes – or possibly off your toes and onto your arse. After being assaulted by hooligans near Hyde Park, she decided to do something about it by taking up various martial arts, rather than being traumatized by the experience. It's deceiving; she may appear harmless, but she's perfected several lethal manoeuvres that could have you sprawled on the floor – just so you are aware.'

'However, from what we understand,' Mo said, 'with her new inner confidence in mastering these arts, she is not nearly as fearful and reactive as she used to be. In fact, just the opposite, she's now becoming much more caring and compassionate, which is why she took up the career she's now in. Believe it or not, but you may have had something to do with this continued inward transformation that's still going on in her.'

'What are you saying? I don't even know her, so how could I have any influence over her, especially with me being here and her being there?'

'You may be more charismatic than you know, James,' Eli said. 'She's really drawn to you. In fact she's all over you.'

'Ah, so I do know her! I thought so. She must not have given me her real name, though, since I don't remember any Julianne. Was it just for a night?'

'No,' he said, 'there have been several nights!'

'Really; you don't say! So when will I get to see her so I can know which one?'

'To be honest, you haven't actually met her,' Mo said – 'not really. Though you have never been formally introduced, she has been with your body for some time. In fact, she knows it really well, more than you may wish. Or possibly, just as you would wish!'

'She wouldn't be the only one,' I said with a laugh.

'But in this case, it's her job!' Eli said.

'To know my body -- what is she, some back street hooker near Kings Cross?'

'No, of course not; your comatose body could hardly respond to such services, even if there was an opportunity. Remember, it's in the hospital now.'

'Let me explain,' Mo said, 'since Eli keeps holding out on you. Are you ready for this? Your consolation prize, Julianne, is a nurse at the hospital where your body is!'

'So that explains it! And I would say, most cheery – if not intriguing!'

'In fact,' he said, 'if you were to ask it, your body would tell you she's your favourite nurse. And why not, she's the one who spends the most time with it, and is by far the most dedicated. She's relatively new to her career and very idealistic; she believes she could make a big difference in any patient's recovery. A most committed health worker who is willing to go beyond the call of duty.'

'Especially for you,' Eli said, 'we think she has a thing going for you! Well maybe not you, so much as for your body.'

'I can understand that,' I said with a cocky grin.

'Fortunately,' Mo said, 'she's taken it upon herself to give your body special care. Perhaps she feels sorry for it, considering the shape it was in.

'Or possibly,' I said, 'because my body appeals to her. Notwithstanding the wounds, I'm sure it must still be relatively good shape.'

'We understand, Mo said, she's very impressed with what she's heard about your remarkable climbing achievement in the Andes. She thinks you must be courageous, but also a tad demented for attempting such an extraordinary expedition all alone. And I think we all agree she's absolutely right about that.

'Inwardly, I would describe her devotion as being more spiritual rather than religious, although, if properly understood, there probably wouldn't be a distinction. During most of her youth she faithfully attended Church of England services with her family. Recently, she's been attending early Morning Prayer services at Westminster Abbey. Who knows, maybe she's praying for you!'

'From what we understand,' Eli said, 'she was energetic, though a bit misdirected at times from those she hung out with in her high school. Guess that's normal; boys wanted to be with her, so what could she do; she didn't want to disappoint.

'After dropping out of her Fine Arts degree programme in music and theatre, she decided to transfer into nursing, which was a big surprise to all her friends and family. Compassion and healing won over drama, although she can still do that rather well when it suits her.'

'From what we've been told,' Mo said, 'Julianne has matured a lot since working at the hospital the last couple of years, while at the same time, adapting a more contemplative life. This may have something to do with her disillusionment with a relationship she has that's been on and off for years, but never really on. Not to say she doesn't like to have fun at parties with wine, laughter and lots of admiring men where she often finds herself to be the center of attention.

'Increasingly though, she has less time for vapid talk, looking for more meaningful discussion in the midst of the frivolity. If she can't find it, she prefers to go home to read a good book, which has put a bit of a strain on some of her friendships recently.'

'You know something else, James, she thinks about you a lot. Of course, that's not quite the same as saying she thinks a lot about you, since she doesn't know you. But nevertheless, you intrigue her as few men have. After hearing how your body was discovered by a forestry helicopter crew who happened to be flying by, she firmly believes it's not by chance your body survived the fall. This she considers to be a miracle. And of course, she's right about that too, even more then she realizes and far more than you realize.'

'Sure, guess I must I'm damned lucky, if you can call lucky lying in a coma for God knows how long? Even if I become conscious in my physical body again, I may need to live out the rest of my days as an invalid or worse.'

'What happened, James, had nothing to do with luck,' Mo said. 'In fact, providence is present in your life more than you'll ever know or understand. You are not only fortunate, but you have been bestowed with a unique opportunity few humans will ever receive.'

'So are you saying this was planned? The Almighty set me up for a fall?'

'Or maybe,' he said, 'at some subliminal level, you did. Isn't it interesting; you awoke in a fitful panic at the end of your dream that infamous night, feeling you were about to fall off a mountain ledge. And then just a few months later, there you were, half way around the world, ready to take your plunge. What drew you there?'

'It's a mystery to me,' I said. 'It just seemed to happen; but not at all what I intended when I booked my ticket to Chile.'

'In any case, there's more to this,' he said. 'As we've often discussed, the real you, the James within, intended this adventure in his own muffled and muted way, even while dwelling in the Lowlands. You're coming over here could have occurred in any number of ways, but at some level, you chose the most direct way because for you it was the most natural way.

'Think about it, you were an accident waiting to happen! No

climbing companions, precious little climbing gear with few emergency provisions. To top it all off, you selected a suicide Mountain, not telling anyone where you were going. So you must recognize your part as co-creator in the set-up, be it blame or credit, as you choose to believe.'

'Fine, sure, okay,' I said, 'perhaps there is something to what you're saying. It's possible there has been a certain lack of responsibility on my part regarding proper preparation, although I did have a satellite phone, which I apparently lost in the fall. But I don't want to talk about that now; let's get back to my nurse. Is she hot? I need to know that.'

'What do you mean by that term,' Mo asked? 'That can carry a lot of dubious connotations. You may wish to describe her as such, but I'm not sure I would; too limiting and objectifying. There's a whole lot more to her than what meets the eyes.'

'And since you're an academic of exquisite tastes,' Eli said, 'I would have expected you to ask what kind of poetry and music she enjoys, what books she reads and kind of discussions she engages in. Surely that must be far more important to you than just her body,' he said with a straight face.

'No, not really,' I said. 'Okay, all that too, but what else can you tell me? Is she's on Facebook? I'd like to see some pictures.'

'I'm sure she would be considered very appealing to most men,' he said, 'but as we already indicated, don't let her feminine body deceive you, she can be hard as nails if need be. She wouldn't hesitate to give you a swift knee where it may not feel so good if she thinks you have it coming. Problem is, you may never know if or when you do, since that is her female prerogative in determining when retribution is warranted.'

'Sounds rather high-spirited!'

'Well yes,' Mo said, 'she can be very spirited, but since you're a spirit, that may be a good match; wouldn't you say? Quite literally, you're outwardly spiritual and she's inwardly spiritual; and as she continues to become more inwardly responsive rather than outwardly reactive, you will have less reason to be concerned. In fact, I think she could be about as perfect for you as you could want, provided you both wish to grow and develop in the same way.'

'Which way is that?'

'*Further in, further up,* as we keep saying. Of course, it's always possible one of you could trip up the whole affair. It happens all the time on earth where there seems to be a propensity to sabotage relationships before they come to fruition. So when you go back, it will be important you discover how to live less by your mind, and more by your heart, as she's now beginning to do.'

'So how would I do that? I'm supposed to make my living using my mind, not my heart'

'It's for you to discover, Mo said. 'But if you are willing, I'm sure Julianne could help.'

'That's because it's more of a female thing, since they're more right brained.'

'And maybe,' Eli said, 'that's why you may need someone like Julianne to help you get in touch with your heart, ever before you return. If you let her, we think she would be very good at this.'

'So how would she be able to teach me anything here, she's on the wrong continent and in the wrong zone?'

'Women have their ways, as does Julianne.'

Of course they do, I said sarcastically. So how do you both know so much about her?'

'You should know, James, we have connections, really good connections.'

'In this case, with someone who is well acquainted with Julianne,' Mo said, 'as good a source you'll find anywhere – tells us whatever we need to know.'

'Well then, maybe I need to meet this source of yours so I can find out if you're not just making this all up. So how can I make contact; do I need some reverse Ouija board?'

'If you don't mind,' Eli said, 'we prefer not to say.'

'Okay fine, if you must, keep your secrets, but I thought you just said this dimension has no secrets.'

'This is really more about withholding information for your own good,' he said with a laugh.

'To me, withholding information sounds much like the definition of what secret is supposed to mean. So what else did this classified source of yours say about Julianne – if it's not too big a secret?'

She's a very straight-up, no-nonsense type, Mo said, perhaps more than you are accustomed to with your prior roommates. So be aware; she has little patience with those of contrive airs and conceit.'

'Nor do I, since that's not my style.'

'Are you sure about that?' Eli asked. 'Have you ever tried, when it was to your advantage, to tell clever philosophical vignettes to make an impression, or how about assorted witticisms while attending sophisticated dinner parties? Have you ever bragged about your outstanding achievements while on a new date; perhaps with a little name dropping thrown in for good measure? I'm not judging you or implying there's anything bad about that, especially if that's you. I'm just saying such tactics may not work very well with Julianne if she suspects you're being pretentious.'

'So what's her problem,' I said, 'she should know when she's with a Renaissance man.'

'Perhaps she's a bit sensitive to this because too many in her drama classes kept getting carried away with their role playing. She's more interested in the understated qualities of the inner being. So whenever you're around her, you may wish to stifle any temptation to assume any persona other than your own, otherwise she is going to see right through you.'[1]

'But really, I would never indulge in such self-aggrandizement – unless, of course, it helped me snag a little companionship for the night.'

'Ah, I see,' said Mo. 'You know; we conducted a special *PROJECT JAMES* reconnaissance operation while you were still living in the Lowlands. Knowing your modus operandi among woman, we advise you maintain your needy patient mode for as long as you can with Julianne when you get back. This will give you some extra time for her to know you at your humble best. That's the man that's going to win her.

'As Eli said, try not to impress her with anything other than your authenticity. That may work with some, but not with her. Not to say you shouldn't be proud of your achievements and passionate dedication toward scholarship. Just don't flaunt it. She already knows about that, so the less you say, the better. If you think you need to strut your stuff,

---

[1] Considering what later occurred (Book 2, Chapter 2), it's amusing, if not prescient, for Eli to have made this comment.

she will consider you insecure; a really big turn off for her. She much prefers unassuming, confident men. But then, what woman doesn't?'

'Are you saying I'm insecure?'

'Why do you ask; are you insecure?' Mo said laughingly.

'Only when I don't get what I want from women,' I said, smiling. 'But carry on, tell me more. Tell me more about her family background?'

'Her father was and still remains a strong role model for her. A very solid man whose qualities she hopes to find in her future man. He was considered an outstanding instructor in a fine arts school in London; much admired for his talent and personal integrity. Likewise, her mother is very talented in music. Recently her father completed his career as Headmaster and now is retired. They now spend most of the winter in Melbourne, Australia where they have a flat.'

'Sounds like a decent family;' I said, 'certainly better than what I had for much of my youth. No wonder she has high standards in finding a suitable relationship.'

'If you wish to meet her standards for such a relationship, we suggest you relax and be genuine. Whether you realize it or not, you are at your best when you don't think you have anything to prove.'

'That sounds too easy.'

'Only because you've never tried it,' Eli said. 'If you do this, she may come to believe you're the man she's been waiting for.

'But if you're not careful, Mo said, Julianne's always ready with several zingers. According to our source, while still in university, she once gave an arrogant literary student a lesson in Shakespearean poetry, with the line: *God has given you one face and you make yourself another.*'[1]

'Most jolly – and witty; I like that. I'm sure that would deflate a bloke should he have any designs on her. But I think I'd be up for the challenge. If she used that line on me, I'd quote to her a line from the same scene: *To a nunnery, go.*'

'And what if she did?' Eli said.

'It certainly would be most unfortunate for her,' I said.

'And possibly,' Mo said, 'it would be even more unfortunate for you.'

'Perhaps; I guess the question still remains whether she'd want to be in a relationship with me. After all, I'm not exactly rich, am I?'

---

[1] Hamlet, Act 1, Scene 3

'I guess it depends on how you define rich,' Eli said. 'Fortunately for you, money isn't her primary criterion. She's more interested in finding a man that's has more substance than his outward possessions. Not to say a little financial stability wouldn't be a consideration for her. She wants a family and would like to know she's secure if she's no longer working. But for now, you have her attention as her special patient. Like we said, she's grown rather fond of you, or at least your body.'

'It's a good thing,' Mo said, 'since you're not exactly Mr Congeniality these days, are you?'

'Likely I'm not, which means she must go for the strong silent types,' I chuckled.

'Yes, very silent, but in your case, no longer so strong,' Eli said. 'Nevertheless, you may be pleased to know that all your parts, particularly those you deem most vital, are only temporarily disengaged. Provided your body survives, you will likely be restored to full capacity for what you consider so necessary.'

I smiled, 'most reassuring;' I said. 'If not, I would have had to jump off that damned chasm again; this time for good. Speaking of the jump, what happened when I first arrived at the hospital; was Julianne there to greet me?'

'She was assisting in the Emergency unit that day,' Mo said, 'and among the first to attend to your body. Although, I must say, the good doctors in Santiago did an excellent work in stitching the mess together and so there was little left to be done when you arrived in London except give you more tests, wire you to their life support machinery and insert the plug into the wall.'

'Much of the assignment has been assumed by Julianne, who took to your body right away as her special restoration project. As the days passed, she made it her business to find whatever she could about you, questioning every visitor who came by to pay their last respects to what they thought was you. No one in the hospital has been more longsuffering and dedicated to your recovery than her; even whispering encouragement into that vacant head of yours.'

'I'm most grateful for her efforts,' I said, 'but a lot of good that will do while my body continues to atrophy each day.'

'You may be surprised,' Eli said. 'Do you realize that each of the seventy trillion cells in your body, with their astonishing complexity, have their own conscious awareness? Specialized medical researchers are only now beginning to understand and appreciate the significance of what's going on in these micro universes. Vibratory sensors are contained in each of the microtubules contained in each of your cells, and they, believe it or not, respond to Julianne's impassioned prayers. You probably won't normally hear this from the medical community; nevertheless it's true, there is strengthened resolve within each of these units when a healing intention is expressed.

'This seemingly mysterious spirit/matter nexus in the microtubules will gain acceptance as evidence for cellular intelligence increases. Although, there continues to be resistance to whatever implications suggest something more is going on besides mechanistic processes.[1] Much of what happens in the cells has yet to be comprehended; but when it is, it could do much to threaten prevailing paradigms. Already much has come to light with cutting edge sciences, such as in the new discipline of Epigenetics.'[2]

'Eli's right,' Mo said, 'in spite of what some intransigent scientists fear as having metaphysical implications, many others are prepared to concede there is may be more at work in this realm of consciousness than what they previously considered possible. There's something extraordinary and visceral that operates deeply within the conscious intelligence of each cell. What occurs to one cell is instantly known to all, a perfect example of how quantum mechanics functions within biology.

'This ought to be obvious to the medical scientists, but unfortunately, it remains largely outside their medicine chest. The tendency in traditional Western culture is to either glaze over these less established

---

[1] Microtubules are one of the components of the cytoskeleton in the cell's cytoplasm. One of their primary functions is to assist in cell division but there are other functions that go far beyond this, where each contains ionized water molecules that some scientists believe register conscious impressions.

[2] Dr. Bruce Lipton, developmental biologist, and former professor of biology at Stanford is one of the foremost pioneers in this new disciple. One of his first books *The Biology of Belief* provides an important description of the implications of what we are learning on this subject. I return again to this subject in Book Four of this narrative.

modalities, or oppose them if results can no longer be ignored. But then, it's always been that way in a world that only knows how to work from inside out, outside in.'

'Obviously, Mo, your views are completely contrary to the medical community's approach to wellness. I suppose that's your right, but what does this have to do with Ms Nightingale?'

'I was about to make the point,' he said, 'this young woman is not only very bright, but much more open minded than many in her profession – which is most fortunate for your body. Even though she has been trained exclusively in the allopathic pharmaceutical remedies, she suspects there is much more to healing than injecting and ingesting drugs. In all fairness, it should be recognized many medical doctors also acknowledge there are limitations to the old order, and are beginning to recognize certain complementary approaches and procedures where there is substantiation.'

Julianne has done a little studying into healing practises such as acupuncture, homeopathy, EFT, and reflexology, which she considers much less invasive, and perhaps, even more effective in working with the body's natural healing processes. She doesn't say much about this because it may sound hokey to the some of the more orthodox practitioners she works with. No one wants to be ridiculed or censured.'

'Okay, that interesting, but what's that doing for my body,' I asked.

'Perhaps more than you, she or the doctors may imagine,' Eli said. 'If not those specific approaches, at least her spiritual connection with your body has had much to do with your body's survival and remarkable progress to date, especially during the first couple of critical weeks. We believe with her strong commitment, she will continue to exert a positive impact towards a relatively speedy recovery when you re-enter your body. As Mo was saying, every living fibre senses the impact of her heartfelt prayers whenever she projects her healing intent. Her loving kindness brings emotional strength and light to each microtubule that exists within each cell of the body's organs.'

'Wonderful,' I said, 'though I'm not sure I understand how her prayers can have a causal connection with my body – sounds psychosomatic to me.'

'How can it be psychosomatic if you're not aware of her suggestions?

Yet what you say is true in the sense that your body's cells are aware of her healing message and touch. It's a spiritual connection and so in this sense, they are naturally susceptible to psychosomatic effects. In fact, on a cellular level of consciousness, we suspect your body may be getting a feel-good charge now and then with her feminine touch,' he smiled.

'Well, whatever happens in my body or in my room, hopefully I will be aware of what she did for me when I return so I may express my deepest gratitude to her.'

'If you go back, I'm sure you will express much gratitude to her.' Mo said, 'but for now her sustained focus continues to revitalize your cells, which could result in you slipping back into your earthly suit sooner rather than later.'

'So how certain are you I'm going to make it?'

What's there for you to make? Your body, however, will make it if and when it's ready,' Eli said, 'but as we've said, it's always possible it won't. But we think with Julianne's special attention, the odds are getting better all the time. Imagine one fine evening when we're sitting around the fire, with me playing my guitar and Mo reciting his favourite Celtic poetry, then suddenly, the first thing we know, zap, you're gone: just like that. No more James, at least not here.'

'Assuming that happens,' I said, 'then at least I'd be able to meet her right away and see for myself how interested I may be. But what happens if she doesn't have any appeal to me? You say she looks great, but not every man's tastes in women are the same.

'Perhaps you should be more concerned instead with what appeal you will have to her, Eli said with a smirk on his face. I think that's what's really at stake.'

'Okay, fair enough – I get your point. However, should there be some intimacy in the future; do you think we'd be able to sustain a functional relationship for more than a few months? Considering all the women I've been with; really, what are my odds? I think I have reason to be wary and concerned.

'For whom: women or yourself?' Mo said, chuckling. 'But seriously, James, I have no way of knowing how things may work out. How could I? That will depend entirely on you as much as her. At this point, all

I can say is that conditions seem favourable, or we wouldn't be telling you about her.

'And yet, at this point, you're not completely in alignment with her since you both view life much differently. She approaches life from within, you from without. You may think this is just the result of left brain/right brain orientations, but there's more to it than that.[1]

'Compared to Julianne, you are more mind oriented, examining ambiguities, weighing, analysing and creating new complexities where they may not have existed before. It's what philosophers do, but it may annoy her if that's all you do. It's not a deal breaker, but we suggest you keep things simple and get to the bottom line as quickly as you can. That much she understands and respects.'

'I'm not sure if life is as simple as a bottom line – that's sounds rather black and white. But I don't suppose any of this will make that much difference if we have enough going on in bed; that's the real bottom line – even if we drive the hell out of each other the rest of the time.'

'But I'm not sure love is that simple either, Eli said. And yet, consider the benefits to being in a relationship where each isn't as perfect as the other. Perspectives are only perspectives, but relationships require mutual understanding, awareness, and above all, respect. It's the way we can grow into beings of higher consciousness. Julianne may be perfect for you, but that doesn't mean she needs to be perfect – any more than you need be perfect to be perfect for her. Think of a relationship as an opportunity to learn from the other, especially when being tempered in the crucible of life's adversities.'

'Oh, I like that,' I said, '"tempered in the crucible of life's adversities." Very good Eli; sometimes you surprise me with how well you can wax poetic!'

'Or, it may also be stated, "tempered in the crucible of *love's* adversities,"' Mo said, 'since love, when tested, forms a crucible to temper our affections into what they're meant to become. But it's also possible to experience relationships as a living hell. There is nothing noble or poetic about being with someone who totally vexes your soul,

---

[1] The old paradigms of the lobe's limitations are being questioned as it becomes increasingly clear there's nothing in the brain's respective right/left hemispheres that can't function in either

day and by night, just as you vex theirs. Not everyone is meant to be together. However, I don't see that outcome with you and Julianne. With some conscious effort, it's possible your relationship could become exemplary.

'Astute as Eli and I may be in judging character, we haven't been assigned a crystal ball, and so we can only assess probabilities based on what we know, which isn't all that much. Souls are too complex to make definite predictions, so I suspect it will be rather entertaining to watch how things work out from the sidelines.'

'Obviously, we'd like to see you win Julianne for a long term loving relationship,' Eli said, 'rather than just another notch on your bedpost. That would be a shame – she deserves much better.

'Though secure within,' Mo said, 'she still needs to be treated with dignity and respect, just like any other woman. And though she may never harbour hard feelings towards you, your body could experience some hard feelings over some of your less circumspect remarks. What I mean, James; she's been training for her black belt.'

'That's interesting,' I said. 'I like the feisty types; makes for kinky bed partners.'

'Is that so?' he said.

We continued to talk about this most delightful young woman after deciding to take another hike along the summit ridge. Though I tried not to appear too obvious about my interest in Julianne, I had to admit, I was already enchanted with this intriguing young woman. Most peculiar, I thought; my body had met her, but I hadn't. Peculiar indeed!

I had to laugh at myself. Eli was right; I was envious of me, or at least of my body for all the attention it was receiving from her. Most ironic! Still, I told myself, not to get too worked up, at least not until I had the chance to do my own due diligence.

Much to my delight, I was assured by Mo that I would soon have the opportunity; soon I would meet my special nurse.

CHAPTER 11

LAMENT TO LOVE

Amare Et Sapere Vix Deo Conceditur:
Even a god finds it hard to love and be wise at the same time.[1]

For the rest of the day, I found my mind drifting towards this young woman; or was it my heart? Though we may never have met, I wondered if we ever bumped into each other on the street or in the Tube; perhaps even in some coffee shop, such as the one below me. That was possible if she lived not far from my flat, as Mo claimed, though I still wasn't sure how he would know that, unless it was from that mysterious source he had.

I couldn't help but happily imagine her attending to my body. I'm sure her intimate sponge baths would have been very pleasant, but likely not for her. It was rather humorous: all I had to do was lie there, mouth shut and eyes closed and her hands were all over me. Once again; another irony! Perhaps Eli was right; not trying to make an impression sometimes worked better.

But what if caring for my body was more than just a job to her, but a genuine desire to know me, mind and soul? With her being so

---

[1] From an ancient unknown Latin source.

curious about me, finding all she could from visitors, perhaps there was more going on than just physical attraction. What if this encounter also meant something else, perhaps having to do with destiny? But now could that be?

Unfortunately, I sometimes think too much and spoil the moment. Even as I delighted in these ironies, an old familiar dread began to grip me as I thought; would this fledgling romance, the one that had eluded me all my life, be denied me like all the others? With my penchant to sabotage meaningful relationships, I had a sinking feeling I'd find a way to blow this one too; most likely the very first chance I got. I always did; that seemed my fate, and I felt powerless to do anything about it. I asked; from whence came this venomous psychosis that so often beset me – some ancient curse? I had no idea, and that's what was so frustrating.

The more I thought about my failures in love, the more upset I became in not being able to understanding why that happened. All too often I would become unhappy with the women I lived with, yet I wasn't sure what caused me to become so easily provoked. Just as regrettable, I often became angry with myself. How would I ever be able to break this recurring default pattern if I didn't first understand what the bloody hell was wrong with me.

As humiliating as it may be, I knew I was coming to an important juncture in my life. I was finally recognizing I had to talk with someone. But I wasn't sure if I was yet willing to admit my problems were of my own making, even though I suspected they were. In the past, I assumed every altercation I had was more about them than me, and that my only fault was in allowing crazy women like them into my life. But whatever the cause, I knew something needed to happen before it was too late, where someday I'd end up old, bitter and chronically depressed. I could see it; sitting alone at night, feeling sorry for myself, while wallowed into old books of deep existential despair.[1]

After sulking most miserably through the night, by morning I was ready to confess how dysfunctional my life was with women, which, of course, my mountain priests already knew. In spite of Eli's antics, I had

---

[1] I thought of works by various Existential Philosophers, such as Jean-Paul Sartre. His book *Nausea*, (1938), for whatever profound philosophical merits it may have, brought me into a dark Weltschmerz.

com e to trust these other-worldly beings more than anyone else I knew back home. I realized that if I wanted to make a fresh start, I needed their help to exorcise these nasty, self-deprecating demons. Forever may they be cast into the *lake of fire*!

As if this was part of some larger choreography, the opportunity presented itself after they arrived in the morning without me even having to broach the topic. The sun was still rising as we sat down at the table to have tea and the Portuguese sweet bread Eli baked yesterday in the old woodstove oven. The stage was set when Mo said, 'So James, do you want to talk more about Julianne? – I think you do, so let's hear it.'

'Okay, I admit she's been on my mind quite a bit, especially all you had to say and the exceptional picture you painted of her. But you know; I'm probably not the man for her. She'd probably be better off with someone else because ...'

'-- the prospect of losing another relationship terrifies you,' Mo said, interrupting. 'That's ignominious fear, and it's not a good enough reason!

'I suppose you're right,' I said, 'but as I look at the world, it becomes rather obvious how elusive love can be there. Perhaps I'm not looking in the right places but I don't see a lot of functional partnerships. Where there is some evidence of happiness, they still don't seem to last for long. It's rather difficult not to become cynical when you realize how fickle relationships are, and how things will likely turn out. Especially for me! Sometimes I wonder why I even bother.

'Well, actually, we have a rather good idea why you bother,' Eli said.

'Of course, but there's got to be better ways to achieve the same ends. But since I don't know what they are, I don't wish to hurt this lovely young woman or myself with all the pain that's involved in these breakups.'

'Doesn't sound like a good place to be,' Eli said, 'where that's all you expect and what always seems to happen. Have you ever asked yourself why that is?'

'If I knew the answer to that, I'd stop doing whatever causes these vicious cycles that spiral me downwards into despair. I realize I must share in some of the blame, but not all of it. Sometimes I think my

241

biggest problem is not being selective enough, and so I keep allowing these wrong types into my life.'

'Quite possibly you're not the first that's done that,' Mo said. 'As the good bard observed, *the course of true love never did run smooth.*[1] So who are these wrong types that keep attracting themselves into your life?'

'I'm not sure: perhaps they're women who just want different things out of life than I want, and so I set myself up for failure.

'Could you give us an example?' Eli asked.

Sure, there are lots to choose from, but there's one that was particularly agonizing at the end – at least for me. For once, I was in love this time; I mean really in love. She was a bright young woman who just graduated with a commerce degree at another university in London. I was about to graduate with my doctorate and so was diligently searching for a lectureship to begin my career. At the time, my financial situation wasn't the best, not that it ever was.

'After a few months, I finally received an offer from a private undergraduate school in Glasgow. I almost accepted the position, even though I didn't care for the idea of moving so far from London where I would no longer be able to participate in my old philosophical milieu. Also, I had much bigger long term plans and expectations for my life, where I would be instructing and advising graduate students who were actually serious about their studies rather than just earning credits towards their degrees. Still, it was a place to start. The only thing that held me back was this young woman. She wasn't prepared to come with me, and I wasn't prepared to go without her. I really thought she was the one.'

'Ah, so is this where the young live-in girlfriend dumped you for the wealthy entrepreneur?' Eli asked.

'Is there anything you two don't already know about me? Why need I even say more, you already seem to know everything there is to know?'

'Not everything,' he said, 'only what we need to know, it's not as though we spent weeks and months reviewing your classified files stored in some dingy celestial attic; even if there is such a place in the sky. So please, carry on with your story.'

---

[1] William Shakespeare, *A Midsummer Night's Dream*, Act 1, Scene 2

'I'm still not sure why that should be necessary. But anyway, you're correct; even though I passed on the position for her sake, she had no problem passing on me – but not for my sake. As a commerce graduate, she was probably less than impressed with my financial situation, especially when I asked her to help pay for part of the monthly rent.

'As I said, money was tight for me, since I no longer had access to student loans or scholarships. But that didn't seem to matter to her; she wasn't prepared to help out, even though she had been living with me for close to a year. I don't know, maybe she thought she had already paid me enough in other ways – and perhaps she did, although I didn't see it that way. In spite of all this, I still believed we could make things work if only she would gave me more time to find a teaching position to get established, hopefully in or near London this time.

'Then one day I came home and she was gone – along with all her possessions and a few I thought were mine. Didn't even leave a note! I later found out some rich stiff had come along, even older than me, but had done exceptionally well as a partner in a development company that had offices in London and New York. Perhaps she considered his luxury flat near Canary Wharf to be more comfortable than my love nest over the coffee and deli shop. There was a time she thought it was charming, with its wall to wall books. Somehow, it must have lost its quaint appeal – as did I, most obviously.

So what was the girl to do? Of course she bolted -- for the good life and a flat with multi-million pound view! However, with her interest in business, rather than in philosophy, I'm not sure how long the relationship would have lasted anyway – nor do I particularly care anymore. So there it is; another sad vignette in my troubled love life.'

'Unfortunately, there will likely be even more unfortunate vignettes in your life,' Mo said, 'unless you're able to identify what lies at the bottom of your relational problems. Maybe there is more to it than you think. Perhaps it's not just about money, or the lack of it. If so; are you prepared to discuss this now?'

'What do I have to lose; except more of my wounded pride?'

'Then let's proceed,' he said. 'But first allow me first to give my perspective on intimate relationships between women and men. This time I need you to listen. Last time you didn't permit me to finish what I had to say on this subject.

'By all means,' I said, 'the mic's all yours.'

'The first thing you need to understand, James, is that love is the highest expression of who and what we are. This is because the Infinite Source is all that is. When you realize you are one with all that is, nothing can be more fulfilling. That's enlightenment! That's love! And so I say to you, never allow yourself to become disillusioned; don't give up on love no matter what disappointments you've experienced in the past.

'Always remember, love is the essence of what we are. Obviously the ego mind doesn't understand this, nor does it wish to. Yet it's divine love which unites the yin with the yang, without loss or compromise to identity, only completion in the other.[1] When essences intertwine and oscillate within the oneness, the yin becomes more yin and the yang becomes more yang. Where would the universe be without this union: the dynamic of creation? There would be no creation, since creation is love's eternal enactment!'

'That's splendid Mo,' I said, 'but it hardly rings true with my experiences. I'm sorry, but I've been jilted too many times to not be cynical about relationships. As I've already admitted, some of my problems may have had something to do with me, but it seemed the better I treated them, the less they respected me. And so I would react in anger, even if I didn't say anything.'

'So with that being the case, how well did you fare with your more militant feminist lovers? I understand from what you said, there was a love/hate thing going on between you and them.'

I love strong women, I said, 'perhaps because I love to subdue them, as in Shakespeare's *Taming of the Shrew*. Although, it's possible I may have overreacted at times when provoked. That doesn't make me

---

[1] According to traditional Chinese philosophy, Yin is the negative/passive/female principle in nature and Yang is the positive/active/male principle. Carl Jung termed these concepts as *anima*, being the female image in a man's psyche, and *animus* being the male image in a woman psyche. Together they form the complimentary whole.

a misogynist for telling them what they needed to hear. I just want a level playing field, is that asking for too much?'

'What did you say you thought they needed to hear?' Mo asked.

'Lots of things; but they would never listen; their minds were already made up. I made the point that if they called me misogynist it was because they were misandrists.[1] Not surprisingly, most women don't know what the word means, or that it even exists. In fact, many of them seem to think it's a joke, and then laugh. When's the last time you've heard a feminist use the word? I'm sure there are lots of more interesting things I could teach them, but I'm not that interested anymore, which is probably why they resent me.

'Did you ever compliment them,' he asked, 'even when you didn't always agree with their perspectives? Maybe they just wanted to be accepted for who they are and what they believe.'

'That's another thing,' I said, 'you must be very careful with your compliments, especially when it's about their body. They call it objectifying, I call it flattery. They can say whatever they wish about my body, I don't mind; so what's their problem?'

'The problem is you're no longer at a sea port on the Mediterranean,' Eli said, 'but in a politically sensitive culture.'

'You're certainly right about that. But aren't I doing them a favour so they need not take themselves so seriously? Too often humour is vastly underrated among these warriors. They really need to lighten up with all their demands and conditions.'

'But first ask yourself,' Mo said, 'whether the unconditional love you were demanding was even possible if your love remains just as conditional as theirs. I don't want to be too direct here, but isn't it true, your amorous life is more about scratching an erotic itch than anything else? Where's the unconditional love in that?'

I remained silent; Mo was nailing me hard again. I couldn't deny it: too often I was a player, finding in the end, I was the one played, and perhaps deservedly so.

'You've come to a point in your life,' he said, 'where you need to decide what is most important for you. We suggest next time you

---

[1] Misandrist or misandry means distain for men, the counter to misogynist or misogyny.

become romantically involved with someone, connect with her inner essence first, and not just her body, it's much less painful that way! Bodies don't attach for long, but essences sure do. For men on the earth plane, the outward form seems to be a necessary condition to love, but it can never be sufficient for a lasting relationship.'

'Perhaps, what you're both saying is true, but you must understand, it cuts both ways. Many women such as this young ex-roommate, seemed more interested in external appearances and trappings than, as you say, love's inner essence.

'I find this especially the case whenever I find myself getting too close to the less accessible, higher maintenance types. What seems to be of most interest to them is what I can provide them; which in my case, is never sufficient. I suspect it may have something to do with the bottom line on my tax form, such as it is. So if these women are so decidedly underwhelmed by what I have, rather than overwhelmed by what I am, that must make them as shallow as me when it comes to love.

'Your words, not mine,' Eli said.

'Well perhaps I should rephrase that; all I can say is that without a lot of money, there seems to be no loyalty or commitment. First chance that comes along, they're off with some big swinging dick with the luxury Jag, Rolex and an upwardly mobile career. Well fine, if that's all they're looking for they can have it. To hell with them; I don't need them. The only difference between us is that their exploitations are more crass and flagrant than the simple charms of love I desire. At least with me, there's no second guessing what I want. It may only last a night, but it's never at anyone's expense.'

'Yes, that much is clear on the outside,' said Eli, 'but how do you feel later? Is there a hidden cost; perhaps some other price you pay?'

'That's possible; I often ask myself why I feel so inadequate after they leave in the morning. In so many words, they seem to ask, *will you still respect me in the morning*? Sure, why not, and the next one too; but how about me? I could use a little respect in the morning as well; with or without a Ferrari. Is that too much to ask? Unfortunately, it seems being a good lover isn't enough these days.

'And I'm sure you are,' Mo said with a smirk, 'not that I actually need to know that. Let me ask you though; if outward appearances aren't sufficient to sustain love for either you or them, doesn't that tell you something? Possibly there's a lesson for you why these affairs never last for long. If, as you say, they're so externally superficial, don't these women have a right to what they want as much as you? If you didn't respect them for anything more than their sexual appeal; why should they respect you for anything more than your monetary appeal?'

'I'm not sure that's a fair question; I give a lot more than I take and they know it! And if you say they give me sex in exchange, then I guess we know what that makes them.'

'From what you seem to be saying,' Eli said, 'it appears they must think what they have to offer is more valuable than what you have to give, and so in the end no one is satisfied with these dubious transactions.'

'But you know,' Mo said, 'if you aren't cutting it with these less altruistic women; that may not necessarily be bad, because if you found these arrangements to be to your satisfaction, it would mean you had no interest in discovering the true essence of love. Many men don't care about this. But it's not a nuance, it's what's basic. It's what you were searching for when you felt drawn here to discover the *something more* that has been missing. I'm not saying you've found it yet, but I'm most confident you will.'

'So leave your mistakes in the past where they belong,' Eli said. 'In reality, they weren't mistakes at all, but *learning experiences*. In the end, they will help you move beyond to what's been holding you back in establishing meaningful relationships. As we keep saying, we learn by contrast, whereby we discover what we want by experiencing what we don't want. That's why you are now beginning to finally find what you want in life.'

'You mean Julianne?'

'Possibly, but that's for you and her to decide, not us. Perhaps there are still other women who can teach you what you need to know and experience. Didn't we say it's a large universe? It's your life and your freedom to do as you please, and with whom you please. No one is going to judge you, though you must bear the consequences of whatever actions are not of love, but of fear.

As you will soon become aware, love expresses itself in many ways, just as there are many words for these. It will be interesting to see how

247

your love life unfolds when you return to the earth plane. Perhaps Julianne will be involved in your drama, but life may also provide you with several other cliff hangers, each contributing to your personal growth.'

'While the sun remains shining brightly overhead, there're a few other cliff hangers I'd like to experience. Since venturing further towards Argentine, one hop at a time, I thought I may skip towards another range which, according to my topographical map is over the border.'

'Go ahead, maybe next time I'll join you,' Eli said. 'Your outward escapades reflect the freedom you are feeling from within. When you return, we'll see if we can view your love life from a higher vista.'

After returning from an exhilarating time on various peaks on the easterly range, I found my friends sitting outside on the deck with a half empty bottle of port. Eli took a big drag on his cigar and said, 'sit down matey and help us polish this bottle off. I hope you don't mind, but Mo and I were discussing your love affairs while you were on top of the world.

'We don't wish to make light of your past liaisons, as fanciful as some may have been, but you shouldn't feel guilty if you don't have all the answers to questions of love, because you likely never will. We clearly understand why many of these relationships have disappointed you and caused you great pain at times. So we're really on your side – as we're on theirs.

Relationships are too complex and deliciously unpredictable to completely know all the dynamics of what's going on. It's the glory of being a god in human form! Maybe you've heard the ancient saying, *Amare et Sapere Vix Deo Conceditur; even a god finds it hard to love and be wise at the same time*'?

'Good to know I'm in good company,' I said.

'As dysfunctional as some of your relationship may have felt at times, Eli said, they provided you with valuable lessons, helping you develop in ways that may not otherwise have been possible. Not just romantic relationships, but all personal interaction provides opportunities to learn and grow. Undoubtedly, you've had some conquests, some loses, some gains, some disasters and I'm sure; lots of thrills. But ask yourself, what have you learned and what have others learned from you.'

'Though we realize you may have suffered at times,' Mo said, 'have you ever considered all the women you've rejected, and how they must have felt? Is it possible some found you too intellectually aloof and emotionally detached to love? Please, don't feel defensive with these questions, we're not judging you, but you may wish to give some thought to this.'

'That may be rather excruciating to think about. My attitude is; when they're gone, they're gone, I don't even think about it after, it's less painful that way.'

Even though I was often uncomfortable with Mo and Eli's direct questions, I knew they were doing me a favour by cutting to the chase that I may clearly see things for what they were. I had neither spoken of these intimate personal affairs to anyone before, nor had anyone held a mirror before me to see myself in this way.

'We don't wish to be difficult,' Mo said. 'I realize these are painful questions, but you need to find a way to stay out of these swampy romances that keep sinking you. The truth is you aren't in the Lowlands anymore; you're above that, so you need to stop believing you have to fight your way out.

'I wish I could forget all the fights I got into. Not the brawling type like when I was a sailor. That was fun and easy back then,' I laughed. 'The next day everyone would be over it and we would be friends again. Great sport! With women, however, conflicts are never fun or easy. Even worse, they never seem to get over it, even when they pretend to!'

Well possibly it's because you're not that easy to get over, Mo said. But then, why wouldn't they feel resentment if they feel used and jilted.'

'Fair enough, but I'll be honest with you; sometimes I just want to get laid with no strings attached, then move on as quickly as possible before getting stung by the queen bee. But make no mistake; whenever I get attached, they all become queen bees. And then comes the inevitable sting, and I die another death!

'It's a vicious cycle in these swamps, but I can't seem to find my way out. Perhaps my problem is that I don't know how to read their minds, but how am I supposed to understand what they want if they won't tell me?'

'Did you ever ask?' Eli said, 'or did you assume they should be able to read your mind?'

Why bother, I'm not sure even they know what they want, other than what I want. As you say, we're only scratching each other's itch. But to be honest, it seems we all end up itching more by being involved in this sport. We're all trying to score – wherever, whenever and however we can. So I tell myself not to take these relationships so seriously; it's all in the game, right? But sometimes I wonder if it's worth it. There's got to be some other game that's less brutal; perhaps rugby or bullfighting.'

'But, Mo said, 'when you continued to, as you say, move on to the next and the next, were you not only moving on from body to body rather than soul to soul. How did you see them, as bodies or souls?'

'It depends on their body,' I smiled; 'with some it's not easy to see past their bodies.'

'I suppose not, Mo said, but if you had seen them as souls first and bodies second, perhaps things may have turned out differently. Did you ever think to ask any of them if they were prepared to travel on the same journey with you? Do you know if any of them were standing by your side when you gazed out your hovel's window, searching through the dark mists of the Lowlands? Maybe they too wanted to catch a vision of this elusive Mountain? Sorry to disillusion you, James, but possibly some of them were looking for something more than your body.'

He then paused, perhaps to give me some time to think more about what he said.

'That's a most provocative thought, Mo; I just assumed they just wanted from me what I wanted from them and nothing more.'

'That's too bad,' Mo continued, 'because now you'll never know. Is it possible some of them saw in you what you reflected in them, something more than just thrashing about in the sheets for a night or two? What if they were seeking the same Mountain as you, the *something more*, but not knowing which direction to look? But you didn't ask them, and so in the end they came to see you as you saw them, another toy; fun to play with until you're bored, or it gets broken.'

'Well, I guess it's as you say, we'll never know, and yet not all were just toys for me to play with. Some I wanted to connect with more deeply in ways that would last, it's just that I didn't know how. It was frustrating, but I could never understand why I was never able to satisfy the ones I cared for the most.'

'Is it because you were only able to love their bodies, not their souls,' he said, 'just as you could only offer your body, but not your soul. As Eli was saying, moving from body to body, but never to their souls.

'But I always thought it was they, not me, who didn't wish to connect.

'Possibly there's more to this than you realize,' he said. 'Is there something preventing you, not them, from establishing a lasting relationship?'

'And what would that be; what could possibly be holding me back?'

That's something you will have to find out for yourself. But let me ask you; in all honestly, is there something in you that fears their souls, even as you love their bodies?'

I had no answer to Mo's question; both provocative and unsettling. I suppose I could have said that's because they only were only bodies to me since the soul is just a metaphor. But I knew better now, and so that would just evade the question.

After a few moments, I got up and paced the floor, deep in thought. At last I said, 'I think you may have me there, Mo. I'm really not sure – possibly it's because I'm afraid to open myself to those who cause me to feel the most vulnerable? Those I cared for the most, I don't allow in very far. You know, I don't think I've ever admitted this to anyone before, especially myself. But still, I'm not sure why I would fear these relationships, there's little else in life I fear, not mountains, academic bullies or storms on the high seas.'

'It's true,' he said, 'you don't understand why you fear the women you love the most. At least your mind doesn't understand, but your heart knows. It's the secret you've been avoiding your whole life.'

'I'm sorry, but I don't have secrets; at least nothing I'm aware of that's of any importance. But let's say I did; would this secret be about something serious?'

'Yes James, very serious,' Mo said. 'There's more to your fears than you realize; so serious even we can't discuss this with you. But if you're prepared to listen carefully, I'll tell you what I can so you will be prepared to face it someday. Please hear me out because you're probably not going to like what I have to say.'

Mo certainly had my attention now. I sat down again, and braced myself for what he might have to say.

'What lies below at the root of your problems with women is an insidious fear that has long persisted and will continue until it is recognized and dealt with. The problem isn't your wonton licentiousness per se; this is only a distraction you unconsciously created for yourself over the years to prevent you from seeing what resides below. And you are right, James; you feel especially vulnerable towards women you wish to be closest to, because you know that if that happens, they may hurt you. Yet these fears are only manifestations of what lies much further below.'

'That's an interesting hypotheses, Mo, but I'm not convinced a nasty monster is lurking somewhere deep in my subterranean consciousness. That makes no sense, why would I fear what I most want; to love and be loved?'

'Then ask yourself what causes you to use women to shield yourself. What has been stalking you most of your life, that you deny? You may whatever you wish, a monster or a dragon, the kind that breathes fire when it gets angry. Until you are able to discover for yourself what it really is, we can't say or do anything that would help you. You would deny anything we may suggest, and in the end, it would be counter-productive.

'Okay, if you don't want to tell me what this is about, I can't make you, but at least give me a clue. You can't just set me up like this and then leave me flapping in the wind. Not exactly fair, is it?'

'All I can tell you, James,' he said, 'is that it has to do with a certain relationship in your life that didn't last for very long. Not nearly long enough.'

I was flummoxed. Which relationship; I've had so many. Should I be feeling guilty? I suspected there may be something to what Mo was saying, but had no idea what. Perhaps he was right, possibly there was something hidden and suppressed down so deeply I couldn't see or feel it anymore. If so, what could that be?

I looked at Eli, but there was no clue what this was about.

At last Mo spoke, 'as I said, this is something you will have to deal with at some point in your life. But not yet; you're not nearly prepared. But when you are, it will lunge out at you, and then you must confront it with all your courage. But take heart, when you see it, the answer will be presented to you. That's because the solution is contained in the problem. It always is, we promise!

'Then, once you have purged your soul of this fear, a time will come soon after one bright day when you will enter your new paradise with the woman you've always sought, but could never find.'

He then got up from his chair and said, 'it appears we need more wood. The fire's almost out and nothing's left in the bin outside. So why don't we all take a break and see what dry wood we can find below the tree line.'

Don't ask me how we were able to accomplish this task of gathering firewood, since I have no idea. It was a miracle! But then, wasn't everything I was experiencing in this realm a miracle even though they were all natural in this dimension. Perhaps that's what miracles are; things on the earth place that are caught up in a high frequency on the spectrum.

After all, that's what things are, energy patterns being acted on by other energy patterns. Higher patterns, planes, dimensions, octaves, vibrations; whatever term you wish, can influence lower energetic spheres but not the lower the higher. The miracle, then, is in accessing what naturally occurs in the higher sphere, while still being in the lower. If I were still able to teleport and manifest when I got back, as I do here, it would be considered a miracle, or magic, on the earth plane.

And yet, such an understanding remains unsatisfying, in that this would only provide a mechanistic explanation of effects, but not what lies at the cause of the effects, regardless of dimensions. Perhaps a real miracle would have more to do with a transformation in my personal life when I returned home.

In any case, there's wasn't much I understood about what was going here as we gathering our firewood. But I'm sure it must have had something to do with aligning the frequencies of various forms subsisting in lower dimensional octaves, such as with this wood.

By the time we returned it was already twilight. I expected they would soon be leaving, but once inside; Mo sat down and asked me a rather enigmatic question – which was not all that unusual for him. 'Tell me James, how do you think you were you able to win the war over your ego's determination to remain in the Lowlands? I'm sure it didn't wish to leave since it was a place you knew you would remain outwardly safe and secure, even though you were inwardly unhappy.'

The question caught me off guard. But considering how we had devoted much of the day earlier to analysing my past relationships, I suppose it was inevitable we'd have to broach the topic of the human ego sooner or later. I thought about it for a while, but didn't have an answer to his question, since I had never considered my life in the Lowlands as me being at war with my ego self. Although, I suspected it had much to do with frustrating and sabotaging my relationships.

After splitting a pile of logs outside, Eli joined us as he threw a few logs on the fire then sat down in his usual old lounge chair. 'While still outside, I heard Mo's question,' he said, 'so for what it's worth, let me offer my thoughts on this since you seem to be struggling for an answer.

'Go ahead,' I said, 'since I'm not sure what Mo's getting at.'

'Well,' he said, 'at its beginning, your dream seemed to indicate that it took years before you could break free of your ego's hold so you could leave the Lowlands, and even then, under considerable protest. But that's just how it is on earth; the ego prefers to keep everyone miserable in its land of mists, bogs, swamps, thorns, ruts, and noxious insects.

'In the end, however, you ignored its nattering, though it tried to fight you every inch of the way. Which is why you had so much slogging and trudging through the marshes just to find your way to the Mountain base. It seems your confused and divided mind kept searching for what couldn't be found while stuck in the Lowlands' bogs. At times you would frantically dash around in circles, creating even deeper ruts for both you and your lovers. And yet, your promiscuity did little to assuage these chronic fears of rejection which continued to haunt you.

'Then finally at the end of this stage, there was that peculiar sideshow of yours in the pub. That would be an example of how your delusionary ego-mind tried to distract you from your vision. But in creating such a spectacle, the incident strengthened your vision to *breathe the new air*, as you began to make plans for this expedition. And so it wasn't long after your dream that inauspicious night, you determined at last to abandon the ego's Lowlands.'

'*Breathe the new air*,' I said, 'where did I hear that phrase before? Was it you or Mo who said that?'

'It must have been some other sage,' Mo said with a chuckle, 'but I'm sure Eli's correct; your ego-mind was not appreciative of being forced to leave its familiar milieu behind. That's why it kept trying to undermine your noble quest with its incessant prattle about your life's failures, even as you continued to ascend above them. During your darkest nights in the storms, fear would sometimes grip you, making you wonder if you shouldn't turn back. Yet your heart remained determined, and so you didn't.'

'Isn't it remarkable, Eli said, how it took years on earth before you were able to begin your spiritual ascent. And then in the end, you still weren't able to make it to the Summit, at least not in your mortal form. Most ironic, I would say, how it became necessary for you to fall the rest of the way up!

'"Fall the rest of the way up;" is that what you meant to say?'

'It is;' he said, 'you had to fall a considerably ways down so you could join us up here. But at least you made it, even if that was a bit of a circuitous route. Now all you need to do is allow your heart to carry you even further in. As we keep saying, this is only a resting station for more adventures to higher Summits that will take you the distance further up.

I suppose your right; in a sense, I guess you could say I really did fall the whole way up to this jolly Summit. But what do you mean "let your heart take you the distance further up?" Further up to what?'

'To where you're going,' Mo said.

'And where's that?'

'Further down,' he said. 'You will be able to reach the highest Summits when you return to the earth plane. The Summit will probably look much higher from below, because it is, at least relative to the Lowlands' low altitude. But that doesn't mean things need be difficult for you to access the Summit. Since you've come this far, you will still be here while you are there. It's like you will have bi-located, with your heart here and your mind there, yet united in spirit.

'Even though you may find yourself dwelling on the Lowlands plane once again, you no will longer be *of* the Lowlands plane. There's a big distinction between the prepositions *of* and *on* when it comes to your new spiritual existence.'

'I'm not sure that was very helpful – or logical,' I said, 'but that aside, where specifically does this journey lead and where does it end?'

'Why must it ever end,' he replied? 'As long as you remain an adventurer, seeking something beyond what you have already experienced, the journey is never over, nor can it be. If it had an end, would that not be hell? Fear thwarts and paralyzes one from moving forward. Perhaps this is what perdition means: stagnation where, in one's darkness, the exit door remains hidden.

'Light can't be seen if you keep looking away in other directions. In reality, you don't need to know each twist and turn in the road ahead as long as you continue in faith to follow the light to where it leads you. It's always further in and further up. That's why we always say; wherever you are, follow the wisdom of your heart, and not just the intelligence of your mind. Only in wholeness are you able to discover new adventures your intellect could never have planned or anticipated.

When you left the Lowlands, your heart believed there was a Summit for you to ascend, though you had no empirical proof it existed. Little did you know back then, it would only be a new beginning, launching you upwards to new heights, even to the stars! Savour the journey, James! Though you may at times wish to rest along the way, as you take in the spectacular views, know the adventure is never over. There's nothing to regret and nothing to fear that it may end, because it never does.

'Unfortunately, many on the earth plane consider the body's death to be the end or, at best, an eternal ennui of religious tedium that if you had your druthers, you may prefer annihilation. But as you well know, that's simply not true. Wherever you are, is the starting position to wherever your soul wishes to continue on its merry journey. There are always more marvels for you to see and experience on the many roads of paradise. Believe us, wherever you decide to go will always be towards the highest and most noble adventure, at least until the next and the next.'

'Those are most inspiring words, Mo, but I doubt that's how I will experience my life when I return to the earth plane.'

'Well then, here's a quote for you,' he said, 'from a very special book Julianne has been studying: *for you know that when you return to the level ground from which you climbed, you will be different as a result of having made your ascent. The hard work is done. What you gain here you gain from what is beyond effort and learning --- what you have gained will never leave you but will sustain you for forever more.*[1]

'When she read that passage,' Eli said, 'she thought of you, although she still isn't sure how it applies to you. Perhaps one day, after you return to the *level ground* in London, you can explain it to her.'

'This quote must have come to you from your inside source, right?'

'Indeed it did,' he said. 'She even wrote it out so I could give it to you. Very, thoughtful, just like Julianne.'

Oh, so you're saying Julianne's interlocutor is a she?

'Most definitely; very much a she – in some ways, she even looks like Julianne.'

Before leaving the cabin that evening, Mo stood at the door and said, 'you need not be concerned, James. As the quote says, by the time you find your way back to your worldly problems, they will no longer seem like problems. There will be no reason for you to wallow in the guilt and fear of the past that so often had you stuck in the ruts of the Lowlands. But as I said, before you return, you must first find the dragon and confront it, so that at last it may be conquered. And when you do, the conflict will be no more.'

After they walked out the door and vanished into the cool darkness, I settled in again by the smouldering fire, contemplating all that had been discussed today. I noticed a copy of Homer's *Ulysses* on the hearth, apparently left there for me to read.[2] As I browsed through certain passages, fond memories returned to me from when I first read this epic while sailing through the Aegean many years ago as a merchant

---

[1] From *A Course of Love*, Mari Parron, Book 3, Chapter 11.

[2] The *Iliad* and *Ulysses* by Homer are considered the oldest extant literature in the Western world, dating back to the 8th century BC.

sailor. (I remember, after reading this, I was constantly watching for the beautiful sirens as we passed through the rocky islands).[1]

It was difficult, however, for me to concentrate for very long on the passages. I still couldn't stop thinking about the elusive dragon that may be lying in wait, ready to devour me. Would I be able to slay it, or would it slay me first?

As I thought about it, the more I felt I would never be able to hold on to Julianne. Before long, she'd leave me, just like the rest, provided I wasn't smart enough to pull out first. It was a game of pre-empting the other; a most insane game of fearing the fear of rejection. But maybe that's what these dragons of fear do. When you play with them, they breathe their fearful fire before eating you alive – until the next time.

The next morning, after my companions arrived, we sat on the deck with a fresh pot of rooibos tea, enjoying the sun and the wonders of nature's splendor.

'Isn't this jolly?' Eli said. 'Here you are James, having the best of both worlds, the wonders of earth's splendour along with the splendours of us. What more could you ask?'

I just looked at him blankly without saying anything. I wasn't in a good mood, especially for his humour. As if he didn't know what more I could ask. How about this woman I'd probably never be able to have?

'So, James,' asked Mo, 'what do you wish to discuss today? Are we finally finished talking about your wretched life on earth,' he laughed, 'so we may finally move on to more significant things in the universe.'

'Such as what?' I asked, with some irritation.

'Oh, I don't know,' he said, 'perhaps we could discuss the synchronistic spins of uncoupled electrons and why nothing on the earth plane is as it seems.'

'And perhaps that's the only certainty there is,' I said, where everyone and everything keeps changing. After a while, it all seems like life is one big illusion.

---

[1] Sirens were beautiful but dangerous creatures that Homer and other poets wrote of. Often they would lure sailors away with their enchanting voices, causing shipwreck on islands such as Anthemoessa.

'Much like what the mystics stated,' Eli said, 'and as Einstein inferred.'[1]

'Perhaps it would be best if we do spins and uncertainty another,' I said. 'I had a miserable night after we talked about that damned monster. I think you and Mo must have stirred something up that's bigger than me, so maybe you could try to settle it down for a while.'

'Obviously, it's getting ready to do battle with you, Mo said. That's why it's necessary for you to prepare yourself. Let me assure you, when you are strong enough to stand up to it, it will disappear. It has no defense in the light. As it's written, *perfect loves casts out fear.*[2] Light is love's expression and so once you become sufficiently enlightened, you will look upon it, not in fear, but in love. And when you do, it will be transmuted into love. Then you will see much differently all the women you thought you feared.'

'Including Julianne?' I asked.

'Especially Julianne,' Eli exclaimed. 'When this transformation occurs, you will no longer fear anyone's rejection. As you discover how to love and accept yourself, others will love and accept you for who you are, just as you have always in essence been. And then you will likewise accept everyone as they are, even those you may perceive as being enemies. This perception will change your world.

'Even before you arrived here, you were beginning to discover how differently things appeared. With the new vision, you had a new purpose. The more you listened to your heart, the more you sidestepped the muddy ruts as you raised your head to see past the obfuscating fog. And as you began to ascend the Mountain, life became exciting again, notwithstanding some setbacks scaling up the steeper precipices.'

'I suppose that's true; certainly one must occasionally look upwards when ascending, however, I'm more concerned I may fall back down into my old ruts when I return to my body.'

'But why would you want to go back to your old misery, Mo said, 'when you don't have to?'

'Perhaps I won't know any better.'

'It's most probable you won't,' he said, 'at least until your mind

---

[1] Eli earlier quoted Einstein as saying: *Reality is merely an illusion, albeit a very persistent one.*

[2] *There is no fear in love; but perfect love casteth out fear;* 1 John 4:18 (KJV)

catches up with your heart. Then it's possible everything will change for you, especially if Julianne is in the picture. But as we continue to say, without the heart's guidance, the mind remains confused. It may take some time before it relinquishes its control to the heart,

'And what if it doesn't?'

'That would be most unfortunate,' Mo said. 'It's your choice though; the mind won't abdicate its power to the heart until you will it to do so. Not that it should go into exile; the heart requires the mind as much as the mind needs the heart. Ultimately the mind is to serve the divine inner knowing of the heart, which in turn, serves the mind with its inspired guidance.

'That's why we remain confident things will work out, proved Julianne still remains in your life after your recovery. Remember what I quoted to you before from Virgil.

Yes, of course: *Omnia Vincit Amor: love conquers all!*

'And when this happens,' Eli said, 'you will be able to resume your inward ascent, even while you remain on the earth plane. And so, the Lowlands you lived in will no longer be as it had been for you. Gone will be the marshes, swamps, bogs and ruts because, in your heart and mind, you will remain standing on the Summit's solid terrain.

'That's not to say you won't continue to hold on to whatever gratification and prestige you believe you deserve in the Lowlands. But eventually, you will no longer consider these accruements worthy of your time or effort, especially once you recognize they were merely illusions that reflected who you thought you were. Yet these attachments will still serve to remind you what baggage you no longer wish to carry any further on your journey.'

'That's fine Eli, but if everything I've striven to achieve has served its purpose and the world has no more meaning, why would I even want to bother living on earth any longer? And what about the C-X75 Jag I've dreamed of owning some day?

If you truly desire and believe in this dream,' Eli said, 'it may come to you, and you will soon racing along on the Autobahn with all the Mercedes, Lamborghinis and Ferraris. But if you really wish to enjoy the ride, don't settle for just that. Remember you have been created and designed for much more than just fast cars and fast women.'

'But if it's not fast cars and fast women, then what purpose could life possible have? I'm not sure I even know,' I said jokingly.

Actually you do,' Mo said, 'or at least your divine Self knows. We know you're not serious – not entirely, but still it's a good question to ask because the mind needs to be reminded what we came here for when we incarnated on earth. Without the heart's true understanding, the mind soon forgets what's real by chasing after the false idols it creates. Even among the world's greatest philosophers, too few give much consideration to this question. Only those who have discovered how to unite their hearts with their minds truly know, because only they can know.'

I think you may be overstating that, I said. There are many scientists and business people who function in their minds are perhaps the wisest of all.'

'Yes, so it seems' Mo said, at least those with passion; scientists who love to discover and create new things by their research; entrepreneurs who love to create new wealth by discovering new goods and services for humanity. They didn't accomplish any of these tasks with only their minds; they did it by engaging their hearts with their minds, whether they realize it or not.

'Only the heart, which is the very soul and centre of one's being, knows what it truly desires to be happy. And though most think they know what they want, they really don't, they only know what their ego tells them, which is always a lie.'

'And yet I think everyone, including me, already realize we all just want to be happy,'

'Obviously everyone wants to be happy,' Mo said, 'but what the ego says is necessary for happiness is never the case. It's sad how few understand how to find it. What many assume will make them happy, is often what makes them most unhappy, since they look to the outside where it can't be found or experienced. Happiness is an inward quality, and so must first be experienced within the heart before it can be outwardly expressed and experienced.'

'Historically, though, the world's primary challenges have not been about happiness,' I said, 'but related to survival through securing food and shelter.'

'Which, at that time, he said, 'was sufficient for happiness.'

Obviously, this isn't sufficient for my happiness, my needs are a bit more, ah, *delicate*. But if you find me the right woman, I'd be very happy – for a while, I laughed.'

'But then,' Eli said, 'maybe there is no right woman for you; at least until you are right for a woman. Though you may consider women to be your biggest problem, many might say you are their biggest problem. When it comes to living side by side with humans, wherever they are on God's green earth, life's biggest challenges are found in relationships, just as they are also the greatest opportunity for humanity to grow in virtue and wisdom.'

'If so, then I should be a saint by now,' I said.

'Perhaps you should be, but you're not,' Mo said, 'although one day you may be if you are willing to go down that path. For now, it's more important you first recognize the cause of these problems. It's never about the conflict without; rather, it's the conflict within, just as it has always been for nations, tribes, and families.

'In fact, all conflicts are symptoms of inward fear and alienation. As we've said, that's the reason why so few know who they are. And as long as they don't care to know, they never will; especially when they listen only to voices that are equally lost and alienated within.'

'Whether they're lost, alienated or just alien,' I said, 'it seems I too may have heard a few of these extraneous voices on the way up here.'

'There are many voices we can choose to listen to,' Eli said, 'both within the head and without, but all that speak only of fear are delusionary. In this confusion, there remains only one Voice that speaks peace into the heart. The problem is; it can only be heard when the mind's fears are silenced. This is the divine Voice of the Spirit, audible only to the ears that wish to hear its message more than the voices of distraction.[1]

'That's why,' Mo said, 'it's so important that you discover your Self, as I keep saying. Though you may forget who you are, as is inevitable on the earth plane, still you will hear the Spirit's Voice quietly reminding you who you are.'

---

[1] This reminded me of the saying: *He that hath ears to hear, let them hear.* Mathew 11:15 (KJV)

'I can't say I remember hearing this Voice,' I said, 'although, I must say, I still haven't forgotten the sweet and enchanting voice when I first scaled up towards the Summit.

'Actually you've been hearing the Voice all your life,' Mo said, 'more than you know. It has come to you in many ways; some difficult, some pleasant, but most often through the lessons you've learned. As for the enchanting voice you thought you heard near the summit, just remember almost anything is possible in this spirit domain.

'It was almost seductive. Actually it was seductive. Possibly I only imagined the voice of a beautiful mountain nymph waiting up here for me. What do you think? Or maybe it was my special angel – should I have one. Doesn't matter, I'd love to hear her soft voice again, but I'd probably scare her off once she read my intentions.'

If you ever hope to see her, you'll need to attune yourself to her domain. But behave yourself; she could just as easily tune you out of her domain.'

'But what if she wants me to misbehave?'

'Then I guess that's for you to work out with her,' Mo said. But you may find she speaks only to your heart in a language of sublime impressions. Then one day, after you return, you may find she's by your side, speaking to you still.'

'That's a jolly thought,' I said. 'But perhaps we shouldn't get too carried away with the angel metaphor. I mean, isn't that what angels are, metaphors for all the perfect women that don't exist?'

'I suppose, if that's all they are to you,' Eli said. 'But then, I'm not sure how satisfying a metaphor is. Though you may be touched by a metaphor, still you can't touch it.

And yet, I said, even if angels should exist, I'm not so sure how touchable they might be.'

'But what if Julianne is your special angel, at least on earth?' Mo said. 'If you approach her respectfully, you may be able to touch her. Certainly she has touched you – possibly more than any woman.

'Now wouldn't that be a switch? I said, smiling. 'Rather than my special angel descending down to me from on high, I'd have to descend down to her! In which case, she may regard me as her special angel.'

After they left that evening, I continued to sit by the fire, as I considered all we talked about these last couple of days. Yes, there seemed to be promises of love, yet with the risk of these promises being broken. All this intensive discussion about love and relationships was making my mind weary, so I placed the empty bottle of rum on the floor, and climbed the stairs to my loft. Perhaps by morning, it would all be sorted out.

CHAPTER 12

LAMENT TO WORK

Whatsoever thy hand findeth to do, do it with all thy might[1]

Before I knew it, the sun was shining brightly through the loft window. Likely it was late morning by now, judging by its position in the sky. I wasn't sure if it had something to do with the bottom half of the contents of the bottle I consumed last night, but I had slept much longer than usual. More probably, my mind needed a little extra down time to process all the unresolved love issues that still festered in me.

Or, more delectably, perhaps one of my angels came by to visit me in my dreams; the one with the alluring voice. After all our talk about angels, I wondered if she might have whispered something I wanted to hear, thereby keeping me in bed for so long.

I went down to brew a pot of coffee just as they walked in through the door, bringing with them a variety of breads, cheeses and meats. A great way to start the day, I thought. After eating, we settled in by the fireplace to continue where we left off last evening.

---

[1] Ecclesiastes 9:10 (KJV)

'So James,' Mo said, 'how are you feeling about things today? Did you finally get over your past love affairs so that we may move on to other subjects with a little less drama, or are you still wallowing in past regrets?'

'Discussing these various situations was most helpful,' I said, 'but I'm not sure I can make all the painful memories go away that easily. It would be wonderful if that was all there was to my situation, but unfortunately, my personal challenges aren't limited to the women who've come into my life. So if you don't mind, please indulge me once more before we move on to other matters, as you say, of greater significance.'

'As you know,' Eli said, 'we're here to offer you our inerrant opinions. What you do with what we say is up to you.'

'Inerrant or not, I found what you both said yesterday to be most informative. I've never spoken so openly to anyone before about what's so personal. I must say, you and Mo have earned my deepest trust. In as much I'm able to make sense of otherworldly perspectives; I'm prepared to listen to whatever else you have to say.

'That's fine,' Mo said, 'you'll soon comprehend more of what we have to say as your conscious notches up to higher planes of spiritual understanding, and so I'm sure things will become more obvious to you the longer you're here. So tell us, what else is causing you grief besides the misunderstood women in your life?'

'Misunderstood at times, certainly, but just as often misunderstanding,' I said, 'but apart from that, there is still one other major life crises I struggle with. It's the difficulty I'm having in establishing a professional career; and because of that, sufficient income to have a respectable living. As I've already indicated, things didn't pan out as I anticipated in finding an acceptable professorial position in London.'

'But do you not lecture in one of the more prestigious institutions in Britain? I don't think many aspirants come this far in so little time. In fact, few students attain doctorate degrees this soon in their lives. And when they do, they often have to settle for less than what you've been offered.'

'That may be,' I said, 'but I'm not at all certain if I'll even have a career when I return. I may have achieved a modicum of respect in being associated with such an institution, but even after all the work and effort I've applied to get this far, I still find myself caught in a vocational impasse. It's most frustrating, but with all the budget cutbacks and the way the system works, it will likely be difficult to receive tenure in the foreseeable future. But I'm growing impatient, I need to keep moving along rather than standing in a queue to nowhere, waiting for someone on the faculty to retire or die.

'The fact is; all I have to show for myself after acquiring this very expensive education over eleven years is part-time employment with part-time pay. I'd be better off teaching in a secondary school somewhere in the hinterlands, for which I'm over-qualified. I even had to apply for a new credit card to make this trip, so now I'll be paying usurious interest rates each month since I have no savings, only debts.'

When I return, if I still have a job, I'm sure the administration will want to retain me as an instructor for as long as they can, which may be forever. That way they can play me off against the other instructors coming into the system who are competing for the same classroom time. Now and then they'll throw me a bone by sponsoring me to present a paper at some symposium.

So what can you do, what can you say, when there's no certainty at the end of each semester? Everything remains so tentative. All you can do is hope that at the beginning of each new semester, there will still be enough enrollment and courses in the curriculum to teach. You just don't have any way of knowing from semester to semester.'

'I sympathize,' Mo said, 'but I'm not so sure all that much has changed in the system over the years.'

'Even so,' I said, 'it seems we keep getting screwed over for more urgent and meaningful capital expenditures such as refurbishing the elegant executive administration offices in the East Wing. But I won't go into that now; I don't even wish to think about the money that's being squandered at the expense of more important items such as my livelihood.'

'So how did you get involved in this line of work,' asked Mo, 'since you seem to be less then enamored by its contingencies?'

'I love philosophy, but don't enjoy the politics; nor do I wish to be just another drone working for the institution. I need to be inspired -- like when I was a security escort for the Miss Nude pageant. The best job I ever had, even if it was just for a day!

But that aside, what most motivated to go the full distance with my studies, were a couple of exceptional instructors I had during my first years of studies. It wasn't exactly what you would call the *School of Athens,* but at times we may have come close to it with our many discussions over tea.[1]

Each exuded a seasoned charm and intellectual piquancy, without any specific bias other than towards the pursuit of truth. What impressed me most was their genuine appreciation for wisdom, rather than just knowledge. For me, this set them apart as true philosophers rather than just pontificators of ideas. Unlike many instructors I encountered, they didn't need to be right; only wishing to be open, incisive and fair in their analysis; which is why I considered them such ideal role models.

'Later, in my last year of undergraduate studies, I met another professor who also made a great impression on me, but for different reasons. He claimed to be from Portugal, but didn't look or sound particularly Portuguese, at least from what I remembered while docked at the Port of Lisbon. After I told him I had been a merchant sailor in the Mediterranean, he became very interested in knowing more about my experiences and where I had sailed. I found his insights into the history of sailing most remarkable, dating back to the earliest days of trans-Atlantic shipping. Apparently he had also done some sailing at one time, although he wouldn't say when, just that it was a very long time ago.

'Often we'd go to the local Ale House, and he'd tell me in great detail about Columbus' sailing adventures, including some of the infamous relations with the Caribbean natives. He also seemed to know a lot about Magellan and his ill- fated attempt to circumnavigate the world.

Many of these stories went into very vivid detail – perhaps too much so! I wasn't sure where he got his information, but at times I suspected he was making it up. Possibly he was just extrapolating certain facts

---

[1] In reference to Raphael's masterpiece fresco (1511) of the famous Greek philosophers of antiquity, with Plato and Aristotle most notable position in the centre.

to embellish his own interpretations, like some amateur historians are known to do while writing historic fiction.

'Though he was an instructor in physics, he was always probing me with philosophical questions it was difficult to coherently answer. Prior to meeting him, I was considering studies in theoretical physics but he talked me out of it and into philosophy. As it turned out, this was sage advice, since I was never particularly talented in mathematics. Perhaps he sensed the philosopher in me, something I had never even considered. In any case, he seemed to have a keen insight into life's affairs, including that of mine.

'It was uncanny how well I connected with him on so many levels, considering how young I was at the time and how little I knew about the real world. He often overwhelmed me with his broad knowledge on everything; or so it seemed back then. I also remember he had a peculiar nickname for me. Apparently, I reminded him of someone he once knew a long time ago. So whenever we met at the pub, he would call me Sebastian, or just *matey*. I also remember he never drank bitter, only rum; the dark Caribbean variety.

'After serving as an interim instructor for a short time, he suddenly and mysteriously disappeared. He didn't tell me he was leaving and no one in administration knew what happened to him; where he went or if he intended to return. He was a bit of a mystery to everyone; nothing about him was certain. I'm still not sure how he secured a lectureship position there; in fact, I'm not even sure if he even had the proper credentials to teach; not because he wasn't bright; in fact, he was brilliant – seemingly knowing way too much for a mortal!'

'Would you by chance happen to remember his name,' asked Mo.

'I don't recall his last name, just that it sounded Portuguese. Since we were friends, I just called him Miguel. Why, do you ask?'

Mo smiled and said; 'you never know, perhaps we'll be able to locate him someday.'

'I hope so. Sometimes I wonder if he didn't show up just for me, even for that short span of time. I know that may sound rather far-fetched, but he really did change the course of my life by inspiring me to pursue philosophy. For some time after, I saw everything in a much broader, universal light. A most fascinating character, I must say! So if you ever hear anything about him, please let me know; I'd love to be able to track him down someday.'

'And possibly you will,' Mo said, 'perhaps sooner than you think – if he doesn't track you down first.'

'So was there anyone else,' asked Eli, 'who helped illuminate your path while in your graduate studies?'

'Most certainly,' I said. 'While enrolled in my Master's degree programme at the University of Calgary in Canada, I was influenced by a highly regarded world class philosopher named Dr. Terrance Penelhum, who specialized in subjects as diverse as Hume, scepticism, religion and immortality.[1] With amazing clarity he was able to understand and delineate opposing positions and then posit cogent arguments for each side without compromising his own personal convictions.

Though he was retired as Professor Emeritus at the time I met him, I found his insights most helpful as my unofficial thesis adviser, offering me profound new perspectives into philosophy. When I return, I'd like to have a chat with him about my experiences here. The last I heard he was still writing, and even speaking, now well into this 90s.

It was about then, during my graduate studies, an overall shift in my awareness began to occur, albeit tentatively, as I slowly moved beyond narrow rationalism towards a broader, more inclusive understanding of reality, as with my old friend Miguel. Possibly this was because, as you say, I began to catch glimpses of my Mountain in a metamorphic parallel world.[2]

Coincidentally, this is where I also learned to climb the most challenging mountains in the Canadian Rockies, where I spent many weekends being inspired by the beauty and majesty there. This was a

---

[1] Terence Penelhum, Emeritus Professor was an internationally esteemed philosopher and prolific writer of scholarly books in philosophy and religion. In the early '70s he founded the Department of Religious Studies at the University of Calgary. After graduating from Oxford and Edinburgh, he accepted a professorial position at the University of Alberta in 1953. One of his recent books I found very intriguing was *The Paranormal, Miracles and David Hume* (2003). Also I thought his book *Survival and Disembodied Existence* published long before I was born, was also most profound.

[2] Perhaps, Ouspenky's term *Tertium Organum*, (third logic), would apply here as I briefly outlined earlier in chapter 7

turning point for me; my studies were now taking on new meaning, which I was eager to explore.

'After graduating with my Master's Degree, I was given a referral from Dr Penelhum that I be admitted to Edinburgh's doctoral programme in philosophy. Unfortunately, I ended up assigned to a thesis adviser who evinced very different qualities than what I was accustomed to. And so, for the next few years, things did not go well for me!

'His disdain towards those who didn't share his understanding, made him as intransigent as the 15th century Spanish Inquisitors who enforced the Roman church's theocratic dictums. He didn't wish to be challenged by subordinates, believing his philosophical precepts should be as self-evident to me as they were to him. I still wonder how I made it through that ordeal, considering the adversarial approach he took towards my thesis' presuppositions.

I couldn't help it; even though I was intellectually sceptical about many things George Berkeley wrote about, his off-beat Idealist arguments resonated with me. My Weltanschauung was rapidly shifting away from its old moorings, releasing me into uncharted territories that I didn't always understand.'

'I expect it must have been rather difficult for you to be on your own at this time, Eli said, especially when you weren't sure where this journey may lead you as you formulated your thesis.'

'Admittedly, it was rather confusing and stressful at times. I suppose, if you wish to use my dream allegory, you may say I was caught in the long transition between the Lowlands and the Mountain. My advisor wanted me to focus more on Hume's sceptical approach, along with Ayer's positivist repudiations towards all things spiritual. It seemed the more I progressed along my road less traveled, the more our relations deteriorated. At a certain point, I suspected I would be denied my doctorate if he were to remain involved as my adviser. And yet I wasn't prepared to compromise myself or back down.'

'From what I understand you're saying,' Mo said, 'perhaps by then you had become more interested in understanding the whole, rather than just analyzing the parts. In this regard, it may be assumed you were rapidly moving past the bogs, towards the Mountain base that would eventually lead to your ascent.

'I never thought about it in that way before, but certainly there was some rather nasty mud wrestling going on in the swamps over more than just nuances of philosophical discourse. Perhaps you're right; I may have already gone well beyond the borders of the Lowlands where he was not comfortable. In fact, things were getting personal, which is why we kept clashing over everything, including sports and politics. These weren't the old drunken brawls I once enjoyed at the seaports. Thought civilized, nevertheless they still were brawls and it wasn't certain who would win in the end — though it seemed certain neither of us would come out unscathed.

'It didn't help he was an ardent and militant atheist. Although I still considered myself an agnostic, I was becoming less sure about this all the time. Perhaps it was his antagonistic belligerence that drove me in the opposite direction. It was ironic, but as I studied Augustine and Aquinas, the more I found myself arguing for the very positions I once assailed.'

'On occasion, I would take a copy of Pascal's Pensées with me while riding on the bus or in the tube. For whatever reasons, I felt drawn towards this seminal Frenchman of the Renaissance, even though I didn't always agree or relate to his more religious discourses, yet I respected the clarity of his philosophical statements. At the very least, he helped give me a clearer vision to see beyond the Lowlands' murky fog. Whenever I contemplated the Pensées, I felt something stirring within me, something I had previously ignored or denied.

'At various times, when I had enough of my advisor's arrogant condescension, I would read a provocative selection I came across. It especially annoyed him when I would quote to him: *There is enough light for those who desire only to see, and enough darkness for those of a contrary disposition.*[1] Implying, of course, he was too in the dark to understand what Pascal and I could clearly see.'

'I can well imagine how these vignettes of wisdom would have helped your advisor see through his fog,' Mo said, facetiously.

'I'll admit; I was often cocky and presumptuous, as though I had all the light and he, in his obstinacy, had none. Obviously, we were on a collision course. He, with the academic steam roller coming at

---

[1] Pensées; Section 7

me, ready to flatten my world, and me standing on the road all alone, shooting him a bird. My clinched fists, pitted against his powerful machinery, mattered little, but when I got angry I didn't care; I was a scrapper and not one to back down. I guess that's still an issue with me at times.

'Are you still angry at him?' asked Mo.

'In retrospect, I think I would handle the conflict much differently now since I understand how things work in the system. Most probably, he thought he needed to rein me in to prevent me from falling into a black hole of solipsistic Idealism, as he perceived it. Had I given him the benefit of the doubt, I might have realized that his intentions weren't so bad. Still, I think he could have been less doctrinaire, while encouraging me to develop my own emerging views.'

'From what you're saying,' Mo said, 'it sounds like it was a rather lonely struggle being up against someone you needed to have onside to earn your degree.'

'It was, but things didn't begin this way when I began my scholarly sojourn. As an undergraduate, I fit in with everyone else, dismissing anything religious as superstition or spiritual nonsense. Everything in the universe was rather straightforward. Life is much easier when you're flowing along with the mainstream; you don't have to think that much when there's no one to oppose you.

At that point, it seemed I was destined to have a promising career, as I continued to earn scholarships, while making connections at conferences with influential scholars from across Britain, North America and Europe. I worked hard, although I found the course work to be relatively easy --- at least until I made it into the doctoral programme.'

Obviously, this was a time of deep intellectual frustration of me, as I became increasingly concerned about what to believe about ultimate reality. I wanted to break out of the old beliefs of the established mold, while coming up with new expansive concepts with my free thinking. In the end, this is what got me into trouble!

As you may guess by now, my thesis was rejected after giving my oral defense. Ostensibly, this was because I was insufficiently critical of what they regarded antiquated Idealism. I suspect I offended some of those on the reviewing committee for being too critical of Hume and some his harsher empirical perspectives, which I considered to be intellectually stifling. But that was just me – obviously, not them!

Certainly I didn't do myself any favours in bringing Berkeley into the argument to critique Hume. I thought since Hume came after Berkeley, it was only fair this time Berkeley have an opportunity to rebut Hume – through me; his willing provocateur.

'And so, that's how I arranged a segment of my thesis; a kind of a Socratic dialogue between Berkley and Hume. At one point, Berkeley reminded Hume, most cogently, of the logical necessity of an omniscient Presence to maintain the existence and order of the universe with divine, eternal perception. Such audacity – conjuring the Bishop to affront the committee's secular sensibilities!

'I thought it was rather humorous in places, especially where Hume broke his foot kicking a stone, while attempting to refute Berkeley.[1] Most clever, it seemed to me, but not so much the examining committee. Apparently, in serious scholarship, that's not how things are presented. I suppose I should have known better, but I couldn't resist having a little fun for the sake of my sullen adviser. In the process, I thought they may appreciate my bold and novel approach to scholarship.'

'So why where you such a big fan of Berkeley all of a sudden,' asked Eli, 'especially after being an agnostic most of your life?'

'Well, I'm not sure how much of Berkeley I actually embraced, but I was impressed with how he attempted to posit a uniquely logical explanation for how reality was unified, when everyone else settled for a fragmented universe. Rightly or wrongly, I challenged Hume's empiricism and sceptical enquiry as possibly having a disintegrative effect with its resultant plurality.

I may have overplayed my hand on that one, especially when I suggested his empiricism was precursory to the fragmentation that

---

[1] This was a parody of the following famous quote by Boswell's in his biography called *The Life of Samuel Johnson* (Book 3, published in 1791). *After we came out of the church, we stood talking for some time together of Bishop Berkeley's ingenious sophistry to prove the nonexistence of matter, and that everything in the universe is merely ideal. I observed, that though we are satisfied his doctrine is not true, it is impossible to refute it. I never shall forget the alacrity with which Johnson answered, striking his foot with mighty force against a large stone, till he rebounded from it — "I refute it thus.*

occurred in the twentieth century. The committee, with its political disposition, definitely didn't like that, preferring to blame Edinburgh's own Adam Smith and his *Wealth of the Nations*.[1]

I have a strange inclination to be contrarian at times, taking positions I don't always believe in myself, just to give the philosophical thought police a hard time. But in my oral defence, I was sincere about my thesis' veritable stand, believing to be self-evident, well prepared and presented. In my zeal, I attempted to find a credible approach to systematically unify reality into an integral whole. I thought I had the makings of a universal theory of how everything hung together.

'And for this,' Mo said, 'you had to do more time? – I'm not surprised!'

'Sure did; another year of bloody hell reworking my paper, which in my mind, already was an abiding achievement of innovative scholarship. But at least I got another kick at defending myself against these, what I considered; pompous sophists. In the end, they relented and accepted my defense, probably because I sufficiently compromised myself to give them what they thought they needed to hear. Possibly it was regarded as more "measured and balanced" as I heard someone say.

'I was also told there were a few phone calls from various scholars, encouraging them to consider the merits of my thesis. In any case, it was the biggest ordeal of my professional life, having to appease, assuage and mollify their insular *groupthink*.'

'Did you remain bitter about this after?' asked Mo.

'Does it sound it? Perhaps I still am, since I hate being pushed around and compromised. We used to have ways of dealing with bullies at sea. However, as I was just saying, I've mellowed a bit after acquiring some empathy as an instructor. In retrospect I don't think anyone harboured any personal ill will towards me. From what I can tell, most consider me a rather likeable chap, albeit a tad belligerent at times when the street fighter surfaces.

---

[1] *Wealth of Nations* was first published in 1776 in Scotland. One of the world's classics on economics, Adam Smith provided the intellectual foundation for free market economics. The book is also a social commentary. Interestingly, both philosophers were from Edinburgh. Hume died the same year Smith's book was published.

'To his credit, even my adviser told me not to take things personally; he only wanted to thicken my skin and sharpen my mind, though I'm not sure that was the case, knowing his aversion to all things transcendent. Most likely I agitated everyone's sensibilities with my lack of deference to their established orthodoxies. And with my supercilious attitude, I probably was too full of myself to handle things as well as I could have, for which I paid a price.'

'I think it's true,' Mo said, 'the challenges you encountered during this period were the early stages of your preparation to ascend your Mountain. Though you may not yet have heard an audible call, I suspect you felt something reverberating through the chambers of your soul. However, it may still have taken a number of years for you to begin your ascent after sloughing through the Lowland's marshes.'

'I like the way you put that Mo; it's almost poetic the way you construe the dream's metaphors.'

'To some extent, is it not true that we're all poets?' Eli said, 'even if we don't always perceive life nearly as poetically as we should. Perhaps one day, you too will become a poet and writer, employing rich imagery for what you remember seeing on this side. Simple descriptions won't be adequate when attempting to portray the significance of your experiences here.

'Thoughts that carry the greatest impact consist of impressions communicated by dynamic bundles of images, much as those perceived in your dreams. This is why we're always referring to its metaphors as being the ideal representations of your journey's outward experiences.'

'I don't mean to get too sidetracked to this topic,' Mo said, 'but it's also why poetry is the highest form of communication on earth, since its visual images express the inward richness in the heart, far beyond the ability of the cognitive processes. That's why Socrates once said *poets are the interpreters of the gods*. Whatever can be elicited by descriptive words will serve to convey the meaning of higher realities, since universal meanings are implicitly enfolded within these envisioned impressions. Higher thoughts often come to us in vivid images and symbols, evoking meanings hidden within the subliminal recesses of the soul.

'I'm not exactly sure what that was supposed to mean, Mo, but at least I understand how well epic poetry is able to communicate this exquisite imagery you speak of. Home certainly did this for me, even when I was an adolescent. Unfortunately, by the time I graduated with my doctorate; the romance of sailing the high seas was lost, as I struggled to understand things rationally, not poetically. I would arrange and then rearrange the universe until I was satisfied, but I never was for long. And then you two came along and toppled my apple cart.'

'We're always pleased to topple neat and tidy carts that misrepresent reality' Eli said. 'It matters little what fruits are displayed; if they're spoiled, they will cause the buyers' minds to become ill and delusionary. That's why carts need to be toppled sometimes. Not that we're vandals; we don't go around doing this for fun; well not always – except in your case. Perhaps when you return home, you will do the world a favour pushing over whatever carts of rotten fruit are stuck in the Lowland's muddy ruts. They are everywhere, especially where the surface is the most boggy and flat.'

'And how do you propose I get away with this anarchy? I'm not sure there are any university grants available for upending the established academic order.

Begin with the way Socrates did it, Eli said. No one can learn anything when they stop asking questions. Isn't that what children do and real philosophers are supposed to do when no one else will? Each new answer must lead to new questions and if it doesn't, the cart gets stuck in the mire of smug satisfaction, and soon hubris rot sets in to spoil everything.'

'But before we get too carried away with apple carts, Homer and poetry,' Mo said, 'I'd like to hear what happened to you after you graduated.'

'Certainly; so where was I? Oh yes; after finally earning my doctorate, I thought I would set the philosophical world ablaze with my brilliant philosophical innovations. It didn't take long, however, for reality to settle in when I discovered there were no institutions of higher learning ready to offer me a position, at least none worthy of my intellectual prowess.

Finally, about six months after returning from Edinburgh, I found a temporary position back in London. But it's been three years now, and I'm still stuck in this subpar situation with little promise of anything that would lead to a professorial career. I suppose, if necessary, I could find extra work during evenings and weekends with some part time bartending as I did as a student over ten years ago. And then what; get a job sailing with a contraband shipping outfit out of Crete? Now that's something to philosophize about!'

I should have stopped rambling on, but I carried on with my litany of grievances about the system, various administrators and obstinate faculty members along with all the useless committee meetings I was expected to attend.

During this time, Mo continued to glare at me without saying anything, making me feel more uncomfortable the longer I carried on. An empathetic nod of the head now and then, acknowledging the various injustices that had befallen me, would have been appreciated. I can't say he was actually glowering at me, but it sometimes felt that way.

Finally I got the message; even though I seemed to enjoy twisting in the pain of my woes and misery, I needed to find some resolution for what I had stirred up within myself. This would be a good time, I thought, to get away and recalibrated my attitude. Conveniently, it was time for my routine afternoon hike.

'Excuse me gentleman,' I said, 'but I need to get into the great outdoors for awhile. If you don't mind, I'd like to have a couple of pints of Pilsner when I get back.'

'We'll check in the cellar, Mo said, but before you go, I want to remind you that these various problems you speak of are only symptoms of the human condition. Even among the most accomplished, there is guilt and self-loathing, often off-set with hubris and cynical arrogance.'

'And what about me;' I said, 'are you saying I too have been complicit in this behaviour, albeit cloaked in some pretense of respectability?'

'Only to the extent you sometimes abdicate your higher vision to your base illusions. But why would you wish to give yourself over to the pain and misery the ego mind creates in order to sustain itself. It makes no sense. Yet it seems most everyone participates in this insanity, at least to some extent.

Like darkness, the separated mind becomes a phenomenon on to itself that has no true existence, only self-deceit. As with you sometimes, the ego often creates a persona of arrogance to hide its fear. It cares not for love, except to use it for its own advantage. Its biggest fear is unconditional love, which immediately vanquishes it; just as the presence of light instantly vanquishes darkness.

'When you understand the egos tactics are designed to pre-empt the guidance of the divine Self, you can see how humanity continues to undermine its well-being by identifying itself with failure and victimhood. After a while, it lashes out irrationally and becomes very seditious; which explains how Hitler built his Third Reich in Germany. After being defeated in World War 1, he capitalized on the collective resentment of the German's psyche. The Jews were a convenient target to hate because of, among other things, their astonishing success in most areas of life.'

'If you are aware of Russian philosopher, G.I. Gurdjieff, Eli said, you may appreciate what he meant when he said that the last thing humanity wishes to give up is their *suffering*.[1] This insane propensity inflicts upon itself the various *poor me* delusions it enjoys clinging to because of how real and special it makes the ego feel. After all, victimhood is familiar and even comfortable, in a sick sort of way, when problems are inevitably someone else's fault. It's obvious how right Gurdjieff was about all this. The ego is always finding creative ways to use its suffering once it's found how to leverage perceived misfortunes towards whatever payoffs and perks its able to solicit

'For many who wish to dwell upon their misery, there exists a perverse pleasure in being wretched. Some seem to think this makes them exceptional, even superior, especially if they can blame someone for their condition or neglect. At some point, should they become sufficiently hostile, they may organize into a collective of vengeful militants, demanding their perceived rights. As the anger continues to smoulder, guilt is assigned to those they wish to blame for their plights and alleged misfortunes.'

'This is not to discount the many injustices committed against the oppressed where revolution becomes inevitable,' Mo said, 'particularly where there is totalitarian oppression. However, throughout history many revolutionaries knew how to aggravate and exploit dissatisfaction against the existing orders, only to create greater oppression with

[1] See Gurdjieff, Appendix 'C'

totalitarian regimes. Russia was oppressed by its Czars, but nothing compared to the Bolshevists and their presumed liberators; Lenin and Stalin.

By fulminating resentment, tyrants strategically catapult themselves into power as leaders of the insurrection. History repeatedly shows how wars are festered after there's a sufficient aggregation of resentment, hate and envy. Unfortunately, much of humanity continues to writhe in this same bitterness, seeking a balm of vengeance that further agitates the inner pain and torment. Yet this outward discord is but a macrocosm of the inward discord caused by the tyranny of the humanities collective ego which, in its insanity, seeks to destroy its host.

As I headed to the door, I wondered if there wasn't some inimical tyrant within me seeking to destroy my relationships and career. Too much of my life was occupied with concerns that probably didn't count for much and yet I couldn't seem to let them go. So what was this that had taken over my life; my ego, karma or something else?

'When you return later this afternoon,' Mo said, 'we can continue this discussion as we examine the dynamics of free will and determinism. You may find that helpful.'

I left the cabin and made my way up to the summit ridge, wondering what he had in mind that may be so helpful. With all my griping and grumbling the last couple of days, I suspected this may turn into more of a lecture than a discussion about me needing to take more responsibility for my life's destiny. I wanted to believe I was free to do whatever I wished with my life – be it lecturing, bartending or sailing; nothing was in the cards or determined in the stars. Unless there was more to it; had the dye already been cast?

CHAPTER 13

NOT MY FIRST RODEO

Live so that thou mayest desire to live again –
that is thy duty - for in any case thou wilt live again![^1]

I walked against the brisk cold wind blowing across the Summit ridge. By now I had learned how to respond to whatever weather conditions I may encounter, in any way I chose. Generally I preferred to experience the elements as I normally would in my earthly body, yet without any discomfort. I noticed how the temperature had been cooling recently with the Southern Hemisphere now entering into the fall season. The dark foreboding clouds seemed to reflect the turbulence of my inner melancholy.

There was much for me to consider and reconsider. As strange and peculiar as life had become in this present state of existence, I was aware of the unique opportunity I had been given to begin my life anew. But would this be the first time I began? I remembered we had recently discussed the topic of reincarnation, which I always found to be problematic and confusing.

Eli assured me, saying, with a laugh, 'it's really not that difficult to

[^1]: Friedrich Nietzsche (1844-1900)

figure out, James, at least not according to playwright Henry Miller, who wrote, *sex is one of the nine reasons for reincarnation ... the other eight are unimportant.*[1]

'But apart from that important criterion,' he said, 'it's also easier to comprehend the nature of incarnating when it's understood the nature of consciousness is inherently divisible. Even though each soul becomes individuated in its own awareness, still it remains unconsciously connected to a greater whole, which in turn is part of a greater whole, all the way to the Source.[2]

'I'm not sure if you're serious or just playing with words,' I said, 'so give me an example, if you can.'

'Certainly,' he said. 'Consider certain ancient traditions speaking of a single soul incarnating as both male and female after splitting upon creation. Thereafter, each divided conscious entity seeks to become whole again, reuniting with its soul-mate, though few actually find their completion while on earth.

'Are you making this up, Eli?' I said. 'That's really straining the limits, even for you!'

'It may sound rather far out at first,' he said, and I can't say I believe such a split happens to one soul. But still there's a connection for procreation to exist on earth, something like in the myth of Eve being formed from the rib of Adam. This impulse to reunite may be understood as the basis for how sexual energy is derived, even though the specific mate may not be found for several millennia. At some point, however, each soul will have acquired the necessary experiences for an optimal union. When the two eventually find each other, they will be mutually enriched after reuniting as matured souls, now truly understanding the nature of love after its long absence.

'After this occurs, incarnation on earth serves no further purpose, unless they wish to add greater texture to the relationship with more tempering in a lower dimension, together or separately. However, at that stage, further advancement can generally be accomplished on the

---

[1] Quoted from Henry Millers' memoir; *Big Sur and the Oranges of Hieronymus Bosch,* (1957)

[2] After subsequently discussing the topic of Holons, this became much easier to understand.

spirit side without enduring these rigours, although it will seem to take much longer to progress.[1]

'But whatever else may be the benefits to the soul's incarnation on earth, be it once or several, most of our spiritual growth is provoked by those in our lives who give us the most grief, as we likewise reciprocate the favour by contributing to their misery. Life can seem tough sometimes, especially when we project our own unhappiness onto the other. And yet, through these ongoing experiences, we discover more about forgiveness, tolerance, patience, grace and understanding, than by any other means, as we advance towards greater fulfilment of our being.

'If we don't learn our lessons here on earth, we will need to incarnate for as often as it takes to get it right. As I'm sure you've read, many of the ancient Greek philosopher would speak of how we must all first drink from Lethe, the river of forgetfulness,[2] before incarnating so we may begin each life on earth without the baggage of previous lifetimes holding us back.' There are no deadlines for returning, it's up to us; freedom always prevails, even when we don't want to be free.'

'If this is true,' I said, 'my soul must have already had its fair share of trying to get it right, only to forget about it.'

'Well, who knows,' Mo said, 'perhaps this lifetime will be the one you get it right so you no longer need imbibe the waters of Lethe's banks again.'

'That may be optimistic,' I said with a laugh, as I left to go on another hike that I may think more about this and everything else we had been discussing. I wasn't so sure I'd be ready for my final ascent to wherever I was headed after my body's death, be it soon or after returning home. Though my life here on the Summit was blissful, there were times my mind would return to my less than blissful past, such as with these last few days.

For this reason, Mo kept encouraging me not to cling to the unpleasant memories, since what happened no longer existed. And yet,

---

[1] This is a fascinating and exotic topic which I will later explain more fully in subsequent narratives regarding what I discovered about the complementary nature of the sexes.

[2] Plato refers to this underworld river of oblivion in *The Myth of Er*, in Book X of *The Republic*

for some reason, I felt compelled to revisit whatever issues had troubled me throughout my life. Was it my old karma still haunting me that it may hold me back?

But what if I was able to break these old patterns by adapting the light and happy attitudes of my new friends? Nothing ever seemed to bother or upset them when they were being serious; not even me! If only I could have this same insouciance, possibly I would arrive back home just as carefree; all my problems would be gone because I would have no awareness of problems, only solutions.

Realistically though, my life probably wouldn't be much different or any easier than before I left. And so, once again, I'd be standing in line trying to elbow my way into a faculty position. When recognition and acclaim didn't materialize, I'd become cynical and dejected, just like when I was passed over by someone last year who was far less qualified than me. Perhaps what I needed was just a little sip from the Lethe River to start fresh.

I knew I had a choice, however. How many of the available teaching positions posted by scores of North American campuses had I even bothered to apply? None, since most seemed to be small community colleges I wasn't interested in, preferring to wait to be recruited by a world class university, befitting the world class philosopher I perceived myself to be. I didn't want just a job, but a career. After all, not many could do Kant like me; even fewer understood his *Critique of Pure Reason* as did I.

Besides, Eli was right, relative to the age of most professors, there was still a high probability I would have a fulfilling professorial career if I was prepared to wait it out. Or possibly, there would something else out there, even more fulfilling, allowing me to apply my philosophic skills without enduring all the bureaucratic nonsense. Unfortunately, at this time, there wasn't a big demand for *Philosopher Kings*.[1]

As I continued further along the ridge, I thought again of how Mo glared at me while I as venting my frustrations about my life on earth. Perhaps, in his inimitable way, he was saying the past had been my choice, not a fate determined by the gods and anyone else. But then,

---

[1] A concept Plato advocated in *The Republic*, whereby only wise philosophers would rule the people.

what about karma, wasn't one's life a consequence of past choices, both good and bad?

I realized not many care for the notion of karma, perhaps because it's too Eastern an idea for Western sensibilities, particularly among most in the Judeo-Christian religious traditions. And yet the Christian adage, *you reap what you sow*, sounded very much like what I understood karma to mean.

I couldn't say I believed in karma, but then, I couldn't say I didn't either; I really didn't know what to think since it had never been discussed in all the years of my education. I guess it all depends on what is intended when using the word. I just knew it wasn't considered the kind of concept a good agnostic should seriously entertain. Had anyone brought it up in the classroom, I would have treated it with jest or outright denial – that's generally how we handle whatever phenomenon we don't wish to discuss.

It's not that philosophers always need to have all the answers; we need only ask clever questions for others to answer so we may ask even more questions. Maybe that's why there are fortune tellers: to get answers to questions no one else wants to respond to, even if the answers may be considered ridiculous. But at least they have answers for everything, especially my love life.

I laughed to myself as I thought about my so-called fortune teller back home; the one I visited whenever I wanted to be amused. Probably, I amused her too. In a way, we had become rather improbable friends. I often admired how she always had an answer in her crystal ball, when so few in my department had any balls, including myself. Generally, though, I disregarded everything she said, except the women I slept with; which she said had to do with my past karmic debt.

I laughed to myself; perhaps she and I should form a special psychic/philosopher symbiosis and go into partnership. I would put questions to Socrates, Plato and Aristotle and she would channel their responses to me as I recorded and edited the transcripts, along with my comments. Then we could publish these sessions under such titles as, *Afterlife Afterthoughts* – a bestseller for sure, especially if I could get them to talk about sex! Especially Plato; what a laugh that would be! As they say; *nice work if you can get it.*

I stopped for a while and sat down on a stone as I recalled what a Buddhist friend of mine had to say about life after death. After living at an ashram in Tibet for several years, he returned to London firmly convinced of his new beliefs. He tried to get me to understand his enlightened views, but since I didn't believe in life after death at the time, he was wasting his time.

But I still remember him saying a few things that got my attention, perhaps more than I let on. 'How well you understand what goes on after death,' he said, 'depends on how well you understand the essence of the soul. There's much more to this than you think, since the soul is not limited to time and space. First you must appreciate incarnation isn't about the body, which is what everyone in the West seems to think. Rather the flesh body is but one representation of the over-soul, whereby other individuations of this soul may incarnate concurrently on earth or somewhere else.

'Think of the individual, he said, as being a tributary where part of the soul stream separates to go its own way and yet its essence remains intact with the stream, united as one where the whole is in the part and the part is in the whole. In this, identity is never compromised, but is vastly expanded.'

These were intriguing concepts, I thought; but not very credible – at least not to a sceptic like me who had no appreciation of what the soul was other than a metaphor for self-awareness!

How things had changed! Now here I was, in a spirit body, wondering about everything and if there may be a parallel for what he said in the dynamics of the *New Physics*. Anything seemed possible, considering how electrons constantly split, reformulate, exist at once in several places, respond instantly to the spin of its *doppelganger* split half, as if it's one, while seemingly separate. But then, if space is an illusion as we think of it, nothing would be separate, even though it appears that way.

Ah yes, the weird and wacky world wide web of quantum *superpositions*.[1] Who knows, perhaps the soul behaves like this too, seemingly an individuated

---

[1] The double slit experiment is briefly discussed in Book 2 Chapter 8. It was the first and perhaps most obvious demonstration of quantum superpositions. Various physics have argued this is an indicated of the role of consciousness in the collapse of the wave function.

unit of consciousness, and yet integrally entangled as a singularity in a soul-group, or whatever you wish to call it. If so, then all are one, enriched by the other's unique experiences and qualities, ultimately residing in God the transcending Source. Would such a supposition be too much of a quantum leap? – Maybe on the earth plane; but not here.

I remember Mo once suggested there is nothing in the subatomic world that isn't connected; all is a vibrant one in the vortex of the infinite void of all that is. The paradox is that the void isn't actually a void, since the infinite is enfolded in the *implicate order* as the un-manifested universe of *nothingness*. From this emerges the manifest, explicate order, which is perceived as the universe of everything.[1] And so it is with us, since we are all of one Source, essentially contained and unseen within the enfolded (implicate) universe as one, and yet expressed as many in the unfolded (explicate) universe of manifested experiences.

I really didn't understand what he was saying, and I still wasn't sure how much I comprehended. These were deep thoughts I was challenged with at Summit U. For one thing, I wasn't sure if I was ready for all the mystical implications of their interpretations, possibly because I was still trying to understand the nature of the soul with only my mind. And yet it no longer seemed such a ridiculous idea to believe we are souls that reincarnate in vessel forms – with my current vessel now docked in some hospital in London.

For those, who believe in reincarnation, such as my friend, I could understand why certain ideas about it may sound appealing. Especially so, if it's believed everything has been prearranged according to some higher cosmic plan that we hatch with others while dwelling on some higher spirit plane. But still I wondered; why would anyone want to come to earth, knowing what they may be in for.

Unless, of course, it's necessary for the soul's conatus to develop into what it is destined to become.[2]

---

[1] See selected quotes by physicist David Bohm regarding these notions in Appendix 'A'

[2] The concept of conatus means *to endeavour* in Latin. It has been used by philosophers throughout the ages with varying degrees of meaning. Descartes defined it as *an active power or tendency of bodies to move, expressing the power of God.* Bergson names this principle *élan vital, (vital impulse).*

It seemed to me, however, there must be a better way, considering how earth sometimes seems like hell. I remember suggesting to my Buddhist friend, somewhat cynically, that if this cycle of rebirth actually occurs, it must be some kind of hilarious set-up for the gods' amusement. If everything is prearranged for us to be born into certain families, communities and countries with various economic, social, religious and cultural conditions, then they should take some of the rap for when things go wrong, which happens to be most of time.

He said we all contrive our parts in this drama, along with all the other players in the script who, with us, enact their assigned roles.[1] To me that sounded much too deterministic. Why would I choose to participate in this theatre unless I was able to change the script before it was too late? Perhaps these were absurd questions to absurd notions. After we parted, I chose not to give more thought to such odd speculations – until now.

Mo and Eli frequently discussed incarnation in reference to the oscillating progression and regression of human history over the last few million years, not just since 10,000 BC. According to them, the spiritual dynamics of the soul's evolution, devolution and involution always exist in dimensional universes.

'Most who choose to incarnate on the physical plane of earth,' Mo said, 'come to evolve and expand the quality of their soul to a greater depth than what would be possible in the spirit dimension, where there are few if any resistances. At higher levels of awareness, the soul tends to be drawn mostly towards those circumstances and souls that add substance to its essence.

'But not all progress; often devolution results when the soul forgets why it came. That's why, throughout the ages, the earth involutes into new complexities of existence within the tension of the polarities of evolution and devolution. For these reasons, it's not for us to judge our lives as being good, bad, fortunate or unfortunate. If it's understood that eras and lifetimes are experienced to develop new facets of character and substance, or accomplish some other objective, then it's possible to

[1] Mo may have been alluding to Shakespeare's line from *As You like It: All the world's a stage, and all the men and woman merely players.*

make more sense why anyone would wish to live yet another lifetime on earth.

'Though often crude, gritty and unrefined, earth remains on the cutting edge since it's in an exquisite zone between light and darkness, reality and illusions. As a pearl forms as an irritant in the oyster's shell, this is how creation on earth emerges from the contrast of all that happens and is experienced. As William Blake once wrote; *without contraries there is no progress.*'[1]

I got up and continued my walk, still deep in thought, as I approached the high end of the summit. I've always had an excellent memory, but now it seemed photographic. I still amazed myself at how well I remembered what Eli and Mo said, even if I didn't understand it all.

In any case, if what Mo said was true, then it seemed karma should be understood as the process of progressing or regressing, rather than being a punishment or reward. Out of the consequences of past experiences, a new go forward plan emerges, providing for further development in accordance with what we intended before incarnating on earth. Perhaps I could think of myself as the pearl Mo referred to, living as an irritant in the oyster shell of my life where new thoughts, innovations and expanding desires formed to create and form something of value.

According to Mo, our earthly lifetimes are brief segments on the continuum of our existence that are meant to actualize the divinity within. Really, just flashes in the pan as we progress towards the Infinite Source. That's why difficult lifetimes may be understood as opportunities for overcoming whatever nasty stuff bogged us down in the past and whatever else that prevents us from making headway. If it seems we regress, it's only a matter of lifetimes until we move forward again in a time of no-time

Mo's confessed that while he was on earth, he was undecided on most of these questions. At times, I wondered how clear he was even now, since his answers often seemed ambiguous and puzzling, a bit like that of my Buddhist friend. He didn't seem to like the word reincarnation, preferring to speak of embodiment or bestowal, which probably meant something different to him than what I was able to understand.

---

[1] William Blake, English poet (1757-1827), *Marriage of Heaven and Hell.*

But then not much of this was that straightforward to me either, except I understood I was no longer in my biological body. Which would mean, if I were to return to my biological body, I would be reincarnating in a slightly used, (and abused body); quite literally. I wondered if I possessed a spirit body something like this one prior to coming into the physical dimension over thirty three years ago. If so, where did that body come from, and what did it, (I) look like? And how many have I had? Do they still exist, as latent thoughts conceived in the mind of God? These were just some of the concerns I had.

Obviously, I didn't understand that much; still needing much clarification on these enigmatic questions about personal existence. I wasn't sure though, if my companions wouldn't just end up creating more confusion in my mind since they seemed to enjoy stretching me far beyond my rational capacity.

As I continued to reflect on these matters, I made my way along the ridge back to the cabin. So much of what we had been discussing remained beyond the scope of my formal education, since for years now I dismissed all beliefs about immortality. There's lot's to dismiss when you're an agnostic. It's easier that way; you don't have to work through the issues, just deny what beliefs you don't understand and then feel superior towards those who need this crutch. At least that was my attitude as a sceptic during those days.

As I approached the cabin, I stopped for a moment and reflected on all I had been thinking about on this hike. Though there remained many unanswered questions, I knew there always would be since it's not possible to receive answers until one is capable of understanding them.

This time on the ridge, however, had helped bring more clarity into my life, whereby I resolved to no longer mire myself in the ruts of the Lowlands. I could remain jaundiced about my life's shortcomings, or I could become supremely grateful for what I had discovered in this body that I may begin anew. My choice, my destiny!

And yet, I suspected there was something holding me to the past. Was it karma – demanding I pay for some dreadful sin committed in this life, or past life, I had no way of remembering? Roman Catholics required penance for release, but I had no desire to buy my way out by purchasing their Indulgences.[1]

Enough questions, I thought; what I needed now were some real answers before I become more neurotic. I made my way down the slope to our charming abode, to hear what they had to say.

Eli must have known I would be coming down the summit ridge. Just as I stepped onto the cabin deck's old wooden planks, he handed me a bottle of Czech Pilsner, as requested. We sat down in the bright sun. Most of the clouds had blown towards the eastern horizon, just as my earlier gloom had blown over.

As I pushed back on my chair and put my feet up on the railings, I happily guzzled down the first beer, feeling very content. Whatever karma might mean, I still had the free will to think whatever thoughts I wished to entertain. Rather than feeling bad about my life not being perfect, I could just as easily focus on what was right. And at this time, there was much that felt right about my strange existence here.

But what might it be like once I returned home, I wondered; would it be business as usual, or would I be able to take this light and happy state of being with me, regardless of whatever problems still remained there? And if my physical body died, then none of that would matter anyway.

Finally Mo joined with us outside, carrying his tea. Were you able to clear your head by breathing in the new air?

'Yes,' Mo, 'I think I'm gradually becoming clearer about my existence here, but still have some questions about karma. If it's not just a mental construct or belief, how does it relate to free will and determinism? If you would, I'd like your opinion on how it all fits together.

'Before I give you my views on this,' Mo said, 'I'd first like to know what you think.'

'I really don't know what to think. It seems the karma concept, like predestination or fatalism, can be used to provide an easy rationalization

---

[1] The Catholic Church's sale of Indulgences was contrived to mitigate God's punishment for sins. It was abused in medieval times to extract payments from those fearing God's wrath after death. Reaction to this corruption gave rise to Martin Luther's Protestant Reformation, beginning in 1517.

for not taking responsibility for what happens in one's life. But on the other hand, it may explain why I've had these albatrosses hanging from my neck for so long.'[1]

'Since we've spent much of the last few days talking at length about your problems, tell me what you think is the biggest obstacle that prevents you from being where you wished to be in life?'

'Everything seems like such a struggle for me, even when it shouldn't be. I'm considered intelligent, with a very high IQ, yet nothing has come easy for most of my adult life, particularly with my relationships with women. It seems that when things are too easy, I find a way to make them more difficult, as if I need to raise the bar to prove something to myself. That's why I keep taking on the most difficult challenges I can find, be it women, scholarships, career or climbing impossible Mountains.'

'And yet,' Mo said, 'even after achieving what few others could have achieved, do you not still consider yourself a failure?'

'Often I do; but isn't that insane? Just because I haven't yet found the position and relationship I desire, doesn't explain why I'm always dwelling on my lack of success, rather than my accomplishments. Which is why I may sometimes come across as arrogant, perhaps compensating for my insecurities.

'Is it possibly,' Mo said, 'what you're experiencing in life is as it should be, not because it was predetermined, but because it is in accordance with your current state of evolved consciousness. What if your perceived failures aren't mistakes, or even bad karma, but opportunities you unwittingly created for yourself to discover what your soul needs to continue with its ascension?

'But why do I have to make life so difficult, as if I'm punishing myself? I can't think of any reason to do that, apart from the trouble I created as a boy while living in various foster homes.

'During our earthly years', Eli said, 'we often experience failure in love, finances, family, recognition, to name but a few of these disappointments. It's called life; precisely what we all come to earth

---

[1] Samuel Taylor Coleridge Taylor's metaphor found in *The Rime of the Ancient Mariner* (1798), meaning a burden to be carried in penance for some past misdeed.

to experience that we may experience contrast while making our way through the confusing field of illusions.

'But what if, no matter how hard you tried, things always turned out to be failures until the day your body died. And yet, all this time your failures were helping you discover your Self, a celestial being of divine resplendence. Would that be failure?'

'With your physical body now in the hospital,' Mo said, 'some would say you failed to make your ascent, and yet that's not true, you have been ascending towards something new and exciting far beyond the summit.

But I can hardly take that back with me. Other than receiving a splendid esoteric education at your unaccredited university, I'm not sure what I'm supposed to do with this "something new and exciting" when I return. I suppose I could join an ashram in Tibet like my friend or become a priest somewhere; but I'm not sure my heart would be in either. My desire is to be a philosopher, lecturing to the brightest minds in the world. And yet, the way things are going, my fear is that I will fail at this too.'

When I asked you what you thought was your biggest obstacle in life, you said it was struggle. And you were right, but it has only been a struggle because of what you just identified as the cause of all your struggles.'

'And what did I identify as the cause?'

Just listen to you James,' Mo said, 'you just said; "my fear is that I will fail." Don't you realize fear and failure is a vibratory match? You struggle because you fear failure. What has ruled your life has been fear; not love. That's why you can't experience a loving relationship in life, that's why can't have a good enough teaching position. If you can't love in relationships, can't love your work, then it's because you struggle in fear of failure

And so you must refuse to fear failure by learning to live your life from love. Only then can failure become your back door to success. In fact, more often than not, it's the only door to success.

'Lovingly embrace your perceived failures as opportunities to discover something new that will lead you to where you wish to go. Unless you live life from all angles you will never understand or

293

appreciate what success is, even when you are successful. It gives you the contrast you need to move *further in and further up*. You may not realize it, James, but that's how you made it up this Mountain.'

'I'm not sure I understand what you mean,' I said.

'Failing to cross the chasm is what brought you to this new Summit, your biggest achievement in life so far. Not to mention the other incident when you failed to make your descent, trapped and stranded on the west ridge. But this seeming failure is what gave Eli an opportunity to exhibit his agility in a way that prepared you to discover your own ability to teleport.'

'Which, of course, is how I came to discover I was a spirit existing as a spirit body!'

'Many are dying to find that out,' Eli said with a straight face. But you didn't have to, since you found another way.'

'This why,' Mo said, 'you should never consider anything you've done in your past to be a pointless failure, when in actuality, it's another approach towards achievement. For example, you failed to make it all the way up, and you failed to make it all the way down. Both were necessary for you to be where you couldn't have otherwise been.

Even the conditional relationships that seemed to have failed you at home, helped provide the contrast you needed to find the true unconditional love you seek. As we often say, in various ways, light can only be experienced as light because darkness has given light the necessary contrast required to experience its own illumination. Darkness has no reality unto itself, only the absence of light's reality. Likewise, fear has no reality unto itself, only the absence of love.'

'Ask yourself,' Eli said, 'how would you have even known you were successful unless you first experienced failure as the absence of success? Each seemingly wrong turn, or fall, in your case, can create new and meaningful vistas to view life. We would like you to keep this in mind when you return to pursue your future career and relationships. Remember, you will remain happiest when you call forth your heart's desires, rather than struggle with your mind's fears. That's when you become who you really are, because then you love you, when you're most aligned with the essence of your divine Self.'

'From now on,' Mo said, 'try to view these failures as opportunities to choose again! That's what free will is for: to choose again. Choose to love rather than fear. It's the most under-rated, under-valued and under-utilized gift humanity has, even though determinists would like to convince you that you're deluding yourself.'

'I've know many who take that position,' I said, 'but I've always wondered where the concept of freedom comes from if not from one's innate capacity to experience and feel it. And furthermore, why even bother trying to convince others against thinking they are free if they have no choice but to think they are free. To change someone's mind about this or anything else is a choice whether they wish to be convinced or not convinced. I've seen a lot of fancy dancing around these questions, but never have I witnessed a satisfactory answer. My department is full of determinists; I don't even try to argue with them anymore. What's the point; they're determined to prove their thoughts are determined!'

'I guess that's their choice,' Mo said, with a wry grin, 'freely and willingly determined. Word plays aside, there still is some truth to what determinists say in reference to those who remain asleep in their complacent state of consciousness, or should I say unconsciousness.

'When one forgets they have choice, they react as though they have no choice. But to react is not the same as to act. There is no freedom in reacting; only with intention can one truly act. Because everyone has the capacity to be intentional, everyone has the capacity to experience freedom by exercising their will.

'Without being aware of the Self's inherent freedom, it is easy to fall into a deep slumber and become a mere pawn to fears to life's circumstances. Regardless of what happens, you're neither a pawn nor a victim, even if it sometimes feels that way. Unless, of course, that's what you choose to believe. Even when the decisions you make don't go well, you're still free to *choose again*. When you choose to see things differently, to see through the eyes of love rather than the eyes of fear, nothing can remain the same, particularly when your inward vision is illuminated by the heart's divine light.'

'That's why there's nothing you've done in your life that should be considered a failure,' Eli said. 'Your setbacks are what made your inward discoveries possible. As we said, your failure to cross the chasm is what made it possible for you to cross over the great Chasm. It's what brought you to this Summit, allowing you to view life from the vista you sought as you left the Lowlands behind. You achieved what some would say was impossible. Some failure!

'Too bad I can't add that to my curriculum vitae, I said.

'Who says you can't; and while you're at it, don't forget to mention how you're able to ascend four or five mountain peaks, even before breakfast. What other man can do that?'

'When you put it that way,' I said, 'it would seem my karma is working out rather well.

'If karma is experiencing the consequences of who you are and what you've become, let me be the first to agree,' Mo said. 'Whatever we may call it, what is sow within, is reaped without. But what is reaped is not always known until the soul returns home. Should one incarnate on earth again, their character will be determined not by fate, but by what they chose to become. That's their karma!

So what have I become? What's my karma; have I made any progress since the last time I was in spirit?

Indeed you have, from the day you were born, Eli said. But the greatest progress was made you began to go within to see visions of the Mountain, although you were hardly aware of what you were doing. This was really a call to love. That's when you were being most true to yourself. As Shakespeare so wisely put it; *this above all: to thine own self be true. And it must follow, as the night the day, Thou canst not then be false to any man.*[1]

'Because you were true to these visions, you could not be false to yourself or anyone else. That's why you couldn't fail, even if the broken and battered body in London suggests you did. But you didn't fail it either,' he said with a grin, 'what other man's body gets more loving care from such a beautiful woman?'

'No offence to you or Mo, but that seems a very good reason to go back,' I said, smiling.

Indeed it is, Eli said, that you may learn to live life with love and not fear. But what if you could find love here? Anything is possible!

I didn't know how to respond to that, but we had already moved

---

[1] William Shakespeare; *Hamlet*, Act 2, Scene 2

on to several other topics as we continued to chat into the evening. Normally they departed much earlier, but they understood how important it was for them to help me sort out my life.

As they got up to leave for the night, I thanked them for being so gracious in hearing my lamentations these last few days. This really had gone on rather long.

'We are pleased to be of service,' Eli said, 'as we say, you only receive what you give. *Buenas noches, amigo. Mañana* is a new day, a day without end.'

As I climbed to my loft to rest my weary mind, I thought how, in all my adult years, I never had confidants I could trust more than these two. I was also grateful to be on this surreal adventure, learning about myself, even while my body remained comatose in a hospital half a world away – having its own special reasons to be grateful. I was beginning to think that my life was charmed, not because of past karma, but because of who I had become in the present.

Now that the Lowland's dark veil of fog and fears were lifting from my mind, I really had nothing to complain about. What I considered significant problems in my life, were now but residue from past illusions.

As I drifted off to sleep, I thought about how my life in this realm, at first so bewildering; had become my new world. And yet, I wondered at times if this too was but another episode I was still dreaming in my dream.

CHAPTER 14

A REALLY NEW REALITY

For you see, so many extraordinary things had happened lately,
that Alice began to think that there were very few things that were impossible.[1]

I don't always recall the precise order of certain discussions since they often arrive in quantum bundles, requiring me to connect the dots later. So please ignore whatever inconsistencies you may find; I've attempted to provide as much coherence to these strange narratives as possible.

Without me being aware of what happened after I returned, it took some time before I learned how to access my field of memories. Strangely, the whole continuum of occurrences presents itself at once, like viewing a long river from the sky. I then focus on a segment to recall and relive. Though I have a very precise imprint of what I

---

[1] Lewis Carroll, from *Alice's Adventures in Wonderland*, published in 1865.

experienced, still I struggle at times to arrange the proper sequence of events.[1]

Be that as it may, in this segment, I recall sitting outside around a fire outside on a cool and cloudy evening, presumable in fall, talking with my friends about how it's possible to make quantum leaps across dimensional boundaries. Occasionally I would poke at the embers smouldering in our campfire as I watch the flames flare momentarily while the coals glowed brightly in the dark. I could do this for hours while reflecting on whatever profound or frivolous thoughts may flitter through by my mind. For some reason, it seemed the most meaningful discussions often occurred around our fires, both inside and outside.

Though I didn't understand everything they tried to explain about this new reality; still I was eager to learn all I could since I knew I'd never be exposed to these teachings back home. This evening, however, my mind kept wandering back to my life at home and what it would be like there now.

Eli must have sensed my inward distraction; and so after throwing more wood on the fire, began to talk about us visiting my body in London. I was still conflicted about doing this, thinking it may be a little like identifying someone's corpse in a morgue. In all honesty, I was probably more curious about seeing my nurse who, they said, continued to care for my biological mass with her assiduous devotion.

At times I would think about her, yet remained concerned whether she would be my type, although I could hardly remember what that was – in fact, I may be open to most any type by now. In some ways, it kind of felt like I was being set up for a blind date, which for me, had never gone very well. I wondered if maybe they using her to bait me to

---

[1] Time can seem a bit wonky when apprehended outside the sidereal sphere of the Earth plane where we are generally restricted to our dense perceptions of physicality. Experiencing time outside of time is a very curious paradox which I can no longer comprehend. There are too many logical inconsistencies, at least from the limited conscious of the earth plane. Just try to imagine what the third dimension must look like from the perspective of the second dimension! How I came to recall all the precise events and discussions I've chronicled in this series will be disclosed in the fifth book.

go to the hospital so I would finally see my body to bring final closure to what happened.

I was still having some difficulty at this point reconciling my former beliefs with this new reality. Perhaps they just wanted to demonstrate to me that it was still alive, albeit marginally, so that I would realize there remained a possibility I may return to my former body and my former life.

More probably, though, they just wanted to make sure witnessing its presence would make an indelibly impression. Then, in the future, if I was back in this body, I would know for sure I was distinct from the body, the one I had so adamantly identified with as being me. Not having to face my body seemed the easiest way to avoid being proven wrong again, although I knew the truth about this. Old beliefs can be tenacious when so much pride is vested in being right.

Though I could teleport, I still didn't know how it was possible, even as I became more comfortable doing what I shouldn't be able to do. Generally, I put these questions out of my mind like many of us do with things we don't understand, such as how a little silicon and a few wires enable computers to do magical things, or how it is possible to instantly speak to someone across the world through the air waves with a small device that also plays games and movies while making bank transfers.

One more thing; I was apprehensive about teleporting half way around the world without knowing my precise destination; what if I got caught on the continuum of some space/time warp, if there's such a thing? Who knows, perhaps there really is a Bermuda type of triangle out here that can suck you into its dark vortex where you remain caught.

Perhaps I had read and watch too much science fiction of how things can go wrong when navigating through new dimensions of space. It seemed to be an occupational hazard. But little did I realize back then I would one day be caught in a zone that was stranger than science or fiction! Likely Eli was reading my mind again as I thought this.

'It's really not that much different James,' he said, 'than what you're already doing here. There's no degree of difficulty when teleporting in a spirit body. Whether twenty feet or twenty thousand miles, it's all the same, since it literally happens in no time. It is 100% safe; with no reported casualties! Obviously, there can't be, when your body is immortal spirit.

'Furthermore, you can never get stuck where you don't want to be, since your intentions are the only guidance system there is. There is nothing between you and where you want to be; no black holes, no vortexes; nothing! Just as when you first transported yourself to the big rock; you're here and then you're there in the same moment.'

'Just like magic,' I said. 'At least that's how it felt.'

'Except this magic, which only seems magical, is contained within natural law, operating on an alternative plane called quantum reality. When you understand this, the space/time continuum won't seem like such a big deal. Though teleporting across the world may seem amazing to you, it isn't that hard to understand when you realize everything is a form of conscious energy, including your body. Be it the density of physical mass or the lightness of your spirit body, it's all the same, only the expressions are different.

'Sure,' I said, 'that's jolly but I still can't understand how it's possible for the body to instantly be beamed, and then reformulated somewhere else, like some tawdry episode out of *Star Trek*. That may make for good fantasy, but it blatantly violates everything we understand about physics. For one thing, we realize things can't move faster than the speed of light. Just ask Einstein.'

'Well maybe we can arrange for that later,' Eli said, 'when you're more prepared to discuss advanced physics with him. Realize Einstein didn't know everything; in fact, he would tell you he still understands very little.'

I assumed Eli wasn't serious about meeting Einstein; that would be unbelievable, considering we were on Earth rather than in some celestial dwelling above the clouds. And yet weren't my friends also from some other domain? Actually I really wasn't sure where they were from since they never seemed interested in telling me, at least not yet.

'I realize,' Mo said, 'this maneuver may not make much sense if you see your body they way Western culture perceives it. Many Christians in the West still await a massive physical resurrection. However, it's not that way at all. In reality, everyone is a non-physical thought form conceived in the Mind of God, preserved for all eternity because God's thoughts never die. Although, it true, some sleep until they're ready to be awoken, as with you when you were taking a nap down in the ravine for a couple of weeks.'

'Just a thought form conceived in the Mind of God? I'm sure both of you would have hit it off well with Berkeley, but probably not so well with Darwin.'

'From our lofty perspective, Mo said, no one in the world has even come close to getting it all right, although some have it more right than wrong. But those who unite their minds with their hearts have a more adequate understanding of how thoughts can manifest as forms.

I've always been sceptical of interpreting reality as being about forms, particularly Plato's. Perhaps we can invite him to drop in for tea some afternoon to see if he's still big on his old teachings, as you both seem to be.'

'I suppose we could if he wasn't busy,' Eli said, 'but I understand he's training Husky dogs for snow sledding in Alaska. It was something he always wanted to do to enrich his character in ways his mind couldn't.'

I laughed. 'Right, of course he is, Eli. Mush!'

'Well to be truthful, he's not,' Eli said, 'but we know she is.'

'It just keeps getting better,' I said, laughing. 'I wonder what he calls herself – maybe someday I'll go to Alaska to look him/her up. Perhaps we would have an interesting chat about transgender issues from his/her exotic perspective.'

'James, my clever sceptic,' Eli said, 'you may soon find your new reality gets much stranger than Plato mushing her dogs through the snow. Get ready for a major paradigm shift that will change everything for you. Until you become expansive enough to allow for it, you will continue to remain confused about the ultimate nature of reality. Obviously, none of this was taught in your courses back home.'

'It's certainly a shame,' I said, still chuckling about Plato. 'I think this story may raise our enrollment about as fast as it would lower our credibility.

'But let me finish what I was last saying about God's thoughts,' Mo said. 'Note I didn't say we are *just* a thought in the Mind of God, as you suggested. No thought of God is just a thought. Every divine thought is of supreme importance, because everything is part of the whole, just as the whole is in every part; even you and me.

'In this sense, the essence of reality is based on what may be considered a *thought of God*, just as everything in our conscious awareness may be considered a thought. Can anything be conceived without a thought? Not really! In all infinity, nothing can exist other than that which is thought that's in relation to another. All proceeds from the one Source from which all thoughts are created and made manifest through relationships.'

'Which would indicate God must have created hell as well as heaven,' I said. 'So how do you reconcile that with a benevolent God?

'All of humanity,' he said, has the ability to think whatever thoughts they wish to think, which determines what is created on earth. That's why this information we are giving you is so very important. Hell would cease to exist on earth and in the lower spheres, when hellish thoughts are replaced with heavenly thoughts. But that's man's free choice, not God's! So what are you creating with your thoughts James?

Maybe we should talk more about Plato and his Huskies,' I laughed. 'Certainly, discussions about God's thoughts don't often occur among my colleagues at work.'

'You're right, they often don't,' Mo said, 'except in ridicule. But compare their attitude with what was said by someone more intelligent than all of them put together: *I want to know God's thoughts, the rest are details.* I'm not sure what context he intended that to be understood, but in any case, Einstein certainly had a way with words, not just numbers.'

With the flames having subsided to the occasional flicker, I was now thoroughly mesmerized by the hot glowing coals, as we all sat there in silence for some time. Finally I said, 'carry on with what you were talking about, Mo; I'm listening, even if I'm not always sure what to make of what you're saying. I understand Berkeley and even some of Einstein, but I'm not sure I always understand you.'

'Actually you do, Mo said, more than you realize. But to help you, visualize a ray of light proceeding down from God the Source. We may call this the *Ray of Creation*. This concept of an emanating ray or wave, is not well recognized or appreciated outside the esoteric traditions of the ancient Gnostics. Nevertheless, it has merits. Think of a beam of pure light emanating outwardly as it passes through various filters of lower dimensions; diffused and assimilated into each new atmospheric plane. The ray reaches down into the lower regions of the universes, but is never compromised; even when the recipients distort, twist and obfuscate its essence.

I think Thomas Aquinas said it most succinctly, said Eli: *all things are received according the nature of the recipient.*[1] Think of this in terms of each receptacle and recipient of the *Ray* that is animated in accordance with its evolving nature. In this is expressed an expansion of infinite variety. But here is always the possibility of significant devolution, such as occurred on earth when man chose to experience his life as a state of separation from the Source of his existence.

This is depicted in the Creation myth and illustrated in William Blake's poetry: falling from innocence to endure the hells of experience, then eventually regaining innocence in a state of higher consciousness. This outcome is only possible by going through the fires of experience. The states may be summarized as: *Innocence - Experience - Higher Innocence.* What this means, when applied to the Ray of Creation, is that the density encountered by the Ray is what causes the light to become increasingly less brilliant, once it leaves the Source of its effluence.'

'And so,' I said, 'what you are suggesting is that when humanity develops the capacity to receive more light, more light from the Ray of Creation will be retained on earth within the souls of its recipients.'

'Well stated,' Mo said, 'that is why reunion, or redemption, as some religions call it, is the constant story of humanity's sojourn on earth while being restored to wholeness from the illusory distortions of the ego's thought forms. By reuniting with our Self, or as Christian scripture calls it, the *Mind of Christ*, we return to the Source of our being.[2]

And in becoming whole, we transmute the twisted thoughts of hate to love, falsehoods to truth and darkness to light. It's not possible there could be anything outside of the divine thought that's not an illusion because a real thought can never leave its source. All else is varying degrees of insanity as evidenced in hell's disconnection and separation. But no matter what, we can never remain lost to God, only to ourselves,

---

[1] Thomas Aquinas, (1225-1274), Italian philosopher, theologian and priest with the Dominican order

[2] 1 Cor. 2:16 (KJV)

because we will always remain a thought in the Mind of God. It can't be otherwise, because God's love can't be otherwise. And in this, all are eventually reunited with their Self's Source.'[1]

After being an agnostic for several years, I wasn't accustomed to these concepts or language. I wasn't hostile to these ideas, just indifferent and so my reticence to discuss such ideas would have been evident at first. In these early days of my stay, I often pushed back towards a more familiar philosophical mind orientation that I was comfortable with. Perhaps that's why Mo suggested we defer our deeper spiritual discussions to a later time when I was more receptive to understanding more rarified concepts.

'There's no problem,' I said, 'I really don't have anything against God, should he, she or it, exist somewhere up there. However, these are rather lofty thoughts you're tossing about; perhaps a little too archaic for the 21st century. I think humanity has moved on to more immediate concerns that are addressed by science and the social sciences; such issues as sustainability, social justice and saving the planet.'

'Ah yes,' Mo said, 'with a hint of opprobrium in his voice, if the world wants responsible stewardship, there needs to be an examination of underlying motives rather than identified with the latest cause célèbre. Such activism may be well intended by some, never lasts when it too becomes associated with the faddish social conceits inspired by judgement, fear, anger, hubris and blame. All you need observe is what happens when idealism is trumped by a mindless mob imposing their agendas. Remember the Bolsheviks, Maoist and thousands of others? There's really not much that's new out there, just the old patterns morphing into new forms of dissent.

'So where are the real revolutionaries? Have they all been crucified or did they just get rich and powerful after the revolution? Throughout history, the world has been plagued with ideologies whose bitter fruits

---

[1] Obviously, Mo was a Universalist, once suggesting I read George MacDonald (1825-1905), who was a poet, author and minster in a time and place where Universalist notions were scarcely tolerated. Often his literature, in such books as *Lilith and Phantastes,* centered on how all would eventually go from darkness to light. *His writings inspired many authors, including: Lewis, Tolkien, Chesterton and Twain.*

eventually decay into the forgotten soils of time. When causes aren't rooted in humility, love and truth, they invariably lead humanity into cynicism, serfdom and ultimate destruction.

Be sure to keep your eyes on ideological movements that are based on deceit and watch how quickly the zealots descend into a strident frenzy demanding everyone think like them, particularly when they overcompensate for their doubts and what they know to be untrue'

I was going to change the topic about then, but it was obvious Mo wasn't about to stop until he got it all out.[1]

All human conflict is only symptomatic of a deeper problem more serious than most realize. It's the conflict within. As I'm sure you realize, relationships are most strained when souls become alienated. Humanity was created to exist as in the unity of God's Oneness, not for war as often happens when it sees itself as being separate from their neighbour.'

Conflict between the nations, tribes and families inevitably occurs when the mind and heart are separate. No one has a clue who or what they are, and for that matter, who anyone else is either. The mind acting on its own is always confused, resulting in a perpetual state of alienation within and without.'

'I can see where you are going with this,' I said. 'Marx thoroughly discussed the problem of alienation in *Das Kapital*.'[2]

'Indeed he did, but unfortunately he had no idea what he was talking about; he only understood external socio-political conditions, or what he called scientific materialism. In presuming to solve the world's problems with external economic solutions he only created disaster for much of the world.'

'I have a few Marxist friends who would beg to differ.'

'Then let them beg all they like. How many tens of millions of his victims were and still are forced to beg? A trip to North Korea and a few remaining regions in the world will soon demonstrate that. Until one understands what's within, they can't understand what's without.

---

[1] As it turned out, Mo had good reasons for having strong feelings on this topic that will be later be revealed in a subsequent narrative

[2] Published in German by Karl Marx in 1867; foundational to communist philosophy and economics.

Marx seemed to think he could cure what he regarded as alienation, by taking away everyone's freedom for their own good so they could be liberated into his socialist utopia. He sensed, however, the transition may be a bit messy for a while.'

'Unfortunately, on that he wasn't wrong,' Eli said. 'As things turned out, a bloody lot more messier; the worst humanity has ever endured, which he likely would have blamed on all the religious and imperialist *reactionaries* not seeing things as he did.'

'Do you suppose,' asked Mo, 'if he knew his ideology would result in over 150 million deaths, directly and indirectly, throughout the world in the 20th century he would have written what he did?'

'I'm not sure, I said; perhaps he would think it was a small price to pay for liberating the world from itself.'

'Or perhaps' he said, 'for the fame and respect he thought he may garner for himself among many of the revolutionaries and intellectuals in the world. What amazes me, even after all that happened last century, is the huge following his ideology continues to have. This would include many in China, Vietnam, North Korea, Cuba, Venezuela, and Russia; not to mention intellectuals throughout the free world on university campuses such as yours. I suspect however, there may be far less of a buy-in from the starving proletariat in Zimbabwe ruled by a Marxist tyrant.'[1]

I didn't say anything, but I remembered the graduate level course I took on Marx several years ago. The professor and most of the class fawned over this so called liberation ideology they insisted on calling scientific, although I doubt if many of the students read much of *Das Kapital*. I know I didn't, at least no more than what was required. Perhaps no one told them the failed revolution was over, at least in the free world.'

'But many say the problem wasn't the Marxist ideology' I said, 'but how the revolution was implemented and mismanaged.'

'Yes of course,' Mo said, with more than a tinge of sarcasm, 'mismanaged in every single region and country that befell its curse. And isn't it wonderful how all these self-styled intellectuals still think

---

[1] Robert Mugabe, President of Zimbabwe

they can make the revolution work; just give them your power and freedom and they will tweak the system.

'What this should demonstrate, most graphically, is you can't fix inward alienation by outward material force. The real revolution has to start from the heart or things become more disastrous. Fear alienates within and then separates; love unites and then brings wholeness. History illustrates this, as do the events of today. I keep saying; the alienated mind recognizes only the confusion of fear, which invariably leads what we've witnessed.'

'I think most intellectuals in my university's social sciences would say your perspective is imperialist and reactionary.'

'Then I say to them, consider the evidence of history and how bitter movements, in the end, always yield bitter fruits; loving movements yield fruits of love, joy and freedom. When activists presume the underlying social problems are not spiritual in nature, but material, they will demand their material problems be solved with material means and thereby make a much bigger mess.

'But then, this isn't surprising; how can they hope to solve their spiritual problems when they're convinced they're only material beings? They can't, but they never seem to learn, and they never will until such time they realize they are spirits that came into the world to temporarily manifest in what appears to be material form. When this is realized, they may apply spiritual means to resolve their spiritual problems, since the deepest longings always turn out to be spiritual in nature. Again: *as within, so without.*

It all started with Descartes, but not long after his arrival on our side, he recognized the folly of unwittingly creating a dual distinction between matter and spirit.'

'So are you telling me matter doesn't matter,' I asked?

'It only matters how you perceive matter,' Eli said. 'When we understood it to be something inert and apart from spirit, it leads to the illusion of separation. That is when humanity banishes itself from Eden. However, when matter is rightfully understood to be a physical vibratory manifestation of spirit, then spirit is rightly understood to be the substrate of all that is. Your spirit body appears to be material because it is; only existing in a higher vibratory state. Try to think of it as being part of a higher octave than what exists with your biological body. In that sense, both appear to be physical, even though both are essentially spiritual.'

'This sounds a little too Eastern for my Western sensibilities,' I said. 'That's something you may find in the *Bhagavad-Gita*!'

'Indeed you may,' Mo said, 'so let's take another less Eastern approach; an analogy from science. Think of the *solid* iceberg that sank the Titanic. In truth the ice was only crystallized hydrogen and oxygen atoms which were also invisible, vapour mist in the air at one time, without material form or substance. But notice what an invisible electromagnetic pattern can do to another electromagnetic pattern when its form is altered with some cold air. We call this physicality, and it sinks ships.

'Likewise, a thought in the mind of God, when perceived through the filter of our consciousness, crystallizes like ice, as an electromagnetic pattern of solidity. In fact, this is what we do, whenever we collapse the wave into what we believe are material particles.[1]

'So now, try to imagine matter as being patterns of crystallized thought forms we derive from our divine Source through the agency of our minds, which in turn, are derived from the divine Mind. Unfortunately, the world is in the habit of interpreting material manifestations as being inherently solid, independently *real* and separate. Anything suggested to the contrary, seems too ridiculous to consider from the earth plane's perception of reality.

'Fortunately, the *new physics* has now taken us beyond that illusion. Word is getting out, and at some point public opinion will catch up with what has been discovered, though probably not for a while yet since there is much resistance within science. There are still too many materialist prejudices in the scientific world that militate against humanity's spiritual enlightenment.'

'So what do you want me to do with this' I said. 'I'm still not sure I'm in total agreement with these extrapolations. Quantum mechanics is a relatively new discipline, so we shouldn't rush to conclusions where there is no consensus based on hard science.'

'Once you discover what this new dimension of reality means as

---

[1] I refer again to David Bohm's term *frozen light* as quoted in Chapter 8.

you experience it more,' Mo said, 'you will understand reality is not limited to earth plane's "hard science." You could even have a vital role in expediting this message to the misguided thinking of those who currently hold sway in much of the Flatland world. Unfortunately, they still influence the world to see itself not as it is, but as they see it.'

'You're sounding rather extreme, Mo; not all intellectuals are misguided, though a bit eccentric at times. Overall, I think objective reason keeps everyone on course.'

'Are you sure about that,' Mo said?

'No one's perfect,' I said, 'which is why we have peer reviews. It helps when there's a panel of informed experts who can verify and endorse whatever is being posited, or dismiss it as bogus, if necessary.'

'What if, Mo replied, these esteemed panels did nothing more than engage in more *group think[1]* to preserve the status quo of conventional thought? How long do you think any of their rationalizations would hold up before another peer review panel in fifty years, or in only five? Money, politics and progressive social trends wouldn't have anything to do with how truth is interpreted, would it? Or, perhaps, have everything to do with it?

'Don't get me wrong, though, I agree panels have a valid place provided they don't shut down opposing views, especially the ones that aren't currently in vogue. My point is these panels are not necessarily the repositories of truth they often present themselves to be. And so it is wise not to put too much confidence in their pronouncements, especially where dissent is not tolerated.

'It seems to me, I said, that you have some serious trust issues with the world's most respected institutions. Fine, that's your business, not mine. So don't ask me to sign up for whatever contrarian message you wish to proclaim to the world.'

'That's fine; we're not yet ready to sign you up for anything,' he said. 'You don't even know who you are yet. Nevertheless, it would be a shame if you didn't by the time you return. Ask yourself who could be in a better position to tell the world all it need to know; what they are and where they're going. Anyone who has the bullocks to ascend this mountain has what it takes to tell it straight up.'

---

[1] Another Orwellian term coined by George Orwell.

'I'm sure anyone who holds a mirror up to their face can see what they are. What they make of it is up to them, not me.'

'The message Mo speaks of,' Eli said, 'albeit a bit circuitously, is the *good news* of salvation for those lost from within, and to their world without. There are no ecclesiastical intermediaries to stand in the way. It's about the direct encounter with the numinous Presence that some call God the Father, or the Source of all.

'Many see no meaning or purpose in life. That's very depressing! Especially for them! That's why everyone needs to know how they are as immortal gods woven into the tapestry of life. Humans aren't the wretches they often think they are as lost fragments in a meaningless universe. Rather, all humanity is part of the infinite wholeness of all that is. So, James, are you willing to tell them this, or are you going to keep it a secret?'

'Depends; what's the pay?' I asked ingenuously, attempting to bring a little levity into this overly serious conversation.

'The job pays well, Mo said, infinitely more than money. How much more is up to you since you only receive what you give. If you give of your enlightenment you shall receive enlightenment tenfold – maybe even more if you do overtime.'

That's jolly and most splendid, but seems a little lacking in substance. I had something more material in mind since it really is a material world back there. I'm not sure being an emissary to enlightenment or anything of that nature is going to pay the rent.

'Lilies of the field, birds of the air, James, when you understand as they do, you are already rich,' Eli said.[1]

'And so this will be your mission' Mo said, 'to establish a new world order. But this time guns and swords won't be required since they were never very effective in overthrowing the old order of fear and alienation. Though it may take another two thousand years for the message to sink in, humanity will ultimately return to the knowledge of what they are, and have always been; immortal spirits – not lumps of biomass waiting to die.

'It's the greatest message you could offer those living out their lives, yet quivering in the shadows of death. After you return to the earth

---

[1] This was in reference to Matthew 6:26-33.

plane, there will be more than you can imagine who will want to hear of your experiences here.'

'But what if I don't wish to say anything?'

'Then fine,' said Mo. Do as you please; I've never believed you could do this.'

I was taken aback. 'Oh really,' I said, 'and why not?'

Because, I know you can! I don't have to believe it.'

'Oh,' I said, 'okay.' I wasn't expecting such a strong endorsement from Mo, especially after I opposed much of what he said today. It was also inspiring and affirming to hear him give his oration with such rousing conviction about the hope he had for this world.

His message was much different than what's found among in the intelligentsia back home. Existential angst and despair, in all its *Weltschmerz*, is still more fashionable than messages of divine hope such as Mo offered.[1] If I did what they wanted me to do, I'd look like a complete idiot, completely out of touch with the *realism* of their reality.

I took some time off from our discussions to relax in my loft, still thinking about Mo's rather unconventional views about life. But then, why not, everything else was unconventional about him, with Eli being no exception. One thing that was concerning me the most was how determined he seemed to have me champion his otherworldly perspectives after I returned. I could only imagine how well this would go over with the Tenure Selection Committee.

In fact, it was most audacious and extraordinary for him to have any such design on my future. Why should I risk my career to save the world from the mess it created for itself? This was about his vision, not mine! Besides, how could I possibly tell anyone about all the strange events occurring here to me, let alone convince my intellectually ossified

---

[1] Once again I refer to the works of Jean-Paul Sartre, (1905-1980), French Philosopher and writer who remains popular with many so consider themselves intellectuals. A sample of Sartre's philosophy is evinced in *Being and Nothingness* (1943); *L'homme Est une passion inutile,* (Man is a useless passion); *'Je suis condamné à être libre'*, (I am condemned to be free). In the past, I would identify with his philosophy during my darkest moments as I did at times with accompanying expressions of art.

colleagues about there being a spiritual reality that transcended the material world.

And then, as an afterthought, tell them how wrong they are about almost everything. A very tough sell, indeed! In fact, it was already hard enough for me to admit what I was experiencing here in this spiritual world, so how the hell would I be able to convince anyone else? The very notion was absurd.

But as I lay there, I thought, why not make something of this in a way that may be perceived as provocatively avant-garde, if only for my amusement. After all, I was already on the set of *Theatre of the Absurd*.[1] I started to think; what if I could write a satire about the strange incongruities I was encountering here. That made me smile; what a great idea!

With some imagination, I could create a modern version of *Through the Looking Glass*.[2] In it, I could hold up a looking glass to all my colleagues I would name *Tweedledee* and *Tweedledum*, to whom my existence here on this side would only be in the imagination of the *Red King*. But then how surprised they would be when they looked and saw that the mirror didn't reflect who they thought they were, but only spirit beings like me.

Obviously, if I did something like this, I would have to come up with a pseudonym to protect my identity. Perhaps Monsieur Cheshire, after Carroll's *Cheshire's Cat*, would be a very good name; where I could escape ridicule with a mischievous grin suspended in the air. After a short sleep, while thinking about this, I stepped down the loft's stairs roguishly, my imagination still caught up with where this satire could go. Perhaps I should become a writer someday; it may be amusing to think up lampoons like these.

I found my companions still waiting for me outside on the veranda.

---

[1] *Theatre of the Absurd* (*Le théâtre de l'absurde*) related to absurdist fiction plays written by various European playwrights in the 1950s, portraying existential themes regarding the meaning of life.

[2] Lewis Carroll; *Through the Looking Glass* (1871) was preceded by Alice's Adventures in Wonderland. References to the Red King, Cheshire Cat, Tweedledee and Tweedledum are among the characters in Carroll's writings.

But then, I could never be sure if they had truly waited for me, or if they somehow knew when to materialize back into my zone.

Taking a bottle of bitter Eli handed me, I said, 'I've been thinking; should I someday pick up this gauntlet of yours, what do you suppose would happen? I wouldn't have a career for very long, would I?'

'Who knows?' Mo said, 'maybe not in the way you think, but what if your career could become something far more interesting and illustrious than what you have now?'

'And what may that be?'

'The answer is obvious -- at least to us,' Eli said, 'you could become a writer and tell the world all you've learned about this side of existence.'

'Ah, you mean like a playwright?'

'That may be a good start,' he said, 'whatever you do, follow your heart's leading rather than heed your mind's fearful caution, since it never trusts the heart.'

'And through your writing,' said Eli, 'you may find your inner world will return you to your exquisite world of immaterial matter.'

'Now there's a delightful contradiction in terms,' I said laughingly, "immaterial matter," I think that may be very good immaterial matter for what I was just thinking about regarding *The Theatre of the Absurd*.

'It only seems a contradiction because some words, like matter, don't always mean what you think. Just wait till you travel to London with us, then you will understand how wonderfully disincarnate you are, without even having to compromise the incarnated experiences of the senses.'

'I'll never figure that one out,' I said. 'Everyone is aware sensations are registered by the body's neurological network, and then processed through the brain into our conscious awareness. But obviously, that doesn't seem to be the situation here where we have all seemingly lost our brains, if not our minds.'

'I don't mean to be disrespectful,' Mo said, 'because I realize how extensive your lectures on this topic have been in your Philosophy of Mind classes. You've even had neurologists come to your classes to give guest lectures about the material basis of the mind, so I'm sure you must consider yourself an expert. Yet all you've been able to come up with, like all good philosophers, are more perplexing questions about the nature of the brain.'

'May I remind you,' I said, 'it's only by asking appropriate questions, we learn.'

'Yes, he said, but questions are all you will ever end up with on this, if you don't have an adequate understanding of what the mind is. Along with most who study the mind, being rooted in Western dualism, you have believed the mind to be merely a phenomenon in the material brain, just as pain is a phenomenon of the nerves. However, since that's obviously not the case here, you will remain confused until you accept what should be evident to you by now.'

'Which is what?' I said, now feeling a little defensive. 'Certainly I consider myself an authority on this topic and don't appreciate being told I had an inadequate understanding of the mind.'

Ignoring my protestations, Mo continued, 'sensations are perceptions processed in the mind, which are not always linked to the neurological network. Isn't it interesting that even while on the earth, it can be demonstrated that the mind, even without external stimuli, has the means to experience neurological sensations. Ask anyone who's in a deep hypnotic trance experiencing sensations, or, perhaps more interestingly, those experiencing sensations in phantom limbs.'

'This is because consciousness is essentially a mental experience, not just an experience of the nerves. The body's brain and nervous system are adaptations of mental patterns for physical experiences, designed to function in the reality of the third dimension, which is often obstructed. As such, these sensory organs interface with the mind, but they are not mind.'

'So you're saying, around here nerves and brains are obsolete?'

'Not obsolete, because the earth gives a basis for the spirit plane's experiences. All planes are of one creation and therefore exist as layers of one ultimate reality. Although earth's physical plane flows out of the spiritual, there is a loop back from the material that can give substance to spiritual experiences on the spiritual plane.

"You mean like with sex?' I said, trying to be provocative.'

I would say that's a very good example, Mo said. It's why sex prevails in heaven for some and not for others, based entirely on one's experiential preferences while dwelling on the earth plane. And that's why, none of the intermediary organs adapted for the physical plane are required on the spirit plane, unless you decide there's some reason you want them, sex organs being one notable example! Love's essence always creates form around the desires of the heart's affections.

'But on the other hand, why would you want to give form to a liver when you don't need it? And yet, the physical body, as it is experienced on earth, influences the appearance of the spiritual body, according to the physical preferences the soul adopts while on earth. And yes, in case you were wondering, external manifestations of sexuality can be greatly influenced by what's considered sexually appealing on the earth plane.'

'That's an interesting theory, especially the sex part,' I said with a laugh. 'But then, why would the mind even bother to create the brain, when, according to you, the mind doesn't need a brain to operate?'

'That's because,' Eli said, 'the physical brain, in most cases, serves as a transducer to modulate spiritual consciousness for the physical plane's adaptation.

'What do you mean in most cases, I said, 'either it does, or it doesn't.'

Most interestingly, Mo said, there are rare cases, where surgery and CT scans reveal images, where individuals, some of superior genius intelligence, who were born without a brain. In fact, I did plenty of research on this while I living on earth, even interviewing several brain surgeons who had no explanation and were visibly annoyed that this should be possible.'[1]

'I'm not sure how you expect me to believe that. But then, what do I know? I still don't have an explanation for how I'm able to instantly teleport from one location to another, with or without a brain. I thought it was a mind trick of yours at first, but after a while, I could no longer rationalize the trick away.'

'But of course,' Mo said, 'there is no rationalization or better explanation than understanding teleporting as an experience of your mind. But it's no trick. As I suggested earlier, the body is a mental construct, although that doesn't make it any less experientially physical. It's easy to dematerialize and then rematerialize in another location

---

[1] Dr Bruce Greyson, Professor of Psychiatry, University of Virginia, discusses this and other related topics, in a lecture he gave in 2014, titled: Is *Consciousness Produced by the Brain?* A video of the talk may be viewed on YouTube under: *Does Consciousness Need a Brain?*

when it's understood that all materializations are constituted in the mind as mental events.'

'To manifest anything,' Eli said, 'all you need is the will's focused intent and not get concerned about how it happens because you wouldn't be capable of understanding. Let's just say it involves switching gears within the octave. So enjoy this materialized sausage that was intended, grilled, seasoned and especially prepared for you,' he smiled.

After taking the sausage he cooked, I placed it in a bun filled with Mo's special German sauerkraut. After one bit, I said, 'this sausage is the best I've ever had since Oktoberfest in Munich. In fact it's even better. Everything here seems to taste better than I can remember – including this ale,' as I took another swig. 'But I still don't understand why our senses are more acute in this realm without a sensory nervous system to communicate sensations?'

'Did Marconi require wires for his wireless radio sets to transmit sound?' asked Eli.[1] 'What a concept that was in the day! Suddenly sound could be carried and received through immaterial radio waves rather than through material wires. Impossible! At least so it seemed. We may think of the wires as analogous to the body's brain and nervous system: all considered indispensable – until it's found they're not.'

'But let's not take this analogy too far,' I said, 'it soon breaks down, as do most analogies.'

'That may be,' Eli said, 'but the bottom line is, everything you desire has a heightened sensation if this is how you wish to receive it. And so it must be, since consciousness has no wires or dense materiality to get in the way of what your soul wishes to experience.'

'I can think of something I may desire to experience with heightened sensations,' I said, 'provided it won't blow any of my fuses.'

'So I guess it's a good thing there are no fuses in your spirit body, should whatever opportunity you're thinking about present itself, or herself.

But it's not only here in this spirit domain that wires may be circumvented,' Mo said. 'You may not realize this, but everyone on the earth plane is capable of experiencing heightened neurological

---

[1] Guglielmo Marconi (1874 –1937) shared the Nobel Prize in Physics in 1909 for his work in the development of wireless radio transmission.

sensations outside their body. And there's no need to crash headlong down a Mountain to experience this phenomenon. Once again let me emphasize that consciousness does not originate on earth but emanates from Source where divine Spirit animates form into its unique existence. It can be rather fluid since it's the nature of Spirit; where no walls are erected to obstruct the Mind of God.

'Except for closed minds, but those walls are built by those who wish to remain imprisoned with the belief that the mind is confined to the body's brain. As a result of advanced cardiopulmonary resuscitation technology, this false belief is beginning evident, where more and more observe their bodies lying on their operating tables from the ceiling, even as they take leave. And then, many see it again when they return, just as their bodies are being revived.

Do you realize, Mo said, there are now over thirteen million reported cases of NDEs? Some of these include sceptics, who discovered how unconfined they felt while floating away. It makes it harder for them to dismiss the spirit realm when they recall all they observed going on in the room while being perched above their bodies.

'One need not be induced with drugs or fall into a coma to disengage from the body during deep delta wave sleep. These experiences, however, can easily be forgotten or distorted later on, especially after being processed by the mind's rational beliefs. That's why many disincarnate adventures are remembered as being nothing more than bizarre dream episodes.

'Among the willing, there are some who are able to experience out of body soul travel while remaining fully conscious in a theta brain wave state.[1] However, we don't recommend this for anyone who is not divinely shielded from whatever lesser astral forms may attempt to encroach upon the bodies of susceptible souls.'

'There may even be times,' Eli said, 'when you think you're living such a dream here with us. But if this is merely a dream you're experiencing, it's a damned good one, no less real than the dream you've dreamed on earth for over the last thirty three years.'

---

[1] Theta waves occur while in a trance or lucid conscious dreaming with electroencephalogram (EEG) readings of 3-6 Hz. Delta waves record 1-2 Hz occur in sleep and unconsciousness.

'A most provocative thought,' I said, 'but how would I know which life was only a dream?'

'Well, let me ask,' Mo said, 'if we're going to compare dreams, where does life feels the most real; where there's pain or where's there's pleasure? Where do you feel most alive? By the way, have you ever tasted such a good sausage?'

'Not since the last one Eli grilled,' I said. 'But in this domain he shouldn't be taking any credit for this.'

'Really?' Eli said; 'and all this time I thought it was about my culinary acumen.'

'In spite of Eli's self-congratulatory assessment,' Mo said, 'I'm sure we can give him some credit. Don't you like his selection of seasoning and how he over-cooked your sausage to perfection?'

'Very much, I take it all back; Eli you're a great short order chef. But let me get back to your previous question. It's ironic, but as I continue to dwell here, things seem to become more substantial, with an exquisite richness than I've ever before experienced, including Eli's sausages, they keep getting better too.

'They haven't changed,' Mo said, 'even Eli's sausages are the same, but you have – in as much as you allowed your inward capacity to appreciate whatever is there to perceive. Though Berkeley may have said, *to be is to be perceived*; perhaps we may also say, *to perceive is to be*, especially when you get good at it.

Another provocative thought, keep them coming; I'll try to remember them when I return to teach. So if I had to choose which dream to live, it's becoming most apparent I'd prefer this heightened state of sensation, compared to my drab daily life on the earth plane. I can hardly imagine what it would feel like to be here with a woman that I loved, especially with the sensory enhancements you were just referring to. No offense intended – both of you chaps are very fine companions, but only in the absence of someone fairer.'

'And perhaps', said Eli, 'one day, possibly even before you return, you will find how all sensations, and I mean all sensations, are perceived in a more rarified state of receptivity in the spirit body.

This is also why our wines taste so exquisitely delicious,' Mo said, 'even without us having a fruit orchard or wood casks to ferment the grapes. We know a few things about good wine and so our wine cellar is evidence of our discrimination. So it would be a shame if you didn't have the capacity to appreciate this; as you say "delicate solera bouquet."

'In fact, the longer you live in the spirit body, he said, the more sensitized you may become to this superb plane of existence, if you so choose. Once your soul begins to attune to all its hidden spiritual aptitudes, you'll think you're in heaven because by then, you probably are,' he chuckled. 'Life is never stale but forever joyful, expanding as we expand, allowing us to create as we were created.'

'Let me make the point once again,' Eli said, 'none of this diminishes the importance of existence on earth, whether you consider it a happy or unhappy dream. This is why, as we recently discussed, many return to incarnate of earth again to have more opportunities for spiritual growth. And so that's another reason why this lower plane of existence is not to be negated or dismissed. Contextualize your life as a holon, that's continually being transcended with new facets of exquisite character that are subsumed into new holons of expansive reality.'

'Holon; what's a holon?' I asked. I don't remember anyone at university ever speaking of holons in the past.'

'And they likely won't in the future either,' he said. 'But we'll get into that more later on; for now, just think of it as a conceptual device to better understand the dynamic relationship of the part to its whole. It is how all intonations of earthly experiences enrich your life in the higher dimensions.

'It's also why Eli and I can still enjoy our time here with you on earth, even while remaining in a higher vibratory plane of existence. Higher spiritual octaves are able to include the lower earth plane octaves without compromising their transcendence. Higher always includes the lower, even as it transcends it. This is how Jesus, after his resurrection, was able to eat fish with the disciples in his spirit body. And how you too, even in your spirit body, are able enjoy all the earthly delights we have provided you on this Summit.'

'Jolly,' I said, 'but in lieu of the fish, I think I'd prefer another one of Eli's culinary delights though, if you don't mind, not quite as well grilled on the outside this time. They're very good, though a tad spicy for a Brit; wouldn't you say? Or is that how they prefer them in your locality? Perhaps I can drop in sometime to see how you do things there.'

'One day, I'm sure you will,' said Eli, 'but till then you'll have to be content with your Munich sausages on earth.'

'Seriously though,' Mo said, 'while your physical body remains alive, it's not possible for you to enter our realm. However, if your body doesn't recover in London, then you will advance towards our neighbourhood, far beyond what you are experiencing in this in-between zone. Whenever the time is right, you will depart Earth and spiral your way up to higher spheres where you will most belong. Yet you won't be alone, you will be among those you are most bonded with in your common affections and consciousness.'

'Anyone I know?'

'If you are lucky, maybe us,' said Eli, smiling, 'and all those for whom you have the deepest affections in this life and those prior. Your closest affinities will be towards those who occupy the same domain of consciousness as you. You may be surprised how many of these relationships you've accumulated over the ages; it seems you're a rather popular bloke.

As may be expected, you are always closest to those with whom you've been the most intimate; the ones you most wish to be with. This would be like you standing at the centre of concentric rings, and everyone else is spread out around you in proximity to your affections, just as you would have it on earth, but seldom do.'

'As pleasant a thought as this may be,' Mo said, 'it would be a shame for you to leave the Earth when there remains so much for you to accomplish. Though we wish you could stay with us indefinitely, your stay in this realm of existence is only a time of reorientation; a time whereby you may prepare yourself for your new earthly mission – should you choose to take up the cause, I might add.'

'I'm glad you're still saying I may actually have a choice with what I do in my life,' I said, perhaps with a little more acerbity than I intended. 'Good to know it's not just part of someone's agenda.'

'Of course, everyone's destiny is their choice,' Mo said. 'God's universe is a benevolent universe of love and so it must allow for choice, even if it seems there is no choice, because love would have no meaning without choice.'

'That was a little confusing the way you put it,' I said, 'but I think I understand what you're trying to say: I'm a free man in my mind, even if it doesn't always seem that way.'

'You are more free than you realize,' Eli said, 'and the further you move up in the scale of consciousness, the greater freedom you will experience. Even when your body is incarcerated, your awareness can't be imprisoned since love has no boundaries.'

'I hope this reference to prison isn't meant to be some omen for what the future holds when I return.'

'When you return, he said, you may at first feel incarcerated, but eventually, as you become increasingly aware that you are more than just a body, you will be able to go anywhere in your spirit, although, that may take several years to learn'

'It seemed to me,' I said, 'this wouldn't be much consolation to all the political and religious prisoners being held to rot in all the cells of the totalitarian regimes across the world.'

'But what if,' he said, 'their soul's consciousness was able to fly away to more pleasant environs, even while in prison? Wouldn't that help, if that was possible?

I suppose it would, but for now I'm going to fly off to a few new pleasant environs I have yet to explore on the peaks of the west range. Maybe I'll get a view of the Pacific.

As I walked towards the summit ridge, I thought how much of this conversation was completely contrary to many of my former beliefs. But then, as I've often observed, even my being here was contrary to those beliefs. So much for beliefs!

The old reality was slipping away as new discoveries pre-empted my previous patterns of learning. The problem was, this transition was so sudden; at times it left me confused trying to assimilate my new spiritual reality with the past. I wondered how Einstein would have handled this. If only I could talk to him, maybe he could help. After all, wasn't he the one who had all the answers?

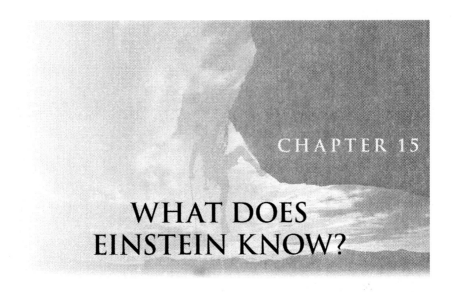

WHAT DOES EINSTEIN KNOW?

Reality is merely an illusion, albeit a very persistent one[1]

The next day, Eli and I spent the morning climbing and hiking along a ridge he wanted to show me, located on a distant mountain range that I hadn't noticed before. There were several spectacular glaciers towards the east, most inspiring in their bright, icy majesty! One of the mountains in the far distance stood out above all the rest, and though I didn't realize it at the time, it was, and still is for that matter, the highest mountain in the Western Hemisphere. Most impressive! I needed to climb it while I still could, which is precisely what we did a few weeks later.

But there was also another mountain Eli pointed out to me that appeared to be one of the highest and most formidable of any I had seen so far in the Andes. He only said it was my special Magic Mountain, and the further in I went, the further up I would go. A most curious statement, I thought! After that, he didn't say anything more about it,

---

[1] Albert Einstein 1879-1955, Nobel Prize in Physics 1921

even when I asked. That's the way things often worked here; the more I wanted to know something, the less information I got.

Shortly after returning, we resumed our discussions over a large bowl of thick and hardy vegetable soup that Mo had prepared while we were gone.

Most delicious! I can tell; fresh out of our garden.'

'That's right,' Mo said, 'it materialized straight out of the garden market in Santiago where I do most of my shopping. Someday I may show you how to do that. But for now, I'd like to pick up on something fresh you said yesterday. It was about Einstein's equation $E=MC^2$, as it relates to the speed of light. It really is a most brilliant formulation in as much as it approaches the realm of higher dimensions, and yet it's not able to go beyond the temporal world's space/time continuum.

'But then, no calculation, not matter how brilliant, can apply to a broader field transcended by a more inclusive holon of reality than earth's perception of time and space. It's not just me saying this; some quantum physicists today question how his equation applies to the subatomic level of reality. Many believe it doesn't.

'We, however may intuit orphic time since it is perceived not with clocks, but within our very being. Even on the earth plane, this may occur at times. Though, you continue to experience earth's environment on this summit, yet you're not limited to its frequencies; just as you weren't limited by geographical constraints while teleporting to the mountains you visited this morning.

'Yes, I have to admit, things do tend to move along rather rapidly in this dimension, seemingly in no time flat.'

'Yes, very fast indeed; as you can attest. In fact, so fast, even the word *fast* doesn't apply. However, the term *immediate* does since there's nothing *mediate* to pass through between here and there.'

'And yet,' I said, 'this doesn't change the fact that physical objects aren't able to exceed the speed of light.'

'That may be true on one level of perception,' Eli replied, 'but only for what seems to exist within the limitations of the third dimension. Have you ever heard of non-locality and quantum entanglement? Niels Bohr, Werner Heisenberg and their Copenhagen gang can be thanked for bringing to our attention these new underlying realities of subatomic events.'

'Of course, I'm very familiar with these theorems,' I said, 'but there still is plenty of controversy on the interpretation of the data; possibly there always will be.'

'Certainly,' Mo said, 'but this is how science progresses on earth, nothing is ever settled, since a more expansive picture is always emerging to interpret and reinterpret the facts. Only scientism's junk science says things are settled for various political, corporate or ideological interests, demanding it be so.[1] All I can say, science is going to be even less settled in the near future as things become increasingly wonky in the physics laboratories.'

'From what I understand,' Eli said, 'Einstein couldn't buy into the implications of what Bohr and his colleagues advocated in quantum theory. As he called it: *spooky action at a distance.* I think most physicists today agree Albert was wrong in dismissing the equations behind these quantum quirks. As you know, physicists regularly split an electron where it's demonstrated each half goes its own way, and yet the counter half instantly responds to the other's change of spin, no matter where they each happen to be relative to each. Yes Albert – very spooky indeed!'

'And yet,' Mo said, 'in this supposed scenario, can it even be said electrons are disconnected? In fact, can anything be understood to be apart when the Source is the substratum of all that is.[2] When you take the limitations of time and space out of the picture, odd things seem to happen. But only odd according to the obstructed experiences of sentient consciousness on earth or, for that matter, any other physical planet.'

'Wait a minute,' you said *any other physical planet.* Are you telling me you believe there may be life on other planets?'

'Believe – what's not to believe?' Mo said. 'It's only a question of where you find it. When you understand that the universe is created by

---

[1] I found Mo to be a most gracious man, but on the topic of *Scientism* and the politics of *settled* science, he had nothing but contempt for what he considered to be foolish departures from empirical science. The discussion came up repeatedly, in slightly different contexts, as you will read further along.

[2] Sir Arthur Eddington once stated: *the substratum for everything is of mental character.* See Appendix 'A'.

Mind, or let's say the Mind of God, you realize there can be no limits to infinite expansion because the Source is infinite. Put another way, how can a thought be limited since there is nowhere it cannot be. You can't keep it in a box, though many try. With Mind being infinite, there's no requirement for time, space or matter. God thinks Thoughts, and so it is.'

'Is that not anthropomorphising God? I said. 'In fact, it most obviously is.'

'You could be right James; these words may easily be misunderstood as being anthropomorphic in nature – creating God in man's image. Unfortunately, it's often the best we can do when communicating with words. Higher understanding can only function when we are able to communicate with nonverbal thought forms. You haven't discovered how to do that yet, though this may soon happen when you become inspired to have inner knowledge, or gnosis, without words.'

'And how would I manage to do that?'

'Maybe the question isn't about *how*, Eli said.'

Before I could ask Eli what he meant by that, Mo continued to explain what he wished to say about anthropomorphisms: 'This is why, when we attempt to explain reality in finite terms, we need metaphors and images we are familiar with, because ultimate reality is not explainable in conventional terms. Descriptions may be employed either as signposts to deeper meaning, or they can distort what we wish to communicate when taken literally. Only when words are put aside by going within, are we able to discover intimations of what has been called the *Numinous*.[1]

'And that's what I mean," Eli said, rather than asking *"how,"* understand there is no "how" – it just is.

'Is what?'

What I just said; an inner *knowingness* or gnosis. It will come to you when you are ready, but it can only be experienced according to one's

---

[1] The word 'numinous' originates from Latin, later developed in the 20th century, particularly with theologian Rudolf Otto, in this work *The Idea of the Holy* (1917) where he describes it as the *Mysterium Tremendum*.' Aldous Huxley, in *The Doors of Perception* (1954) also discusses this term at length. The idea relates to an ineffable encounter with the Divine but also has other variant meanings.

capacity to receive. You know it's the Numinous when you don't have specific words to describe what you are inwardly sensing. That's why mystics often remain silent.

Though finite *man* can never fully know the infinite Source, nevertheless he can intuit the Presence of Infinite Source, through the portals of his heart, from which being essence is derived. What comparison can the finite have with the infinite?[1] There is none but the void from which infinite potential emerges.

'If this much was understood, humanity would no longer seek to know about God, but rather seek to know God. There's a big difference between *knowing* and *knowing about*. When it's understood there's no *about* it, there's no need for idols, icons or anthropomorphic projections of a big guy in the sky.'

'In my experiences,' I said, 'it seems that's where religion always seems to get stuck. More than anything else, it was these ridiculous anthropomorphisms that turned me away from all this in my younger years. Zeus, Jove, Jehovah, or any of the other gods, with all their foibles; were much too human and capricious for me to take seriously. Which is why, any talk of God seemed to be too foolish to give credence.'

'But didn't you tell us you said a little prayer to Zeus the night you had your special dream?'

'I wasn't serious. But isn't it interesting, here I am anyway, far up on my own Mount Olympus – so which one of you is Zeus?'

'Whoever you wish,' Eli said, 'but I'd stay clear of Mo; you never know when he's lightning is going to strike.'

'That's evident, I said. But it's also evident how many religions talk about God in much the same way, as an externalized image appearing in man's image.

'But science isn't much better,' Mo said, 'when it represents life to be nothing more than a three dimensional material event. It's a shallow and idolatrous representation of reality, since life, in essence, is spiritual.

---

[1] As a philosopher, I was most intrigued with this subject, and so it was with great interest when I came across a book called *The Supreme Identity*, (1950) by Allan Watts. For those who may be interested, It contains a very profound chapter simply called the 'Infinite and the Finite' that draws from various sources such as the ancient *Upanishads*.

Though the moving parts may appear outwardly material, none of these cause life, they only respond to life's inward spiritual essence. No scientist in the Flatlands has, or can demonstrate anything to the contrary.'

'Those are rather strong statements, Mo,' I said.

'Indeed they are, Eli said, but after seeing things from the inside out, I would have to agree with Mo. There really is a lack of understanding about the basics of life. But then, I was as ignorant as the next bloke, having not been lucky enough to fall on my head off a mountain to be properly instructed by two sages possessing infinite wisdom.'

Further to what I just said, Mo continued, errors in perception also occur when what is observed through the lens of microscopes is understood by the same principles as what is observed though telescopes. But they really are two different universes, one within, and the other without, and yet they are one, since what is within, is within what's without. So rather than basing the interpretation of what's out there from what's *in there*, it's assumed all that exists is only the 3D read-out of external appearances. And yet, what's going on in the subatomic universe is anything but a 3D read-out.

'I think it's also becoming increasingly obvious to many astrophysicists,' Eli said, 'that many of the former time/space assumptions no longer form an adequate basis for understanding the universe. For example, what physical laws are known to provide a basis for the Big Bang's theoretical *singularity,* or which of these laws provide a basis for the *black hole* theorem?

'It becomes evident things must be interpreted much differently when these question are asked and no adequate answer is found. But then, what can you expect when sidereal time and space are made subordinate to a subatomic world that doesn't acquiesce to Newton's laws.

'Which is why Einstein called it *spooky*,' Mo said, 'he didn't like it, but in the end, it's the only basis by which reality will be understood. Not that it ever will. All emanates from Source, and therefore all is spiritual.

'What's missing,' Eli said, 'is an understanding that all creation exists as conscious perception, just as Berkeley put it. And therefore, at its base, all existence is spiritual in nature, rather than the outward shadows of physicality.'

'Shadows;' I said, 'is that supposed to be an allusion to Plato's shadows on the cave walls spoken of in his *Republic*?'

'That may be a fair comparison,' he said.

'But I think that allegory has fallen out of fashion these days.'

'Likely it has,' Mo said, 'but then certain cosmological theories such as *The Big Bang,* for whatever its merits, may soon fall out of fashion too.[1] It makes little rational sense when tied to the limits and mathematical equations of the earth plane's three dimensions. There are a lot of assumptions built into the hypothesis that become increasingly dubious when subjected to the limitations of 3D computations. Just my opinion, but I suspect the shelf life of the Big Bang theory, as it is currently posited, is about to expire. Or to put it another way, the theory will not explode, but rather implode, likely with a fizzle.

For some time now, there has been plenty of dissension in the ranks of the astrophysicists but whatever new cosmologies come along will continue to be constrained by postulates within their linear/sidereal parameters.

'So Mo, with your contrarian disposition, are you taking another shot at Einstein? It's my understanding he helped formulate the idea of the Big Bang.'

'At first Einstein participated in the theory's formulation, he said, 'since it seemed to work so well with his initial Theory of Relativity. Interestingly, at one point he attempted to debunk the Big Bang in a relatively unknown manuscript he wrote in 1931.[2] Einstein was a great scientist, although he had some blind spots, especially related to quantum theory.'

---

[1] The Big Bang theory postulates the universe originated roughly 13.8 billion years ago from a 'singularity' (thought to be the origin of time and space). The theory has nothing to say what happened when or before it supposedly 'happened'. More and more physicists question the existence of a singularity or the Big Bang itself. One such physicist is Saurya Das who recently challenged the total concept in a prestigious physics journal, creating a bit of a stir in the cosmological community.

[2] The paper aligned with the position of astrophysicist Fred Hoyle who twenty years later advocated an eternally expanding universe.

'My understanding is he's back with The Big Bang theorem again,' Eli said, 'with the proviso the explosion is not to be understood as a material event. The "singularity" from which this universe supposedly exploded into existence wasn't a speck of dense matter as scientists say, but more like a condensed thought form, expanding into the infinite expression of time's fourth dimension. The event, for lack of a better term, would also be one with the manifestation of form in the continuum of space. Only in this semblance of understanding, would his understanding be correct regarding the Big Bang.

'That's most interesting, since astronomy has always fascinated me. Pardon the pun, but I'd love to have a better scope on this.'

'Someday I'm sure you will be able to view the variegations of the greater cosmos, in as much as you are able. But even in a higher state of consciousness, you will only receive an intimation of what's there, although this comprehension is able to expand as you progress in your spiritual evolution. The more you understand what's within, the more you will understand what's without.

'To further boggle your mind, James, you may find the universe of the Big Bang is only one in a myriad of universes. When you have a sense of the magnitude perceived from vistas much higher than what can be imagined from these Mountain tops, you may be surprised how differently things appear. There's no end to discovering the nature of reality. What is viewed through the 3D lens of the Hubble telescope is only a hint of the infinity that lies beyond.'

'Rather than waiting for *someday* to occur, I'd prefer to take a peek through this inter-dimensional lens of yours, so I may see what you see – just a sneak preview if I may.'

'Sorry James,' Eli said, 'but this Mountain isn't high enough. Besides, there still is too much earthly haze here for you to see much of what's out there. You will have much better views when your body is dead enough for you to see from these new heights,' he laughed.

I didn't laugh, since I didn't find what he said to be particularly humorous.

'That was supposed to be funny,' he said, 'you should realize by now you can't die, only transition. So what's there to get upset about? Although it can be upsetting for those left behind – unless, of course, they come into an inheritance. Others may grieve for the departed for a time, but generally not as long or as much as most would like to think. And why should they, since no one here gives a second thought after they cross over to view and experience the new reality.

'The best we can do is explain a few things about how life is experienced in a significantly higher state consciousness. But since you're still limited to this middle ground, there's not much we can say since you still don't have anything to compare this dimension to. Although, by now I'm sure you must have a much better appreciation for the inherent elasticity of time/space perception.

'Metaphorically speaking, when you come to join us in our sphere you will be able to view reality through a new telescope – it really is quite the display out there! You may be surprised, however, to find there's no equipment stationed *out there,* since it's already built into one's unobstructed consciousness. So what's *out there* has more to do with *what's in there.*

'Sounds Buddhist to me,' I said. 'So are you Buddhists?'

'What if we were – zen what?' Eli said, again trying to be clever.

Just then, Mo came to join us outside on the deck. 'Mo, would you say we are Buddhists?' Eli asked. 'James wants to know.'

'I don't know, since there are no religions where we come from. But if we were Buddhists, I suppose it would along with several other traditions, in as much as they contain truth,' Mo said. 'So why do you ask?'

'Because of what you and Eli keep saying; you know, about reality being within rather than without. I'm not sure if that's not rather simplistic.'

'But if you're viewing the universe without a telescope,' Mo said, 'that's not such a bad thing. It's just as Eli said, whatever is *"without"* is because of what is *"within."* Depending on how you define reality, that shouldn't make *"without"* any less real. I'm not sure if such a view makes us Buddhists or not. If you like I'll ask the Dalai Lama his opinion when you go back.'

'So why would we spend billions on astronomical research and outer space exploration?' I asked. 'From what we can see, there's a whole lot of what's *out there* that would have to come from within. I'm not sure I'm large enough to contain it all. Astronomers examining the stars and planets can tell you how vast the cosmos is, not to mention the experiences of astronauts and evidence of probes going all the way to Mars and even past Pluto.'

'To access the Internet, you don't have to know everything that's available, do you?' asked Mo. 'Try not to worry about it, you're not expected to understand everything we're saying; hardly anyone does, especially those who look to the physical. You won't be able to grasp the relationship of subject/object dynamics until you are outfitted with the necessary equipment to comprehend what will always remain incomprehensible to a world of limited capacity. Once you're higher up and further in, you'll have a much better idea.'

'I think I may already have an idea what to expect,' I said, 'having ventured on a few of these trips while in Ecuador where I had an encounter with my own *Don Juan*.[1] He had some *good stuff* that sent me to some very far off places. So if you help me find a way to expand my consciousness while I'm here, perhaps I'll be able to take another magical tour through the cosmos.'

'It may have been interesting back then, but what we have is a much more exciting trip,' Eli said. 'The really *good stuff* is pure mind, sans mescaline or anything else that's not part of your soul. As you become increasingly attuned to your soul's essence, you will experience your consciousness expanding to new highs without any external assistance. If it wasn't for your body in London demanding you return to it, you may never wish to leave this bliss.

'So when do we get to do this?'

'Don't you realize you're already on this trip you want to take? Your experiences have not been induced, and so they can only advance and expand as much as you are capable. Otherwise there would be discord between what you are within and what you experience without and you wouldn't be much good for anything after you returned.

Assuming you do return, you will gradually recall much of what you have experienced on this spirit plane when you unite the feelings you had with a cognitive understanding of what they mean. In other

---

[1] Don Juan was a Mexican shaman that Anthropologist Carlos Castañeda's spoke of in his book; *The Teachings of Don Juan*, (1968).

words, your mind will have to catch up with your heart, before you can understand the significance of what happened. When it does, you will be able to recreate all that you experienced on this plane.'

'But how would I? Obviously my brain in London isn't getting any of this.'

'It doesn't need to, since your conscious soul is getting it,' he said; 'what more do you need? The unified *you,* that which thinks with the mind and feels with the heart is the essence of your soul. Everything will be preserved, as in a hologram programme, even if it takes years before you access it.'

'That's most encouraging to hear,' I said, 'but where is all this information stashed if not in my brain lobes? Is there some storage unit in the sky?'

'There actually isn't a location since its non-local. Remember, the universal field of consciousness we have spoken of is where your memories exist, accessible to you whenever you wish to recall them. Try to think of it as the Internet *cloud* where you store your computer files. The analogy isn't perfect, since you'll likely need some assistance to access this amorphous cloud of experiences when you return.'

'So who has the key to my files?'

'You do,' Eli said, 'encoded and inscribed within your soul. Whenever you want to access these memories, you need only go within.'

'But how?'

'Don't worry about it;' Mo said, 'help is always made available for those who seek. But don't be too surprised if it comes, not from us, but from someone much closer to home.'

'Who could do such a thing,' I asked, 'the local witch doctor?'

'Or perhaps,' Eli said, 'there's someone more lovely – to cast her bewitching spell.'

WHAT DO I KNOW

Space and time and matter – and at the bottom we reach symbols.
Its substance melted into shadows[1]

The next day our conversations continued to meander over many topics; including scientific, esoteric, spiritual, historic, and so on. I was particularly curious in knowing more about their understanding of what they refer to as the *Infiniverse*. If what they said was true, humanity has very little idea what the cosmos is about, but I would have to write another book even to attempt to explain what this all may mean. So I will leave that for another time, should I live long enough to tell their stories.

In fact, I thought someday I should write a science fiction series and capitalize on what l was learning here. Sir Arthur C. Clark would have nothing on me.[2] Though he may have been a very skilled writer and futurist with his prodigious mind, I'm sure even he couldn't have imagined what I was about to experience.

It was later that morning our conversation took a surprising new

---

[1] Sir Arthur Eddington, Swarthmore Lecture, 1929 (see complete quote in Appendix 'A')

[2] Prodigious author of science fiction including *2001: A Space Odyssey.*

twist as we sat outside enjoying some freshly baked sweet breads with our tea. It was less comprehensive than our discussion about the cosmos, yet of greater interest to me.

'It's been some time since we discussed your nurse,' Mo said. 'What do you think – are you ready to meet her yet?'

'Ready? But of course, it's been a long time since – you know.'

'Actually we don't, but never mind. Rather, let me ask if you would be prepared for her to meet you, presuming she would be willing?'

'I'm not sure I understand your question,' I said.

'What I mean is; just because you may be ready for her doesn't necessarily imply she would be ready for you, at least in a relationship. What is she rejected you?'

'But why would she reject me, especially after caring for my body all this time; wouldn't she be rather attached to me?'

'What makes you think she would care only about your body?' he said. 'Do you think it's possible she may be interesting in something more than your body? Something more than what you were interested in before in your relationships, that being the soul.'

'Also,' Eli said, 'there's the question of how interested she would remain if she knew of your long string of relationships? Many women are looking for something that lasts more than a few months, which now brings us to the question Mo asked you to consider.'

'You mean, *who am I*? Don't worry; I'm still working on it. It's a tough one; not that easy to come up with answers. Perhaps the real answer is *I'm nobody*.'

'Your ego is the *nobody*,' Mo said, 'though it likes to think it's *somebody* when it presumes to be you. However, you're not alone with this; all human nature has the same issue with this mind illusion. As we've said many times, the ego is not who or what you are. Does the word *nothingness* still resonate in your mind?'

'Of course, I can still hear it in my mind,' I said, 'just as clearly as that night in the mountains.'

Then repeat it again three times whenever the ego tries to deceive you into believing it is you. I know this may sound peculiar, but the ego is insane, not wishing to be recognized for what it is: *no-thing-ness*.'

'Maybe it's not the ego that's insane, I said, 'but attempting to answer your question.'

'That's because you're thinking about what defies analysis, Mo said. 'No amount of thinking will bring a sane answer to knowing yourself, although it will at least bring the question into your awareness. That's why I asked it.

'But while you remain working on it, we would like you to also consider a much different question that may be even more difficult for you to answer.'

'More difficult, how could that be?'

'You need to think about this long and hard before trying to answering this question: what do women want?'

'Oh that's easy,' I said with a sly grin.

'Okay; so what's the answer?'

'Me!'

'Of course they do, James,' Eli said, 'except those who don't. So to help you find some intelligent answers to this question, let's narrow it down and consider what qualities you think women find attractive in a man? Then at least, you may have a better understanding of what Julianne may be looking for – besides your body.'

'To be honest, I'm not sure what women want in a man; I've never asked them, but I'm not sure they know themselves. Besides, they're all different; you never know where you stand. Generally it has to do with their mood.'

'From what you just said, I don't doubt you've never had a conversation with a woman on this before– which is why you may need to give more thought to this if you ever hope to resolve your relational issues.

And while you're at it, Mo said, I have a third question you may find even more difficult to answer.'

'You both sure are full of question aren't you; as if I didn't already have enough of my own?'

'You once said,' Mo continued, 'without questions, there are no answers. So the next question for you to consider is: what qualities do you wish to find in a woman – other than the obvious? In other words, what inward attributes should she possess in order to establish a lasting relationship with you?'

'That may require a lot of thought,' I said with a smile, 'I normally don't look at women that way.'

'We know you don't,' Eli said, 'and that's why we're asking. You're right; it likely will require some serious thought for you to understand what you truly want. Then again, it may be nothing more than your mood and temperament, as you say. In any case, take your time; we don't need answers from you right away. Actually, we really don't need your answers at all. But you do. That's why we first asked you to consider what women want; you may find, in essence, the answers aren't all that different.'

'Isn't it interesting,' Mo said, 'that even as a philosopher, continually asking questions about the nature of the universe, it has never occurred to you to ask something as basic as what each wants from the other in a relationship? I think it would be safe to say, that by your own admission, whatever you imagined you were looking for in the past didn't work. Obviously you've never given it a lot of thought, or any thought.'

'No, I suppose not, but let's not dwell on the past.'

'You're right,' Mo said, 'dwelling on the past is never very helpful, especially if that's where you stay. Still, we'd like you to question your assumptions about women, so that in the future you won't have to carry with you what hasn't worked in the past.

'Then perhaps, you will have a greater appreciation for *who* they are, rather than just *what* they are, especially in reference to meeting your needs. Once you do this, it may help you think more deeply about these questions. If you can do this, it may be easier for you to establish an extraordinary relationship in the years ahead.

'But before your mind starts to overanalyze what women want and what you want,' Eli said, 'first listen to what your heart tells you, and not just your mind, since it doesn't know anyway.

'It's not possible for you to attract what you really want until you come into alignment with the desires of your heart. If you allow only your mind take charge, it will become so preoccupied with questions you won't even be able to hear the heart's answers. It's an occupational hazard you philosophers have, since it's easier to come up with questions that don't require nearly the same inward introspection.'

'That's a matter of opinion,' I said; 'an answer can't be an answer unless the question was first asked. Socrates' mastery proved how a good question cuts to the chase, leading to a truthful answer.'

'I'm not saying questions aren't important,' Mo said, 'they most certainly are; in fact, we've just asked you two more very significant ones. I'm only objecting to the tendency to take the lazy way out by seeking answers that don't require inward discernment. Proper answers will require an intuitive response from the heart, not just a cognitive analysis from the mind.'

'I think we all agree,' Eli said, 'the purpose of a good question is to lead to a good answer and so an answer is only as good as the question asked. But I think our point is; you don't get very far with that in matters of love when seek only cognitive answers without examining the intuitive answers of the heart. Didn't Socrates say *the unexamined life is not worth living*? The mind doesn't know how to do this; it's incapable, only the heart can do it.'

'Perhaps he did say that, at least according to tradition.'

'Then should we not also ask whether an unexamined love is worth having? Mo asked.'

'But how is it possible for one to examine love? I'm not even sure I know what pure unconditional love is or how to define it. So you tell me, what would you say are the attributes of love?'

'I'm not sure love has attributes' he said, 'though its effects are readily evident. Perhaps it's that by which everything else receives its attributes, even fear, which is its absence. It's often said that God is love, but that's not saying love *is* God; only that love is *of* God. If we acknowledge love is of the heart, the centre of one's being, perhaps we only need to understand what God does through each expression of life. The heart's yearnings are often more difficult to discern than finding answers to things like algebraic questions where possibly only the mind is engaged. Discovering one's true affections requires much heartfelt honesty, and sometimes painful introspection. Sometimes what one really wants, is the least evident.'

'If you recall our earlier discussion, James,' Eli said, 'I believe it was agreed how few people in the world realize what they want. They tend to drift along mindlessly waiting for others to tell them what they should be wanting. It's why the world can be such an unhappy place; not many go to the effort to examine the depths of their hearts. But then, how can they if they don't know themselves and what their purpose is?

'And yet everyone is made aware of what they should want. Governments, religions, family, friends and advertisers all presume to know what's best. But in the end, it comes down to what they want *from* others, not *for* others. I know this may sound cynical, but what they really want is not service but servitude. It's a big vicious circle; yet it seems to work for society in its own twisted way.'

'But think of the advantages, Mo said. This makes things so much easier; no one has to go to the effort of discovering what they want since that's already determined for them. In order for them to find what they truly want, they would first have to know their true Self, that being the full union of the heart and mind.

'Who has the time or inclination for that? It takes much courage, honesty and determination to find what the heart wants, especially when the separated ego-mind keeps screaming for all the things it supposedly wants. Power, money, prestige, gratification, vengeance, pain and suffering; these are the insane desires of the unhinged mind, none of which make any sense to the heart, since all they do is keep humanity in bondage to itself.

'Which, is precisely what the ego wants; since it derives its bogus existence from the external illusions and idols it is allowed to create. Yet there is no peace with any of these, and so the search goes on without end or satisfaction. *Vanity of vanities, all is vanity.*[1]

'So what would you say,' I asked, 'are these deepest yearnings of the heart that are so difficult to understand?'

'At the deepest level,' he said, 'the soul's basic yearning is relational, to be one with one's Self, through the Source, the All that is. Everyone wants to love and be loved. But one is only capable of loving to the degree they are able to receive love, but they can't do this until they love themselves. See how it's all tied together; love is all about union.'

---

[1] Ecclesiastes 1:2 (KJV)

'When you understand giving and receiving are part of the same reciprocal process, you will recognize the essence of all relationships, not only between men and women, but with everything. It's the dynamic that creates and maintains unity since everything in life is relational in nature.'

'Sounds a lot like sex,' I said, 'giving and receiving love are implicitly experienced as one, and at once.'

'That's because serving and receiving are a vibratory equivalent,' Eli said. 'Anyone who understands this universal principle will want to give at least as much as they receive, knowing it perpetrates a cycle of creative expansion. Out of this, the soul's abundance emerges, and what woman doesn't want to be loved out of a man's inner abundance?'

'I'm not so sure I agree with that. Based on my experiences, I think women's attraction has more to do with a man's outer abundance.'

Perhaps you only experienced what you were anticipating, Mo said. It may be a hackneyed phrase, but still it's true enough; we create our own reality, based on what we choose to believe about ourselves. That's the reality that's projected on to the world. That's why we want you to discover who you are while you're still here with us,' Mo said. 'Provided you continue to ask the question of who you are; the answer will be known – not in words, but in knowingness.

'Also, as you do this, remember the other questions I gave you. Whatever answers you find aren't for us; they will be revelations from you to you. When you ask the appropriate questions, you will find the appropriate answers, provided you look to your heart. But they can only be known once you know yourself. Remember, your heart is an expression of your soul, and your soul is an expression of God.'

'I confess, in the past I haven't given too much thought to what I want in a relationship, possibly because I already resigned myself to not being able to sustain a relationship for more than a few months. Failure in love has become an established pattern for me, and so I fear I may never have what I most want. Whatever I was receiving didn't seem to satisfy me for long any more than I was able to satisfy them.'

'So maybe,' Eli said, 'it would be a good time to ask why this was.'

'As we discussed before, there were lots of reasons. But for some, I don't have a reason. They often said I was distant, and perhaps I was,

but I really don't know why they would say that, I was very intimate –
at least in bed.'

'If you knew yourself,' Mo said, 'you would know why they said
that. But then if you knew who you were, the real you, there would be
no why for you to know. This is where things get interesting, because
it's only through relationships we come to know who we are. That's
the part you've been missing. Nothing can exist alone, nothing! Not
even you. Nothing exists outside of relationship! Furthermore, love, in
its essence, can never be known until you're first in relationship with
your Self.

'I know you're probably tired of hearing us say it, but only when your
mind and heart are united as one in relationship, can you be in relationship
with anyone or anything outside yourself. But when this happens, you are
whole and your life is transformed. Then are no limits to becoming more
of what you are, when your Divinity, your Christ, your Self, as you prefer,
continues to expand into what you are eternally becoming.

'In this sense, you can never discover all there is for you because
you will never exhaust all the possibilities for who you may become
through relationships. You are a unique and distinctive expression of
Infinite Source with an infinite capacity to extend the essence of your
being into new variegated expressions of being. When you come to
understand this, not just in your mind but also in your heart, you will
have discovered who you are, the god within.'

'Most inspiring words, certainly worth considering – if only I
understood what the hell you were talking about. But how is this
supposed to relate to my relations with women? You say I'm missing
something, so tell me again, what am I missing, other than the love of
a good woman?'

'What you are missing James, is your identity,' Eli said. 'Your
identity has to do with your relationships. For you, at least in the past,
it's all about what's on the outside. How can you recognize the essence
of the woman you seek if you're not able to recognize your own? And so
how would it be possible to know which woman could align with you?
But once you discover who you are on the inside, you will understand
the true substance of what's outside, whereby you may enter into a
mutually loving relationship.'

'I realize we've discussed this before, but tell me again what am I supposed to look for in a woman, other than her necessary sexual allure and appearance. A great personality is wonderful, but I'm not sure that's sufficient.'

'And yet what you have deem *necessary* in the past, has never proven to be *sufficient*,' Mo said. 'Why do you think that is? Have you ever considered what it would be like to wake up to someone who's in relationship with your soul, and not just your body; a soul mate whose presence helps you become the man she wants to love more than anything.

'Or would you prefer an outwardly beautiful woman who stifles you by pulling you down to her level by? Even if she gratifies you, you may wish to walk in the other direction – very quickly. However, if you find a woman who shares your vision, then you have the spiritual basis for a true loving relationship, not to say you can't also have what outward qualities you deem necessary.'

'That's fine, but your emphasis seems too platonic with these ideals. That's not what a man's after and so it's not natural. You may think I sound shallow, but that's not how the human race gets to be procreated.'

'But is that all you're interested in James,' he said, 'contributing to humanity's progeny? Let them carry on, as they inevitably will, but wouldn't you prefer to have a love based on what's more spiritually substantial than just her face, breasts and posterior. If you give special attention to her inward qualities, then she may give more attention to yours, such that whatever other attraction you have for each other may last for more than a night or two. Then you may appreciate everything else that's desirable about her, perhaps more than what other men would see or recognize.'

'Do you have any specific suggestions how I should go about this, and see beyond by normal criteria of appeal? I think, after all these years, I may be kind of stuck on what's outside.'

'Gaze into her eyes,' Eli said, 'then imagine going beyond, as you look deeply into her soul. What do you sense? Keep searching until you sense her inward voice speaking to you in silence. What does it say? Is she a mature and generous soul? If not, what do you prefer? Declare to yourself what you want and what you don't want. At least that way you'll become aware of what you're looking for, should you ever be tempted and overwhelmed with only external appearances.'

'That may be rather intense;' I said, 'I'm not sure how many women would be comfortable being undressed in that way.'

'You may be surprised,' he said, 'but generally a women prefers that a man to notice her inward qualities before becoming fixated on what's below her neckline. So look into her eyes first and then she will know you're not distant. If she returns your gaze, then you know she won't be distant with you, since she will also be searching for what lies below the surface of appearances and what you outwardly project. Unfortunately, most are too fearful to allow their lovers to see them as they truly are within, and so don't know each other, only what they see when they outwardly undress the other.'

'I'm not sure I'll remember this tip since it's rather counter-intuitive to the male instinct. Too bad there's no angel here I can practise this technique on before I have to return home.'

'How do you know there isn't?' Mo asked. 'Should you find your angel, allow her to look deeply into your eyes, through to your soul, as you do the same. You may be astonished what you discover there.'

'And what, to my surprise, are you suggesting I might discover?'

'You may discover yourself,' he said, 'for only in love can the Self be found. And only in the Self can you know who you are, because that's what you are.'

'I'm not sure I could allow myself to become that vulnerable to a woman, especially after all they've put me through in the past. Besides, this gazing into each other's soul sounds a bit too personal for my preference; there are other parts they have I'd rather gaze on.'

'Probably you've never noticed the superb nature most women have to nurture and support? It's something you may not have experienced, since you don't see these qualities in yourself, and so you don't recognize this in your lovers. But ask yourself what kind of woman you would allow inside you, someone who just wants what she can get, or someone who is capable of unlocking your true passions?'

'I don't think I've ever been with a woman who needed to unlock my passions; they're readily available for the taking.

'You keep thinking about sex, but that's the easy part,' Mo said.

'If that's all that attracts you, what about all the other time you're with her not having sex? We're only trying to help you to consider the deeper passions of the heart that undergird everything else; not using relationships, but creating relationships – something to think about, James!'

With that said; they both rose from their chairs and walked to the door.

'Just so you know,' Mo said, 'we won't be here when the sun rises tomorrow; or the next day either. We decided it would be best if you have time alone to ponder these questions more and all we just said. As you concentrate over the next few days without any distraction from us, you may be surprised what you find in the depths of your being. And be sure to help yourself to whatever other surprises you may find in the depths of the wine cellar.'

As I watched them make their way up the summit, I heard Mo singing the old Irish hymn, *Be Thou My Vision*.[1] I think the words were supposed to be a special message for me. He could be subtle at times, yet direct. I would be alone for the next few days to find a vision for my unexamined life, something Socrates once said wasn't worth living, I assume, without a vision.[2]

Judging by the moon, it must have been past midnight – most unusual for them to stay this late. While climbing the stairs to the loft I reflected on what they asked me to consider. I suppose this one another assignment in my Summit curriculum. But how would it be possible for me to focus on such abstruse personal questions for so long? There's no animal, I thought, other than man that would fret over such inconsequential matters. Well, perhaps not so inconsequential to Socrates.

During the next few days I went on several walks along the ridges of several surrounding Mountains, hoping I would get a fresh view for my life too. It always amazed me how I could materialize on these peaks so effortlessly. (If I may use the term *materialize* in reference to my spirit

---

[1] The original words are attributed to Saint Dallán Forgaill of the 6th century.

[2] In Plato's *Apology*, Socrates is reported to have said at this trial, *the unexamined life is not worth living.*

body). Even now, I can still hardly believe I did anything so impossible and so surreal, like some comic book superhero.

On one occasion I noticed an oblong shape indentured in a sheet of ice on a mountain, making me curious if this may lead to a cave inside the mountain. Then I realized this was the other side to the ominous mountain Eli had pointed out to me as being my Magic Mountain, inferring it may have significance for me one day.

After being alone for several days, I was becoming increasingly restless. Whenever I looked within to find answers, I found what I came up with would slip through my mind as quicksilver. And I too would slip away, generally into facile thoughts about nothing in particular. Examining the unexamined life was hard work!

Then one morning, without notice or warning, as I was lighting a fire in the old stone fireplace, they unexpectedly burst through the door.

Not surprisingly, I was delighted to have them back and anxious to share how my inward quest was progressing. As it turned out, they didn't seem to be that interested, saying it was my business, not theirs. And yet they seemed very pleased I was making this effort and I hadn't given up.

Never before had I concentrated for so hard and for so long; I'm sure if I had a physical brain it would have been utterly exhausted by now. Mo suggested I was probably working too hard because I was relying on my mind more than my heart. I suppose he was right, philosophers tend to be more concerned with what's going on in their local head, rather than what's happening in their non-local heart.

I suspect, like me, most of my colleagues live much of their lives on the surface of mental engagement rather than allowing themselves to be informed by the deeper promptings of the heart. These are often held in suspicion since they don't seem rational, at least to the mind's analytical standards. Perhaps that is why we, as philosophers, occupy ourselves so much with pure logic and linguistics rather than including the broader, significant concerns of the heart.

I say significant, because from what I came to understand, the heart is the only portal we have to access our divine Source. However, the head is preoccupied with the established brain wave patterns of its thoughts. I suppose that's why Mo would often say beliefs were of the mind, while faith was of the heart. He also made the point that the terms *belief* and *faith* are often used to mean same thing, when actually they're not. The mind has mental beliefs about everything, mostly wrong, but knows nothing of the heart's faith, which is never wrong when listening to its divine Source.

As is evident from all I've represented so far, Mo and Eli were adamant that heart and mind were never meant to function separately, because only in their unity, can divine wisdom be know. And yet there often seems to be a bias among various professional philosophers and scientists that only the reason of the mind can know what's worth knowing.

As we discussed this topic over lunch, they stressed once again how imperative it was for me to remain united within if I ever wished to know myself. Part of the reason for me having this time alone, they said, was to show how futile the mind was in discovering who I was.

'And yet,' I said, 'I've always been so calculating in my professional life, even if things didn't always work out so logically in my personal life.'

'Then I recommend,' Mo said, 'you begin to call into question your mind's fixation with reason when it refuses your heart to have its say. Teach it a lesson by doing some of our yoga breathing exercises, and then go into a deep meditation to silence its chatter. Realize the mind engages in its clever self-deceptive ruses to avoid admitting it doesn't know what it is, where it's going, what it's doing, or what it's talking about. On its own the mind is lost, since it doesn't possess a moral compass or have the internal guidance system of the heart. That's why it needs to cooperate with the heart to get its bearings.

'The ego-mind says you shouldn't listen to your heart, it will make you irrational, and so you end up doing stupid things. And that's true, without the rational faculties of the mind the heart often lacks the analytical grounding necessary to function properly. That's why it's never a case of just the heart or just the mind but the union of heart and mind. That's wholeheartedness, that's fullness of life and that's wisdom. The union of the mind with the heart makes the mind more rational, not less rational, as the heart become wiser with clarity of reason. That's why the best bridges are often the most beautiful, just as the best poems are often the most coherent.'

'I'm not sure how well bridges and poems illustrate your point,' I said, 'but I think I have an idea of what you're saying. We function with rational bridges to get where we are going but it's the poem that makes the trip worthwhile.

Well stated James, I think you understand better than you realize.'

I didn't say anything, but it was becoming clearer to me that many of my more regrettable experiences in life were a consequence of my rational judgements not allowing my heart to inform my mind. I often dismissed my intuition as irrational, which may explain why my love life continued to fair so badly. I wasn't listening to the wisdom of my heart, and so I wasn't able to access its unconditional love. Had I done this, things may have turned out much differently with the young women in my life.

As I thought about it more, I became aware of how well the ego and mind collude against the heart. Why couldn't I see this before? Though I may have sensed this whenever a woman walked out on me, my ego-mind remained inveighed against them, full of judgement, always convinced it was right. Whenever I split with a woman, I was assured it was that "bitch's" fault, not mine. Then later it would turn on me, and say it really was my fault. With the ego-mind, you can never win. It's insane. At least until you engage the heart, which always knows the truth, because it knows love.

I now realized if I wanted to find and sustain a stable lifelong relationship, I would have to get my mind and heart to work together. But I also understood if there was one essential quality I needed to find in a woman, it would be to find someone who was patient enough to teach me the real inward meaning of love.

When Eli first brought this up, I told him facetiously that I was quite confident I could teach her more about love than she could keep up with. What he meant, however, was likely something quite different. But I knew what I really wanted was a woman who could show me unconditional love that I may learn how to respond unconditionally rather than react with fear of rejection.

I wasn't sure how realistic that was. One of the painful things that kept coming to me during the last couple of days of deep introspection, were the utterly stupid and destructive things I did to sabotage my relationships before becoming too attached. I couldn't understand it; what was in me that defaulted to this debilitating psychosis? I can't say I was particularly conscious of what I was doing; in fact, it wasn't obvious at all.

Though I hadn't met Julianne yet, I wanted to believe she had the qualities I was lacking that would save me from this destruction. This was hardly fair to expect this from her, and yet, if what they said was true, she already exhibited unconditional love towards me each day she provided special care for my body in the hospital. I wasn't sure why she would do this, realizing I would never know what she did or if my body would live long enough to thank her.

It was hard for me to believe, with all the disappointments I had endured with my relationships that someone like this would come along for me without me even asking. But I was still careful not to get too worked up about entering into an ideal relationship that may never happen. Too much had gone wrong in my past.

Meanwhile, later that morning, we discussed their theory of the complementary nature of man and woman. In extensive detail, Mo spoke of how the sexes directly correspond to the spiritual qualities of love and wisdom, with goodness and truth being subsets of these. At the base of this paradigm, were essence and form, the inward and the outward. Interesting concepts, I thought, but still a little too esoteric to take that seriously.

'Do you realize,' Mo said, 'in some ancient traditions it was believed man was created as a representation of truth and woman a representation of love? This would mean man is created to give the outward expression of truth and woman to provide the inward content of love; meaning, truth is the outward form that contains love's essence.

'Of course,' he said, 'it is never just one or the other; each contains elements of the other's central features. Yet these qualities remain dominant in one or the other. This is why man is usually more mind centred and woman usually more heart centred. Man's orientation is to be more externally active, analytical and calculating; woman more inwardly receptive, nurturing and affectionate. When man and woman enter into a union, the two complement each other as an expression of a wholehearted human being.'

'Unfortunately,' Eli said, 'things seldom work out that way; not because union is untrue, but because the world is not true to union; not true to truth and most of all, not true to love. Without enlightenment, humanity is confused about almost everything.

That's why we'd appreciate it if you bring some enlightenment to the world, it needs it now more than ever just because there are so many lacking direction and purpose.'

'I'd be pleased to help out where I can, but wouldn't it be a good idea for me to have some of this enlightenment myself first before trying to spreading around what I don't have. So how do I get this enlightenment; when I don't even have a Bodhi tree to sit under?'

'You need not find it,' Eli said, 'it will find you when you discover how to open the divine portals of your heart. That's where the light shines through; from the heart, not the philosophy of the mind. That's why a woman such as Julianne may help open you to enlightenment if you let her. Such a relationship would be more than just another tryst or cherry to pick for your body's salacious appetites; it's about you rediscovering your yin complement so you may find greater wholeness in your latent yang.'

'So I get more yin for my yang.'

'Or more yank from your yin,' he said.

'However you think of it' Mo said, 'this is exactly what you're looking for, whether you're aware of it or not. After years of being frustrated and disappointed in your love affairs, it's really the union of souls you're seeking and not just the yin and yang of bodies constantly colliding. Remember what I said about the complementary nature of the sexes?

'I do, but that was rather abstract; it would be more helpful if you would give an example to illustrate your point.'

'Alright then, how about you and Julianne; she has a wonderful capacity to love and nurture and you are very capable in discerning truth from falsehood with your logic. Your outward intellectual form of truth includes an emphasis on knowledge and reason; hers is love, as is evidenced with her compassionate care towards your body. But as I said, each of you share in both qualities of love and truth, albeit imperfectly, but your orientations are focused primarily on truth or love.

'If you share these strong attributes with each other you will bonded in a dynamic union that your truth will become more truthful and her love will become more loving. And by this, you may discover yourselves in a mystical union where your distinctions dissolve and fuse into wholeness.'

'Should the stars line up for you and her,' Eli said, 'at least metaphorically speaking, this relationship could turn out to be more meaningful than anything you've ever encountered. It may surprise you that you would be capable of such a relationship, considering your history with women. There are several ways to achievement enlightenment, but this could be your special approach and perhaps hers too.

'So how's this going to happen with her in physical form and me here in spirit form? It would seem there is an incompatible issue here.'

'Don't worry about it,' Eli said, 'as we've explained before, she's in spirit form too, just like you, but with a physical covering in her earthly manifestation. You may soon find you're able to connect with her on a level that you would never have imagined possible.

'For now though, we only wish to set the stage when you return home. How you feel towards her now could make a difference in how you respond to her when you return. It's rather difficult to find someone when you're not aware of or what you're looking for. But once you are aware, I'm sure you'll find a way.

'That's why we asked you to engage your mind with your heart that you may know what you are looking for, because up to now, you haven't known. Your heart already knows what it wants, and so you won't even need to think about it. If you give it a chance, it will guide you wherever you are, here or back home.'

Though I was interested in what they had to say as it related to Julianne, I wasn't sure how seriously to take Eli since it appeared he was much too young to know much about relationships. Even though I knew not to judge by outward appearances, still there was a credibility gap. But at least I could accept what Mo had to say, considering his older, sage-like persona. And yet in fairness to Eli, how would I know how old he actually was and what relations he might have had with women on earth.

Later on that day, I thought more on what he said about love and enlightenment. It was true, how would I understand what to look for in love after years of closing my heart while opening my zipper. It's amazing how wisdom can go unnoticed when it's too obvious to recognize. However, that wasn't something I was about to concede to him.

'When we go to London,' Mo said, 'we trust you will see Julianne as she is within; there's much more to her than an enticing appearance.'

'With all this build-up,' I said, 'I'm a bit concerned I may be disappointed; as happens all too often. And so I'm not sure these expectations I have are fair to her or to me.'

'There are no promises on our part,' Mo said, 'love makes its own choices. But if you decide not to follow through, at least there are no fees, forfeited deposits, penalties or obligations on your part. You may find Julianne isn't your type, that's fine, just move on then before she finds you're not her type. It's a two way street and I'm sure she will have plenty of options if she so chooses to exercise them. Once the lights flash back in your eyes and the real James shines through, she may decide you aren't quite what she's looking for.'

'But really,' I said, 'what's there not to like? Seriously, are you saying she may prefer the stiff in the hospital bed over the real me?'

'Well, at least she knows the stiff is harmless,' Eli said.

Actually, my greater concern is what Julianne will think if she hears rumours of my past. If she does, I hope she won't think I'm a serial philanderer just because of what others say. You know how it is; people like to talk.'

'Indeed they do,' Mo said, 'but then, Julianne isn't looking for a celibate monk. She may find your scallywag swagger enticing when the seaman overshadows the staid professor she thinks you are. I'm not an expert on women, but I understand some are attracted to this piquancy for reasons they don't always understand.

But beware; she can become most indignant towards any man who demeans women with base comments. And rightly so! She wants to be respected for who she is rather than what her body is. Yet like most, she believes herself to be a body, and so enjoys the admiration her body receives, as long as she doesn't feel objectified.

'I can sympathize; I know how that feels,' I said. 'Happens to me all the time, but with the right women, I put up with it.'

'I'm certain you do,' he said. And though Julianne may sense she's more than her body, she still enjoys the attention she receives when she's being ogled by certain men or envied by less attractive women. As I said, this contradiction occurs because she identifies herself as being a body rather than a spirit. But she can hardly be faulted for this misperception since that's how most of humanity views itself.

'However, she's now beginning to understand things differently since embarking on her spiritual journey over the last year or two. There are times when she's alone with your body, she wonders if there might be more to you than what she sees; whether you exist in another dimension.'

'I've been accused of that more than once on a date; possibly when I get too intellectual for them.'

'But at least now you really are in another dimension,' Eli said, 'and so if you're able to get through to Julianne in some evidential way she would know you are conscious outside your body.

This would likely convince her that the body is not what we are, but what we possess, or more correctly, what seems to possess the soul. This may change everything for her because whether one believes they are a body, or have a body, makes a big difference in how one perceives their self. Once you realize you're not the outward clothing that you leave behind, you won't identify so much with what you aren't.

'Even though,' I said, 'clothiers often like to quote the famous Latin phrase: *Vestis virum reddit; clothes make the man?*'[1]

'That nicely sums up how the world thinks,' Eli said. 'If it's not the clothes, it's something else on the outside to show; never on the inside: a sports car, a degree, a profession, a pretty woman. ... Oh sorry James, I forgot – that's you, or at least what you were,' he laughed, along with Mo.

'No offense intended,' Mo said, 'in fact, we hope when you go back you'll have all this and more, provided you can handle everything.

---

[1] Marcus Fabius Quintilianus, (35 – 100 AD), Roman rhetorician born in Spain.

But before we leave,' Mo said, I wish to make a few more points about Julianne.'

'Please continue,' I said, 'provided you don't get too distracted with these laughing matters.'

'Distractions here are only diversions that lead to a more comprehensive understanding of life.' he said, 'since the path is seldom a straight line. Often it's as circuitous as was your path to Julianne – even before your body arrived at the hospital.'

'What do you mean; are you saying we met somewhere before? I don't remember sleeping with anyone named Julianne, unless you mean being squeezed together in the underground tube.'

'It's possible you may have bumped into each along the way in London,' he said, 'but that's not what I'm referring to. Rather, I'm suggesting there may be something far more significant going on, such that, when you look deeply into her eyes, as I suggested, you find a mystery hidden within; perhaps one that involves you. Also carefully observe her demeanor, character and personality. Then ask yourself whether you also sense her presence on some non-physical plane.'

'I'm not sure that makes a lot of sense,' I said.

'Regardless, we just want you to be aware there may be considerably more to Julianne than you think,' Eli said. 'And no, we're not operating a match making service; that has never been our line of work – at least up to now.

Nevertheless, with freedom being what it is; whatever you decide to do with Julianne or she decides to do with you, is perfectly acceptable since there's always another lifetime. Who knows, one day you may wake up and decide you wish to live the rest of your life as a celibate monk in the desert. But for now, the most important part of your curriculum is to discover the essence of love. In fact, this is the most important part of anyone's curriculum – even for desert monks.'

'But since we can't actually teach what love is,' Eli said, 'the best we can hope to do is help you find someone who can demonstrate it to you. That's the difference between learning and discovering. When it comes to experiencing the actual yin/yang dynamics of love, you will require someone prettier than us for your practicum. It's up to you, but we think Julianne would be an excellent facilitator.'

'About now, I'm ready for any attractive facilitator you can find me. So when do I get to meet her?'

'Technically, you can see her anytime you choose,' he said, 'since we aren't your wardens. You now have more freedom than you've ever experienced before on earth. If you don't mind though, we suggest it would be best if we help you find your way there and back again.'

'Of course; I'd hate to get lost en-route.'

'Then it's settled, Mo said, 'we can go in a few days when she works the night shift again and has plenty of time to spend with your body. I'm sure you will find it interesting to witness how well she relates to it while it languishes there in its forlorn state.'

'Whenever you're ready, I'll have my bags packed --- I'm looking forward to this adventure that I may finally meet a real woman with a real body of flesh. Although I'm not sure what I'd do with it, except, as you say, objectify it as the object of my affections. Which may be a rather lame excuse on a date, but at least she will be real. I'm not even sure I'd know what to do if I met a real goddess in this dimension,' I said with a laugh.

Mo and Eli looked at each other, grinning, which made me suspicious they knew something I didn't, as generally was the case around here. But I didn't pursue it, knowing I'd never get a straight answer. Maybe it was just an inside joke, but still I had to wonder; was there something they were holding out on.

THE PRESENCE

For he shall give his angels charge over thee to keep thee in all thy ways.[1]

Duffing my stay, at least to this point, there were no other beings I encountered on our summit, or the remote mountain peaks I visited, other than my two companions. At least not that I was aware of! But then, the question of whether there may be someone else prowling up here, took on a strange new twist for me late one night.

It was an odd feeling, but as I sat by the fire reading late one night, I felt someone's presence nearby. I sensed it only for a short while and then it was gone. At the time, I dismissed it as my imagination, since I just finished reading a creepy murder mystery. After that, there was nothing more; at least not for a long time, perhaps weeks.

Then late one night, I stepped outside for a few minutes to examine the sky's constellation while picking up an armload of firewood stacked outside. When I went in, I found the fireplace blazing even though the fire was very low when I had gone out. I sat down in my chair while looking into the fire, much amazed. And then, there it was. The presence – it was back.

---

[1] Psalms 91:11 (KJV)

At first it seemed eerie as I continued to sit there but as my impressions continued to grow, I wasn't frightened so much as intrigued by what I sensed; a very soft and warm feeling drawing closer and closer to me. Most peculiar, I thought – and a little exciting.

My mind told me it was just me conjuring another fantasy, wishing to have a young woman near me. But this time the sentience didn't go away like last time, as I allowed myself to embrace the feeling rather than dismissing it as I had last time. The feeling became more palpable, and yet gentle, as I began to consider whether there may be a feminine spirit wanting to spend the rest of the night in the loft with me.

Then I thought of the phantom presence that hovered near me while I first completed my ascension to the summit. I recalled the soft feminine voice that spoke to me, directing me away from the chasm towards what turned out to be the most accessible approach. Would this be the same sweet spirit?

That seemed just too good! Imagine, this celestial babe still wanting to be with me. Hmm, I thought; I wonder what would happen if she suddenly manifested before me. What kind of relations could I expect to have with her? But what if she was an angel, I thought, smiling; she'd likely be too *religious* for what I may have in mind.

Though I still had difficulty believing in angels, the idea of spending some quality time with a higher being, appealed very much to my imagination; provided, of course, she was a feminine spirit. To fulfill my exaggerated desires, she would have to be very beautiful, preferably without any wings to get in the way. My musings soon turned into salacious fantasies, although my dour rational mind warned me not to get too carried away indulging in such delusions, even if they felt good.

Certainly it was a preposterous notion, too unprofessional for a self-respecting philosopher to even consider. Still I couldn't resist; my whim was telling me a very special visitor was here in the cabin with me, not on my lap, but very nearby. What if she wanted to share the night with me; couldn't she just appear? On the one hand, I suspected anything may possibly happen in this realm of existence; and yet I continued to struggle reconciling my desires with my rational beliefs. Perhaps I was trying to reason too much rather than allowing myself to feel. And then, even as I was considered this, the presence suddenly vanished, totally gone from my awareness.

I never mentioned anything in the morning about what happened last night. Again, nothing more happened for a long time. And so after a while, I assumed whatever it was I had imagined, must have dissolved into the aether from whence it came, or perhaps, as I often joked, the pixie dust had finally worn off.

But then one evening as I was watching my companions fade away over the summit and into the twilight, I felt the same peculiar stirring nearby. I didn't move, but continued to stay outside in the glowing luminescence of the full moon, wondering what I may be sensing this time. When nothing more happened, I finally stepped back inside to sit by the fire to resume reading *Alice in Wonderland*.

The book, along with its sequel, *Through the Looking Glass*, appeared on the mantle yesterday, likely placed there by Eli. Some time ago, he told me Carroll's books would help open the windows of my imagination, to prepare my mind for what may be in store for me while on this plane. For whatever reason, I had never read these stories before, and was surprised how the surrealism was able to loosen my mental rigidity, transporting me into a world of delightful fantasy. At the time, I didn't realize then how much Alice and I would have in common in the days ahead.

While I was reading the part about Alice's tea party with the Mad Hatter, and the other strange companions attending, I sensed my own attending companion drawing closer towards me. Again, I felt the warmth, as I put my book down, no longer able to concentrate on Alice's party. I felt certain this time that the phantasm was real; it was no longer possible for me to ignore the feminine essence wafting about in my sphere. Once again I wondered if it may have any amorous intent: a most delicious whimsy I would imagine at times after the last encounter.

I became restless, or perhaps excited, so I went to the liquor shelf and poured a half glass of gin and walked out onto the deck outside, wondering if she would follow me. I smiled as I looked up towards the moon and asked what magical spell was being visited upon me. I was feeling amorous, and wanted so much to reach out to the spectre, but there was no form to grasp, although I imagined a very beautiful angel standing before me. Casting reason aside, I went back in and climbed the stairs to my loft, hoping she'd be sitting on my bed waiting for me in her translucent silk gown.

No such luck! Of course not; I laughed for allowing myself to be suckered in again by my unbridled passions, still yearning for what wasn't there. How easy it is, my mind told me, for the imagination to play its tricks when we really want to believe something, even as foolish as this. Obviously I allowed myself to get caught again with Alice and my own world of *wonderland* fantasies.

And still I couldn't help but try to conjure her presence into a luscious form, be it material or spiritual, it didn't matter. Now that's a bit weird, I thought, if not confusing; imagine trying to materialize a spirit when, technically, I wasn't even material myself.

I then laughed; thinking about how, even back home, I sometimes had problems materializing a date for the night. When hard up, I would sometimes indulge in erotic visualizations, but never with a celestial being that I would never have imagined to exist. And yet, that's exactly what I was doing now. As much as it offended my rational sensibilities, I couldn't deny the warm presence I had felt during these visitations over the last several weeks, even if it is just my imagination.

It was apparent I was developing a double mind, befuddled by the realities I thought I was experiencing and my philosophers mind. What was real and what wasn't; maybe I should go ask Alice. After I considered everything several times over, I couldn't let go of the feeling that these visitations were more than just delusions of my mind.

Was there actually a spirit out there existing in a vibration higher than mine, be it a ghost, angel or something else? Since I was too embarrassed to speak to my friends about these exotic, and perhaps erotic, visitations, I had kept everything to myself. But now, after this last visitation, I decided it was time to discuss what was going on. Hopefully they would have something helpful to say, although I expected Eli wouldn't be able to resist having a little fun with it first.

The next morning I was ready to tell them, but for whatever reason, the time never seemed right. Perhaps because I still felt too uncertain whether these supposed experiences were real or only the delusions of a desperate, love sick man. So instead, I asked what they thought about angels, hoping that may give me some clues to help me understand this phantasm.

'With you both claiming to be familiar with how things are supposed to be on this spirit side,' I said, 'I am rather curious to know if you believe in angels, guides, guardian angels, archangels, etcetera, like most religious people?'

Why not?' Eli said. 'In fact some of my best friends are ...'

'No seriously Eli, aren't angels just figurative metaphors; figments in the imaginations of the old and feeble who seem to think they need celestial assistance to make it across the street! Then, of course, there are children who sometimes say they talk to these imaginary friends while playing in their sandboxes, but then, they imagine all kinds of other things such as elves, fairies and dragons.'

'Well, who knows,' he said, 'perhaps some children, with their pre-nascent memories, still communicate with higher beings. Why not? There are also many adults who do the same, often without being fully aware of it. Even you called out the night of your pub incident to a Greek god on Mount Olympus. Someone must have heard you, and maybe that's why you're here with us now.'

'I suppose, in some fashion, I requested some divine intervention that evening since I was feeling so frazzled! So if gods, angels, and what have you, exist out there in some form of virtual probability, there's a big credibility gap they need to deal with if they wish to be taken seriously by rational thinkers like me. Don't they care how badly they're being misrepresented by religion and culture? Most of what I see and hear out there seems to be pure unmitigated nonsense! For example, why would any of these presumably magnificent beings need wings to fly around? Blimey, even I can transport myself through the aether without having to flap feathers about. They're for the birds and possibly Clarence too since that was such a big deal for him.'

'Who's Clarence,' Eli asked.

'When I was a student, some of my friends and I would watch old British, French and American movie classics by connecting my computer to the television. That's how I medicated my mind after studying too long. In any case, Clarence was some hapless angel character in an old movie classic who would literally hang out in the trees, waiting for an opportunity to do some special good deed so he could earn his wings.[1]

'This was an exemplary old flick that well reflects a by-gone era that only Hollywood could come up with in all their feel-good schlock, at least when compared to the more jaded conventions of modernity. But I'm not sure if religious representations, with their effete angelic imagery, are any better than Clarence. At least he wasn't kitsch.'

'At one time I too had the same misgivings about angels,' Eli said. 'Often it seems what religious people say about higher dimensions is an unfortunate parody since there's little in the world for them to relate their higher reality. This is much like trying to demonstrate the cyber complexities of a quantum computer to a headhunting tribesman in Papua New Guinea who would have no way of knowing there was more to it than it's outward casing.'

'You may choose to believe in angels or not,' Mo said, 'since they don't need you to believe in them to exist. Yet isn't it assuring to know you have friends in high places, especially when you really need them.'

'Such as when falling off a cliff and needing a helicopter to rescue your mangled body,' Eli said.

'Quite possibly,' I said, 'but how do I meet these obliging friends of mine when I'm not in trouble? It really shouldn't be that much trouble for them; especially while I remain here in a spirit body between worlds.'

'But, as we've said, you're always a spirit,' said Mo, 'whether you're contained in your earthly vesture or as you are now. However, you still remain connected to your physical body by your ethereal silver cord as it has been called.[2] And as long as you remain attached to the earth plane, you won't be able to perceive higher entities, even in this dimension, unless they transduce their energy down to you.

'Realize however,' Mo said, 'if a celestial wishes you to see them, you would, even if you didn't want to. All they need to do is attune their form's frequency to manifest within your vibratory octave. It's

---

[1] *It's a Wonderful Life*, (1946) James Stewart, Donna Reeves

[2] *Remember Him--before the silver cord is severed and the golden bowl is broken.... and the dust returns to the ground it came from, and the spirit returns to God who gave it. Ecclesiastes 12:5, 6 (NIV)*

rather simple, but unless they do this, you may not even realize they are present.'

'What if I ask them nicely, would they come then?'

'It would have to be for some purpose other than your amusement,' Eli said. 'It's similar to them vibrating on FM radio frequency while you're tuned in to AM. Their transmitters are equipped with both FM and AM frequencies, along with many other bands they are able to tune into. Perhaps you saw them at times when you were a young boy, though you probably wouldn't have realized who they were.

'When you return, you may be able see them from time to time, although you likely won't realize it since they seem no different than anyone else. No wings, no shining auras: just mixing it up as ordinary earthlings, wearing street clothes and clutching their Starbucks' coffee while waiting to catch the bus. They seldom announce themselves as they reportedly did in Biblical accounts.'

'But why would they?' Mo said. 'No one today would believe them anyway, even if they blew their proverbial trumpets. Besides, if they got involved with such theatrics, they'd probably get arrested. They really don't like to create scenes that draw attention to themselves unless there's a good reason. Look at what happened to Sodom and Gomorrah, their appearance didn't seem to help much.

'I suppose not,' I said, 'even as a myth.'

'Not even as a myth,' he said, 'but when angels do appear in real life, it's generally to accomplish some specific purpose such as answering a call for help in a way that wouldn't otherwise have been possible. Since it's much better for humanity's conscious development to rely on faith rather than sight, they try to remain inconspicuous. Seldom does anyone realize what's going on behind the scenes when they intervene. Even you slept through the whole rescue drama.'

'I guess I must have,' I said, 'since I don't remember the slightest thing after my blackout. It's my understanding though, many religions seem to think angels were created as special orders of immutable existence, forever remaining as they are and always will be.'

'Not possible,' Mo said, 'nothing remains static; all is vibrant; all is alive. As for being special; they're not, no more than us. Where love rules, all are one, all are the same in essence; no one is special though everyone is unique and distinct within the character of their being. It can't be otherwise because all are of one divine essence, even though we're all individuated souls; even you. Or I should say *especially you*,' he chuckled.

'So rather than think of angels as belonging to a different celestial species,' Eli said, 'recognize they have unique functions of service to assist lower dimensional beings. Angel means messenger, so generally that's what they do, give messages that teach lessons in many different forms.'

'So if I'm a lower dimensional being, you must be angels since you say you're attempting to assist me with my reorientation programme. If so, you sure don't act it – much too much like me'

'Unless we're fallen angels; you know, the type you can relate to.'

'Touché,' I said.

'With all due respect,' Mo said, 'how would you, of all people, know how an angel is supposed to act when you're not even sure if you believe in them, apart from Clarence and others you may have seen in the movies? We may not be accredited angels or even official guides,' he said, 'but that doesn't mean we can't help you with your orientation study programme at Summit U.

'Even while providing real knock-off Habana contra-band that you can see, taste and smoke,' Eli said – 'here; have another.'

'No thanks, I've already had a few too many;' not that good for your health, you know.'

'So are you afraid your spirit might die and go to Earth, he chuckled? From what I understand, things generally work in the other direction.'

'Frankly, I'm still not sure which direction I'm going – or coming. Life or death on earth, while here and there and back again. So what do you think is next for me? I'm still confused since you still haven't made it clear what I'm supposed to expect.'

'No, you're absolutely right James,' Mo said, 'we haven't been very clear; but only because we don't know what's going to happen next. Mostly, it will depend on what decisions you make here and whatever else happens to your body in London. Nothing's fixed in a free will universe. But from what we've been given to understand, you'll likely remain making trouble on earth for at least another fifty years.

'But with James' edgy zest for extreme sports and mountain cliffs,' Eli said, 'it's possible he could be back this way much sooner. We hope not though, since there's still plenty to be done in the world, even if that's bad news for the Flatlands.

'Are you sure you don't want another, James?' Eli said, 'rolled them myself with a little help from Fidel and his serfs. You know it doesn't really matter; you're still a spirit because, as I said before, that's what you've always been and shall remain. The good thing here on this side is the spirit body always remains in excellent health which is why I can smoke as many of these as I please, even though it may have killed me, or at least my body, when I was a chain smoker much of my life. But even if it did, who cares; I no longer have any reason to worry about that or anything else.'

'Alright, one more and then I'm done – for now. My concern is not with this body, but my earthly body when I go back. How do I explain to everyone how I managed to become addicted while being unconscious? It took years for me to kick the weed habit after I was a sailor.

'Don't worry, we won't tell your body if you don't. He'll never notice the difference,' Eli said.

'Yes, but addictions are of the mind as much as the body, right?'

'Perhaps, but how can you be addicted when you can't even get a buzz here,' Eli said, 'unless, of course, you want to. Here a weed is just a weed, never a need.'

'Fine, but if I start chain smoking when I go back, it will be your fault. After struggling to get that damned monkey off my back, I would prefer not to fight these demons again. Perhaps I need to find better company to associate with here – preferably without any bad habits.'

We spent much of the day engaged in more of our often rowdy and sometimes disjointed discussions about anything and everything, including, among other things, multi-dimensional universes and my current state of spiritual existence in this plane. Certainly there was nothing organized like the syllabuses back home. If they had a systematic curriculum, it was less than obvious to me what that may be.

In fact, they didn't even seem to think it was even necessary to delineate subject disciplines, as though everything should flow together in one entangled interdisciplinary web: physics, math, religion, art, philosophy, psychology, astronomy, anthropology and good cigars.

Whenever I tried to systematize things, they insisted these were merely artificial divisions of thought, which is separation. But separation, they said, is nothing more than creating an illusion of fragmentation and thereby alienation, since a part has no context or meaning when detached from the whole. Nothing is real; nothing exists except in relation to everything else which means all is a part of a greater whole, much like the idea the *Ray of Creation* and its source.

This chaotic approach troubled me at first, at least until we had a thorough conversation about *holons* and what that means. Thereafter, I began to have a better appreciation of how everything in the universe should be understood as simultaneously being a part and a whole, which is just another part for a greater whole, all the way to the Source.

Or, as I understand it now, the many in the one and the one in the many, as Jesus seemed to have once implied it.[1] The many are *one* in the Source, while the Source remains eminent in the many. By this, it is recognized how everything flows seamlessly across all multi-dimensional lines of perceived separation.

Mo indicated orthodox academia is not ready for such integral notions because the *a posteriori* orientation is not balanced with an *a priori* perspective. And so everything falls apart when viewed separately.[2] Perhaps that's why I had never heard about Arthur Koestler's and Ken Wilbur's contribution to the understanding of holon concepts, even though there was an academic *Chair* endowed at Edinburgh University, where I graduated, bearing Koestler's name.[3]

---

[1] *That all of them may be one, Father, just as you are in me and I am in you.* John 17:21 (NIV)

[2] *A posteriori* reasoning is inductive or derivative from observed facts, whereas *a priori* reasoning is deductive or presumptive rather than observatory.

[3] Arthur Koestler (1905-1983) coined the term in his book *The Ghost in the Machine* (1967) and did much to develop the Holon concept. The *Koestler Parapsychology Unit* was established at the University of Edinburgh in 1985.

Ken Wilbur's book, *Sex, Ecology, Spirituality: The Spirit of Evolution* I believe is the most exhaustive detailed work there is on the topic of Holons, although the Holon principle shows up in many of his other writings such as *A Brief History of Everything*. There are a few brief discussions on the Holon concept further into this narrative.

A couple of years after I returned home, I thoroughly studied the inherent layers of concepts, until I had a firm grasp of the relational dynamics. I tried to share some of these ideas with my colleagues, but received only dismissive remarks about it being too metaphysical for serious consideration. From what they said, I strongly doubted if any of these critics bothered to study the concepts of holons, which seemed strange, since the implicit logic made a great deal of sense to me.

There was nothing metaphysical whatsoever about the concepts; they were completely rational, which, for the reductionist, suggested the universe was integrated, not fragmented, as they seem to favour. It appeared they had already drawn their lines in the sand where they didn't need to connect the parts with the whole, or effects with the cause.

It must have been after midnight when Eli and Mo wandered off again into their twilight zone. I remained outside under the stars as I watched the last of the red embers in the pit turn to ash. Though the flames had gone, its warmth remained, much like the sweet presence that still lingered in my mind.

When I say sweet, I imagined catching a faint whiff of a fresh rose, just as I had in the presence of my phantom visitor. But of course, no flower could grow or exist here. I smiled as I thought about this and the tricks of the mind. I wondered, though, if this was a sign she may show up again. Or had my cold rationalism finally chased her away.

With the coals now completely burned down, I went inside to do a little more reading before retiring to my loft. I lit a fire and the kerosene lanterns. I found I could read in the darkness when I focused, although I preferred to enjoy the warm glow of the burning oil lamps reflecting off the log walls.

Obviously, being able to see in the darkness was proof I was seeing with more than eyes. So I wondered, were my eyes redundant to the internal vision of the soul? I was still trying to understand what it meant to be in a spirit body rather than a physical body. From my experiences here so far, anything may be possible. But then, was it not obvious my physical body back home was redundant to the greater spiritual ability of my soul.

On the mantle over the fire place I found a copy of Alfred North

Whitehead's book *Science and the Modern World*.[1] We recently discussed some of Whitehead's more challenging concepts in his *Process Philosophy*, but I found, even as a philosopher, the concepts very difficult to comprehend. I remembered Eli said he would try to find me a copy to read.

As I turned the pages, the writings still remained as abstruse as when I was a student in graduate school. I thought that without all the murk and sludge in my physical brain's neocortex, I may have more mental lucidity to understand these concepts. Apparently not, but since I was too stubborn and proud to back down from an intellectual challenge, I kept sloughing through the pages as best I could.

I wondered how many on either side of the line understood what Whitehead was trying to express with his unique insights. At times I wasn't sure if he even did. Possibly he was confused, but no one knew or could tell because his writings, though profound, were often too oblique for most to understand.

It seemed to me that reality shouldn't be this difficult for mortals to access. But then, perhaps Whitehead was of such a rare spiritual genius that he was among the few who could access the higher layers of reality, primarily reserved for those dwelling in the higher dimensions of conscious thought.

As I continued to read, I wondered why they wanted me to read such intellectually challenging material at this time. Was my mind being prepared for some new challenge I would soon encounter?

Later the next day, I told Eli I was struggling with Whitehead's expositions, so needed to take a break by reading other curriculum material. He suggested I take a look at Plotinus' *Enneads* and, if I wished, he'd try to find me a copy. I thought this was an excellent idea, since I always meant to study this ancient *neo-Platonic* classic, even thought I didn't get too far with it in my undergraduate years. At least now I had the time and inclination to do it justice.

---

[1] The book, *Science and the Modern World,* published in 1925, provides a challenging philosophical alternative to the Cartesian dualism of modern scientific methodology. Later, Whitehead published *Process and Reality* a highly regarded work in the development of his school of *Process Philosophy.*

And so later that evening, while sitting down by the fireplace to read, I noticed a copy of the *Enneads* placed on the mantle. I was delighted to read what Plotinus had to say about truth, beauty, logos, goodness and the ultimate transcendence of *Oneness*. Still, I wondered about Plotinus' position on the topic of creation. Is all reality created *ex Deo*, out of God, as he says, rather than the orthodox Christian position of *ex nihilo*, out of nothing? Perhaps it depends on how you look at it. All and nothing, are they not really the same? Nothing being the infinite void from which all energy is constantly being manifested and re-manifested into infinite forms. That would include universes along with the creation of spirits like us.

But then, I thought, who the hell cares about such questions, other than professional philosophers and theologians. For me though, I was still thinking about the voice saying "nothingness" to me in the night and how that had impacted my life so many years ago.

I read into the early morning, feeling greatly uplifted as I continued to penetrate deeply into Plotinus' *Second Ennead*, and I don't mean uplifted as in levitating out of my seat. I already did that stunt. In any case, the more I read the more affinity I felt towards the inspired words of Plotinus. There was something transcendent about his writings that inspired me to feel more alive and aware towards the numinous nature of reality. It was gratifying to comprehend what previously was only faintly perceived. It was interesting that a number of the questions I had grappled with in this new reality had already been addressed by in his writings almost two thousand years ago.

In some areas, however, I wasn't sure his words were making things that much clearer for me to understand. Even though I was in spirit form on this Summit, I still struggled to understand the coherence of the body-soul dynamic. But at least I no longer thought of these questions in the context of spirit versus matter. I was now able to recognize spirit as being both inner soul essence and matter as a projected expression of spirit: or to put it another way, a pattern of spirit form. Yet if spirit was implicit to matter, what was implicit to spirit. This was something I continued to think about as I read.

Then, as though I was being answered by him from across the

centuries, I noticed where he wrote: *If a fire is to warm something else, must there be a fire to warm that fire?*[1]

That's it, I thought; as I put the book down; a most profound question! I gazed into the fire and asked; what is it that lights this fire? For that matter, what is fire in its essence, and what is the flame that continues to burn in me, regardless of what body I occupy? Was it the warmth of love in all its mystery?

As I closed my eyes to dwell on this thought, I felt a warmth, but it wasn't from the fire, but from within me – an involuntary response to someone who had entered the cabin! Yet no one was here – that I could see. Yet a wave of sweet desire swept over me. Not exactly what I'd call erotica so much as a warm and gentle ardour. My ghost was back! Or perhaps it was my angel – my ghost angel.

I have no words to describe the convoluted sensations I was experiencing; perhaps this is the stuff poets attempt to put into words. I didn't understand; how can you have feelings for someone or something whose form you've never seen, not even with a picture? But as with last time, I felt the same soft, peaceful and femininity that seemed to enshroud me. Though I desired to draw her closer towards me, I wasn't certain how to do this.

So I said, 'who are you?' Silence! 'What have you come for?' More silence. 'What do you want from me?' Still more silence. I said nothing more but sat there for some time, wishing to be more enfolded in the sphere of her presence. Finally, I decided to go up to my loft to see if this time she would follow me there. I basked in an aura of vibrant sensations I sensed, or imagined, enveloping my body as I lay there on my bed. Soon I drifted off into a deep and peaceful state of soul slumber, perhaps similar to the state after my fall, though there was nothing traumatic about this; quite the opposite.

When I awoke in the morning, I felt nothing of what may have happened, although I recalled the enchanting spell that had been cast on me before my slumber. Had I experienced a romantic rendezvous with my ghost last night in my dreams? I couldn't say, but nevertheless, it was a pleasant thought. Maybe something would surface again later, as sometimes happens in dream recall.

---

[1] Plotinus's First '*Ennead*': Second Tractate

I continued to lie in the light of the morning's sunrays, relishing the feelings of being charmed last night until I heard the clanking of kitchenware downstairs and smelt the aroma of freshly brewed coffee. Obviously my servants had already arrived to cook breakfast. Eli entered through the door with an armful of wood as Mo was preparing something on the stove.

'What are you two devils up to this morning with all your commotion? Until then, I was trying to recall a most pleasant dream that …'

'Deviled eggs, of course,' Mo said. 'We haven't had any since you first arrived on the Summit. How do you like them, hard or easy?'

'I like it when things are easy, but not overly.'

'Ah, you mean neither this nor that,' Mo said; 'the devil's recipe for complacency. But that's not the way you got up this Mountain, is it?

'No, it wasn't easy,' I said, 'I had to be one tough egg to make it this far, especially after my shell got cracked on a very hard rock below.'

'So that's how you got to be so scrambled,' Eli said in jest.

Our banter, lame as always with Eli, carried on as we ate what Mo prepared on the stove, along with an assortment of meats and cheeses. Later he admitted he cheated because deviled eggs were too difficult to make, and so he just manifested them. It's true, he said, 'the devil's way can sometimes be a lot easier.'

When we finally settled by the fire for our morning session, I thought I'd open with a certain question I wanted to ask for some time. 'If you don't mind me asking,' I said, 'I'm very curious where you two are from. Perhaps it's time you tell me what your fixed address is and when you're finally going to invite me over for dinner.'

'We would love to show you around,' Eli said, 'and I'm sure one day we will, but at this time you're not yet sufficiently wired for our neighbour's frequencies. Like the angels we talked about yesterday, we can go down because we're within a higher holon that contains your lower plane. You're still in a lower vibratory plane that's too slow and limited to contain the higher.'

'Holons again,' I said. 'Give me an analogy of how this works.'

'It's not difficult to understand,' Mo said, 'but analytical minds have a way of reading into things, thereby making them a lot more complicated than need be. So let me give you an example even a philosopher might understand. Think of a Russian Matryoshka stacking doll set where each smaller doll nests into the larger and then the next into the next and so on. You can always put a small doll into a larger one, but not a larger doll into a small one. The larger includes all of the smaller dolls in the set, thus transcending what was contained. What could be simpler?

'There is much more to understanding the relationship of parts to the whole, but we can discuss that later with the vast implications of where these premises lead. For now, this should give you a starting point with something very basic. Often the most profound philosophical concepts are the simplest.'

'I'd like to know more about these dolls in your dimension. It would be interesting to see how they stack up.'

'Even if you were able to handle their higher frequencies,' Eli said, 'the experience would probably make your future life on earth bloody miserable and you may not wish to return to the earth's plane. But as you often hear us say, your dense world provides unique challenges and opportunities for your soul to prepare for the refulgent states of being in our realm.'

'So if I can't go to where these being are,' I said, 'still I think it would be splendid if some of the prettier angels would deign to lower themselves to my level, if only to give me a smile and wink. I'm not really that far down the scale am I? I mean, if they can go all the way down to help the distressed, why not here too?'

'Just curious,' said Mo, 'but why are you so interested in seeing angels all of a sudden?'

'Well, okay, I wasn't going to bring this up before, so promise not to tell anyone; I don't want this getting around, but I think someone, possibly an angel or ghost, is prowling around here at night. I'm not sure what she has in mind, but I sense her presence late at night before I go to my loft. She must really like me because I feel she's coming on stronger to me all the time. I wish she'd appear to me, but maybe she's doesn't trust ex sailors.'

'What makes you think this prowler is a she?' Mo asked.

'Because that's what I wish to imagine – so stop trying to ruin my little fantasy. Trust me, I know these things; this presence feels very feminine; delectably so.'

'And you can extrapolate all that from just feelings?' Mo said. 'I must say, not bad for a philosopher! So what happened to your analytical mind?'

'It's taking a much deserved rest,' I said. 'Besides, if I allowed it to interfere, it would spoil everything, just like before when she suddenly left after I started thinking too much. Though I imagine my angel, or whatever she is has a beautiful radiant face, with a long slim body, wearing one of those slinky white satin dresses; still there's something more to the attraction I can't explain. The feeling is much different than I've ever known towards a woman. It's rather strange, but I feel drawn to her in some inexplicable way, as though I already have a mystical connection with her. So how would you explain that?'

'Your consciousness has been steadily expanding ever since arriving here in your current octave,' Eli said, 'which is why your frequency is now able to align with certain subtle energies as with your visitor. Later, as you notch up your vibratory alignment, you may witness her inner essence pattern configure into what appears physical.'

'So are you saying this spirit could manifest just like that?'

'She already has manifested, he said, but not to you; not until you're able to achieve closer vibratory alignment with her. But then, what would you do if you had such an encounter? You're hardly accustomed to being in such class.'

'I don't know, maybe I'd ask her out; problem is where do you take someone so far up? I suppose we could go to her cloud, but then what? I'm no angel. I can't even play the harp. So what do you think about this phantom, and why she's stalking me?'

'Stalking may not be the right word,' Mo said, 'perhaps it's just some secret admirers openly trying to get your attention as best they can.'

'Let's start with just one for now, okay – at least until I get the hang of this. So fine, she's got my attention; now what?'

'What do you want?' Eli asked.

'I'm not sure what I'm allowed to want, but I'd be open to whatever suggestions she may have for us, no matter how un-angelic. But first I need to meet her and find out why she keeps coming by at night. Not that I mind. Actually, I rather like being haunted by her.'

'I don't blame you for wanting to meet her, but as Mo said, you first need to come into alignment with her. Provided you are able to make the vibratory connection, there's no reason why you wouldn't eventually be able to see her and possibly many others on this side. To enter that domain, however, you will need to do more inner, transformational work, since this is more than your outward perception; it's about your inward spiritual receptivity.'

'But if an angel can meet me on a bus or in a coffee shop, why can't she do the same here?'

'Possibly it's because there are no buses or coffee shops up here, or maybe she's not even what you would call an angel. But if she is, maybe she doesn't wish to meet you physically, at least not until you're ready. Perhaps she wants you to first ascend to her level where you are able to join with her as a vibratory match. That doesn't necessary mean she's being a snob, maybe she wants to entice you to ascend further up and further in to where she is.'

'But didn't I already climb high enough up this Mountain?'

'I guess not,' said Eli. 'Obviously she thinks you still have a ways to go.'

'Okay, fine. So just tell me what I have to do, and I'll do it.'

'Be patient James,' Mo said; 'there's no hurry. It's coming since you're already doing all the necessary preparation; just stay on course. You made it this far on your journey, but there are still higher Summits you need to ascend to before you are able to meet this entity.'

'... my ghost angel?'

'As you wish,' he said, 'but when you're able to align with her you might find she is neither ghost nor angel.'

'That's fine, as long as she looks as good on the outside as she feels on the inside.'

'Like we always say James; *as within, so without.*' I'm sure you won't be disappointed.

'I suspect you both know more about this minx than you're letting on. So what's her name?'

'Should you meet, be sure to ask,' Eli said with a grin, 'though I doubt you would believe her.'

'Why wouldn't I? Can you at least tell me a little of what she looks like? How could I have anything in common with her if she's some alien or ephemeral celestial being from another dimension?'

'We're all spirits that emanate from the same Source,' Mo said. 'That obviously would include your visitor, regardless of how she appears.'

Suddenly Eli jumped up in excitement, his chair falling over in the clamour. 'Oh my God!' he shouted; 'there she is James, looking at you again through the window!'

I sprang up. 'Where, where?' I cried out excitedly.

'Oh bloody hell – sorry James; you just missed her! That's most unfortunate. I know, try running out back and see if she's waiting there for you in the shrubs.'

'Damn you Eli!' I was about to slug him, but wasn't sure how effective that work here.

'Still looking for love in all the wrong places?' Mo asked.

'Nice set up, Eli,' I said. 'Wait till it's your turn!'

'Made you look,' he said, laughing.

A bit embarrassed with getting taken in again, I got up to open a pint of bitter that was sitting on the window ledge. 'But look what she brought me – left nothing for you though.'

'Sorry James, but I placed that bottle there earlier,' Mo said, trying not to laugh. 'But you go ahead, James. Have it anyway, at least it's real.'

'I'm not sure who or what's real around here anymore, no matter what side of the window pane.'

'On whatever side of the pane or plane we may exist,' he said, 'we're all created and individuated as discrete beings. You name it: humans, angels, guides, guardians, archangels, cherubim, seraphim, ghosts, aliens or whatever other exotic beings may proliferate throughout the stars. Call them whatever sounds good to you, they don't mind, they all know who and what they are.'

'I'm pleased for them,' I said, 'maybe one day I'll figure out who and what I am too, as befitting a philosopher that doesn't get taken in so easily. So tell me, while we're on subject; if we're all of the same essence, what is it that differentiates souls where some are good like me, and some not so good like Eli?'

'Everyone becomes uniquely individuated according to the quality of their soul's character,' Mo said, 'based on the cumulative choices they've made through the ages. Certainly nature and nurture have an influence in earth's dimension, but it's how we respond to life's circumstances is what causes us to become what we're constantly becoming. It's mainly through relationships you grow, function and survive.'

'But are you still regarded as humans in your dimension?'

'If we seem as human as you,' Mo said, 'that's because we are or at least were. It depends on how you define human. The biological term *"Homo sapiens"* hardly applies to a spirit, although the human experience was derived from where the spirit essence intersected with matter, the higher vibration with the lower.

The most obvious difference is that our former humanoid suits have been laid aside, having served its purpose, whereas yours is still laying somewhere in London, patiently waiting for your return. Since you are still connected to your earthly vessel with the allegorical silver cord we talked about, you're not at the vibratory level where you are able to enter into our realm that transcends, yet includes the human dimension.'

'So better luck next time should you plunge down another chasm,' Eli said with a laugh.

'Eli, I'm not sure death is a laughing matter, especially when it's about mine.'

'Consider the state of those to whom you are talking. Do we look dead? I hope not – never felt more alive, and so there's no reason to get all morbid.'

'If we make light of this, James,' Mo said, 'it's because we're all much lighter when unburdened by earth's heavy load. In fact, so light you just want to laugh when you realize that what is called death was just a means to get where you wanted to go.'

'No disrespect to you,' Eli said, 'but the transition is a laughing matter for those whose bodies have died. But when death is feared, it can indeed be a very cruel joke until you realize there was nothing to fear. Setting your worthy and honourable body aside at the end of its earthly phase is hardly the same thing as losing your soul. After the acorn germinates, and the tree begins to grow, the seed returns to the elements, having served its purpose in preserving the conatus of the tree long before giving form to it.'

'Okay then, so tell me, when your acorns died, how did you manage to come here to be with me all this time? Did heaven, hell or some planet called Zog punt you onto this purgatorial plane so you may pay for your past misdeeds?'

'We come and go as we please,' Eli said, 'but this isn't purgatory, unless you consider it purgatory, which it may be for some. Other than that, I don't know if such a state actually exists. Certainly I haven't come across it. Have you Mo?'

'Only once, when I was in a rather unfortunate domestic situation a couple of lifetimes ago,' Mo said. 'My marriage wasn't hell, but it wasn't heaven either so perhaps it was something in-between like purgatory. But I learned from it, and I'm sure she did too. Perhaps the notion may be considered a projected state by those who think they need to purge themselves of something they did. But I can think of many better things to project.'

'So now that we have that settled or unsettled, can you now tell me more about where you disappear to when you leave at night?'

'You wouldn't believe us if we told you,' Eli said.

'Try me, I'm curious. What's the big secret?'

CHAPTER 18

CHAMPS-ÉLYSÉES

What no eye has seen, what no ear has heard
and what no human mind has conceived[1]

Though I recognized my friends had lived on earth at one time, I wasn't able to find out much about where they called home. Certainly they weren't aliens from some distant galaxy on the other side of the universe; they had too much earth grit for that. Based on some of the things they said, I suspected they were from whatever dimension humans transition to after they depart their biological bodies. Perhaps because they didn't seem like they were afterlife types, I had never broached the topic of life after death. It still seemed hard for me to believe they were no longer of the earth since there seemed to be no big difference between them and me.

It was early the next day while we were having coffee outside and talking about my life in London. I decided it was finally time to bring up the subject they seemed to have evaded – at least up till now.

'You know,' I said, 'I've told you all about where I live and how good the sandwiches are in the deli below, I think it's now time you

---

[1] *I Corinthians 2:9 (NIV)*

both tell me a little about where you live and what twilight zone you wonder off to after twilight.'

'Of course,' said Eli, 'you're right. That's what we do; we transition off into the twilight zone. But it's where you're from too, you just don't remember!'

'Can you be a bit more specific Eli, without making this into another riddle?'

'It's a fair question,' Mo said, 'but there's not much we can tell you at this point, or it may indeed seem like a riddle, even more than it is. We don't wish to confuse you with words formulated in your physical sphere of existence, so there's not much we can say except that it's a rarified plane of existence.'

'I think you will find me more than capable of understanding what you have to say. I'm a rather quick learner.'

'We know you are,' said Mo, 'but this isn't about learning, it's about understanding a deeper level of reality than what your mind is capable of processing. It would be like trying to understand Whitehead in the first year of primary school.

That's also why we have encouraged you to study various books to engage your heart, that you may catch a few fleeting glimpses of the ineffable.[1] These will help open the portals of your imagination to see into the celestial sphere, but only dimly. Too often modern philosophy applies only rational thoughts to mystery, which is why it so easily becomes confused. Only by experiencing this domain within, will you understand what's perceived without, all else will be speculation.

'We can say however, our domain is not to be construed as a geographical location, twirling about in space, but rather a state of being, manifesting in a variety of densities along the Ray of Creation, from the most rarified to the most opaque. We can also say that each soul exists in unity with others who share in the same quality of affections and purposes. These relationships reflect one's inward essence; which is why one feels in perfect harmony with kindred spirits.'

'Splendid, that's not a bad start, tell me whatever else you can, even

---

[1] These included portions from various writings of Pensées, Enneads, Cloud of Unknowing, Meister Eckhart, Upanishads and the Gospel of John.

if it's only a caricature of the higher reality! I'm sure there are many who will want to hear about this.'

'Some may,' Mo said, though few would believe you, even if you could explain it. But since you're so interested, we tell you a few more things as long as you realize there's so much more to these higher domains than we can begin to describe. We only hesitate because whatever we tell you may seem so trite, that it misrepresents the hidden reality.

'I recognize this, but tell me what you can about this place, or as you say; state of being.'

'The world has many names for this domain of existence: Heaven, Paradise, Beulah, Nirvana, Valhalla, Happy Hunting Grounds, etcetera, the list goes on. Yet these are only names, and so can't reveal the true nature of the celestial sphere which may be characterized as total peace, happiness and contentment.'

'So if everyone is a state of this perpetual celestial bliss, wouldn't that get rather boring after awhile, if not annoying? Personally, I don't trust people who go around smiling all the time.'

'Everyone is as happy as they wish to be, just as on earth. Except in this state there is every reason to be happy and no reason not to be. Understand that happiness is a result of inward qualities such as love, creativity and relationships. Essentially, it's what you make of it, since happiness can never be imposed from without. In the lower dimensional realms, what is taken to be happiness is a perverse desire for misery, fear and pain, as so many on earth seem to prefer.'

'As for me,' Eli said, 'my dimension needs no name, so I just call it home. That's what it felt like the instant I arrived: the perfect fulfillment of my most inward desires.'

'That's why the name doesn't matter,' Mo said. 'Call it whatever you please; it's a sense of belonging and union, based on what you are within.'

'Still, I'd like to have a name for purposes of discussion, since I can hardly call it home while my body remains bound to the earth. And I'd prefer not to use the word heaven any more than hell. Both names have the same religious associations, even though they have opposite meanings.'

'So why are you uncomfortable with the word *heaven*?'

'Ever since my early years, I've thought of it as an unctuous fantasy to bait the gullible and naïve masses to behave in prudish ways I could never relate to. As I said earlier, I often associate the name with pale effete angels and pudgy little cherubs we often see depicted in the medieval and renaissance paintings. They were a big hit then, but I think the world has moved on beyond the whole otherworldly scene. I'm sure though, many religious people expect to see goofy things like this when they die.'

'And so, any notion of heaven to me seemed to be nothing more than *pie in the sky*, far too trite for anyone with enough intellect to think for themselves. That's why I've never cared for the word *heaven*.'

'Then why not choose another name?' Mo asked, 'perhaps something with less religious connotations, since you have problems with that one. It doesn't matter what you call it as long as the meaning you give it points beyond itself. So can you think of a name you're more comfortable with? Remember though, whatever moniker one may ascribe to this domain, can never represent its true essence and transcendence.'

'Sorry, but I don't have the slightest idea what to call your home. Until recently, I was very sceptical of its very existence.'

'Maybe I can help you here,' Eli said. 'I believe it wasn't long ago I saw you reading Homer's Odyssey.'

'Yes indeed; thanks for leaving me a copy. Ever since I was a boy I've enjoyed reading exquisite tales of Greek mythology.'

'And why do you think that was?' Mo asked

'I'm not exactly sure. I just know when some of my late father's books found their way to me, including the leather bound classics; I wanted to read them all. I think that's when I first got interested in mythology, though there was much I didn't understand back then.'

'Just curious, James, but what did you like most about these books?' he asked.

'I think more than anything, the books scribed by Homer and Virgil held a sentimental value that seemed to give me a vague connection to my deceased father. I repeatedly read the same pages I was sure he had read so long ago, wanting to share the same thoughts as him. Then later, when I was a sailor, I took his leather bound book of Homer's Odyssey with me, and read it again with new wonderment, thinking he may also have been reading it as he sailed through these same Aegean islands.'

I paused for a moment as I reflected on these fond memories, then finally I said: 'This is most curious; I have no idea why I'm telling you this; what does this have to do with rebranding heaven?'

'Perhaps more than you realize,' Eli said. 'Do you remember the term Homer used in the Odyssey to describe Paradise?'

'Of course, *Elysian Plains* or, as the French say: *Champs-Élysées*. In fact, everything in Paris seems to be associated with that name; more than anywhere else, they made it famous, even if they don't always realize what it means.'

'So wouldn't you like to make the name famous for the rest of the world?'

'What do you mean? There already was a movie produced by that name not long ago.'[1]

'All the more reason for you to tell everyone what if actually means,' Mo said, 'and how close you came to being there while your body was in a coma. Also, considering how you sailed among these mythical islands, the name is superb. Who knows, maybe even way back then, you were searching for Élysées.'

'Okay, why not?' I said. 'Let's go with Élysées. Perhaps someday it'll catch on, as it did in the past.'

'Ah yes,' Mo said, '*the Elysian Fields*. I like it; a most heavenly choice! Homer is considered to be among the first to have used the name. The nomenclature possesses a refined and illustrious history. Poets throughout the ages talked about the Elysian, or Elysium, as an afterlife paradise, including Virgil, Plutarch, Dante, Blake, Keats, Shakespeare and several others.

'As you indicated, the name has also found several expressions in modern culture, including Paris' famous *Avenue des Champs-Élysées* and *Palais de l'Élysée* of the French Republic. The name is even in their much beloved pop song, *Aux Champs-Élysées*.'

---

[1] *Elysium*, released in 2013; starring Matt Damon and Jodie Foster. The wealthy and powerful live on a gigantic space paradise called Elysium located in Earth's orbit.

'So assuming we're all in agreement,' I said, 'we'll refer to your home territory as Champs-Élysées, or alternatively Elysian Fields, being the Anglo version.'

'To keep things simple,' Mo said, 'let's drop the champs/fields and go with Élysées, Elysian or Elysium, as you prefer. For my part I've always been more partial to Elysium, the more common Anglo name.'

'Ever since I spent time in Paris several years ago,' Eli said, 'I grew accustomed to the French version, and so you may at times hear me pronounce it as Élysées.

'Some consider the name to be neo-pagan,' Mo said, 'which I suppose it is, having originated several thousands of years ago in Greece.[1] As venerated as the word was through the ages, Homer's depiction was only a limited earth bound symbol, reflecting his times and environment. But, we may now expand on that and think of Elysium as a higher vibratory state of being, rather than suggesting a place somewhere past the stars beyond the blue. The name has an interesting mystique that points to whatever transcends the seas and plains of earth.'

'Mystique; that's what I'd like to hear more about; so tell me of all the mysteries that lie beyond earth's seas and plains?'

'As we just said, there's not much we can say that you would understand, until you're able to comprehend the greatest mystery of all. When you do, you will ask no more, you will just know. Then you will no longer wait for Élysées; Élysées will come to you.'

'So what is the great mystery of which you speak?'

'*Nosce te Ipsum: Know Thy Self.*'

'Oh, that again; fine, I'm still working on it; it's quite the conundrum. But for now, just tell me in simple terms, what goes on in Élysées. What kind of things do you do to amuse yourself when you're not here confusing me?'

'Use your imagination,' Mo said, 'Elysium is a very large tent with infinite capacity and diversity to extend itself into the *Infiniverse*. So when

---

[1] The name may have its origins with the Greek verb *eleuthô*, meaning *release* for the souls of heroes and virtuous men. The mythical locations vary among poets such as Homer, Hesiod and Virgil. *Some traditions considered this a realm of the netherworld, others certain eastern islands in the Aegean Sea and later, a place on the Black Sea.*

you ask me what goes on, what am I supposed to say, especially when there's no end to things that are seemingly happening everywhere all at once, at least until you decide what you wish to focus your attention on. Even then, it's possible to split your focus on many things all at once.'

'Okay, but I'm not sure how that would be possible without being diagnostically ADD. Regardless, just tell me what happens when one arrives on Elysium's golden shores.'

'I suppose it's different for everyone,' Mo said, 'but most souls coming to Elysium find themselves enveloped in a sphere of pure light and love that manifest in many divine forms, depending on the recipient. It is that encounter with divine transcendence that causes so many to plead not to return to earth, even when there is every reason to continue with their journey's there.'

'I can experience that intimacy with God the Source at any time when I open the portals of my heart to receive all the love I'm capable of receiving. But for whatever reason, that wasn't what I experienced when I crossed over this last time. Rather, I found myself sauntering dreamily through an open glade surrounded by mist that reminded me of an area we called *A'Ghàidhealtachd* in the Scotland Highlands.'

'The next thing I knew, knights came charging over the glen towards me, all armoured on their powerful steeds. And yet I had no fear, just an overwhelming fascination of what was unfolding around me. They even had a spare mount for me to ride. At first I thought it was all just a dream, and so allowed myself to believe I must be one of the knights who had lost his horse in battle.

'As you may guess, this was an exquisite and most splendid re-enactment of a fantasy I harboured as a young lad, when I wished to be a courageous knight. As we rode through the fog towards the castle, I felt I was one of King Arthur's Knights of the Round Table.

Soon after dismounting, we entered the Grand Hall and sat down to a large sumptuous feast in my honour. The beautiful Queen Guinevere, who sat beside me, whispered in my ear that this was my homecoming being enacted as my life's most cherished dream, and yet it was not a dream. Then suddenly everything became clear and I knew who I really was, much like coming down from a mind altering drug trip, not that I would actually know that.

'Everyone was having a most jovial time, with me being the centre of attention. I couldn't have asked for a more joyous reception, wenches included. And by the way, guess who Sir Lancelot was?'

'I give up, who?'

Mo looked over to Eli, as they both laughed.

'Eli?'

'And most convincingly,' he said, 'just as I pictured the brave knight to be!'

'It was most splendid,' Eli said. 'I too was caught up in this same fantasy as a boy, while reading about Merlin, Sir Galahad, Sir Gawain, and of course, Sir Lancelot. Even as an adult, I'd read whatever I could find on the legends of King Arthur. You should know by now our imaginations are not diminished in the spirit realm, but are unleashed to create as never before, just as William Blake envisioned in his poems.

You can't help but have a lot of fun playing these roles when new arrivals take everything so seriously. Nowhere else do the experiences and events of earth have a greater import then during such occasions, since they provide a bridge into ascendancy. In this sense, we all bring some of earth and its trappings along with us until we grow out of them.'

'I have no doubt you'd fit right in Eli, considering all the pranks you get to play on unsuspecting souls crossing over.'

'Never a dull moment,' he said, laughing; 'almost as much fun as pranking you.'

'In a way,' Mo said, 'these incidents aren't far removed from the various plays we script and act out during our lifetime on earth. Shakespeare wrote in Hamlet, *All the world's a stage, and all the men and woman merely players.*[1] Though the plays on Earth aren't always so much fun, at least we get to teach each other some of the lessons we came to learn, even if we scripted them long before entering onto the earth's stage.'

'In which case, I'm curious to know if you both knew each other when, as you say, you played your roles on Earth.'

'No, but I had a reason I wished to acquaint myself with Eli after crossing over. So what better way, then as a knight? We've remained good

---

[1] William Shakespeare; *As You Like it*, Act 2, Scene 7

friends ever since, and on occasions, we sometimes participate in more King Arthur adventure games with other aficionados for amusement during certain transition enactments. As you can appreciate, earth with its history and adventures provides ever expanding experiences there. The lower and higher dimensions are inextricably entwined, forever creating, contributing and exchanging the substance of life.'

'So who was King Arthur, other than a legend?'[1]

'You may be surprised, but there actually was an historical person behind the myth. I didn't believe it at first, but later I found the story was built on the semblance of a local Romano-Brit king named Riotamus from the late fifth century who, ostensibly, was defending Britain from the invading Saxons. No one gets a bigger kick out of playing himself whenever the opportunity arises. Obviously he's very good at this.'

'And I'll bet as Sir Lancelot, Eli gets an even bigger kick playing Queen Guinevere's lover whenever the opportunity arises.'

'I do,' Eli said, 'and so does she.'

'Sounds like everyone must have a lot of fun there.'

'At least for those who enjoy a good time,' he said, 'although at first, too many try to make something religious out of it, at least until they discover Elysium is all about happy relationships. Personally, I prefer to hang out with the party crowd, it kind of makes up for the unhappiness I often felt on earth. But is this not the way life should to be,' Eli said, 'with much laughter, love and happiness? Every joyful fantasy you ever had on earth is still waiting to be played out there. This is the actual reality and why it's rather a shame the word *heaven* has accumulated so many dour associations and ridiculous distortions from the earth plane's way of thinking. But I suppose that's to be expected in earth's vibratory zone – ludicrous caricatures of harps, golden pavement and emasculated angels hovering over us, wings aflutter. I agree with you James, these images give the average debunker like you an easy target.'

'Since my department is full of sceptics,' I said, 'perhaps I should warn them about you in case you happen to be in charge when they

---

[1] Geoffrey of Monmouth is presumed to be the first to write about King Arthur, (approximately 1130) in his *History of the Kings of Britain*. Most scholars agree the book is not historically reliable.

arrive. So what kind of enactments would you perform for them when they cross over?'

Eli laughed, as he said, 'You've read *Dante's Inferno*, right?'

'You wouldn't actually do that would you?' I said, as I laughed?

'Oh I don't know, it may be kind of fun – provided I could get away with it. But I'm not sure the staging authorities would trust me with that theme, especially after some of the skits I pulled off recently.'

'I can only imagine,' I said. 'When I finally come over, Mo, please don't let Eli organize a Halloween Party for my return. I may take it seriously and assume I made a wrong turn while sailing across the great divide!'

'That would be scary indeed!' Eli said with a chuckle. 'You shouldn't be giving me any ideas. If I can get away with it, I may try to organize something like that for the pope when he crosses over.'

'Just to be safe, I think I would prefer Mo to be in charge of making arrangements for my greeting party – what do you say; how about some dancing girls?' I laughed.

'Anything can be arranged if it helps facilitate the transition process. I've observed certain guides who seem to have a little too much fun staging various scenes for new arrivals. Some, such as Eli, have a slightly sadistic bent, where they can hardly wait to scare the hell out of certain NDE visitors who don't believe in anything other than their ego's illusions.

'That's right,' said Eli, 'fire, pitch forks, devils, you name it: the props certainly get everyone's attention when they arrive. More often than not, they return to Earth with an altered perspective on life. Not surprisingly, most are much better prepared next time they return after their final departure.'

'I can see where you would fit right in there with the other rascals. Being such a prankster, you'd be a natural for these stunts. But is it legal to go around spoofing these unsuspecting arrivals?'

'Most certainly,' Mo said, 'nothing can be illegal where there's no law but the law of love. There's also another type of enactment,' Mo said, 'other than a Halloween motif, that can also be very scary. Often it's for the benefit of the very religious who are fond of saying that when they go to heaven all they want to do is forever worship like the angels.

Saying that makes them sound very pious and admirable when trying to impressing others.'

'Forever; that's a hell of long time. Why would anyone want to be confined to singing and chanting forever more? Five minutes in church would be too much for me, unless some bird across the aisle was giving me the eye; then maybe ten minutes.

'Besides, what kind of narcissistic god needs to be worshipped in ceaseless adoration? I would rather be annihilated with a good dose of Socrates' hemlock or be entertained in a lascivious hell where scoundrels and rogues slink around doing more interesting things than sitting around being religious.'

'I agree,' Mo said, 'and perhaps that's why, if I'm not mistaken, Nietzsche is quoted as saying, *in heaven, all the interesting people are missing.*[1] But as it turns out, that's not true.'

'Just look at Mo and me,' Eli said, 'it doesn't take too long for even the most devout to come away with a different perspective as they quietly slink away. Except once when I locked the doors of the church from the outside so they couldn't get out. When I finally opened the bolt, they ran out screaming all the way down the hill. I got into some trouble for that, but it was worth it. Like I said; it's easy to have as much fun you want.'

'And yet, for the sanctimonious,' Mo said, 'it's good for them to experience exactly what they thought they wanted, but actually didn't. After such experiences, they invariable go on to discover how things really are, which generally have little or nothing to do with their religious traditions and expectations. Eventually, everyone comes to understand that worship has more to do with relationships and service towards others, rather than just attending meetings.

'At some point, they begin to realize that the vertical relationship they sought to have with God, was achieved through the horizontal relationships they developed among those who had nothing to do with their religion. In fact, there are a lot of other surprises for the faithful who really had no clue about what it meant to love God.

'That's why it's important not to become too fixated on too many doctrinal words that have taken on misleading connotations. There are

---

[1] Friedrich Nietzsche, German philosopher (1844 - 1900)

many words and ideas that were meaningful at one time, but became sullied over the ages with unfortunate associations.

'For example, the various names given to God over the millennia have often been characterized as a mean spirited, capricious tyrant, including the very name of God. Such representations of power, judgement and condemnation conjure images directly opposed to what unconditional love means. Of course, these faulty projections were often cast about by various religions and institutions that wished to exploit feelings of human guilt and shame to their advantage.

'In fact, some still do when they use their doctrines to spread messages of divine retribution and fear. Quite successfully, as it turns out. Such pernicious beliefs invariably distort and twist the truth, making the simplicity and beauty of love incomprehensible for those who wring their hands in despair, quivering in the shadows of their imagined hells.

'Unfortunately the damage doesn't end there. Many of those who see through the nonsense end up dismissing their divine Source. In doing this, they can't know much about their purpose in life on earth or beyond. But when they connect with all that they are, they connect with everyone and everything, since we are all one with the Source from which all manifestation flows.'

'Okay, I can appreciate how badly humanity gets everything wrong, but what can you tell me about what's right and how things get rectified there?'

'I realize I may not be able to give you the specific descriptions you are looking for,' he said, 'but let me approach the question by explaining how Elysium is able to take what was wrong with the good humanity was able to create on earth.

'The first thing you need to know is that most things are aggregated in collectives, arranged in accordance with the dominant affections of that collective. You may wish to call these centres a kind of *soul family*, or simply *communities* as Swedenborg described it, where things continually flow, evolve and congeal as we sometimes witness in nature. Except in the spirit realm, this phenomenon is based on relationships existing within the same frequency, where no one is out of synch with anyone, or anything else.

'Whenever there's a shift in awareness, spirits become less comfortable remaining in a community that no longer aligns with their vibratory essence. Why would Zulu warriors, for example, want to associate with intellectual snots, even if they could find any in Elysium? But it's not just a matter of cultural differences; these distinctions are mainly degrees of spiritual affections.

'That's why lower regions naturally exist as a necessary extension of the souls who wish to remain separate from Elysium's communities and what they represent. No one sent these souls down there; no one created it for them, and no one but themselves holds them there; it's an outward expression of what they are within. As within, so without.

'But before you feel too sorry for them, understand; they're all in their element, in the spiritual zone where they wish to remain, that being the manifested expression of their deprived affections. It's not a pretty sight, except to them, since they, in their insanity, created and continue to create, the appropriate environment for their soul's depravity.'

'That's rather depressing,' I said, 'so let's go back to Elysium; what are things like in the realms of higher vibratory expression?'

'Imagine, if you can,' Eli said, 'idyllic pastoral scenes in the country, majestic mountains, lakes, rivers, streams, oceans, coastal villages and gardens. It's everything you can think of and far beyond what could be desired. There are colours of unbelievable variations, especially with flowers, all possessing their own special fragrances.

'Yet this is only the starting point, an extension of what's known and experienced on Earth. There's a place, or should I say, a state, which is optimal for everyone's happiness according to each soul's capacity to receive, and then perceive.

'As Mo already indicated, all communities, regardless of where they're found, exist in close affinity to kindred souls of one mind and heart. The illusion of distance holds no more meaning than time does. At will, anyone can be anywhere they wish, just as you are able to teleport at will. All destinations are determined by the intent of the desire to be there. No one in Elysium would wish to choose to be in any place that's less dense or denser, than the vibratory essence of their being.

And yet, everyone has an impulse or conatus, to aspire further in and further up to higher spheres. Even in the lowest regions below, all eventually ascend upwards since their divine essence always remains, even when seemingly lost.'

'But don't these little idyllic communities become a little confining after a while, especially for the more cosmopolitan types like me who prefer big city life?'

'But that's why megalopolises similar to London, Shanghai and New York necessarily exist to reflect the affections of all who prefer bustling cities of boundless vitality, where innumerable expressions of life can be found, including that of art and commerce.'

'Including commerce? You've got to be joking, what's filthy lucre doing in Elysium?'

'I suppose it depends on how you understand it,' Mo said. 'Is commerce not about giving and receiving; that which is implicit in all relationships? Though one is able to manifest most anything, there are always new creations being formulated from the minds and hearts of creators; such as with music and art that have never before been seen or heard. The possibilities for these new manifestations are as endless and expansive as the imagination itself. In fact, all of Elysium's commerce is an expression of creativity that is exchanged in ways that would be virtually impossible to imagine on earth. Obviously money isn't required where the only currency is love and appreciation.'

'That's very nice,' I said, 'and good for them, but why would anyone do anything without receiving compensation for their efforts?

'Can you imagine,' James,' a place where artisans, for example, are eager to share what they have created because they understand, like everyone else, we can only receive what we give. Or, to put in another way, receive in accordance with the reciprocal *desire* to give. With this implicit understanding, no one ever goes out of business unless they wish to do something else.

But one thing you won't find are factories, since the only things that are being assembled are thoughts, both individually and collectively; everything else is a manifestation of those thoughts.'

'So what else won't you expect to find there?' I asked.

;Anything based on fear, deprivation, sickness or anything negative.

Obviously, insurance premiums have little meaning there. The same goes for the arms and munitions industries, except for in the hells where they, in their insanity, are constantly at war with themselves!

But other business, such as architectural firms, remain thriving businesses where great satisfaction exists in designing and creating exciting expression's of form that reflect the collective affections of that region.'

'I'd hate to ask about the status of lawyers or the whereabouts of their predominate domain,' I said with a laugh.

'Lawyers that arrive here,' Eli said, 'tend to bring great clarity of thinking to inter-dimensional cooperation and understanding. Their talents and abilities are not lost, except perhaps for those skilled in litigation. But then, not many of them show up in Elysium,' he smiled.

'Other obsolete or redundant professions include police, military, fire, judges, priests, doctors, administrators, magicians, and obviously, there are no trades. Yet each of these can have several alternate applications, none of which have an earthly description, since they don't exist on earth. There also is much room for scholars, scientists, seers, teachers, facilitators, speakers, designers, tour guides, artists, writers and musicians.

'These, of course, are but a few examples; mostly souls are engaged in various activities they find most fulfilling for which the world could have no name or understanding. The wisest and most spiritually advanced souls are often engaged as spirit guides for those they are best able to relate to. Some like to be called angels, but recently, some prefer being called coaches -- with or without haloes.'

'Whereas the earth plane is built on a foundation of fear,' Mo said, 'Elysium's foundation is built on love. That's the only way if can work. And so, Elysium contains only is created and exchanged in love. Everywhere, there are innumerable occupations, where countess souls engage in fulfilling their talents and aptitudes, while being of service to others who can appreciate what they have created. Writers, for example, can write for the pure enjoyment of writing, while sharing whatever thoughts they wish to express, without having to worry about selling enough copies to survive. Anyone who wants a book, in whatever format they prefer, can obtain it simply by manifesting it once it has been created.'

'So the big payoff, if I understand you correctly, is not in selling copies, but gaining recognition and admiration for what is created.'

'Yes, there may be that, but primarily it's the joy in sharing in what they have created; that's the fulfillment. Since everything is based on relationships, everyone in Elysium wants to be of service to everyone, including one's own self through authenticating expressions of creativity.

And beyond this, relationships are developed, directly or indirectly, between the giver and receiver, once the giver's creations become known. Thereby the artist gains even more fame and recognition than would be possible on earth, since money doesn't get in the way of receiving. That why there are no starving artists, because everyone already has received what they desire.'

'Sounds a little like Karl Marx's dictum: *from each according to his ability to each according to his need.*[1]

'That's close,' Mo said, 'except Elysium has no needs, only desires, which makes all the difference in the universe.'

'In some communities,' Eli said, 'millions of souls dwell, while in others, only hundreds. All is determined by the affections that gave rise to the community, even its size. Whatever else these communities may be, they are not ghettos or cloisters, since everyone is free to be wherever they want to be and/or travel wherever they wish; be it other planets, galaxies, eras, dimensions – even earth, where we now find ourselves with you.'

'So how is one able to keep up with everything that's going on?'

'When you are in the flow of all that is,' he said, 'you don't have to keep up, it just kind of carries you along most happily. All feels effortless, and yet it's dynamic, since this is how life was intended. Nothing is static; everything is constantly changing and expanding.'

'So what would you say, then, is the common overarching feature in this domain that holds everything together, even with the infinite variety of ceaseless activity?'

'Obviously, it's relationship,' Mo said, 'since nothing can exist without being in relationship to something else; not even God since God is relationship just as God is love. It's what makes the cosmos one,

---

[1] From Marx's *Critique of the Gotha Program*, published in 1875, although the phrase was first attributed to Louis Blanc when first used in 1839.

just as we've said before, love is the glue of the universe. Since love can only exist in relationship, it may also be said that relationship is likewise the glue of the universe, being love's expression. As I've said before, you must not think of love as a singular attribute or feature. It is not an attribute, rather it is that by which all attributes exist.'

'Say that again, Mo; perhaps in another way so I'm clear with what you mean.'

'As it is often stated,' he said, '*God is love*, yet love is not God, just as we may say God is relationship, but relationship is not God. There are no adequate words for love, only expressions we understand in relationships. Love is the inward *being-essence* by which all relationships come to manifest in an ongoing dynamic that requires relationships, not only towards other souls, but towards all things, places and events.'

'Sure, that sounds most splendid,' I said, 'if not a little convoluted, but how are we able to find our past relationships when we leave Earth? From what you're saying, Elysium sounds like a really, really big place.'

'That's easy, just go where your heart leads, and where it leads is where you'll go,' Mo said, 'unless, of course, you allow your mind to interfere as it so often does on earth. However, when you allow your heart to lead, your natural guidance system will take you to where you are most attracted. You'll likely find your most intimate relationships waiting to see you immediately; since you can't fail to be anywhere you wish to be. This is so you may continue to develop the affections you acquired and accumulated over the span of your earthly existence.

'On the other hand, if you don't wish to be with some relative or acquaintance you have no interest in seeing, then you need not. And they can't get into your space without your permission. It's that simple!'

'Okay, but I see a few problems with what you say about intimate relationships. What if I had two or three successive wives who happened to die before I get there? Which one do I pick?'

'Who says they want to be picked? As if they're going to want to wait around all that time hoping they would be the lucky one you choose. I hardly think so!

'In fact, Jesus already answered that question when his antagonists were trying to bait him with this issue. He told it straight. No one gets married and so no one is possessed by anyone else. But let's not get distracted with that now. We'll get into this with more depth later on; not surprisingly, it gets a little complicated. For now, realize that you'll be with people of like affections, whatever the relationship may have been on earth, or whatever new relationships you may cultivate on Elysium's side.'

'So you're saying; wherever I end up, everyone's going to be like me? But what if I don't like me?'

'Then I think you may have a problem. Souls who don't love themselves can't truly love anyone else, because love is of the Source and must be experienced from the Source within before it can be expressed. Don't you prefer to be with people who love themselves unconditionally, and therefore are able to love you unconditionally as well?

If they can't love themselves, they can't love anyone else, and so become alienated not just from themselves, but from any other relationship. If this condition isn't corrected, it develops into a state of insanity that continues until they are prepared to follow the light of love into the divine relationship. Then is wholeness restored.'

'That sounds like one hell of a place.'

'Indeed it is,' Eli said, 'so I guess you better learn to like you,' he laughed. 'But once you discover who James is, and what a fine bloke he is, you're going to love him as we do, a divine masterpiece with a few flaws here and keep him humble. That's why it will be easy for you to get along with everyone you encounter in Elysium; your true essence draws together the same quality of souls, although the variety of these characters may remain as richly diverse as on earth.'

'So does that mean there will be a rich variety of women I could date? You know I love variety, at least until I discover what variety I wish to love.'

'As on earth, there's endless variety,' Eli said; 'none are the same; everyone is distinct and unique, yet many have the same in common. There's no need conform to a prescribed mold, which is why the military and corporate establishments could never fit in, even if they had a purpose, which they don't. So when the time comes, you will go to your element.

'If you wish, you may be escorted by guides to help reacquaint you with all those you were closest to on earth and before in Elysium. And while there you may find the variety of friends you say you're looking for. Although, what you consider dating, doesn't happen – much too artificial and shallow. There are better ways for you to find your soul-mate, should you be ready for each other.'

'You mean I have a soul mate waiting for me in Elysium?'

'Or on earth – maybe in both,' he said.

But I'm not sure how a soul-mate could be in two places at once.'

'Then how about in two states at once?' Mo said. 'But never mind; you're not ready for that – at least not yet.'

'However, on this topic of relationships, I just thought of something else about my reception at the castle. It wasn't only the Knights and royalty who were in attendance; a huge crowd of hundreds gathered in the Courtyard to greet me. I had developed strong bonds with most of them over the centuries, but there were many others who showed up to join in the fun and celebration. Many had known of me, without me knowing them. Some of these are now among my closest friends, such as Eli, who still sometimes likes to pretend he's Sir Lancelot.'

'Only at the castle parties,' Eli said. 'When the really old, tired and worn souls arrive, they're shown a time that will forever keep them young and vital. On these occasions they are released from whatever afflictions they may have endured on earth. That's why many of us enjoy serving as guides to help the truly distressed through Elysium's passage to our side of the Mountain. It really makes things interesting, as if things weren't interesting enough already. As we say, we only receive what we give, and so we give them a really good time.'

'So if there's never a dull moment there, then no one must be dull.'

'Except for those with dull affections,' Mo said. 'But if dull is what they are, dull is what they want, and so no one complains. However, when they finally get bored with themselves being that way, and they all eventually do, then change becomes possible. But for that to happen, they may have to return to earth to incarnate for a complete make-over where they can develop more interesting affections. Within in the crucible of earth's contrast, they can change rather significantly in just a lifetime or two as they transform more fully what they were created to become.

And so there really is no excuse for being dull. But as always, it's a choice. Though things are continually changing in Elysium; souls change very little here. Since there are few, if any resistances, life is easy, which is the reason there are fewer opportunities for character development. And so, that's the only thing that's hard, at least in the lower levels of Elysium where the dullest of the dull dwell in their low vibratory state. But in the higher realms are always teeming with life and vitality, since it exists on a high vibration. So much so, that the lower can't even perceive the higher, since it's out of their range.

There are certain teachings on earth, including those of the Apostle Paul and Emanuel Swedenborg, who identified a hierarchy of three heavens. They mostly got that right, except within each of these, there are many octaves that have octaves within octaves; too numerous to mention; which accounts for so many distinctive community aggregates, each expressing their niche along the spectrum.'

'Okay Mo, that's most interesting to know, but let's get back to your story; what happened after your homecoming celebration?'

'Like most everyone else,' he said, 'a past life review was conducted, not for purposes of judging one or anything, but to discuss where to go from here. Think of this as an orientation time, but for some it's an opportunity to rest and heal, especially with those who've endured a traumatic life.

'After that, it's entirely up to us where we wish to be and do whatever we want. This is the stage where most find themselves in their natural community, being the vibratory zone that feels like home. Once there, hardly anyone knows where to start, which is why their closest intimate friends and relatives are there to help reorient them. For some, each new discovery feels overwhelming since they open to more variegated experiences of increasing diversity.'

'I suppose friends and relatives are fine for most, but what if I prefer to find someone more interesting to show me around, preferably wearing something tight?'

'Of course, James – just for you; but before you select an *interesting* tour guide, you may wish to spend some time with those that were closest to you in the past. You can be sure they will be excited to see you again. Wouldn't you prefer to see your mother and father first?'

I didn't say anything; for some reason the idea unsettled me, perhaps because of all the many unresolved emotions about their parting during my childhood.

'After becoming oriented or reoriented to Elysium,' Eli said, 'most wish to find a dwelling, since shelter on earth is considered to be necessary, which, as it turns out, is hardly the case since there's nothing to be sheltered from. Still, a place to call home is desired, and soon they learn to manifest the precise details of what they want for a domicile, at least until they're ready to move on to something new and different.

'When they move on and no one is occupying it, the place eventually dissolves as if it had never been there. Some, who acquire the traveling bug, no longer wish to remain in one place as they once did on earth, since there's no end of things to see and do in the plethora of universes and dimensions.'

'But whatever you do or wherever you go,' Mo said, 'you end up being attracted to whatever you loved most on earth, which is why there's such strong cohesions within the ever expanding circle of those with whom you are in close relationship.'

'Doesn't this feel-good ecstasy become a little tiresome after a while? Perhaps what's needed is a good dose of Kierkegaard's existential angst and despair to give some context to all this euphoria.'

'You're right;' Eli said, 'contrast has its place, especially at the lower stages of spiritual development; but then, that's what earth plane is for. Do you really want to go back to that?'

'I may have no choice if my body wants me back.'

'Oh, right! Sorry about that; I forgot,' he laughed. But there are other existences to choose from where happiness is less prevalent for those who aren't happy with happiness, joy and contentment even though happiness is what we're made for.'

'Unfortunately, it's true;' Mo said, 'for some it's difficult to accept Elysium after being conditioned to accept the world's sorrows from a less than ideal lifetime. After a while, however, most join the party after becoming weary of looking in from the outside. It's all about choices. On the continuum of happiness, there's a vibratory state that's perfect for everyone. But definitely, Elysium is not for everyone – at least until their ready!'

'So where do you think I fit in to all this; should I not return to the earth plane?'

'I think you already know. Do discovery, creativity and expansion give you pleasure, or does anger, vengeance and pain? Whatever the case, everyone ultimately grows beyond whatever gave them joy at one time, especially after they discover new and more profound experiences of happiness. This is like moving past the amusements of childhood to new exquisite pleasures of adulthood. That's why the more you develop your capacity for greater love and wisdom during your years on earth, the greater will be your capacity for receive more happiness in Elysium.'

'Most splendid, I'd say; at least for those in Elysium. But is the inverse not also true for those dwelling in the lower spheres?'

'Yes, of course,' Mo said, 'since nothing is pre-determined other than your freedom. Everyone chooses where they wish to be on the continuum of light. And since we are all creators, the hells will continue to exist as extensions of hellish affections as long as there are souls manifesting what is contrary to the essence of their being. Whatever is not in accord with divine love and wisdom attracts its own unhappy consequences.

'For all those participating in the divine affections of Elysium's splendor, it seems insane that any soul would prefer to remain in darkness. That's because it is insane. Every soul who willfully remains aligned and confirmed in their twisted state of existence continues to manifest life upside down, inside out and backwards, as we too often witness in the world.

'Those who prefer these lower regions, wish to consociate with those in their element whom they remain most comfortable. Often they take perverse delight in tormenting one another, since it gives them an illusion of power. Where else do we witness this in the world? And where do you suppose these leaders find themselves when they depart?

'Likely, not in a good spot,' I said. 'But then, as you say, they will be in their element.'

'This is why,' Eli said, 'the planet always needs more light bearers incarnating from Elysium to prevent humanity from destroying itself, at least until consciousness sufficiently rises to sustain a new spiritual equilibrium. Continued development of sophisticated technologies designed for apocalyptic destruction is making the world more dangerous since power is seldom concentrated among spiritually evolved beings.

'Countermanding the dark forces, however, are increasing multitudes of enlightened souls on earth that actively consociate with Elysium's advanced souls. They understand the soul's purpose is to transform from fear to love, from darkness to light, just as it is to help bring transformation to all other souls. Through the strength of this bond, the earth will eventually be able to dislodge and dispel millennia of accumulated hate, lies and suffering.'

'I certainly hope that happens,' I said, 'but let's leave Armageddon behind for a moment. I have something else I wanted to ask.'

'Certainly,' Mo said, 'what other important questions can we answer about Elysium?'

'Do you have any pictures?'

'Ah James,' he said, 'let's just say the scenery in Elysium is more wonderfully and infinitely diverse than anything you can imagine, where there are unlimited possibilities for greater expansion and creativity. On earth we experience only a feeble foreshadowing of our inherent capacity to co-create worlds with our Creator Source.'

'Actually, I was more curious to see pictures of the women there.'

'I'm sorry, no, we didn't bring photos,' Eli said, 'I'm not even sure how that's done or even if it is, since it's hardly necessary to have image representations when the reality is always available. But anyway, no picture or hologram would do justice to their animated beauty. Remember Hermesianax's adage, "*as within so without;*" it's a principle that most definitely applies in Elysium. Outward feminine beauty is always a direct expression of the beauty within, just as it is with the yang energy.'

'I might add,' said Eli, 'this commensurate relation between inward and outward beauty was often reported by Emanuel Swedenborg, who visited Elysium on an almost daily basis for close to thirty years. He was especially taken by the overwhelming beauty of women whose only attractiveness on earth was within, often inverse to what nature had outwardly denied them.'

'That sounds promising,' I said, 'next time you come across one of these lovely goddesses who's available, let her know where she can find me.'

'Maybe she already knows,' Eli said, 'and is here – visiting you at night.'

'Or maybe staring at me through the window – as you suggested. But speaking of visits; what else can you tell me about the various accounts of those who claim having short visits to Elysium; how credible are these reports? For what it's worth, I've read a few documented accounts of people returning to Earth after their NDEs.'

'Mostly these are legitimate experiences,' he said, 'much like what you are now experiencing, only most go further across the divide. Interestingly, those who have these experiences are from a cross-section of the population; young and old, rich and poor, religious and non-religious, educated and uneducated; it seems to make little difference.'[1]

'As a sceptic,' I said, 'I was never sure what to make of these accounts, but they were always interesting to read about even if some witnesses sounded like religious kooks.'

'Certain reports are suspect,' Mo continued, 'but generally most are credible, even if some travelers may get carried away embellishing their stories with their imaginations. This often happens with overtly religious accounts, where devotees remember seeing and hearing whatever their prior beliefs conditioned them to perceive, such as angels with wings, harps and trumpets.'

'But what you may yet witness here, could turn out to be a lot more bizarre than any of their accounts,' Eli said, 'so maybe you'll be seen as the kook when you return. In which case, you may wish to organize a defense league with all the other misunderstood souls who took a run at Elysium but didn't make it through.'

'Though I may not have made it the full distance, this experience in the Passage is probably good enough for now. I have lots of good things to report when I go back – I can hardly remember when I've had finer wine or better instructors.'

'And I can hardly remember having a better student,' Eli said; 'can you, Mo?'

---

[1] I'm referring primarily to the research done by American Psychologist Dr Michael Newton of the Newton Institute for *Life Between Lives* Hypnotherapy.

'No, absolutely not – likely there's not another quite like him. The best I can remember having.'

'I really am in a class of my own, am I not; being your first and only student. And I must say; the student-teacher ratio here at Summit U has been excellent, as have been the instructors, most notably when Eli rescued me off the ridge. How many would do that? I'll be sure to tell everyone about the good spirits I found up here – besides the liquid varieties.'

'As hard as you may find it to believe, we don't know everything. If fact, we still have a few rough edges so you won't feel intimated.

'No, I don't find that hard to believe at all,' I said with a grin. 'And why I would feel intimated.'

'Not even in our all dazzling resplendence?' Eli said.

'No, not dazzled at all.'

'Then how about those blazing bright orbs you saw?'

'Okay, I will admit; they about scared the hell out of me.'

'If only,' he said with a chuckle. 'Do you realize those orbs were actually Mo and me?'

'So what happened to your flaring aura and halo; did they burn out?'

'Actually, nothing changed except you,' Mo said. 'There was an adjustment in your perception when you suddenly became unencumbered by your physical body. By functioning purely in your spirit body, you acquired the capacity to see us as we are in our element. If you could see yourself in this body from your biological body, you may likewise appear as we did. As spirits, we're of the same ilk, only at different stages along the yellow brick road of becoming what we are.'

'Okay, but when I first saw you and Mo from a distance, I thought I also saw someone standing there with you at the far end of the summit. It seemed to me like a scene from the Mount of Transfiguration story. But then, the next time I looked, there was only the two of you.'

'You're right;' Eli said, 'there was a third who disappeared as you got closer.'

'Was it the same one as a couple of thousand years ago, only on another sacred Mount not as high?'

'No, not him, but don't feel bad, maybe you'll have an opportunity to meet him another time before you return home. But for now, you're going to have to settle for us.'

'Considering your current limbo between earth and Elysium,' Mo said, 'it's much better for us to be your go-between rather than some really advanced celestial being. We're still close enough to the world's grit to understand how you think and feel; which is why we can give you insight to your perceived problems.'

'I agree; it would likely be too big a gap to have celestial guide from way up there come down to counsel me about my past indiscretions. I'm sure with these more refined types; things may get a little awkward.'

'Like having to behave all day in the Queen's regal presence,' Mo said.

'I'm sure a lout would find it difficult to remain in such distinguished company for long,' Eli said.

'Wait a minute, are you calling me a lout?'

'Not at all,' Eli said, 'but some of the women you've known might.'

'I suppose that could be – there may have been a few occasions in the past when I've conducted myself with less decorum than normally befits a distinguished professor. But I think I've learned from my mistakes; wouldn't you say? No more lout – at least for now.'

'What are considered mistakes,' Mo said, 'are actually learning experiences that show the way forward. That's probably why Eli and I received this assignment; we've already had enough of these experiences on earth. Which is why, we're now able to relate to you in a way so you can talk to us about most anything. And who knows,' Eli said, 'perhaps one day we'll find a way to continue our discussions with you after you return.'

'I hope so; perhaps I could try to get my fortune teller friend to be our conduit. Not that I would want her to tell you about my private affairs. I'm not particularly proud of some of my more dubious achievements in my love life.

'We're not here to judge you for what you've learned on earth,' Eli said. 'But damn, all that mindless chasing after women; doesn't that get rather exhausting after a while?'

'It can, but it's never mindless,' I said, smiling. 'No more mindless than a dog chasing a car on a dirt road and getting left behind in the dust.'

'To be honest,' Eli said, 'I also spent a few years on such a road, only to be left in the same dust. But then, maybe that's another reason why I'm able to relate to you so well – perhaps more than you imagine.'

'Oh really; so there's more to this tangled web than just me. Most interesting! Perhaps we could compare notes sometime to decide who the worst scallywag was,' I laughed.

'That would be interesting,' he said, 'but let's not. I don't want to give you any wrong impressions since …'

He didn't finish his sentence; just glanced back at me briefly, then looked away as he went out the door.

CHAPTER 19

LEARNING BEYOND LEARNING

Learning always has as its goal leading the learner beyond learning[1]

B y the next day several questions about Elysium came to me. Because I was increasingly longing for romance in my life, especially after the mysterious visitations I had, I wanted to know more about the women there. Apparently, as I was finding, being in spirit form doesn't ameliorate sexual desire, in fact, it was becoming of greater interest to me.

From what they were telling me, however, I need not be concerned, since I would soon find what I was looking for, relative to what my soul found most attractive, first within, and then without. They didn't say, though, if I'd find her here or back home. But then, what if I could find one here and then another later when I went back. Why not?

I also thought; if Elysium was to be my home someday, it may be interesting to know what else I could expect to find there. Would I find the cars, trucks and motorcycles I was hoping for? In such a domain, what need would there be for commerce? I still didn't understand how

---

[1] *A Course of Love*; Book 3, Dialogues 9:10

the currency of love and appreciation could be adequate substitutes for monetary exchange. I received a few more ambiguous responses after I prodded them further, but nothing they said was very satisfactory.

Finally Mo said, 'certain things, James, can only be known through direct experience. Preconceived notions of how things must be, based on past experience, are not helpful, and will only serve to distort your understanding, whether in Elysium or on Earth. That's why we often find it necessary to speak of how things aren't, rather than how they are.'

Okay, I thought, but at this time, things seemed too skewed to how they aren't.

After breakfast we went outside to discuss more of my questions regarding the affairs of Elysium and how it operated. I found, however, the more they talked, the murkier things seemed to become to me.

In frustration, I put my feet up on the railing and leaned back in my chair and said, 'just curious gentlemen, but what qualifications do you have for this assignment here? Were you required to take a course before coming to meet me? I think it's rather important I know your credentials and whether you're certified or not for this. Though I wasn't actually serious, still I was curious to know what they might say.'

'Our primary qualification,' Eli said, 'is that we were willing to leave the tranquility of Élysées to be with you to give you a hand while you are in this state.'

'But not necessarily limited to the hand Eli gave you to rescue you not that long ago,' Mo said.

'Yes, and I remain most grateful that you both thought I was worth the effort. Although,' I said waggishly, 'neither of you were of much help in getting me off the chasm ledge before my fall, were you?'

'No, not much help at all,' Mo said, 'but I'm not sure how we could have with you still being in your earth's physical body.'

'But then, why would we even want to,' Eli said, 'knowing what an interesting time we could have on this side of the great chasm with you? But in actuality, this is about more than having some fun with you here for a short while. Where we come from, we can have a jolly good time as much we like, whenever and wherever we like. This, however, is your adventure in which we have the privilege of participating, making it part of our journey too. This time with you is very meaningful to me, more than I can say.'

'There's nothing more essential to life than relationships,' Mo said. 'They are foundational to the reality we experience. By joining together, we all have unique opportunities to acquire enriched depths of understanding and appreciation that would not be possible separately. We all benefit in being engaging with each other's actions, reactions and insights.

'Not only do we learn what we teach, we also receive what we give. This is something we keep repeating since it's as true on earth as in Elysium, although these principles are seldom understood in your lower domain. Life is meant to be shared through this ongoing reciprocity; it's how creation multiplies itself. No one loses by giving; there is only gain for the giver and the receiver.

'And so, we are greatly obliged to you, our friend, for allowing us an opportunity to be your guides while you're here. Thought it may seem contrary to how the world seems to operate, yet it's true; we receive as much benefit as you with our involvement here.'

'Well then,' I said, 'if that's the case, I'm pleased to contribute to your ongoing personal development programme in this most peculiar plane of existence. I think I'm now beginning to understand Elysium's mode of commerce.'

'But you must already be aware of how much learn when you teach?' asked Eli.

'I've never thought much about it before, but likely it's true I learn more by teaching than just passively listening to someone, especially when I'm being challenged by some of my brighter students. And yet, this principle, as good as it sounds, still seems difficult for me to accept in a world where it appears everyone wants to take rather than give.'

'And that's why so few truly receive,' Mo said, 'there's a big difference between receiving and taking. So which world would you rather live in?'

'Obviously, I would prefer where there's no need to take, only to receiving in gratitude. Why would anyone settle for anything less than a paradisiacal world, if it were possible?'

'I don't know, but many do,' he said.

411

'As you reconnoitre this Mountain passage to Elysium,' Eli said, 'you will find there are many other mysteries that lie beyond. We can only give you a vague idea of what still awaits you once you are fully released from the earth plane. But even before that happens, you may still experience a few intimations of Elysium's exquisite splendors, provided you have developed the capacity to receive them from a higher vista. After all, you asked for something special in life, and so it will be yours.'

'I'm not sure I remember asking for anything quite like this.'

'And yet,' he said, 'every time you looked up towards the Mountain beyond your hovel, you were asking. After years of being bogged down in the muddy ruts of the Lowlands, you sought to find a new home where you belonged; one that was firmer and higher.

'It was Elysium you yearned for; you just didn't realize it then. That's what your dream was telling you the night of your scruffy pub crawl. Sometimes you pined for a new life during your waking hours, but never so much as when you lay intoxicated in the back of the taxi with your nose bleeding and your bruised face throbbing.'

'Yes, I must say, that certainly was a most inglorious ride home. Now that you mention it, I recall the cab driver suggesting I go find a mountain to climb to clear my head and breathe in the new air.'

'You were wondering where you had heard that before,' Mo said. 'Apparently, it was from him.'

'Of course, how could I have forgotten? But why would he say something as strange as that?'

'Possibly because you needed to hear it,' he said, 'otherwise you may be here with us.'

'You may be right; I remember he made a peculiar impression on me. There was something odd about his demeanor, even a bit magical, like he wasn't of this world. Perhaps he was complicit with me falling into this fantasy. And yet he was a most delightful chap who recently had moved from his native home in Montego Bay, Jamaica.

'I don't know if he found me amusing, but he seemed to laugh a lot with a big jolly smile on his face the whole time, even as he assisted me up the stairs to my flat while I stumbled in a drunken stupor -- wouldn't even take a tip.'

'That is odd indeed,' Eli said.

'I'll admit, after that incident I began to seriously contemplate where my life was headed. Something had to change; that much I knew! And strangely enough, it did. Soon my plans fell in place almost effortlessly, as I prepared for this get away holiday during my Christmas winter break. For some reason I felt I needed to go to the Andes where it was summer and I could climb a high mountain to "clear my head and breathe in the new air" as the cabbie suggested. But I didn't realize this air would be sprinkled with pixie dust, causing me to see the likes of you two.'

'But again, where would you rather live,' Mo asked, 'this Mountain fantasy or the dream in the Lowlands?'

'I'll admit I rather like the views here better.'

'Which is why we called you to join us,' he said. 'We wouldn't be wasting our time if we weren't certain you wished to accomplish something exceptional.'

'How can you be so certain of what I'm not even sure about?'

'Because we realize,' Eli said, 'you have a restless and inquisitive spirit that wasn't willing to settle for what was easiest and most convenient. If you did, you would still be wandering about in the Lowlands' ruts. But in your heart, you wanted to climb to new heights you couldn't even imagine in your dream. You said earlier you thought your life was a struggle, and I suppose it has been. That's because you've always tried so hard to find meaning and purpose in life, although you never did – until now.'

'That's jolly, Eli, and very idealistic; do you know much my student loan weighs upon me whenever I think about it? After all my years of education, the return on my investment on my time, work and money has been less than government bonds. If I could pay off my debts, have a secured tenured position and a good woman by my side, then I'm sure I'd find much meaning and purpose to my life.'

'James,' Mo said; 'you are a philosopher, right? So have you forgotten what the word means? Aren't philosophers supposed to love wisdom even more than the returns on their investment?'

'I suppose,' I said, 'since *philosophus* is a Latin word meaning philia, or love, conjoined with *Sophia,* as in wisdom.'

'So with this being the case, you must be a lover of wisdom. As you know, there are names for those who perform services for monetary reward without actually engaging themselves in the love.'

'That's a bit harsh; are you suggesting I'm prostituting myself?'

'I only make this point to remind you not to compromise yourself for any love that doesn't lead to truth. You wouldn't have climbed the Mountain to come here if you didn't love truth more than money; power and prestige. There was no financial gain for you to heed our call – unless you had found a corporate sponsor.'

'Now there's an angle I never thought of! I could have taken pictures of myself with some company's logo on my backpack.'

'But let me assure you,' Eli said, 'what you received here will have significantly more value after you return home as an enlightened philosopher befitting the School of Athens.'

'Thank you Eli; such hyperbole is most flattering, but it makes me suspicious whether you're trying to set me up for something.'

'If we're setting you up for anything,' Mo said, 'it's your destiny – provided you're willing to accept it. But once you do, you will know why you're here and what lies beyond. What you're about to discover may go far beyond what the wisest philosophers of Grecian antiquity would have imagined in their day. This is why you're here and the reason your earthly body was spared – that you might return to earth as a philosopher worthy of Elysium.'

'So you're saying I still have a lot to learn.'

'No, not learn; we're saying you still have a lot to unlearn. As you unlearn, you can go on to discover what is real rather than learn what isn't.'

'What do you mean *discover* rather than learn; what's the difference?'

'Wineskins, James, it's all about wineskins,' Eli said.[1] 'You can't have old wineskins containing new wine; it doesn't work. The old wineskins won't hold because they were meant for learning, whereas new wineskins are for discovery. Before you can discover what's true you must throw away the false wineskins.'

---

[1] In reference to Jesus' words in Mark 2:22; *And no one pours new wine into old wineskins. Otherwise, the wine will burst the skins, and both the wine and the wineskins will be ruined. No, they pour new wine into new wineskins.'* (NIV)

'That seems more than a little confusing if not contradictory. One can only discover by learning.'

'I'm sure it does seem confusing,' Mo said, 'so let me make this clear. Learning is of the mind and discovery is of the heart. Learning is about assimilating external information from sources which may or may not be true. Discovery engages the heart by accessing what lies hidden within. It is wisdom that flows from Source, conjoining with the mind's understanding. It may be said one can learn through discovery, but not discover through learning. Discovery is so much more than learning, but not only more, it transcends and qualitatively transforms the soul to be ever richer, deeper and more complete.'

'This is why in your dream, you left the Lowlands in the night, meaning the benighted thoughts of what you learned. You had to unlearn all that is not true to inwardly discover what was true.'

'Do you remember,' asked Eli, 'which dark night you became aware you needed to leave the Lowlands to discover your Self?'

'I'm not sure; perhaps it was the dark, drunken, bloody night of my cab ride home.'

'Wasn't there another dark night you recently told us about?'

'I'm not sure there was; at least not that I can think of.'

'Remember that night while you were camping in a mountain meadow?'

'Oh, you mean the voice that woke me up as it repeated the word *nothingness* to me. But I'm not exactly sure anymore if it was saying nothingness or nothing, but in any case, it was something.'

'So what do you think that was about?' asked Mo.

'I still don't know. It was a voice but it had a special quality to it that didn't seem quite human. As haunting as it was, there was no inflection in it, and so it's always haunted me that I had no idea what it was.'

'Perhaps your mind has no idea, Eli said, 'but your heart understood – and then you were never the same.'

'So what did my heart get that my mind didn't?'

'Is it possible a special vibration was encoded that after being repeated three times caused you to receive a subliminal epiphany? Though your mind had no way of knowing what it meant, your heart knew. Only what proceeds from the Source within, exists, all else is separate -- nothingness.'

'But your mind couldn't accept this,' Mo said, 'since much of what you thought you understood had to be acquired as information from without, rather than what you discovered from within. But that night you discovered something you could never have learned. The wisdom of your heart understood what your mind wasn't willing to accept or understand – until now. Learning, being separate from inward knowingness, is *Maya*, the Vedic word for illusion. As heart and mind unite, your separate self merges with your divine *Self*. And then you are whole.'

I sat there speechless, silently looking down at my boots; I hadn't expected this. Had the voice returned – speaking now to me through Eli and Mo?

And were these years of learning really about nothingness, even after earning a PhD? Did it have no lasting value? My mind reasoned that to be absurd. And yet, possibly I had been led to this Summit to discover what it meant to truly discover, rather than just learn more about what others had learned? Yes, that was it, as they said; to know what couldn't be learned – only discovered from within.

'Gentlemen, if you will excuse me, I need some time alone to reflect on this. I sense this haunting voice resonating within my mind now.'

'Take whatever time you need to hear what it's telling you,' Eli said. 'We'll be back in the morning. This is only the beginning; the sounds and visions will become clearer the more you view Elysium from this Passage.'

With that they left for the day, leaving me with only my thoughts.

Often I think too much, and then get vertigo chasing around in circles with my intellect, while attempting to solve the big mysteries of the universe. Life can become confusing after you do this long enough without any resolution. And it doesn't get any easier when your perspectives are deemed to be at variance with the current trends of intellectual acceptability.

To be honest, I've never known where I should stand on a lot of things, perhaps because I'm able to see both sides of an issue and lack any final determinate for the truth. My friends are probably right; I keep second guessing myself because my head is telling me one thing, while my heart tells me another.

But quite literally, what was I thinking all these years? Whose thoughts were they – mine or someone else's? Where do ideas come from anyway – from a few pounds of flesh contained in the skull? That's what I used to think when I had a brain. Obviously I knew that wasn't true now. So what else in my belief system wasn't true – and how would I even know?

As I reflected on what Mo said, I realized he may be right; something in me changed after I heard *the Voice* that night – something I hadn't been aware of until now. I realized that I began to question everything I had been taught, as I struggled to think for myself. These were pivotal years in my intellectual development, while completing my graduate degree at the University of Calgary in Canada. Perhaps this edginess is why I felt I no longer fit in within the intellectual establishment and what beliefs they were prescribing. Likely it's also why I encountered so much difficulty while completing my doctoral studies.

Possibly my heart, in its zest to express itself, was beginning to shake my mind to awaken to what lie beyond the current conventions of rational enquiry. Quite humorously, this is how I impulsively met my fortune teller down the lane. I was walking by when I saw her name on the door with what she did. Without even thinking, I went up the stairs to her studio filled with incense, not knowing where this may lead – perhaps to more voices in the air!

My mind reacted, fearing her influence may cause more paranormal experiences to intrude into my life. Yet the allurement remained and I went back to see her a few more times. But then, after each session, I would retreat back into the old narrow modes of my linear thought, uncritically accepting as I was taught. There no longer was any consistency to my life.

I think maybe that's the part in my dream where the Lowlanders would say *something wobbles in that young man's brain*. And they would have been right, I was confused; everything in my life wobbled. I thought I had heard a call to leave the Lowlands but didn't know where to go. To make it worse, more than once I thought I was in love, enough though I wasn't even sure I knew how to love.

With the heart and mind battling things out, it was either all about my heart or all about my mind, both remained separate and unhinged. In the end though, my mind convinced me only it was real. And so there for a time, most of what I believed to be true was declared by my mind's edict and not that of my heart. And yet my heart continued to insist there was a Mountain out there which I needed to discover, something beyond the graven images of my intellect.

Finally my mind, perhaps out of frustration with my circumstances, began to pay more attention to what my heart was trying to get me to see. And that's when I received my dream! Along with some words of encouragement by my cab driver that night, telling me I needed go where I could breathe the *clear air*.

And so, now here I am – in the Andes where there is enough clarity in the air to make peace between my mind and heart. But I still l wasn't sure how to go about finding this Nirvana. So when my Mountain guides showed up the next morning, I decided I would eventually ask them to explain what was meant by enlightened union.

After we sat at the table for breakfast, Eli got up to take the percolating pot of coffee off the stove, as he asked, 'so James, if you will, please tell us what *the voice* told you last night after we left.'

'Nothing,' I said, 'but isn't that what you would expect from a voice that says "*nothing*." Still, I spent much of the night thinking about what you both had to say about the voice. So where are we going with all this?'

'Where do you want to go?' Eli responded.

'I wish I knew. I asked myself last night how I managed to end up here in this strange passage between worlds, being visited by ghosts or angels, not knowing if I'm going to Elysium or back down from where I came?'

'There's no need to ask,' Mo said, 'just be patient and by the time you graduate you won't care because you'll know whatever path you're on, will be the path forward. It's your journey, and so it has never been trod here before. There is no map, since there is no destination; there's only further in and further up.'

'I'm not sure how well that will help me if I return to London. What then? I may not even have a job, since everything by then will probably have changed.'

'We trust it will, since you will have. As we've said before, more often than you wish, we want you to take this change back with you, along with everything you've discovered. That way others will discover their own destiny past earth's mortal existence. In other words, we want you to be our emissary, and not only ours, but all of Elysium's.

But don't take these words lightly,' Eli said, 'we're absolutely serious. You may not yet realize it, but it's why you came here.'

'Quite frankly, I'm not sure there's all that much you or Elysium can expect from me when I return to the classroom. There are limits to what I can say, and no one receives tenure these days by changing that. You said you want me to rock the boat and overturn apple carts, but I'm not sure that's such a great career move.'

'Let me assure you,' Mo said, 'once you come to realize you are created as an immortal extension of divine Source, you will have changed, as will most of your beliefs about life. Then, you won't be able to not remind everyone of their ultimate destiny.'

'That's splendid! But weren't you listening to what I just said about the politics of tenure? I'm paid to lecture on philosophy, not just stand in front of everyone as a guru with a big happy face, telling the world everything they believe is an illusion, but I have the truth.'

'Don't worry about it, when the time comes,' Eli said, 'you will receive the backing you require to challenge the unexamined beliefs that continue to prevail in Flatland's institutions. You can stand there all day with a happy face, but you will also need to use your intellect to convince the masses they are immortal spirits and not just mortal bodies.'

'That's wonderful. But as an untenured instructor being shuffled around the academic chessboard, I'm not in a great position to tell anyone who or what they are, even if everyone in Elysium understands what they are, If I would even try, it will likely be checkmate for James, and I'd soon be off the board and out of the game.'

'But you need not antagonize anyone when asking serious answers that get down to the basics,' Mo said. 'Simply ask simple questions, as would Socrates. What is the mind, what is consciousness and from whence does it arise? If consciousness is only a function of matter, how is that explained? And what is the nature of this amorphous cloud of

419

awareness that somehow transcends and knows itself? How does that relate to the physical plane?

Further to that, you may wish to ask if there's some underlying grid that allows the brain's parts to function in harmony. If so, what is it? These are very simple questions related to causation that can't be answered by mapping the effects of the brain's responses to electronic prods. As Sir Arthur Eddington once said, *something unknown is doing we don't know what.*[1]

'And can you just imagine what they would say if I asked these so-called simple questions? I can hear it now: "there are no good answers to bad questions." That's what's always said in response to embarrassing questions that have no answers.'

'And that's why,' Mo said, 'it will take someone of your intelligence with sufficient clarity of mind and courage of spirit, to ask the obvious questions that lead to answers that are too simple to answer. At least it seems that way when the only permitted answers are material, not spiritual.'

'I know of no person in their right mind,' I said, 'who would attempt to challenge the established beliefs of neuroscience.'

'Or who would attempt to challenge this Mountain in their right mind,' Mo said.

I could tell where this conversation was going, since I had been down this road more than once with them. So I got up, smiled and said, 'time for my hike,' as I headed towards the door. 'When I return, perhaps we can discuss more mind stuff, but let's not to get carried away with your plans for my life.'

Later when I returned, just after we had lunch and a flash of red wine, Mo was ready to jump right back into the topic of the mind's relationship on earth with the biological brain. Apparently, he didn't think I had a firm enough grasp of what I had studied and taught for years.

And so, after a lengthy discussion, he said, 'what it all comes down to is an understanding of the relationship of invisible causes and visible effects, which in this case, is what underlies the brain's functions. That's

---

[1] Physicist Sir Arthur Eddington (1882–1944) See Appendix 'A'

the approach you need to take when teaching your next Philosophy of Mind course.'

'Which reminds me,' Eli said, 'of what you were reading a few nights ago in the *Enneads*. Remember where Plotinus enquires about the flame and its source, with the line about what *warms the fire*? Was he not asking with this metaphor, what undergirds life?'

'Yes,' I said, 'that struck me as being most insightful to identify a question few consider.'

'So why,' Mo asked, 'do so few of the learned class on earth give any consideration to questions such as these, as if they don't matter? Is it because all they're concerned about is what can be etched on PowerPoint charts? Effects are relatively easy to measure by conducting the appropriately designed experiments. But how do you probe an *a priori* cause when it, by definition, can't be observed or falsified? Where does one go to probe the source of consciousness, when it has no locality?

'So let me ask you; is it for science to pronounce that something can't exist just because it can't be measured? This presumption seems to be implicit in the *scientific method* where the results of the hypothesis have to be falsifiable. That's fine for the physical dimension, but if science remains unwilling to acknowledge there is a reality that lies beyond the limitations of what can be falsified in its empirical assumptions, then they have no choice but to deny spirit.'

'I'm not so sure about that,' I said. 'I think a good scientist understands how little he or she knows about reality. The more we think we know, the more we come to realize we don't understand very much.'

'Fair enough James, you are most correct,' said Mo. 'That should be humbling enough, but I'm not sure I see a lot of humility when so many remain closed to the existence of spiritual reality, which is the very foundation and source of all reality. Is it because it's too obvious to accept?

'From my experiences in the world, very few scientists remain open to non-material presuppositions which is why the world needs a new inquisitor like Socrates that's not afraid to ask the hard questions. It's time to confront the intellectual conceits of those who are determined to keep the discussion closed, lest their bogus sophistries be exposed and undermined. So who's going to step up, James?'

Apparently Mo wasn't going to back down. 'Don't look at me,' I said. 'What do I know?'

'A lot more than you think,' Mo said. 'And before you go back, it will be even more. Your adventure is only beginning. At some point, after you return, it will become obvious to you that these questions that need to be asked; aren't being asked. And more importantly, they aren't being answered. The world needs an uncompromising, take-no-prisoners philosopher to help humanity to ascend the Mountain.'

'But don't you think Socrates would be impressed with all the advancements going in the world these days?'

'In fact we can tell you for certain he's not at all impressed with the dearth of intellectual integrity we witness in science, after being so flagrantly politicized today. Anything can be proven and rationalized with enough data thrown at it. In this era of relativism, too many care only for being perceived as part of the day's fashionable trends without reference to whether it's true or not. In fact there seems to be little interest in truth in a world where only the *avant-garde* becomes the sole criterion for acceptable belief.'

'In that regard,' Eli said, 'it seems little has changed over the course of history. The world cannot remain more or less shallow than its collective consciousness. And so rumour has it, Socrates is considering making a comeback in the world sometime soon.'

'That would be fun to watch,' I said. 'He certainly was the master; just ask Euthyphro.'[1]

'And what if you were Socrates,' Mo said, 'would you do anything differently if you found you were his incarnation?'

'I'm certain it would give my confidence a big boost if I knew I was him or he was me, at least in some diluted form. However, I suspect that by now Socrates would be much further down the path than where I am, considering where he already was when he had is hemlock cocktail. It would have been good to have him on my side when I was attempting to defend my PhD thesis.'

---

[1] A Greek prophet, engaged in dialogue with Socrates, sometime between 399–395 BC.

'Frankly, I'm not sure he would have fared much better,' Eli said. 'Can you imagine him being required to itemize reams of references to back his arguments? As if what he had to say didn't stand on its own merits.'

'That's rather humorous to think,' I said, 'but the whole debacle wasn't so humorous for me. As I already indicated, lack of references for my original ideas was one of the reasons I found myself going against the grain of my intellectual auditors. They insisted I provide more scholarly references for what others had learned, as if quoting what others had to say about what others had to say before them, was more important than my brilliant arguments.

Okay, even if they weren't all brilliant, I couldn't help taking the approach I did. I was inspired to write what came from within, rather than just a synthesis of their old rehashed information. Since I couldn't reference my heart as a source, perhaps I should have referenced *the voice* that haunted me in the meadow.'

'Or you could have referenced Pascal's famous quote: *the heart has its reasons which reason cannot know.*'[1]

'That's a good idea Eli. If I'm ever awarded tenure, I'll use that quote as a subtitle in a paper I deliver, perhaps on the limits of empiricism.'

'I'm not sure how well that would go over though,' Mo said, 'especially where it's believed the heart has no function other than as a biological blood pump.'

'But after all our talk about the inspiration, I think I understand why I remained so resolute when defending my thesis; it had become my heart's passion.

'But after graduation, when concerns about money, career and security became more prominent in my life, I once again began to doubt myself and my ideals. Eventually I became my own worst sceptic and cynic the more I tried to fit into the system. I didn't know what I should believe anymore, or which direction I should go – stay ensconced in the safety of the crowd or move towards the Mountain, if I may use your metaphor.'

'The Mountain isn't our metaphor,' Mo said, 'it's yours, coming to you from a very special dream about you, your Mountain and your

---

[1] *Pensées*, 277, Section IV

reality. But obviously, at that point your mind was going one direction while your heart was going in the other with visions of a Mountain. No wonder you were confused! There was a mutiny going on with the ego mind fearing it may lose command to your heart's intelligence.

'Eventually, your heart won the battle over the mind, or you wouldn't be here. But the mind would be far less confused if it accepted the truce of the heart and join forces to achieve full awareness of your Self.'

'I like your navel imagery, Mo; battle, mutiny, truce, alliance. All I needed back then was a lifeboat, because my ship was going down. But tell me once more about this alliance between the heart and mind. Whenever you've talked about it before, it sounded too abstract and metaphysical for my rational understanding.'

'If its sounds too abstract,' Mo said, 'it's because you're still thinking too analytically with your mind to be informed by your heart's intelligence. You need to be aware of the limitations of the ego mind since there's much it can't possibly know or understand, just as Pascal stated in that quote.

'As we keep saying, the mind is always confused on matters of the heart because, on its own, it has no spiritual connection to Source. Only the heart, the centre and soul of your being, has a divine connection. On its own, the separated mind has no clue who or what it is, yet presumes to become more wise and intelligent as it heaps onto itself more layers of useless information.

'What is considered knowledge, often turns out to have only temporal value, as new information constantly displaces what was formerly considered to be "settled." How many of these facts from a generation ago still stand, and how many of today's incontrovertible truths will remain scientific truths in another decade?

'But as you found out while writing your thesis,' Mo said, 'it is believed we can only learn from what others have learned. The problem is; what others have learned is soon obsolete, since it's only a duplicate of what someone else learned. And so it goes; scholars wishing to sound credible by quoting other scholars.'

'And yet isn't it ironic,' Eli said, 'how civilization's collective mind has never been more prolific with inventing new and better things for the temporal world. Yet all the while, the soul continues to struggle to find meaning and purpose for it all. But only the heart can give meaning, not the mind. As Pascal stated it; *it is the heart which experiences God, and not the reason.*

'As we continue with our curriculum, it will involve less learning and more discoveries. When you listen to your heart, your mind has no choice but to follow because it begrudgingly recognizes its limitations. The process of discovery is an endless and joyful journey, where the air always remains fresh. Do you suppose this is what your cabby was referring to?'

This afternoon on the summit the winds were increasing as dark clouds approached from the west coast, as I took my customary hike along the ridge. As always, there was much for me to think about. It seemed paradoxical; but they were suggesting I should think less with my mind and allow myself to feel more with my heart. And yet, was it not first necessary for me to think about this proposition with my mind?

But then, it's what philosophers do; think about everything. If we didn't, we may all end up becoming poets. I thought about the friend of mine who had recently passed away. He seemed equally adept at both being a thinker and an intuitive; a scientist and a mystic, sharing these divergent abilities with Pascal. I was curious what may have happened to him when he went to the spirit side.

Upon returning, Mo asked me how my trek went, considering how the weather on the summit wasn't very pleasant with the high winds that were driving a mix of rain, sleet and snow. Of course, that's not an issue for a spirit body unless you want it to be. The contrast, however, made me feel content to remain inside, as I enjoyed the afternoon tea by a warm fire, just as I would have on the earth plane.

'You're right,' I said, 'it certainly is a rather nasty slice of weather we're having out there. Speaking of slice, Eli; do you mind if I indulge myself in one your Liverpool tarts? It goes rather well with the Earl Grey – very nice on a rainy afternoon.'

'Sure, have all you want, although I prefer the Manchester variety,' he said with an affected intonation.

'So why don't we have both? And while we're at it, since it's a rainy afternoon, why don't we invite the Queen over for *High Tea*? I'm sure it would be the highest High Tea she would have ever attended.'

'I'm sure she'd be most delighted to join in,' Mo said, 'but there are a few logistical problems with your suggestion.'

'Then why don't we drop in at Buckingham instead,' Eli said, 'and join her there?'

'Can we do that?'

'Can you think of why not?'

'Most jolly; so then why don't we?' I said in my best English, just as the Queen would have spoken it. 'I suppose no one will mind if we remain invisible to them, which shouldn't be a problem, with the exception of a few royal cats that may become alarmed by our presence.'

'So if you two tea matrons are through with your royal musings about tarts, dainties and the Queen,' Mo said; 'may we resume our discussions?'

'Most certainly,' I said, as I selected another one of Eli's tarts, 'but before we get in too deep into the curriculum, I wish to tell you about a friend of mine I met not long after I began my studies in Canada. I just thought of him as I was walking along the ridge, probably because we had just been discussing Pascal and the difference between learning and discovery.

'Though highly learned, he was also a man of great intuition. I was always intrigued by how he knew so much without having to spend time learning. I remember he had a huge library collection of over six thousand extraordinary books, many very rare, but he didn't seem to need them when he wanted to find an answer, since the answer generally came to him.

'I suppose, in your terms, one might say he was able to access *the field* of infinite consciousness at will. I often wondered how he learned to do that, until he told me he didn't learn it at all, rather he discovered it, or perhaps it discovered him.

'According to what he told me, it all began one morning while as a child. Prior to that, he was considered a slow learner, about to be placed in a special needs school for children with learning disabilities. Then suddenly, something very strange came over him while he was in bed, where it felt he was completely outside of time and space. It probably only lasted a few minutes, but it completely transformed him into a much different person. Immediately, and for the rest of his life, he excelled at whatever he set out to accomplish. In fact many have considered him to be the world's most accomplished man.'

'That sounds very much like a *kundalini* encounter,' Mo said. 'It a very rare enlightenment experience, but it does happen; often through extensive yoga training.'

'Yes, that's it. He told me he didn't know what it was, or what to call it, until one day he came across a book on the topic by a mystic. After that he read everything he could find on the topic, which was rather scarce at that time.[1]

'I was thinking; since you both say you know your way around Elysium, I was wondering if you could look him up sometime and give him my regards. He departed about six or seven years ago, so by now he's probably deeply ensconced within Elysium's intelligentsia. Or perhaps he's out collecting butterflies, as he often enjoyed doing while on earth. I certainly hope all is going well with him there.'

'We'll see what we can do,' Eli said. 'So what was his name in this last earth life?'

'His name was Dr Jan Merta de Velehrad, born in the Czech Republic in 1944 and passing over in 2010.'[2]

'I'm sure we'll be able to track him down,' Mo said. 'So is there anything else you can tell us about him?'

'There's way too much to say, but I'll summarize a few things. If you want to know more specifics about him, he's listed in several *Who's Who* publications where his long list of achievements goes on for several columns. He had a PhD in Experimental Psychology from Aberdeen and another Degree in Science, related to physiology, from McGill University in Canada.

'His amazing knack to access whatever information he wanted came in handy whenever I needed to get some inside information on women I was interested in. All I had to do was give him the first name and after

---

[1] Yogi Gupta (1913-2011)

[2] Dr Jan Merta. His long lists of impressive accomplishments are referenced in several books where he is referred to and sometimes quoted. Additional information on him is also available on the Internet.

a few moments of reflecting, he was able to tell me much about her. And not only her external features, ethnicity and family background, but more interestingly, her inward disposition, talents, and affections along with whatever red flag *issues* she may have.

'No doubt about it, he saved me a lot of time and grief when I decided to pass on some of these opportunities. How he did this, I could never figure out, and so I decided this mystery was one of those unsolved curio events, like the voice in the meadow, and so I left it at that.'

'But now,' said Mo, 'you should understand, especially after all our discussions on the *infinite field of consciousness.*'

'I think I'm beginning to understand,' I said, 'but what really inspired me after I got to know him, was his passion to understand the mysteries of life and death. He was particularly interested in knowing more about this spirit side. Maybe too interested! Not long after retiring and returning to The Czech Republic, he began to lose his eyesight, and his body began to shut down. Soon he was hospitalized where he lost all interest in earthly life. In no time he was gone, at just the age of sixty-six.

'I still think it's too bad he didn't stick around longer, since there was so much more he had to say on everything, including scientific, mystical and metaphysical insights. He was adept at weaving new and old paradigms together, by integrated meanings in various fields into new modes of understandings and syntheses. So it was a shame to see him go when he could have had many more productive years ahead of him through his writing and speaking. It was his desire to help the world achieve greater consciousness.

'He also was an adventurer; for many years he held the world's record for the deepest dive in the ocean through Duke University. Besides that, few knew more about the Egyptian Pyramids then him after years of investigation. As an onsite researcher he even slept in the King's Chamber one night, which, he said, would have knocked the circuits out of most attempting this.

'After he retired, I visited him at his home in the historical Moravian city of Olomouc in the eastern part of the country. I noticed there were several framed certificates, degrees and honours hanging on the walls of his large flat that had been bestowed on him over the years. These included Knight of the Bavarian Order of Saint George, Duke of Melk, Prince of Armavir, to name but a few.

'I'm not sure I would have bothered to grapple my way up this Mountain if it wasn't for him prodding me to leave the Lowlands to ascend up here. A scientist, a mystic and everything else in between; it was evident he was a spirit of considerable agility.'

'We've made reference to Pascal several times today,' Eli said, 'which brings to mind what he said about not admiring anyone who possesses a quality such as kindness unless it is accompanied with a contrasting virtue such as courage. It's interesting how your friend had these qualities where, as you say, he could go from one end of the spectrum to the other with such dexterity.'[1]

'Yes, that describes Jan very well. In spite of whatever personal weaknesses he may have had, he was always able to exhibit great scope of mind and spirit.'

'Just wondering,' said Mo, 'have you ever sensed his presence, perhaps while sleeping?'

'Not really, if I did, he'd probably be giving me bloody hell about something or another,' I laughed. 'He would do that at times if he thought it may help me to aspire to a higher plane of understanding. I'm sure I often disappointed him because of my many distractions as a student, if fact, some quite pleasurable. But then, few could sustain the same intensity of focus he demonstrated, including me. There were many enlightened books he lent me that I never seemed to have time to read. He didn't countenance fools well, but for some reason, I got off fairly lightly. Perhaps he pitied me.'

'Or maybe he saw something in you which you couldn't see for yourself,' Mo said.

'I hope you're right,' I said, 'perhaps along with Dr Penelhum, the

---

[1] Eli later found me this quote In *Pensées* where Pascal wrote: *'I don't admire the excess of a virtue like courage unless I see at the same time an excess of the opposite virtue as in Epaminondas, who possessed extreme courage and kindness. We show greatness not by being at one extreme, but by touching both at once and occupying all the space in between – perhaps it's only a flash of the soul from one extreme to the other – but at least that shows how agile the soul is.'* (*Pensées*, 681)

Professor Emeritus of Philosophy I referred to before. Though they didn't know each other, they both encouraged me in their own unique ways, to help me see things from a higher perspective. Considering what we were talking about yesterday, I can now appreciate how they helped me discover truth for myself, rather than just relying on what others were saying.'

'Do you suppose it was any coincidence they happened to come into your life shortly after your surreal encounter with the Voice in the wilderness?'

'I hadn't thought of that before, but possibly there was a reason why they both serendipitously appeared in my life about then. Having recently received my undergraduate degree in philosophy, I thought whatever positions were established by peer reviews were most reliable, since they were, well, peer reviewed. But now, they were making me aware of some of the unquestioned presuppositions I still clung to.

'For years I had been navigating my way through the morass of old belief systems, so it was easiest to simply submit my mind to the contemporary canons of the day. This gave me some assurance of what beliefs were to be most regarded, so I may identify with only the *sophisticated* views of my peers. But after I got to know Jan, I felt more like a sophist than a sophisticate.

'Like I said, more than anyone else, he helped point me in the direction of this Mountain, away from my comfortable hovel in the Lowlands. But also, I'm sure it was his influence that later got me into trouble completing my doctorate. The safe peer reviewed assumptions I had, were undermined and subverted by his unorthodox perspectives.'

'That's interesting,' said Mo. 'So how was he able to undermine the intellectual artifice you had erected over the years?' asked Mo.

'Simply by asking questions; mostly strategic questions designed to unsettle me. Seldom did he posit answers; rather, he just kept asking. He seemed to intuitively know where I was most vulnerable with my intellectual assumptions.'

'That's all?'

'That's all that was necessary. Like Socrates, he knew how to draw the truth out by simply eliminating unwarranted assumptions. His questions were always insightful, challenging me to question many things I had been taught throughout my life. But what they really did was alert me to lazy consensus thinking that often prevails among the intellectual class.

'That's why I was so wary of the examining committee that challenged my thesis. He was the contrarian who first cautioned me against passively accepting the edicts of peer reviews. Too often, he said, the panels served to silence critical dissent once positions were declared and established as being incontrovertible truths, much like the Pope's decrees were once considered infallible.

'After I became aware how much I was compromising myself, I began to question authority at a time when much of academic culture was all too willingly spiraling into a gleeful Orwellian 'Groupthink'.[1] He not only encouraged me to deconstruct faddish assumptions, but to debunk the debunkers who so often go unchallenged while ripping things apart without giving due regard to the intellectual merits of beliefs that may not be in vogue.

'That's when I began to be aware there were many inconvenient questions that no one, particularly the professional debunkers, seemed to be interested in. At times I found myself asking what were often considered ridiculous questions, such as the limits of scientific enquiry; what is the essence of truth; what causes life; and perhaps the most irritating one; what is the universal substrata that underlies the reality we see.'

'Perhaps,' Mo said, 'some of these queries were considered to be too metaphysical in nature, especially in an era that demands all reality be reduced to empirical data. Many of the West's institutions have compromised their intellectual integrity because they allowed themselves to be inundated with wave after wave of new and old sophistries. Few seem to understand how to address ultimate questions which go beyond the confines of science. And so they don't.

'Any political agenda can slip in under the guise of respectable correctness, and can go unquestioned, since there are no external points of reference other than what special interest groups would allow, when seek to sway the masses towards their positions. Just because ideas are

---

[1] An Orwellian term that ridicules imposed conformist thought, often found in collectivist movements. From George Orwell's 1949 novel simply called, *1984*.

endorsed and unchallenged by the mainstream doesn't make them valid. In fact, with the world being so upside down, and inside out, no position should be immune from critical examination, including those of the critics.'

'It often surprised me how dismissive and hostile some reactions could be towards me when I got too provocative. It was like being engaged in partisan politics.

'Of course,' Eli said, 'going against the current always brings resistance, just like when you struggled against the gravity to climb here. But that's how you finally got here.'

'And a steep climb life has been at times, I said, 'the more I struggled to reach the summit, the more doubts arose in my mind. As I wrestled with this, I became increasingly disenchanted with contemporary western society and philosophy.

'Though I grasped what the greatest philosophers from antiquity had to say, they often contradicted the other, leaving me disillusioned, with little hope of finding the truth. As a philosopher, I wished to understand the meaning of life, but all I had to show for my years of education were more questions with few satisfactory answers.

'It confused me further when I met with Jan one last time at his home in the Czech Republic, shortly before he passed away. Perhaps he understood how intellectually disoriented I had become grappling for answers. I never forgot how he challenged me to examine my beliefs to see what I could find there of lasting value. I'm not sure what he was suggesting by this, but it made me wonder if there was anything there.

'He questioned not just me, but how the modern Western world interprets reality, particularly when juxtaposed with the certain ancient teachings. There, he said, I would find wisdom, not of the mind, but of the heart. Among other things, he suggested I begin to study and develop an appreciation for the mystic traditions from both the East and West.

'To begin with, he recommended I study the Baghagavita and Upanishads, along with other sacred Vedic literature. He also asked I read more of Emanuel Swedenborg's prolific works, such as *Divine Love and Wisdom*, along with the writings of other mystics from the Christian West including Meister Eckhart and 16th century Jakob Böhme.

'Had I listened then, I'm sure this would have helped me to develop a more comprehensive philosophical approach to help reconcile the (seemingly) irreconcilable duality between spirit and matter. Unfortunately, by the following year, Jan was no longer around to prompt me.

'And so I defaulted to the same safe thought habits that wouldn't threaten my career path. I returned to being an agonistic and at times an atheist like most of my colleagues since it was much easier that way. I was through with being different; who cares, I thought, it no longer was worth the effort. The world can go to hell and believe whatever it wants to believe. I just wanted to enjoy life, have lots of women, get laid, and still have money left in the bank for future forays.

'That's basically where my search for meaning ended -- at least until the pub incident! Then, with the ensuing dream, suddenly came the turning point for me on my circuitous ascent. I've wondered at times if it wasn't Jan's voice I heard, calling out to me to follow my dream up the Mountain. It wasn't long after that, I finally stopped wondering and began my preparations. And then, when at last I finally reached the summit, I find myself in an altered state of existence with two equally altered beings. More vertigo!

'And suddenly, there you were in your spirit body,' Eli said, with a laugh, 'bedazzled by our eminence. Hardly what you had in mind, I'm sure, as you scoured the earth for ultimate answers.'

'I think I was mostly bedazzled by the Perrier Jouet champagne.'

'Only the very best for our lost and bewildered pilgrim,' Eli said.

You know, said Mo, we may still have some stashed somewhere in the cellar. Certainly worth the climb the climb; but, more significantly, the ascension was precisely what had to happen for you to find what you were really made of. Although this caused you plenty of confusion to find you were a spirit, it lead you to discover all that you could never have learned in a classroom.

'As we've been saying, no one can receive what the soul inwardly seeks through learning, because learning doesn't transform, it can only inform. There difference is between knowing about and knowing. You could have spent your whole adulthood trying to learn what couldn't be learned. Even though you were exceptionally educated, you weren't able to assuage your soul's deeper longings, since you didn't understand what the soul was other than what you assumed to be the brain's sense of personal identity.'

'And so you were a bit confused,' Eli said, 'but confusion is never bad when it reveals how inept the mind is when it comes to understand anything of the spirit. For you, this was an important time of transition; provoking you up the mountain so you may eventually come to discover who you are, as I'm sure you will.

'Perhaps this is what your friend, in his wisdom, was trying to show you. No inward enlightenment or revelation can occur until one is prepared to engage their heart. Perhaps that's why he recommended those writings; to prepare you for this journey.

'Which is why we are here too, though we can only guide you; in the end, you are the one who must decide what you want.'

'I recognize how fortunate I am to have you both as my Mountain guides through this strange world; and better yet, not even charging for your services. Indeed, I am fortunate!'

'It's true, you're most fortunate to have the likes of us volunteering our time,' Mo said, 'but after your stay here with us, you may consider making a donation. In lieu of monetary consideration, we only make a small request.'

'So what do you have in mind; you want me to clean the cabin before I leave?'

'No, we'll take care of that,' he said. 'We only ask you spend the rest of your life spreading our message truth to the far ends of the earth; nothing more.'

'Sure, no problem, I wasn't doing anything much anyway.

'That's true, you weren't doing much that mattered, even though you thought you did. If there's one central message we want you to communicate to the world, it's to tell everyone who they are as a spirit, rather than just separate ego minds with bodies. When they recognize this, they will look within rather than without to find who they are. But before you can pass this message on, you will first need to discover this for yourself.'

'What is it you think I need to discover?'

'Your divine Self,' Mo said, 'it's what you've been seeking;

otherwise you wouldn't have embarked on your Mountain journey. But, unfortunately, most don't know what they seek, that's why they remain in the Lowlands. But as we've said, we can't find this for you, only you can discover the divine Self that's been there always. None of our answers will have meaning until you merge your mind with your heart, the center of your being, the Christ within.'

'When you discover what's within,' Eli said, 'you will know what's without. Remember, *as within, so without*! When you come to discover this, many will want to hearing what you have to say, first by your presence, and then, if necessary, by your words.'

'This would be quite the tour de force, considering I don't even know you're talking about most of the time, especially when you go on about all this religious stuff about Christ, Source and the divine. How do you expect me to enlighten anyone; I've never been anybody's Messiah, nor have I sought to be.'

'Well perhaps you soon will be,' Eli said. 'Lazarus needs a Messiah to raise him.'

'Splendid – then let him find one. So who is this Lazarus and who is this Messiah?'

'Obviously you are – in fact, you're both, provided you get back to Lazarus before it's too late! That's why you need to get ready.'

'For what; where are we going?'

'London! Lazarus is waiting for his Messiah to raise him.'

WHAT GOES DOWN

Sometimes what goes down must come up.[1]

The next day the wind finally subsided, the rain stopped and the sun shone brightly again. Sometimes the weather influenced how I felt, but only because of my lingering attitudes about the weather back home. Today all was well, the rain and sunshine put me in an exceptional mood, with everything in the environment seeming so fresh. After our morning coffee, we agreed we should visit the location where my body had come to rest, just before it was rescued.

While we climbed down, they described the precise details of my rapid descent. From what they said, I was amazed how I was able to survive such a long fall, even though the slope, snow, scree, and shrubs helped buffer my body's impact near the bottom. I was astounded by how close I had come to another precipice off the ravine that went straight down a dizzying distance into a great void.'

'So James, my good aerialist,' Eli said, 'this is it; precisely where your body came to its rest.'

'Bloody, bloody hell; how could I have survived this? This is

---

[1] A quote from what Mo stated later in this chapter.

unbelievable; I can even see some of my dried blood on these rocks, likely as a result of the sharp scree that likely sliced my body open while I was tumbling down. I shook my head, pondering what must have happened after I lost consciousness. 'Are you blokes sure I'm not in a morgue somewhere rather than a hospital?'

'We're rather certain you're in neither,' Mo said. 'Most obviously you're here with us, even if your body is now lying in one of those two places.'

After last night's rain, the rich fragrance of the alpine shrubs and mosses wafted through the fresh, moist air. It always surprised me how keen my senses were in this spirit body, especially when I observed things with intention. Compared to the oblique perceptions of my biological body, it was like seeing by sunlight rather than moonlight.

'That was a jolly long way for a physical body to go down,' I said. 'I think you're right; it's now time we pay it a visit. And hopefully, my Florence Nightingale will stop by to visit while we're there so I may somehow convey to her my deepest appreciation.'

'I suspect there are many things about her you will appreciate,' Eli said.

'If what you say about her is true, I'm sure I will.'

'Our informant checked her work schedule last night,' Mo said, 'and found that she has a few days off, so won't be working again until next week. So let's hold off until then.'

'Also,' Eli said, 'I think we need to prepare you a bit more with what to expect before we launch off to London. We're not sure how you may react when you see yourself; it may be a bit of a shock for you to be in your physical body's presence. You may feel have an identity crisis, such as those with a Multiple Personality Disorder.'

'I suppose under these circumstances, I very well may be beside myself,' I said with a laugh.

But then, this may be not be the first time. On my way up the Summit, I wondered at times if I wasn't losing my mind with a couple of "*mes*" tagging along with the real me, though I'm not sure which one that was. The crazy me was trying to talk me up, while the cringing one, kept wringing my hands, trying to talk me down. They didn't get along very well, arguing the whole way. After all the peculiar experiences I've had since making it here, I think the really crazy James must have won.'

'But then, considering the extreme risks associated with your venture,' Mo said, 'perhaps that's the only real James there is; crazy and extreme. But did you know you would have had guides with you the whole time, whether your body survived the fall or not? They especially like to assist anyone who wants to ascend beyond the Lowlands. However, there are very few souls in the flattest and lowest regions of the world who are interested in finding the Mountain, let alone climb it. In fact, those who refuse to budge are in an even deeper coma than your body lying in London.'

'That's most delightful; whether you mean literally, figuratively, or both. So do you think they're ever going to help me out when I go back home? For the most part of my life, they seem to have been conspicuously absent.'

'Not really,' Eli said, 'they've been there all along, watching you from the sidelines to see how things would unfold, much like a parent watching their child learning to walk. So don't expect them to magically bail you out of all your difficulties! All your circumstances, especially the unpleasant ones, serve to teach you various lessons that prepare you for your next journey and the one after that.

'But it wasn't until you became more receptive to their guidance, that you were helped to find your way out of the Lowlands flying through a pub door.

'Shortly thereafter, your Mountain dream would presage your ascent up here where you were guided up, down and across the steep precipices, both literally and figuratively, as you found new plateaus of growth and fulfilment. These Mountain guides are certified to assist anyone who is prepared to make the ascent.'

'Yes, but metaphors aside, they sure screwed up helping me get across the chasm.'

'Well I'm not sure they told you to try to make the big leap across,' Mo said, 'but of course, it's true, they didn't do much to hold you back either; any more than we did, not that we could have. But I'm sure they already knew your best way up would be the way down. They're very perspicacious. I think it's now obvious that this was your best and most direct route to the Summit.'

'Are you sure there couldn't have been a less messy way to achieve this?' I asked.

'Yes perhaps; but not with you,' Eli said. 'Had you continued your journey after successfully crossing the chasm, you would have reached the summit without your spirit ascended. Then you would have turned around and gone back down to the Flatlands and your life carried on as normal, missing all the fun here with us. Or, alternatively, you could also have just as easily crossed the other chasm directly into Élysées. Another few hours, and your hypothermic body would have frozen on the rocks and ice, finishing off your earthly existence with nothing left for Julianne to attend to.'

'Remember,' Eli said, 'the helicopter didn't just happen to fly past your body after its tumble. Your guides may not have been part of the flight crew, but who knows; perhaps one of them lit a small fire that caused the forestry services to notice your body while investigating. However they set this up, you should send your helpers a thank you note, even if their intervention prevented you from crossing all the way over to Élysées. But then, maybe you weren't supposed to.'

'But at least you found your own secret passage towards Elysium,' Mo said, 'where we could meet you. Sometimes what goes down must come up. By falling, you catapulted yourself up to the Summit, so you may be here with us. Many have to reach bottom before they can rise up. In fact, some of the highest Summits in life are achieved after descending into the deepest chasms.'

Rather than teleporting back to our lodge, we effortlessly scrambled up to begin our morning discussions. Eli made a boiling pot of tea while Mo and I settled in by the fireplace.

'You know, after seeing where my body was found, I can hardly imagine what must have happened after I lost consciousness, and how strange it seems to be here while it's lying in a coma thousands of miles away. I remember one of my Philosophy of Mind students once brought up the subject of comas and whether the patient still has a mind if there is little brain activity being registered.

'Considering my presence here, it's rather ironic how I suggested there could be no mind operating, not even in dreams, if there was no evidence of brain waves since the brain and mind were synonymous. I remember asking if there's such a thing as personal identity if there's no brain activity. It's interesting no one brought up the evidence for out of body experiences or near death experiences as being relevant to the question, as if it didn't exist.'

'So now how would you now respond to your student's question?' Eli asked.

'Although the equipment and EEG charts would indicate my social life to be rather flat these days, I would tell them, if I could, more interesting things are going on with me now than ever before. But still it concerns me what may happen if things don't improve on the charts. I assume at some point the hospital authorities would want to save on their electricity bill by unplugging my bio mass from their life support.'

'You don't need their support for life,' Eli said, 'nevertheless; we'd like to see your body survive so you may return to it when it's ready for you. There's still plenty we have for you to do on earth.'

'Assuming I return to my body, I wonder what it would be like for me to remember my coma state. Will it seem like a long dreamless sleep as I suggested in class, or will I have some awareness of being here with you? And if I did, would there be any sense of time having lapsed, or would this be experienced as just another bizarre dream occurring in *no-time*?'

'Be sure to let us know when you find out,' Mo said, 'since even in the earth body, it's common to have *no-time* experiences. In a more normative state of consciousness, one need only recall how dreams seem so bizarre in the sequence of events and how irrelevant sidereal time is.'

'Certainly,' I said, 'I've observed in the past how many bizarre experiences I was able to protract into a *no-time* slot such as I dreamed about my ascent from the Lowlands. Also, we hear how many, when confronted with the prospect of an impending sudden death, experience their life flashing before them in *no-time*. I think that happened to me too, while on my way down the chasm, though it's rather vague after what's happened to me since. So how are we to understand this; do these experiences actually happen outside of time?'

'In a sense,' Mo said, 'we can interpret time as a creation of our mind's experience, and so our impressions are relative to our conscious state. These vary considerably, as we create mental markers that give perceptions of time. Likewise there would be no awareness of space if we didn't also create markers for perceived distances from, to and between objects.

'Consequently, when existing on a plane of higher spiritual existence, our cognitive awareness of sequential events is neither determined by distance, nor by mechanical clocks or the sun's rotation. Time and space, in whatever dimension they are experienced, remain mental constructs of duration and objectified spatial distance. Impressions are based on what consciousness focuses on in relation to its self-awareness, as the perceiver to the perceived. In fact, everything experienced in time and space is a relational flow, since everything that is, or can be, is entangled within the unity of oneness.'

What Mo was saying made some sense to me, but only because of my supra-rational experiences here. It's difficult to explain this in the context of the third dimension, but the longer I remained here, my consciousness became progressively adept in perceiving things with greater fluidity and expansiveness. Though the sun still rose and set each day, there seemed to be an uncanny elasticity within my awareness of all I experienced from sunrise to sunrise in the Earth's rotation. Other than that, I didn't have any other external points of reference. I had no watch, or desire for one; under the circumstances, it likely would just have confused me.

I got up and went outside for a few minutes to reflect on what we had been discussing. I gazed reverentially at the Mountain's snow and ice, glistening in the sun's light. It felt as though it was calling me to somewhere beyond, perhaps *further in and further up*, as they kept saying.

This was heavy, counter-intuitive stuff, especially for a philosopher like me that always adhered to strict logical propositions. Most of all, I was still having trouble understanding how it was possible to transcend normal sidereal time while in this dimension. Perhaps this is the sort of thing the mind can never grasp because time is too elusive and slippery to objectively perceive without external apparatuses, be it a clock or the sun. I agreed with them, measurements don't tell us anything about the essence of time, qua time. So then, what is the essence of time? Perhaps time is just as impossible to apprehend as consciousness when attempting to observe it by one's consciousness.

As Mo was saying, awareness of time has more to do with the perceiver's perceiving rather than what is being perceived. If this is true, I thought, then everything else about reality is subjective, as Berkeley seemed to infer, since all perception occurs within our minds and not outwardly as it may seem. Still it's difficult to make that discernment until we see past what we think is real on the earth plane. This is where I got lost; certainly the reality I experienced had to be more than just an illusion.

After reflecting on these enduring mysteries, be they in or out of time, I finally went back inside and sat down as Eli was throwing more logs on the fire. I took my seat again and said, 'maybe it's because I haven't been here for long enough, but I'm still having difficulty in understanding the essence of time. It's one of those elusive enigmas often discussed in physics and philosophy. I've read a little on the topic from Augustine in the 3rd century by contemporary Physicist Paul Davis, but never was time and space presented in the same terms you're offering to me.' [1]

'Let me give a broader framework to help you understand more clearly,' Mo said. 'As I'm sure you are aware, time is part of the continuum of space, whereby motion is understood to be a phenomenon that arises within the weave of time and space. Now recognize that these dimensions are experiences that do not exist independent of consciousness, that being, divine Mind.

'I would identify the underlying substrate of time's essence to be receptivity, conductivity and frequency. This gets complicated, so I'll hold off in explaining the intricate dynamics until you're more familiar living in this dimension. This can only be understood by experience, although knowing the appropriate words to help describe the experience is deemed necessary for the philosopher's mind.

'Unfortunately, there isn't a specific word in English or any other language to accurately describe this substratum of which I speak. To understand the basics better, you may wish to read a truly profound

---

[1] *Confessions*, by St. Augustine and *About Time: Einstein's Unfinished Revolution*, by Physicist Paul Davis.

book called *The Unobstructed Universe*, written by Steward Edward White. He wrote about what he believed he received from his wife Betty who had already arrived here by 1940. To describe the concept of time as she experienced it, she would often use the Latin word *orthos*, from the antecedent Greek word *orthosis*, meaning straight, straighten or true. So for our purposes, we may use her word *orthic* to better express how time, space and motion are experienced in this higher dimension.'

'Use whatever word you wish,' I said, 'I don't find these names to be all that helpful.'

'No I supposed not,' Eli said, 'but at least this gives you a new definition to help you move past your old linear mind patterns that still confuse you. The problem is you're still trying to find a universal template for time within the dimensional constructs of the earth plane. The experience of time and space, however, comes from a higher octave that's beyond the limitations of linear sequences. This is why you think you should be able to intellectually grasp time and space as though they exist independent of each other as separate phenomena within the consciousness in which they are perceived.

'Sufficient to say, in your current body's more rarified field of reality, time, space and motion are experienced by a more pliable state of awareness. Wouldn't you say life on earth, when it's most meaningfully experienced, has less to do with the quantitative measurement of years than the qualitative content of those days and years?'

'That much I understand;' I said. 'Quality always trumps quantity with whatever you are experiencing, such as with sex, but I've always found it best experienced with a goodly measure of quantity too.'

'I'm sure you would know,' Eli said, 'at least within the dimensional limitations of your experiences.'

Ignoring this distraction, Mo continued on unfazed, saying, 'This is why time, though quantitatively measured, can only be intuited qualitatively, always in relation to something or someone else. It can never be experienced as something that exists on its own, like an abstract equation of time written on a classroom board.

Your mathematical formulations are not based on the spiritual quality of your impressions but represent time's relationship with space within the limited Newtonian parameters of three dimensions. This relativity becomes more obvious in higher levels of consciousness where $E = MC2$ breaks down to new laws of higher physics such as being examined in certain quantum experiments on earth.'

'But do you realize,' Eli said, 'much of this information on quantum mechanics has been leaked from our dimension? I hope one of these days they catch the rascals – and give them a medal for shaking the foundations in the Flatlands. Who knows, with more tremors, the landscape may one day become more interesting as new overthrusts form. However, it may take some time before a mountain range emerges from below, since there's nothing very solid under the Flatland sandbar except more sand.'

'Do they have any suspects of who received these leaks?'

'The usual,' said Mo: 'Plank, Heisenberg, Jeans, Bohr, and the rest of the Copenhagen conspirators. They've were hard at it throughout the last century, unpacking and disseminating these strange equations. From what I understand, they still have an ongoing influence with all the subatomic research that's still being conducted on earth. Not surprisingly, as in their day, there remains considerable resistance among some physicists regarding the role of consciousness in influencing reality, along with all the metaphysical implications.'[1]

'In case you're not already aware of it,' Eli said, 'I should point out that whenever you teleport to various mountain peaks in *no-time*, you are verifying these quantum discoveries. Should physicists find a way to apply their theorems to new modes of travel, it may be advisable to sell all your stocks in the transportation industry. Intergalactic travel would then begin to catch up to what's already common in the less primitive spheres of the universe.

'There's no relevance to the speed of light, squared or not, when velocity isn't a factor. This is why change can't always be measured within the constructs of higher dimensions of fluidity, where change in *no-time* can only be experienced, not measured.'

'You're confusing me,' I said, 'more than ever with all your talk of *no-time*. If you can't measure time, how can it be experienced?

---

[1] More contemporary physicists such as David Bohm, John von Neumann and Eugene Wigner have also supported the role of the *conscious observer* in understanding the quantum physics.

'Well you tell me,' Mo said, 'when you instantly teleport, how do you measure what you just experienced?'

'I can't answer that. So then, what do you think my experience will be when I awaken from my body's coma state? Is it possible that everything I'm experiencing here will all have happened in *no-time*? If so, how much time did I spend in *no-time*? Obviously, that's self-contradictory.

'One moment I bash my head against some uncompromising rock on my way down the chasm and the next thing I know I'm looking into the teary eyes of my beautiful nurse. If so, then what happened to my in-between reality here? Can I even say this happened if I'm not aware if it?'

'Does a tree falling in the forest makes a sound if no one hears it?' Eli said.

'I'm not sure that would apply as the same thing, but since you brought it up, what's with the tree? Does it make a sound or not when it falls? It's a favourite philosophical conundrum I bring up for debate among my undergraduate students.'

'No sound exists,' Mo said, 'no matter how many trees are falling. Sound must be heard since there can be no sound without its perception. That's not to say there aren't waves reverberating through the aether as a result of the tree's impact hitting the ground. The waves don't vanish just because no sentient being is around to pick up on them.

'You may say the waves are latent sound, but aren't sound per se. Recall once again, what your philosopher friend Berkeley said: *to be is to be perceived*. He was way ahead of his time. We also noted this earlier when quoting physicist John Wheeler: *no phenomenon is a physical phenomenon until it becomes an observed phenomenon*.

'The tree in the forest is another example of the particle/wave phenomena of subatomic physics which acknowledges there must first be conscious observation to collapse the wave before anything can be experientially manifested. Since you are conscious of what is happening to you, what you experience must be real for you, even if you don't remember it later. The wave/particle event is well understood by physicists, but in more rarified dimensions of awareness, the principle can easily be observed and understood. In fact, nothing is more obvious than that in Elysium.'

'Give me an example of what's so obvious there, I asked.'

'Let's say you wish to manifest a dwelling,' he said, 'then the energy particles immediately manifest according to the wave pattern you created with your thought's intent.'

'And I must say, you both did a most splendid job creating this cabin.'

'I'm pleased you appreciate all our hard work,' Eli said, 'but we can't take all the credit for the design; we merely patterned it after your vision for a scaled down version of Skoki Lodge.[1]'

'That sounds rather familiar. Ah yes, of course, I remember that's where I once stayed, deeply ensconced in the heart of the Canadian Rockies. A few years after, our British royalty arrived there for their honeymoon. They may even have slept in the same bed as my girlfriend and I warmed up for them.

'A most pleasant stay it was, so I'm particularly impressed how well you replicated things. Though not nearly as spacious, it still has that same charming alpine feel. I especially enjoy having the loft upstairs all to myself, at least until my visitor decides to return again.'

'Actually we didn't manifest this ex nihilo. We did some improvising while waiting for you to awaken from your slumber below in the ravine. We even did some hammer and nails manual finishing work for old time's sake. Obviously we had to manifest the materials first since there weren't any hardware stores in the neighbourhood. We even added the deck and railing, since we know how much you enjoy sitting outside.'

'Much appreciated! But tell me, what's going to happen to this little alpine gem after we leave? I've grown rather attached to it; perhaps you can rent it to me later when I return to the earth plane.'

'I'm sure it will be long gone before you ever return here in your mortal body,' Mo said. 'When there is no one to hold the field of the energetic pattern that's been consciously manifested, the pattern eventually weakens and its form simply transitions into the field as pure, unformed energy. This is like a chunk of solid ice that melts, liquidates

---

[1] Prince William and Princess Kate also stayed at Skoki Lodge on their honeymoon. (See www:skoki.com for photos)

and then dissolves as a mist dissipating into the air without form, only the invisible energy of hydrogen and oxygen atoms.

'And so, if aligned beings remain in the cabin from time to time, they're presence continues to engage with the underlying vibratory octave of the form, which is why the visible pattern doesn't deteriorate or dissipate. Yet its manifestation can only be experienced by those existing within the holon of the conscious field in which it was created.'

'That's too bad it won't be here for me or anyone else on earth.'

'Not unless you're able to notch up your receptivity to synchronize with this dimensional plane,' Eli said. 'But by then it will likely be long gone.

The next morning we began to seriously discuss our upcoming visit to London. I was more curious than ever about the state of my poor body, especially after yesterday's review of its long trajectory down the precipitous chasm walls. And of course, I was still curious about seeing my nurse, hoping I wouldn't be disappointed. In any case, there was no sense in keeping her waiting but she would still have to wait considerably longer if she wished to know what once was in my physical body – should I return.

'In the interests of scientific inquiry,' I asked Eli, 'would Julianne have any sexual appeal to me since I'm now on a different vibratory plan than her?'

'Would or could?' Eli asked. 'Do you still have a body, or does only the physical one count? The bigger question is whether sexual impulse comes from your consciousness or is it just a chemical reaction that occurs in your physical body?'

'I've always assumed it's just a chemical animal drive to keep the species going, just as it does with all nature, regardless of form or consciousness.'

'Not that it's any of my business, but didn't you already say your invisible friend was able to evoke a certain something within you during her last visit to you in the cabin?'

'Maybe,' I said, 'but Julianne's on earth, not here. So why do you need to know?'

'I don't, but I thought you did since you are asking us about the current state of your libido. Obviously not much can go on in your physical body if it doesn't have someone available to animate various parts of your biology. Contrary to what most think on earth, no sensations can be experienced without the soul; which means, you must have brought your libido with you.'

'Perhaps I did, but what good will it do unless my prowling phantom angel decides to materialize in her beautiful feminine form, as I chose to envision her. She remains as inaccessible to me as Julianne, although at least I will soon get to see Julianne in the flesh even though she won't see me.'

'She sees you as a shadow of yourself lying on the bed,' said Eli.'

'Yes, I suppose so, although that sounds a bit backwards. But I'm sure it's true that physical bodies cast better shadows than spiritual bodies.'

'Seemingly,' Mo said, 'but one's essence always casts the shadows of reality in all you do and say. The shadow is the temporal manifestation; the essence is always the non-temporal, eternal substance. Or as Eddington once again stated it so eloquently: *substance melted into shadows.*'

'I would say is a most enigmatic, if not peculiar choice of words. Nevertheless, I remain a bit concerned about what it will be like for me to perceive this so called shadow of my essence.'

'Ever watched your body on a video?' Eli asked. 'That's just a representation of you. In fact, rather than a video, he'll seem more like a still photo, since he's very still indeed. But what we want you to take away from this encounter, is a lasting impression that your physical body isn't who you are, so that when you return to tell your story, you can claim to have witnessed your unconscious body being separate from your conscious soul.'

'I'd be crazy to reveal that, especially in my Philosophy of Mind class.'

'Maybe,' Eli said, 'but as I've repeatedly stated, you already are a bit crazy, it's why everyone in Élysées you know loves you so much. Who else would attempt such an insane stunt as this expedition? We're rather certain that someday you will be just as crazy and/or courageous to disclose everything in class or in some philosophical symposium about your life here. I'm sure that would be most jolly to watch – perhaps we'll drop in to watch.'

'Yes, of course,' I said, 'you're certainly welcome to attend should I wish to tell my class that I went to the top of a Mountain in the Andes to chat with two light orbs who suddenly morphed into humanoid forms. And then, if that's not enough, they pulled out a couple of bottles of bubbly champagne we shared. And, oh by the way, they are here now sitting somewhere in the back row, critiquing my presentation. That would be good comedy, but not sure it would be a great career move should I say it with a straight face.'

'We hope you will tell your story with whatever face you wish,' Mo said. 'In fact, we want you to do more than tell your story as an interesting anecdote. We'd like you to give some verifiable proof of whatever you witness at the hospital. So when we go there, be sure to take some mental note of things such as names of patients and dates that are on the whiteboards, along with information about which nurses and personnel were working that shift. Remember, you're not supposed to know any of this; you're unconscious, right? So we want you to remember whatever can be objectively verified after you return to your body.

'As long as you access *the field* of your memories, we're sure you will remember everything you wish to recall. But we would also like you to record on paper everything after we return later. There's a reason for doing this that you don't need to know now. With these observations, you will make a convincing case for the validity of your OBE. Many will be interested in hearing this evidence, although there will likely be several others who would rather not know if it goes contrary to their beliefs. Your sceptical friends, who pride themselves in seeing through everything, especially the paranormal, will be eager to debunk you. So why not have some fun with this and provide them a challenge that will leave them stumped.'

'Should I be foolish enough to try this, I would need someone to verify the facts. Since you'd be off somewhere in your own world, who would be there to help me?'

'Julianne could,' Eli said, 'provided she wanted to. But if she was suspicious you were using this as a ploy to keep her interested in you, she may not.'

'Believe me, I can think of better ways to keep her interested.'

'That's what we're concerned about,' Mo said. 'We suggest you save whatever special ways you have until you've established in a congenial relationship with her. But while you are in spirit, see if you can find a way to get through to her without spooking her. If you do, she will then realize you were trying to get her attention. That may endear you to her because it would show you cared enough to try to communicate. So do you think you can pull this off using only your etheric charm?'

'That would be different,' I said with a roguish smirk. 'Generally I rely on my other charms to pull things off.'

'Then this will be a new challenge for you,' he said. 'As open minded as Julianne may be, she might be sceptical of your claims of being out of your body. Remember she's in a profession where they are busy with more immediate matters and often dismiss the reports of patients who speak of their OBEs and/or NDEs. Reports of tunnels of light, relatives and angels are a little too far out to take seriously.

'But then, in fairness, it's hardly their domain of concern. Still it's unfortunate so many medical professionals are notoriously closed minded about anything outside their scientific purview. Some become condescending towards patients who claim various life transforming encounters while unconscious. That's why they have chaplains on staff to deal with these side issues that have little relevance to them.

'Of course, the prevalence of morphine and other chemicals administered to allay pain is always a convenient explanation for whatever purported *fantasy* may seemingly occur in the patience's mind. Much of medical training and practice is considered to be based on hard empirical science without reference to spiritual influences. It's not always the case, but often those taking this approach are outwardly dismissive of the extensive research that has been conducted in this area.[1]

They are the ones who are most convinced the body is nothing more than a marvellous machine, containing an intricate biological network of matter, with no further requirement for a spirit.'

---

[1] As indicated in a footnote in Chapter 17, The Newton Institute has compiled much comprehensive statistical research over the decades in the area of near death experiences and life in between lives.

'Much like most scientists today,' I said, 'but I thought we were talking about Julianne, not medical science.'

'Of course,' Mo said, 'but on this subject, both are related. Julianne is among a newer generation of health care workers tending to be more open in exploring new preventive health alternatives and regimens. She is also coming to appreciate there may be a legitimate place for spirituality as a complementary approach to health treatment.

'This is why she is so committed to you. She realizes there isn't much more the doctors can do for you, except to wait things out while your body remains on life support, since there is no pill to wake you up.'

'Because of her increasing openness,' Eli said, 'she would be an ideal accomplice if she took it upon herself to verify your observations with the hospital records. That way she'll know you weren't just dreaming these experiences up.'

'Could you be more explicit how I'm supposed to know all these details when I return; what if I don't even remember being out of the body?'

'Don't worry, we'll find one way for you to remember. A good start however is for you to make daily entries in your journal.'

'I don't have a journal.'

'Then start one. You'll need it one day. A journal is already being written and stashed away in the *Universal Field of Conscious*. But we'll still have to figure out how you're going to access this field when you return. I'm sure we'll come up with something.'

'Such as what?' I asked.

'I suppose we could try some very graphic recurring dreams of certain things that happened here. That may soften your resistance to accessing the field.'

'You can do that?'

'No, not really, but some of the angel guides closest to you are very good at that. It's kind of like a parent whispering into their child's ear at night. In a sense, they already did this to help you dream your big dream which ultimately led you here, so I'm sure they can help you with this too.'

'And possibly not just your celestial friends,' Eli said. 'If all goes well between you and Julianne, don't be surprised if she plays a significant role in this. She's been studying psychology on her own the last couple of years, hoping to someday become a Psychiatrist or Psychologist. Her main interest at this time is Jung, reading what she can, although she still has much to learn. If she could afford it, she would probably enrol at university again.'

'Who knows,' Mo said, 'one day she may analyse you through regressions, provided you allowed her to do this. Do you think you would?'

'It all depends. If she wants to do this while I'm on her couch, I may be open to almost any suggestion she has to offer.'

'Ah, James,' Eli said, 'perhaps we need to take another break. May I suggest you start to read some Jung tonight? I'll leave you a copy of *Synchronicity* on the mantle; so you can discuss it with her someday – on or off her couch.'

'And by the way,' Mo said; 'we have something special for you; a leather portfolio binder that has your initials engraved in it. We ordered it so you can record what you witness at the hospital. We don't have a laptop, but we can find you a few pens. We'd also like you to journal everything that has happened to you here of significance, including our discussions. The binder is expandable so you can insert additional pages. Before you return, we think there's much you'll want to say. With you now being in this increasingly lucid state, you may be surprised how much you will recall in explicit detail.

'*Buenas noches amigo,*' he said, as he handed me my gift. 'See you in morning.' Without having a chance to say anything, not even thanks; they stepped out the door and were gone for the night.

CHAPTER 21

PREPARING FOR LIFTOFF

A good head and a good heart are always a formidable combination[1]

The next day thing got a bit testy. All was normal through our normal morning discussions; when suddenly midway through, Mo asked me if I had stated my journal entries. I hadn't, but then, I hadn't fully agreed to it either. I wasn't averse to a little writing since I was already planning to make a few notes to help me crystallize my thoughts on what we were discussing. But what he seemed to be proposing, was much more ambitious with far reaching implications.

In the past, they suggested I may wish to write about my adventures here, but now they wanted me to begin everything while I was here, rather than wait until I returned home. Unfortunately, I tend to push back if I feel I'm being pressured to do anything that wasn't first my idea, unless it's related to what I'm being paid to do at work.

So when Mo suggested I had much to write about just to get caught up with the present, I became a bit defensive.

'There's much that has happened,' he said, 'and there will soon be much more, so now's the time to get started.'

---

[1] Nelson Mandela (1918-2013)

'Don't fret,' I said, 'I'll get around to it when I'm ready. But it won't be volumes, probably more of an outline of our discussions.'

'Then that would hardly be worth writing,' he said. 'Do you intend to publish your life autobiography as just an outline too? Is that all your life will be; just a sketch of what it could have been?'

Mo could become rather overbearing at times, especially when he felt strongly about something.

'I think what Mo is suggesting,' Eli said, 'is that it would be helpful to recount all your impressions in great depth. You know – all the things you were feeling, thinking and doing as you ascended the Mountain, and then what happened after you became aware you were in spirit form.'

'At this time I have no intention of scribing the tales of *James in Wonderland* for the public to read. Perhaps one day I'll write something when the time is more appropriate. For now though, I still have an illustrious career to consider.'

'Illustrious?' Mo said. 'It didn't sound all that illustrious the way you were describing it. Regardless, since scholars write books about what they think, it would be most appropriate for you, as a scholar, to write a book regarding your thoughts of being here. There are already enough abstruse books written by philosophers on subjects no one cares about. At least, what you would have to say has relevance to the masses who don't understand anything about life after death or why they came to earth.

'Really James, are there not more significant things to write about than revised syllogisms and modalities of logic? In the words of Hamlet: *There are more things in heaven and earth, Horatio, than are dreamt of in your philosophy.*[1] You may wish to consider this while teaching your classes about the nature of the universe. What Hamlet refers to as being *more* goes far beyond current philosophical enquiry.'

'Mo makes a good point,' Eli said; 'by the time you return home, you will have more of Shakespeare's *heaven and earth* to write about *than are dreamt of in your philosophy*. Besides, wouldn't you want to be known as the ultimate adventure writer?'

'I don't know, being a writer is over-rated unless it makes you

---

[1] William Shakespeare, *Hamlet*, Act 1, Scene 5

rich. I've written enough articles in adventure magazines to know that doesn't happen very often. Besides, scholars are expected to write scholarly books. Writing about my experiences here would be judged as anything but scholarly. So either I write about my adventures as pure fantasy fiction or I write an academic treatise on the subject of delusions, but I'm not sure it could be both.'

'Compared with your life in the Lowlands,' Mo said, 'I'm sure there are times when your experiences here would be considered delusional. Teleporting would be one such example. But this dimension is not about fantasy or delusion. Truth is truth and if you don't write about the truth about this side of life, then who will? No one will ever be able to tell your story like you because this is your story complete with your inimitable impressions and beliefs. It is yours and no one else's.'

'But you're not alone,' Eli said, 'there are plenty of others who have written about their own fascinating OBEs and there are many others who would tell their stories too once they had the courage to do so. As a philosopher that's not afraid to speak out, you could inspire others to tell of their experiences on this side.

'In fact, what you have to tell the world will be considered even more fascinating than their stories, since your experiences here, rather than being for only a few minutes, will have extended over a lengthy period of time. Not to mention all the experiences you haven't yet had -- perhaps more wonderful than you can imagine,' he smiled.'

'Well that may be fine for you to say, but I'm not you. Most certainly it would get me blacklisted, as soon as copies hit the stands. And then no institution thereafter would ever consider me for tenure since universities are infamously sensitive about how they are regarded. Endowments depend on it, and so if I was considered a risk to their reputation, it would be all over for me.

'So gents, I'm sure you must understand my position and why I need to be very careful on how I am perceived as a scholar, especially one who doesn't countenance fantasies. I didn't study for over ten years so I would end up flogging manuscripts of my strange story on the street corners of London, along with the jugglers and fire breathers.'

I could tell my cavalier comments were beginning to annoy Mo. He got up, walked over to the stove and poured hot water into the tea pot without saying anything. Then he pointed at me and said, 'fine, and where will you be in the history books, my friend?'

'Well I didn't exactly mean –'

'It doesn't matter,' he said gruffly; 'I don't even think you have what it takes.'

'Oh really,' I said, a little shocked and astonished with his directness, 'and why not?'

He walked back to his seat and put the pot down to let it steep in the pot. Then he looked at me with a mischievous smile and said, 'because I know you have what it takes. I don't even have to think about it.'

'Oh, well then, that's good to know, but what is it you think I have?'

'What I said: what it takes.'

'What I think Mo means,' Eli said, 'is that you have the ability to make a significant impact on the world – provided you choose to do what it takes. That's why we're strongly encouraging you to begin making your journal entries as material for your future books. When you choose to print them is up to you.

'Believe me, the best is yet to come. Over time you will not only have recorded much of what you experienced here, but what you will have discovered about yourself and the spiritual realm of existence. Then just watch! We predict this will create quite the stir as you reveal to the world what you know about the ultimate nature of reality. It could make heaven one hell of a story!'

'Sorry, but I know nothing of heaven or hell – never been to either.'

'Before you leave this plane of existence,' Mo said, 'you will have experienced something of heaven. As for hell, you already know what that's like without Elysium's presence. If you allow, your mission could turn into a much vaster project than you could believe in bringing Elysium's light to the world. And don't worry, we'll be there with you to lead, guide and assist you, along with other companions you may find in the world to help you.'

'It may be several years,' Mo said, 'but we expect your story will eventually spread in ways that may astonish you. But it's imperative you begin your story now. Once you return to your earthly body, it may be too late.'

'You're putting a lot of pressure on me. Writing a book is not what I came to do when I planned this expedition. I came to climb a mountain in the Andes.'

'And what about the Mountain you climbed in your dream,' Mo said, 'or have you forgotten? Do you think that was about exercise? Or was it about, as your cabbie put it, breathing in the *new air*, the *prana* of enlightenment?'

'To be honest, I wasn't thinking about that dream or my cabbie when I made my travel arrangements; I came to get away from the dreary London winter by having a climbing adventure below the equator. But then, why not; so much the better if I can pick up some enlightenment on the way through. That may help when I'm teaching my classes again. I was wondering though, if your teachings are so enlightened, why don't I feel like Buddha?'

'Because you're neither Buddha, nor enlightened for that matter. However, when discover how to unite your heart with your mind; you may begin to feel like the Buddha, with or without a Bodhi tree. Should this happen, it won't be the result of our teachings; we're merely here to help prepare you to find your own way.'

'In fact the only thing we can teach,' Eli said, 'is a little inter-dimensional cosmology, a few card tricks, clever chess moves, some cords on my guitar and an appreciation for our collection of exotic wines. The rest is up to you. Your enlightenment, however, will require more than fine sounding words since divine consciousness can only be achieved by experiencing union with Source. That's the kind of thing you can never learn, only discover.

'How enlightenment comes is often serendipitous; once the mind and heart unite in the divine, it may be experienced differently. Only love can dissipate the fear that perpetrates the illusion of who you aren't. When the ego dross is gone, all that's left is you; your Self.'

'That sounds delightful,' I said, 'but with all the loving I've had, I should be the Buddha by now.'

'But since we know you aren't,' Mo said; 'you may wish to reconsider what love is and what it's not. When you find it, you will see from the heights of new vistas your academic training could never have brought you. Then you may inspire others to ascend their own sacred Mountains. Though their paths may be different, your life could become a trail guide to the adventurers finding their path to their Summit peaks.'

'Even though it may cost me my career?'

'Or, perhaps make your career,' Eli said, 'and this time on your own terms. Doesn't being on the edge with us fit better with who you are, rather than being another drone, waiting to receive a retirement pension and whatever other entitlements you may be entitled to.'

'I guess it depends what edge you're referring to,' I said.

'The metaphor of *edge* is most appropriate,' Mo said, 'especially for you James, since that's where you plunged down into the depths of the chasm. And it's where you will plunge again. This time there will be no bottom, and so there's nothing to stop or harm you as you are guided through the wormhole of Elysium's Passage. There you will discover the Infinite mysteries of the highest heavens. That's the irony, the deeper you descend within, the higher your consciousness ascends to these new Summits.'

'To put it another way,' Eli said, '*further down* is the same as *further in* which is what's necessary for *further up*. The reason so few are able to find Elysium before they depart earth, is because they're not prepared to be on the edge as you are. Even for the willing, there can be much resistance that obstructs the way. For several millennia, institutions of juridical religion have either stood in the way of the Passage or diverted their adherents away with dogmas and misguided directives.[1]

'As you tell the world about your journey through Elysium's Passage, many will be inspired to follow your steps up these steep slopes, as they open their eyes to see the vision you saw. You may help to remove whatever obstructions of guilt, shame and fear they have placed on their path, by showing Elysium has no obstructions, only unconditional love and acceptance.'

'That's most cheery for those who wish to proceed along their way,

---

[1] Religion means to reunite, as in re-legion. The word means many things to many people, but it may be closest to the truth to understand it as being reunion with God/Source. What man has done with it by institutionalizing it has often resulted in fear, guilt and separation, just as it has often been an instrument for unity and much good. My views back then were jaundiced, but now I realize I was wrong to judge what I often didn't understand.

but I have no intention of being anyone's trail guide towards a Passage I knowing nothing about, be it real or a metaphor. Consider the myriad of scripts and parchments that have accumulated over thousands of years, many written by the greatest philosophers and mystics of all time. These writings contain more wisdom than I could ever comprehend, much less scribe.

'Remember, I'm just a part time instructor, curriculum vitae in hand, searching to find a secure professorship. Besides, what do I really know about Elysium, or what it means to live a spiritual life? Ask any of my former girlfriends; they would say I don't have a clue. And they would be right. So why would anyone want to listen to my feeble contributions?'

'Let me assure you James,' Mo said, 'your contributions won't be feeble. They can't because you aren't. If you had only a fraction of the confidence we have in you, you would realize where your life is going. You know too much now, and so the Lowlands will no longer be able to hold you back when you return. That's why you've been chosen to lead the way for those who are lost or stuck in the Lowlands, particularly in the Flatland regions.'

'As we said before, the reason you have been chosen,' Eli said, 'is because you chose to hear the call.'

'Yes, I remember you once said I've been chosen; most flattered I must say, but I'm still not sure they've chosen the right bloke. Really, I just want to climb mountains.'

'Indeed you do,' Mo said, 'but in more ways than you realize.' There are many who will read about your climbing adventures and want to ascend to where you are. Even some of your old friends in the Flatlands, may look up this way to see glimmerings of a Mountain that had remained out of their sight.

'The world needs to learn about Elysium, not just fables from thousands of years ago. These stories were written for the past but now are considered nothing but archaic metaphors of antiquity. Homer's Elysium, for example, is only a paradisiac afterlife myth in the Aegean Sea reserved for deserving heroes.

'Your writings, however, would speak to humanity in terms everyone can understand, offering hope and purpose to those willing to listen to the call of their inward voice. Believe us James, when we say, there are many souls out there waiting to hear what you have to say, more than you can even imagine!.'

'I'm sure there are many hopeful souls, just as there are many more sceptics in my academic world that would prefer to dismiss whatever I say about the spiritual dimension.'

'That may be,' Eli said, 'but it really doesn't matter, does it? If you could inspire even a small percentage of the souls returning from near death experiences, you could do much to lift Elysium's veil. By making it more acceptable to speak of OBEs and NDEs, several may find the courage to come out of their closets to tell the world what they saw and experienced. Considering the strength of their numbers, they may be less easily cowed by the professional sceptics if someone led the way.'[1]

'Of course this may drive the naysayers crazy,' Mo said, 'but I say to hell with their sniveling condescension. Once the vast magnitudes speak up, there will be fewer bullies to intimidate anyone who has had an encounter with spiritual reality. No one can douse the awakening that occurs among those transformed with only a glance of Elysium. Should your antagonists confront you, it may be rather amusing to watch how you respond.'

'Amusing for you maybe; but not so amusing for me. I'm still not sure why I should take this project; I already have enough aggravation at work, so why should I want more. What's in it for me?'

'It's not a question of finding what's in it for you,' Eli said; 'it's more a question of you finding what's in you for it.'

'What do you mean by *what's in you for it?*'

'What you're made of,' Mo said, 'your substance, the quality of your being; that which you are. Eli and I already know there's more to you than you seem to realize. But if you don't know yourself, how can you possibly recognize what's in you?'

'I'm sorry but I think you lost me with that strange tangle of words.'

'It's not a tangle;' he said, now raising his voice. 'If you would be honest with yourself, it would be most clear! Think about it James! If

---

[1] It has been estimated that there are now over thirteen million reported NDEs in the world, often due to recent heart resuscitation technology. Likely, that's only a small percentage of cases not reported.

you knew yourself you would no longer deny the highest aspirations of your heart. Your real aspirations aren't what you think; they are far beyond the money, power and prestige you thought you wanted to achieve.

Though we may clearly know *what you are*, only you can know *who you are*. We observe your intellect, but that's not who you are. In fact it's your mind that has sold you short of being who you are. What you really are comes not from the mind but from the affections in your heart. They are the reason you climbed this Mountain.'

'Splendid, so if you think you know more about me than I know about myself, then there's no need for us to second guess, just tell me what you know about me and we'll be done with it.'

'As we've indicated,' Eli said, 'only you can discover who you are, just as only we can discover who we are. It's that way for everyone, even though few care to know. All we can tell you about you is what we see, and what we don't see.'

'Okay then, so tell me what it is you see and don't see.'

'Are you sure you want to know?' Mo asked.

'Why wouldn't I?'

Eli looked at me as if he knew what was coming.

'We see' Mo said, 'a man of great love who can't love; we see a man of great vision who can't envision; we see a man of great purpose who has no purpose; we see a man of great accomplishment who can't accomplish.'

He paused for a moment and then said, 'if you wanted, you could change that. You're no longer in the Lowlands! But now you're telling us you don't want to because it may cause you a little *aggravation*. His voice rose again. 'So why do you care what others think? That's hardly what we would expect from a man that's not afraid to be on the edge. Are you not the hero who left the safety of the Lowlands to struggle up this Mountain so you might see and know what others could never see or know? So after all that are you going to be the man you're not when you return?'

I was speechless; it felt like I had just been slammed in the face with a plank. Never before had Mo come down on me so harshly. Yet I knew what he said had a sting of truth. In spite of all the degrees I acquired and all the women I tried to acquire, I knew there was something missing that prevented me from finding what I was really looking for.

After a few moments of dead silence, finally Eli spoke up. 'From what we're hearing, it seems you're afraid of what the critics may say about your story. But really, when has that ever held you back? We know in your past, you've never been afraid of confrontation. When did you ever back down from a seaport brawl? Even when you were too drunk to defend yourself, you were never down for long before you picked yourself and threw yourself back into the fray. And how about the times you stood up for what you believed, both as a student and as an instructor?'

'Hopefully my brawling days are over,' I said, 'especially after that last night at the pub. I'm older and wiser now, so there's no longer a need for me to charge my opponents mindlessly.

'We agree, but there's another type of charge that would be far more effective in defending yourself against provocations. Let's call it *the Charge of the Light Brigade* where you fearlessly extinguish the dark forces with the light of knowledge and understanding.'[1]

At the moment I couldn't think of what to say, except to tell Eli he had taken the word *light* out of context in Tennyson's poem, which was about carrying light weight weapons on horses, though I'm sure he already knew that.

More daunting, however, was Mo, who it appeared, was about to take another charge at me as I braced myself for another onslaught. This time, however, I wouldn't allow myself to be taken down.

'If I'm hard on you at times,' Mo said, 'it's only to help you see and understand what you can't seem to see and understand about yourself. Don't misunderstand me; I'm not saying you don't have great capacity for love, vision, purpose and accomplishment. To the contrary, I'm saying you most certainly do; the problem is you don't know yourself well enough to understand what that means. And so you can't experience what you don't know.

'In the Lowlands, love could only be experienced as outward gratification, rather than inward union; vision was obstructed by the outward haze of material things, rather than seen by the divine inward

---

[1] Eli obviously was making reference to Tennyson's poem.

light. Purpose was driven by career and recognition rather than inward conviction. Accomplishment was about learning achievements rather than transformation of character. You ascended this Mountain to find your love, vision, and purpose that you may accomplish what is already accomplished with. But you have not yet understood this.'

Again, I didn't know what to say. If only he had stopped there, all would have been forgiven, but then he circled around again for the kill.

'But when I see you look back down from the Mountain, towards the Lowlands, worrying about career, money and reputation, I get concerned; very concerned! Of course, you can do whatever you want, it's your life; live it any way you like. But you'll live it knowing you slithered back down to the land of fear and darkness, having denied Elysium's call?

'So tell me, who is the real James? And tell me where he is going; further up and further in, or is he retreating further down and further out? And does he even know the difference?'

With that, he glared at me for a few moments, got up and walked out the door without saying another word. It would be days before I saw him again.

I looked at Eli and he looked back at me. I couldn't tell if he was embarrassed by Mo's diatribe, or just curious about my reaction. Without saying anything, he got up and went down into the cellar, returning with a couple pints of bitter.

'So where the hell did that come from, I asked?'

'The cellar,' he said, as he handed me the bottle.

'No you fool, the outburst; what's Mo's problem?'

'Oh that,' Eli said. 'No, I won't really say an outburst; he just wants to make sure you didn't come all this way for nothing.'

'Why should that be a problem; obviously I have to go down sooner or later?'

'Actually you don't, even when you do. What I mean to say is if you are true to your Self, you will always climb to higher Summits. Even when you return to the Lowlands, you don't have to go down.

'But to be honest, I think what really got him worked up was the way you seemed to be talking about slipping back into the Lowlands, rather than stand firm for what you know to be true. Whether you are conscious of it or not, James, you came here for a reason. Mo just wants to make sure you know what that is.'

'He could have tried a little more diplomacy.'

'And how well do you think that would work? Mo knows you well enough to understand what it takes to get your attention when he needs to. If it seemed he was calling you a slithering coward, try not to be offended, unless you are a slithering coward,' he laughed.

'No, of course I'm not offended, just misunderstood. But why shouldn't I be concerned about my future security, considering all I've been through?'

'Because, James, your purpose has more to do with being true to whom you are rather than being concerned about the approval of those who care more about their beliefs than the truth. Why do you think you came here; was it only for exercise?'

'I suppose there may have been more going on in my subliminal mind, as prefigured in the dream, although the physical challenge was all that I was aware of when I first planned the trip.

'Indeed, there was much more going on below the surface; as you must know by now, rather than suppose. The physical struggle was only the outward expression of your soul's quest to ascend to higher ground to discover who you are, rather than what the Lowlanders say you are.

'And so now it's for you to discover who you really are. But in as much as you become more concerned about your reputation and job security, do you believing them rather than yourself. That's when you slide down the slippery slopes of fear, back into the mire of the Lowlands. Mo sees this as a betrayal of your true Self. You know the old saying: *no one who puts a hand to the plow and looks back is fit for service in the kingdom of God.*'[1]

'Yes, I think I've have heard that quoted before, but what's does *service* have to do with me? I'm not sure I like the word; sounds too much like servitude.'

'Let me put it this way, what do you do back home?'

'Obviously I teach philosophy; so what's your point?'

'Then for you, teaching philosophy is what service means. But tell me, what is philosophy?'

---

[1] Luke 9:62 (KJV)

'As I've said before, it's the love of wisdom: Philia and Sophia combined.'

'So if you, being a philosopher that loves wisdom; will you not be of service to Elysium by speaking its wisdom? Or will you remain silent? That's what Mo is asking in his own inimitable, delicate way. When you aren't prepared to affirm what you know to be true, are you not then in denial of your love for wisdom? How can you be a philosopher when you refuse to be in its service?'

'But I am a philosopher; furthermore, I'm dedicated to teaching what I believe to be true.'

'And that's why we will want to record your thoughts each day so one day you may be able to tell the world, not just what you believe, but all you learned, discovered and experienced here in Elysium's Passage. How could you possibly be in service to humanity, or even to yourself, if you remained silent?'

'You're now beginning to sound like, Mo. Why doesn't it matter to either of you how this exposure could cost me my reputation and career if I say too much about this strange ghost story? I'm not sure why I would want to risk my future.'

'It's your choice how and when you wish to take this risk, not that we see it as a risk at all. We only want to encourage you to keep an account of your thoughts while you're here so you won't regret later on not having done this.'

'Encourage me you say, do you not mean bludgeon me? Even if I make these entries each day, what good would that do when I return? It's not like I'll be able to stick my journal portfolio into my backpack to take back with me.

'Don't worry about the logistics, we'll find a way to get your notes to you so they won't be lost. We'll also make sure everything is transduced to the earth plane octave so you are able to materially receive it when you are ready.'

By the way, thanks for the gift, very thoughtful, you even have my middle name inscribed on it. How did you know it was Gordon?'

'Just a luck guess --- I guess.'

'But what if I don't even remember writing of these experiences that I don't remember experiencing?'

'Likely there will be a time of confusion after you return. That's why we won't return it to you until you're ready to receive it. But even when you journal finds its way back to you, there won't be much you'll understand, at least until you learn to access the universal field. After that, you will be able to confirm and recreate all that you wrote, leaving little doubt what happened here. But if you don't write a journal, you may not access your conscious field of memories simply because you don't believe that's possible. So now do you see why we are being so persistent about this?'

'I'm not opposed to doing some journaling,' I said, 'but I do have a problem disclosing to the world everything that happened. I was thinking about writing more articles for various adventure magazines, as I did a number of years ago. This may allow me to travel to more exotic regions such as the Himalayan Mountains and Amazon rainforest. Magazines don't pay a lot, but at least I could earn a little extra money to enjoy these adventures. Perhaps the first feature could be about this expedition – it would be one hell of a story if I told what happened when I reached the summit. Can you imagine?' I laughed.

'I certainly can, but you would likely need a very thick book to tell even a fraction of the story with all you have experienced here, along with our discussions. In fact, as you write about all that's yet to come, you will likely require several volumes to give a proper representation of what you experienced. And just when you think you wrote all there was to write, you may find other surprising adventures that surface as you access more hidden memories in *the field*.'

'Should I decide to carry on with this ambitious literary project you have for me, it would be on my terms; not yours, and certainly not Mo's.'

'Certainly, James, indeed you are the author of your life!'

'If nothing else, I suppose my story could be sold as fiction. In fact, if anyone interprets my writings as some fantasy novel, they may not be far off the mark, since that's how it often feels.'

'What's important for now,' he said, 'is that you begin to journal as much as you can think of, and then decide later how and when you wish to present it.'

'I suppose that a good place to begin would be about my adventures on the physical side of this reality, where no one is going to freak out about spirits, orbs and voices. Then later, when I secure tenure somewhere, should that ever happen, I can focus on more of the philosophical discussions we've having.'

'You may wish to start with that, but I suspect there will be much more you wish to disclose, possibly a lot sooner than you think.'

'I'm not sure that would be to my advantage'

'I think that by the time you're done here, it will be very difficult for you to hold it all back, especially when everyone wants to hear what you have to say. Before you know it, you could end up with an even more impressive career with a reputation as being a slightly off grid philosopher of enlightened arcana.

'Driven by acute, divinely inspired insights, your peers won't know what to do with you, since it will be so beyond their terms of reference. It's ironic, but have you ever noticed how narrow the box is of those who claim to be the most broad minded, and how much contempt they have towards those who refuse to squeeze in with them?'

'That may be true for some, I said, but they're not all like that. I know many with very broad boxes.'

'Certainly there are, he said, but generally these dwell outside the Flatlands, even if they work there. There are many of these in centres of advanced learning who will remain open to what you have to say. After hearing your message, some may even be inspired to find their way to the Summit. And best of all, you won't even have to find anyone to tell your message to; they will find you. So you see, there's nothing to promote; just be who you are – once you discover who that is.'

'Perhaps I'd be more enthused telling some of the details if I thought I could inspire others to trek up here to catch some of these spectacular views. They certainly are worth seeing. I just don't want to end up making a fool of myself, since I've worked long and hard to earn what I've achieved.'

'Believe me, James, you've never been anyone's fool. Except at times; maybe your own.'

'You're sure I wouldn't ruin my future?'

'Have I ever let you down?'

'No, but you did lift me up – on the ridge during my darkest hours. That's why I trust what you're saying.'

'Indeed I did, but it's nothing compared to the lift you'll be getting later on.'

'I hope you mean financially. You could be my publishing agent for whatever material I decide to release. Perhaps you could pull a few strings and levers from higher up. Do you know of any good publishers where I could cut a good deal?'

'Write the books first then we'll talk.'

He put his pint down, gave me a casual salute as he walked out the door, again vanishing into the aether of the dark night. All alone now, I found a pen with a stack of writing paper on the shelf.

I made a fresh pot of tea and sat down at the old table by the stove. I thought about what Eli said that convinced me to begin writing an account of my peculiar life on the Summit. Though I consented to a write a journal, I would decide later what I chose to release. Perhaps he was right; I may decide to tell all, especially if I receive a sufficiently lucrative contract with a publisher. But if not, I could arrange to publish posthumously; then there would be no risk at all.

I picked up the pen and began to write as I recalled the details of what happened, beginning with my arrival in Santiago. I couldn't seem to stop; it was fascinating to recall all that had happened in just the first few days here with all my impressions. Damn, I thought, this story just might be a best seller someday! I finally put the pen down after I noticed the first glimmerings of sunrise through the window.

It wasn't until at least a week later before I saw either Eli or Mo again. By then, I had accumulated several hundred pages of hand written notes – this was promising to become a very lengthy manuscript, more than I initially anticipated. I noted in detail all the interesting events that had occurred to me, but increasingly I found myself writing a more in-depth philosophical analysis of our discussions. If nothing else, the writing was all the more worthwhile by helping me to develop my own thoughts on what they were saying.

After working on and off for so many days, I decided to take another break outside since the sun was shining very brightly today. I walked far down the easterly ridge and sat down on a ledge to whittle on a long stick I found earlier below the mountain tree line. By now I had learned to manipulate the energy fields of certain objects to accomplish such tasks as using Eli's outdoor knife to craft the stick into a fancy shillelagh. Curiously, I found myself etching various letters and numbers into the wood that had absolutely no meaning to me – at least not yet.

Obviously, I didn't require a walking stick to get around these slopes, or the universe for that matter, but when I was young I enjoyed going into the woods to find sticks to carve. Now, getting away to do something creative with my hands, was a welcome respite for my busy mind. After the last number of days of writing about what they had to say about the deepest mysteries of the universe, today my thoughts began to congeal into coherent patterns that were beginning to make sense.

When I started to write at first, I found myself often distracted by the echo of what Mo had said to me. Really, I thought – no love, no vision, no purpose and no accomplishment in my life? It seemed bloody absurd he would have even suggested this. If anything was lacking, it was his respect! It annoyed me every time I remembered his provoking words until I accepted he only wanted to jolt me to hear what I needed to hear, just as Eli suggested. I couldn't recall anyone talking down to me in quite this way, at least not since I was a sailor being upbraided by a senior officer.

I'm not sure I would have been willing to take such abuse from anyone else, but for some reason, Mo could get away with. As I've said before, at times he could be domineering, even imperious, to make sure I understood what he had to say, especially when I didn't wish to hear him out. However, he had never been this forthright before.

By now I recognized I had brought a lot of my intellectual arrogance with me to the Summit, and so my attitude wasn't always the best when challenged. I remember once, Mo told me that when the spirit is released from the body, a new mind and disposition don't just magically appear in Elysium to displace the former character. According to him, we are still much the same type of beings we were before parting the body, and so it's important to make whatever improvements to our character while we are able on earth. However, from what I understood, it's a lot easier to be more pleasantly disposed in Elysium when the world's irritants aren't so present.

Whether we are on earth, or some other plane of existence, I was repeatedly told that if we wish to be enlightened, it was necessary for us to first transform our lives by uniting our minds with our hearts. No one else can do it for us, not even God since this is a question of our free will! Union is only accomplished by us engaging our will with the divine empowerment of the Spirit. At the time, I didn't understand this too well back then, and so I often became reactive when my ego-mind felt threatened. Which is why I at first resented Mo's comments a few days ago, just as I would have back home.

In spite of that, I continued to reflect on what he last said about me not understanding the meaning of love, vision and purpose because I didn't know who I was. But was that true? I wasn't sure, although I often felt myself fragmented, I suppose because of having lived most of my life within the domain of the ego-mind, and not my heart. I hadn't heard of these teachings of theirs before, but I sure was getting to hear them now, over and over again.

According to them, I needed to give dominance to my heart to lead and direct my mind. Though I was outwardly rational, I knew my ego-mind too often remained unhinged and confused. As Mo would say, the mind is only in its right mind when it's at one with the heart!

Perhaps he realized that if I didn't discover my divine essence on this side, I may never find myself on the world's side and continue to live as only an outward shell of who I thought I was. And so I would never experience real love, have a real vision, have a real purpose or be at peace with my accomplishments.

It was late afternoon, as I thought about returning to the cabin to boil a pot of tea, when Mo quietly walked up from below the ridge, catching me by surprise. I found him to be especially gracious today, as he sat down on a rock nearby, complimenting me on my handiwork. Perhaps he was being sensitive to whether I may be harbouring some lingering grudge towards him. As I continued to whittle, we chatted about nothing in particular. At one point, he asked me what the numbers and letters on the shillelagh stick were supposed to represent. Since they seemed to have come to me from out of nowhere, I told him I didn't know, but was hoping he would.

Then unexpectedly, he asked me the same question I was getting tired of hearing. 'So James, I assume you've had plenty of time to reflect on your life the last number of days; I was wondering if you've given any more thought to the question I asked you some time ago. It's good to ask yourself who you are when you're relaxed as you have been today.

'When not too occupied with other matters, you may catch a glimpse. It's not a case of *knowing about,* but awakening the *knowingness* of who you are within, the gnosis and satori of divine mergence; knowing your Self at once as the knower and the known. As some mystics teach, to *know the knower.'*[1]

'You frequently speak of these esoteric concepts, but often they seem rather solipsistic.[2] To be both the knower and the known; sounds rather insular does it not – if not a bit lonely?'

'But how could loneliness be possible,' he said, 'when the knower's divine Self is known to the self? Then the self becomes one with divine Love, which is the Source of all relationships. What could be more opposite to separateness, alienation and loneliness than this unity?'

'I'm not sure what that's supposed to mean; likely too recondite for my mode of logical understanding. I can hardly imagine Bertrand Russell bothering himself with such matters, but then, I suppose he too had his blind spots.'

'Yes, as a matter of fact, Mo said, 'very blind; but it was his choice.'

'Perhaps I'm still a bit like him, and haven't been here long enough to re-jig my old paradigms to mesh with your spiritual template. Philosophy I can handle, since it's cognitive in nature and that's what I do best. I'm not sure however, if the things you speak of can actually be called philosophy. Maybe more like religion, but unfortunately I don't do that very well. That's why it seems so patently absurd when you suggest I tell everyone to ascend to the Mountain to save their souls.

---

[1] *The Bhagavad Gita* implores: *know the knower.* Likewise, Meister Eckhart states: *The knower and the known are one.* Subject and object meld as one: this is enlightenment.

[2] Solipsistic, from Latin: solus, alone and ipse, self.

Besides that,' I laughed, 'I probably think about sex too much to be able to do this – some Messiah, eh?

'We're not expecting you be a Messiah, just a good philosopher who loves truth, and understands what few on the earth plane understand; in other words, an *adept.*

'There's nothing in my educational background that taught me to think as an alchemist or adept. That's maybe why, even while existing here in a spirit body, it's still difficult for me to think of myself as being anything other than an external body form.'

'That's why it will be very helpful for you,' Mo said, 'to observe your body at the hospital where you can clearly see who you're not. It will make an indelible impression on you to see yourself other than your biological body. Not just for the sake of now, obviously, but for when you return to the earth plane. Once you recall this, never again will you be able to think of yourself as being an outward form. If you did, you'd soon be stuck again in the ruts of the Lowlands.

'Often it's necessary to find what you're not, in order to find what you are. Jesus spent forty days in the wilderness being tested to become fully aware of his divine essence. And when he understood, he knew what he was to do, as will you.

'Possibly you too will spend your own forty days somewhere to discover a few significant things about yourself that come unexpectedly, leading you to a most pleasant surprise. And speaking of a pleasant surprise, I just found out that Julianne is working tonight, should you wish to see her.'

'Most certainly, I would. In fact, I was recently thinking about her as I wrote what you and Eli had to say about her. But I still wonder at times whether she's my type. Considering my upbringing, perhaps she's a cut above me.'

'There's only one way to find out, and that's to go meet her. So when you're ready, we can head back to the lodge to get you prepared for the field trip to London to meet her and your body. We'll see if he remembers you.'

'Yes, I'm sure it will be most extraordinary for us to become reacquainted and find how well we're doing. But I also look forward to see how my nurse is doing. I've seen my body plenty of times, but not hers.'

Now joining us on our way back,' Eli said, 'just think about it; this will be the first time you'll see your complete body all at once, and not just as picture or reflection.'

'And I will also see her whole body at once too for the first time. Are you certain she'll be there? I'd hate to go all that way just to see me.'

'Our source tells us she will be,' Mo said.

'So when are you going to tell me who this informant is that you keep talking about?'

'We don't want to ruin the fun,' Eli said, 'for now, it's more important you meet Julianne. She recommended we should arrive after midnight, Greenwich Time.

'So are you getting excited about meeting your blind date?' asked Eli.

'Blind date?'

'Since Julianne won't be able to see you as you are, she must be your blind date.'

'I suppose, but just remember I have first dibs on her since she saw my body first.'

'Don't worry,' Eli said, 'I'm sure she has eyes only for you. Besides, she's from the wrong side of the celestial tracks; more your earthy type, I'd say. With me being from Elysium, she'd likely find me a bit too uppity and transparent. Nice girl though, I wish you earthlings well.'

'If she knew you were coming by to visit tonight,' Mo said, 'she'd probably do some fussing and preening to look her best.'

'I hope so, but then I'd probably try to look my best too. If she's already attracted to that hunk of biomass lying there, then I'm sure she'll really love my charming personality once I get reinserted. And then, what a lucky girl she will be!'

'Or maybe you could say; what a lucky man you will be and good luck to the girl.'

Eli and I continued to bantering until we reached the cabin. Since there was still plenty of time before our flight, we decided to prepare a special Mediterranean meal. Years ago, as a sailor, I acquired a taste for these ethnic dishes, having spent much time in Turkey, Greece, Israel, Lebanon, Egypt, and Libya, and all areas between. Though the ingredients were manifested, we cooked and spiced everything to perfection.

475

For whatever reason, Mo had a special knack for preparing exquisite varieties of Egyptian repasts. I told him he must have been Moses in a prior life. He only said, 'perhaps I was prior to him, and maybe you were too, if there can be such a thing as prior outside of time. What if we are the same, yet different, as one in the Source of our being, me in you and you in me?[1] What if we are more than just personalities, but facets in One infinite Soul, forever becoming more complete in each other as we live each life?'

That made no sense to me, but by then I knew it didn't have to. As was often the case, Mo was constantly challenging my mind to expand beyond the linear limitations of my rational thought habits.

For now, though, I was more concerned about our midnight adventure. Observing that I had become uncharacteristically quiet after our meal, Mo asked if I was alright, or if we should hold off for another time.

'I'll be fine,' I said, 'although I admit I'm beginning to feel apprehensive about seeing myself in a place other than in a mirror. It's giving me the creeps to think I'll be seeing a living corpse that happens to be me.'

'I understand,' Mo said, 'but just remember what you see is not you, even if you take occupancy of it once again. Still, he's still very special to you because he's your earthly expression.'

'Fine,' I said, 'but what's he got that I don't have?'

'Julianne,' Eli said, with a chuckle. 'But don't worry, regardless of what form your soul resides, be it on Earth, Elysium or some other state of existence, your soul's identity is always preserved in whatever density you find yourself. So it's good that you were able to join us here. Just think of all the fun you would have missed had you slept through all this.'

'Without a doubt,' I said, 'this has been a most remarkable adventure!'

'It's been interesting for us too,' Eli said, 'since we don't very often do this type of thing, in fact, it's the first time we've done anything quite like this on earth.'

The sun was now sinking below the mountain horizon, and

---

[1] Perhaps Mo was alluding to the quote: *I in them and you in me—that they may be completely one.* John 17:23 (KJV)

therefore, according to my calculations, it must have been close to midnight in London. If we were to believe their elusive source, Julianne should be on her night shift by now. Mo suggested we wait a couple of hours for when she'd likely have more quality time to spend with my body.

I became increasingly anxious, as I paced the floor while Mo and Eli continued to play chess. I was in no mood to join in or even advise them what moves they should make, as I sometimes tried to do. Finally, I decided to go for a stroll on the ridge to work off my nervous energy. With the stars shining brightly, I hoped they would shed some light on what may happen to me next.

As much as I had tried to mentally prepare myself to see my body, I still remained very concerned about the implications of this visit. Would it create an identity crises for me? If only I was able to latch onto something more substantial about my state of existence.

But that didn't seem to be the way things worked here, where only the surreal seemed real. I had to wonder if this bizarre outing to London would forever alter my life, as if my life hadn't already been sufficiently altered, more than I would have thought possible prior to ascending here.

As I looked upward towards the clear full moon, I asked if it would give me some of its illumination. With many of the foundations of my world now demolished, what was left for me to believe? Most of what I had erected on its pillars had crumbled down to a heap of rubble.

And now, I was about to travel through time and space through some unknown vortex. Where would it lead, other than to London? I had a feeling that whatever happened tonight, I would never be the same. That was a most sobering thought.

And still I had to smile. Hardly the return trip I had planned last fall – which made me wonder if the airline would refund my return ticket.

After arriving back at the lodge I made a cup of tea and climbed to my loft to lie down on my bed. I practiced a new meditative exercise Eli taught me to put me into a state of theta consciousness, very similar to a deep sleep. I thought it was strange this would work on a spirit, but it seemed to help. I felt relaxed when I finally came down from the loft. Mo and Eli were still playing chess, having a good laugh about something.

'So James, if you're ready' Eli said, 'it's time to catch our departure flight to London. By now Julianne will have been at work for a couple of hours and hopefully will be able to steal away to see *some body* she thinks is you.'

'Very clever Eli: *"some body"*. Alright then, let's not keep them, or I should say, me, waiting in suspense.'

'Have you thought what you may do to try to impress her?' asked Eli.

'I don't know, this may require a different approach, but I'm sure I'd find a way. I always do.'

'But before we lift off, brief me again, so I know all the proper procedures for this flight. After all, London is a very long way off, and I'm still not sure how I'm supposed to find my way without knowing where my landing pad is.'

'It's simple,' Eli said, 'all you need do is to jump on the Non-Local Express and off you go to your intended destination.[1] It will take you the distance in no-time; always departs whenever you're ready; don't ever need a ticket or reservations; never loses your luggage – and best of all, it's free; just jump on board and you're there.'

'Once you've done this and understand how this works,' Mo said, 'you'll be able to travel anywhere you like.'

'Most convenient, I said, but what if there's a margin of error and I get this wrong. What then?'

'That can only happen if your intention is ambiguous. If you're not clear if you want to go to Bangkok or Perth, you probably not going anywhere. All you need is a point of reference where you wish to be – in this case, where your body is located. You can't help but get this right because you can't get it wrong. It's as simple as Dorothy traveling all the

[1] Nonlocal quantum theory suggests, in effect, how teleporting may be achieved through space as demonstrated with electrons, molecules and even small diamond materials. This is a gross oversimplification of very complex theorems in contemporary physics. There is much online information on this for those interested. For the uninitiated, I would recommend *The Non-Local Universe: the New Physics and Matters of the Mind* by Robert Nadeau, PhD and Physicist Menas Kafatos, PhD.

way back to Kansas without even having to click her heels. And don't worry, you won't get lost in hyperspace, unless you want to. It's really no different than you instantly flashing over and about these mountain peaks. '

'Yes, but at least I can see those peaks; I can't see the hospital from here. So how can I intend to be somewhere I've never seen or been to before? Come to think of it, I don't even know which hospital my body's in.'

'You don't need to,' Eli said, 'but in case you become separated from us, I'm sure we'd find you soon enough since all we have to do is intend to be in your presence. So all that is required for you now, is to will to be in the presence of your body – and there you are.'

'Tell you what,' Mo said, 'since you seem to need more specifics, let's all agree to meet in the ward station area near where your body is.'

'It's a good thing we're going undercover,' Eli said, 'you're not that well dressed for a date, are you?'

'But if she's a blind date like you said, I guess it really doesn't matter, does it? Since you were speaking of being under cover, should we take our clothing off before we go? I mean, we don't want to shock anyone with our clothes strutting around the ward, ostensibly with nothing in them.'

'Frankly, I really would prefer you leave you clothes on,' Eli said.

'I thought you would have figured that out by now,' Mo said. 'Remember, your clothes in spectrum are *materialized* projections emanating from your mind, just like everything else found in this dimension. Matter, in whatever dimension it manifests, has no independent existence since Mind is the matrix of all that is.[1] So if you don't mind, please keep your clothes on. Contrary to what Eli may be suggesting, I doubt if Julianne will know what you're wearing.'

'But still,' Eli said, 'you should do something about that rip in the seat of your pants by mending it, or manifesting something new! By the way, the original pair, complete with the rip in the seat, are hanging in a locker at the hospital should you wish to keep the pants as a souvenir.'

---

[1] In light of what Mo stated here, I refer to what physicist Max Planck once said: *There is no matter as such -- mind is the matrix of all matter.'* (See Appendix 'A' for the full quote)

'Thanks for reminding me; without any mirrors or women here, I kind of forgot to pay attention to my appearance.'

'While you're at it,' Eli said, 'try manifesting a new pair of trousers and shirt too.'

'You're right,' I said, 'this is my dress rehearsal for the big city. Give me a moment; to see what's there in my empty closet. I'll find something classy in the aether, just in case she gets a flash of clairvoyance.'

'I've been working on some manifestation exercises recently,' I said, 'so let's see how well I do with my sartorial skills.'

Moments later I came down the loft rather excited with what I manifested. 'So how do I look? I can hardly believe I did this. I was thinking of Sean Connery in the movie *From Russia with Love*, and look at me. All I need now is a cocktail in hand – shaken, not stirred.'

'Most debonair,' Eli said, 'but maybe a tux is overkill for just a hospital visit. Besides, you're making us feel slovenly by comparison. And so if you don't mind, see if you can't find something more casual in your magic closet.'

'Fine then, I'll go for the safari look this time. After all, I am on an adventure. I'll keep the tux hung up in the closet for my next ball with Cinderella.'

As I came down the stairs again, this time Eli said, 'yes, I like it; suits you perfectly, khaki pants and shirt with epaulettes.

'Most impressive,' Mo said, 'like your managing some British colony. So if you two dandies are done with making your fashion statements, I think it's time for us to be going. If you're ready, James – let's be off: ONE, TWO, THR ...'

'Wait, wait ... ... waaaaait, I'm not ready. Let's go over this one more time just to make sure I've got it.'

'You're making this a lot more difficult than it needs to be,' Mo said. 'But then, fear has a way of doing that. Remember, it's like willing to move your hand. You will it, and there it goes unless there is some external restraint. It can't be different, provided you don't override that desire, in which case, you are unwilling to do it. It's the very same approach you use in these mountains, except you focus from within, rather than without, to where you wish to relocate.'

'Okay, but where did you say we're supposed to meet? And how are we all to focus on the same spot when none of us have even been there before?'

'Your intent,' Mo said, 'is to go where we go, so there's no need for you to get too specific.'

'We could go directly to your room,' Eli said, 'but that may be a little much for you to see you, bang on, so let's just meet at the ward station desk nearest to your room. Perhaps you'll find Julianne there waiting for you with a big smile, ready to escort you to your room.'

'In which case, I may ask her to find a room for the two of us with more privacy, since three's company.'

'Right this way Dr Phillips,' Eli said. 'That's right, just step in the NLE transporter room here with us. We'll have Mo programme in the coordinates, push the button, and we're on our way, beamed all the way to London!'

Playing along with the skit, I felt a little more at ease as I stood between Eli and Mo, holding on to their arms for assurance. Perhaps this sounds like I was being a tad craven, and maybe I was, but who wants to end up lost somewhere in infinite space with no way home.

Could I actually go all the way to London without first observing my destination as I had learned to do here? I took a deep breath and said, 'Okay, space cadets –let's do it!'

Continued in Book Two; Elysium's Passage: Surreal Adventures

EPILOGUE

The first part of the narrative is in some ways a long introduction to my ongoing story. I'm not sure where it ends, since there is still so much more to say. Perhaps it will not conclude until sometime after I depart, unless I can find someone on earth to relay how things really are in Elysium and how much I got right. Currently I'm working on the fifth book, which tells of my return to the earth plane and what I'm still learning from my experiences in the Passage.

Let me stand back from the narrative a moment and reflect a bit further on the question of time, space and how I now understand what it means to manifest in that higher dimension. There still remains much for me to interpret and sort out from the limitations of my current perspective now that I'm back home; just so you know I'm not suggesting I have the answers to everything. In fact, I have a lot more questions now than I did before. Prior to having my escapade over the Mountain, I didn't understand what the important questions were, even as a philosopher.

For example, I sometimes ask myself whether my time on that side was an alternate state, or is my current existence back on the earth plane the alternate reality, a mere shadow cast on the walls of time from the spiritual reality within? Or is that too Platonic? But then what's wrong with Plato if you don't have any better philosophical concepts available to interpret this plane of reality?

Is one reality more real than the other, or is it a dynamic of the inward soul coming to know itself by experiencing life outwardly as it manifests in physical form, just as the outward form comes to experience itself by being in-formed by the inward essence of spirit? At least this is how I understood the concept of inform and information being the dynamic of *in* and *form*. Perhaps that's why we come to incarnate on earth; to be *in-formed* that we may appreciate the essence of who we by experiencing the illusion of what we're not.

I can say my life on the Mountain at times seemed to straddle both realities of inner and outer, although I was scarcely able to tell which was which most of time, since it all felt to be one. What I became within, I became without. Which I believe is how a holistic life should be experienced.

What I wrote about in this first narrative is only a fraction of what I experienced during this stage of my stay. Who knows, perhaps I compacted a lifetime or even several lifetimes in a *no-time* warp where time is experienced outside of time. If that sounds like a contradiction, it is, at least on the earth plane. I do know, however, how completely new events occasionally come into my consciousness without context or reference to anything else, or what I thought may have occurred previously. Perhaps I'll just have to ignore most of these incidents until I know how explain them.

At times I'm overwhelmed trying to understand how certain scenes could fit into other events that seem to flow so seamlessly. In fact, some experiences were like a little mini-series with little relation to everything else. But at other times, a missing piece comes to me to insert and link to the other parts, much like a new Scene into an Act of a play, thereby giving the story more coherence.

This is what happened with the mystic voyages I wrote about in the next book segment, *Surreal Adventures*. It took a while, but finally I was able to tie most of it together to find the proper sequences. Had I kept better journal notes, properly organized, it would have helped as points of reference. Unfortunately, when I received my journal, it was a jumbled mess and I didn't have numbers or dates on the pages, since I didn't expected to see these again.

Perhaps in the future, after publishing these narratives, I will publish new editions or books as I add more chapters of what more comes to me; if it does. Hopefully then, we'll have a more comprehensive picture of what went on during my year in Elysium's Passage. For now, thought, I'm attempting to present a credible representation of all I experienced as I continue to glue the pieces that they may logically fit together in this linear arrow of time.

I wonder, though, if maybe some experiences are best left in a chaotic state as they often exist in dreams. Why should it be necessary to always interpret events sequentially, all contextualized in only one direction? What mystical awareness do we lose in separating experiences as slices of partial events moving in only one direction? Do we not make them into something less than they were, by disconnecting events from the aerial view of all that happened and is happening?

I can say now, whatever time is or isn't, my awareness in that state of spiritual consciousness seemed fluid, pliable and vast, as though surveyed from above. Perhaps this was because I had become more aligned with the essence of my soul which was far more whole and expansive than I thought possible.

If I've now lost much of my ability to perceive as I once did in Elysium's Passage, I still relish whatever *Intimations of Immortality* come to me, reminding me who I am and always have been.[1]

---

[1] In reference to William Wordsworth's classic poem: *'Ode; Intimations of Immortality'*

POSTSCRIPT

One last word regarding the publication of the balance of the Elysium's Passage series; as of this date, draft copies of the other segments have been completed. *Surreal Adventures, Mystical Romance* and *The Elixir* I hope to have published sometime between 2018 and 2020.

As for the fifth book; it's now being written by the events occurring in my atypical life where there is scarcely a dull moment. I can hardly wait to begin writing Book Five, which I plan to call *The Return.* Possibly, if may be the most intriguing, judging by what has happened to me since I regained consciousness on this earth plane a couple of years ago.

APPENDIX 'A'

PHYSICIST'S QUOTES

The following quotes by various physicists of the 20th century are a sample of remarkable statements indicating how physics came to view reality in non-Newtonian, materialist terms. (Each physicist is listed according to dates of birth). Many of these quotes are contained within this and subsequent *Elysium's Passage* narratives.

Max Planck 1858-1947
Nobel Prize in Physics (1918)

Science cannot solve the ultimate mystery of nature. And that is because, in the last analysis, we ourselves are part of nature and therefore part of the mystery that we are trying to solve.

As a man who has devoted his whole life to the most clear headed science, to the study of matter, I can tell you as a result of my research about atoms this much: There is no matter as such. All matter originates and exists only by virtue of a force which brings the particle of an atom to vibration and holds this most minute solar system of the atom together. We must assume behind this force the existence of a conscious and intelligent mind. This mind is the matrix of all matter. I regard consciousness as fundamental. I regard matter as derivative from consciousness. We cannot get behind consciousness.

A new scientific truth does not triumph by convincing its opponents and making them see the light, but rather because its opponents eventually die, and a new generation grows up that is familiar with it.

Science ... means unresting endeavor and continually progressing development toward an aim which the poetic intuition may apprehend, but the intellect can never fully grasp.

Truth never triumphs - its opponents just die out. Science advances one funeral at a time.

Both religion and science require a belief in God. For believers, God is in the beginning, and for physicists He is at the end of all considerations ... To the former He is the foundation, to the latter, the crown of the edifice of every generalized world view.

Whence come I and whither go I? That is the great unfathomable question, the same for every one of us. Science has no answer to it.

It is not the possession of truth, but the success which attends the seeking after it, that enriches the seeker and brings happiness to him.

There can never be any real opposition between religion and science, for the one is the complement of the other.

When you change the way you look at things, the things you look at change.

New scientific ideas never spring from a communal body, however organized, but rather from the head of an individually inspired researcher who struggles with his problems in lonely thought and unites all his thought on one single point which is his whole world for the moment.

Sir James Jeans 1877-1946
Knighted in England (1924)

The universe cannot admit of material representation, and the reason, I think, is that it has become a mere mental concept.

Today there is a wide measure of agreement which, on the physical side of science, approaches almost to unanimity that the stream of knowledge is headed towards a non-mechanical reality, the universe begins to look more like a great thought than a great machine. Mind no longer appears as an accident intruder into the realm of matter, we are beginning to suspect that we ought rather to hail it as the creator and governor of the realm of matter.

If the universe is a universe of thought, then its creation must have been an act of thought.

So little do we understand time that perhaps we ought to compare the whole of time to the act of creation, that materialisation of the thought.

Mathematics enters the world from above instead of from below.

God is a mathematician and the universe begins to look more like a great thought than a great machine.

For substantiality is a purely mental concept measuring the direct effects of objects on our sense of touch.

A mathematical formula can never tell us what a thing is, but only how it behaves. It can only specify a thing through its properties.

Modern scientific theory compels us to think of the creator working outside of time and space — which are part of his creation — just as the artist is outside of his canvas.

The old dualism of mind and matter, which is mainly responsible for the supposed hostility, seems likely to disappear, not through matter becoming in any way more shadowy or insubstantial than before or through mind becoming more resolved into a function of working matter, but through substantial matter resolving itself into a creation and manifestation of mind.

Albert Einstein 1879-1955
Nobel Prize in Physics (1921)

Reality is merely an illusion, albeit a very persistent one.

491

People like us, who believe in physics, know that the distinction between past, present, and future is only a stubbornly persistent illusion.

A human being is a part of a whole, called by us universe, a part limited in time and space. He experiences himself, his thoughts and feelings as something separated from the rest ... a kind of optical delusion of his consciousness. This delusion is a kind of prison for us, restricting us to our personal desires and to affection for a few persons nearest to us. Our task must be to free ourselves from this prison by widening our circle of compassion to embrace all living creatures and the whole of nature in its beauty.

The most beautiful thing we can experience is the mysterious. It is the source of all true art and all science. He to whom this emotion is a stranger; who can no longer pause to wonder and stand rapt in awe, is as good as dead: his eyes are closed.

Great spirits have always found violent opposition from mediocrities. The latter cannot understand it when a man does not thoughtlessly submit to hereditary prejudices but honestly and courageously uses his intelligence.

No problem can be solved from the same level of consciousness that created it.

The most incomprehensible thing about the world is that it is comprehensible.'

My religion consists of a humble admiration of the illimitable superior spirit who reveals himself in the slight details we are able to perceive with our frail and feeble mind.

Science without religion is lame. Religion without science is blind.

A person starts to live when he can live outside himself

The only real valuable thing is intuition.

I want to know God's thoughts, the rest are details.

Imagination is more important than knowledge.

Any intelligent fool can make things bigger, more complex, and more violent. It takes a touch of genius -- and a lot of courage -- to move in the opposite direction.

The only thing that interferes with my learning is my education.

The important thing is not to stop questioning. Curiosity has its own reason for existing.

It is clear that knowledge of what is does not open the door directly to what should be ----- for science can only ascertain what is, but not what should be, and outside of its domain value judgements of all kinds remain necessary.

The scientific method can teach us nothing else beyond how facts are related to, and conditioned by each other.

I maintain that the cosmic religious feeling is the strongest and noblest motive for scientific research.

Sir Arthur Eddington 1882–1944
Knighted in England (1930)

Science has nothing to say as to the intrinsic nature of the atom. The physical atom is, like everything else in physics, a schedule of pointer readings.

We are that which asks the question. Whatever else there may be in our nature, responsibility for truth is one of the attributes. It has to do with conscience rather than the truth of consciousness. Concern with truth is one of the things that make up the spiritual nature of Man

We are that which asks the question ---- this side of our nature is aloof from the scrutiny of the physicist.

It is difficult for the matter of fact physicist to accept the view that the substratum for everything is of mental character. But no one can deny that mind is the first and most direct thing in our experience and all else is remote inference.

Something unknown is doing we don't know what.

We have found a strange footprint on the shores of the unknown.

Our ultimate analysis of space leads us not to a 'here' and a 'there', but to an extension such as that which relates 'here' and 'there'. To put the conclusion rather crudely-space is not a lot of points close together, it is a lot of distances interlocked.

Not only is the universe stranger than we imagine, it is stranger than we can imagine.

There is no space without aether, and no aether which does not occupy space.

The revelation by modern physics of the void within the atom is more disturbing than the revelation by astronomy of the immense void of interstellar space.

Science is one thing, wisdom is another. Science is an edged tool, with which men play like children, and cut their own fingers.

Niels Bohr 1885 – 1962
Nobel Prize in Physics (1922)

Everything we call real is made of things that cannot be regarded as real.

If quantum mechanics hasn't profoundly shocked you, you haven't understood it yet.

If anybody says he can think about quantum physics without getting giddy, that only shows he has not understood the first thing about them.

No, no, you're not thinking, you're just being logical.

Our theory is crazy, but it's not crazy enough to be true.

Erwin Schrodinger 1887–1961
Nobel Prize in Physics (1933)

Mind is, by its very nature, a singulare tantum, I should say: the overall number of minds in just one. I venture to call it indestructible since it has a peculiar timetable, namely time is always now. There really is no before and after for mind.

The show that is going on obviously acquires a meaning only with regard to the mind that contemplates it. But what science tells us about this relationship is patently absurd: as if mind had only been produced by the very display that it is now watching and would pass away when the sun finally cools down ---

Werner Heisenberg 1901 – 1976
Nobel Prize in Physics (1932)

Physics can only make statements about strictly limited relations that are only valid within the framework of those limitations.

I assert the nature of all reality is spiritual, not material or a dualism of matter and spirit. The hypothesis that its nature can be, to any degree, material does not enter into my reckoning, because we understand now that matter, the putting together of the adjective material and the noun nature does not make any sense.

Is the nature of reality material or spiritual or a combination of both? I will first ask another question. Is the ocean composed of water or waves, or of both? Interpreting the term material (physical) --- corresponds to the waves, not to the water of the ocean of reality.

The solid substance of things is another illusion. It too is a fancy projected by the mind into the eternal world. We have chased the solid substance from the continuous liquid of the atom, from the atom to the electron, and there we have lost it. Actualities have been lost in the exigencies of the chase.

Our deeper feelings are not of ourselves alone, but are glimpses of a reality transcending the narrow limits of our particular consciousness.

Insofar as supernaturalism is associated with the denial of strict causality, I can only answer that that is what the modern scientific development of the quantum theory brings us to.

The mind as a central receiving station reads the dots and dashes of the incoming nerve signals.

A broadcasting station is not like its call-signal, there is no commensurability in their nature.

In comparing the certainty of things spiritual and things temporal, let us not forget this: mind is the first and most direct thing in our experience, all else is remote inference.

John Wheeler 1911 – 2008
Einstein Prize in Physics (along with nine other notable awards from 1963 to 2003)

No phenomenon is a physical phenomenon until it is an observed phenomenon.

The universe does not exist 'out there,' independent of us. We are inescapably involved in bringing about that which appears to be happening. We are not only observers. We are participators. In some strange sense, this is a participatory universe. Physics is no longer satisfied with insights only into particles, fields of force, into geometry, or even into time and space. Today we demand of physics some understanding of existence itself.

There is nothing in the world except empty curved space. Matter, charge, electromagnetism, and other fields are only manifestations of the curvature of space.

In order to more fully understand this reality, we must take into account other dimensions of a broader reality.

David Bohm 1917 – 1992
Fellow of the Royal Society (1990)

*The world cannot be analyzed into separate and independently existing parts --
moreover each part somehow involves all the others: contains them or enfolds
them. This fact suggests that the sphere of ordinary material life and the sphere of
mystical experiences have a certain shared order and that this will allow a fruitful
relationship between them.*

*The true state of affairs in the material world is wholeness. If we are fragmented,
we must blame it on ourselves.*

*Indeed, the attempt to live according to the notion that the fragments are really
separate is, in essence, what has led to the growing series of extremely urgent
crises that is confronting us today.*

*Thought is creating divisions out of itself and then saying that they are there
naturally.*

*If I am right in saying that thought is the ultimate origin or source, it follows that
if we don't do anything about thought, we won't get anywhere.*

*Difference exist because thought develops like a stream that happens to go one
way here and another way there. Once it develops it produces real physical results
that people are looking at, but they don't see where these results are coming from -
that's one of the basic features of fragmentation.*

APPENDIX 'B'

EMANUEL SWEDENBORG

Swedenborg was a highly esteemed scientist in Europe in the 18th century, closely associated with Sweden's royalty as a friend and administrator (Royal Assessor of Mines). In 1741, at the age of 53, much of his life changed for him as he entered into the spirit side of reality. First beginning with dreams, a few years later he reported his actual heavenly visitations of his soul for most of the next 28 years of his earthly life, which he described as his 'spiritual awakening'. From then on he recorded his celestial visits as he talked with thousands of spiritual entities, not all of the higher realms.

Swedenborg wrote several books with over 18 published works written in Latin on theological concerns. Many of his works are deeply profound, and, for some, rather difficult to read. His most popular and arguably easiest to read is *Heaven and Hell* (1758), a popular introductory summary of his experiences and conclusions.

Given the nature of his experiences and how remote his spiritual discourses were from contemporary thinking at the time, some considered his works to be insane. But this was largely mitigated by his impeccable reputation as a scholar and scientist with the Royal Swedish Academy of Sciences. He also was part in the Swedish House of Nobility (the Swedish Riddarhuset) and Parliament (Riksday).

On a personal level he was characterized as being a very pious and warm-hearted man, speaking easily and naturally. Many literary luminaries became devoted readers of his materials including, Jorge Luis Bores, Daniel Burnham, Ralph Waldo Emerson, Y.B Yeats, John

Flaxman, George Inness, Henry James Sr., William Blake, Carl Jung, Immanuel Kant, Honore de Balzac, Arthur Conan Doyle, Helen Keller, Czeslaw Milosz, August Strindberg and D.T. Suzuki.

There are several books written on him and his works, many of which can be accessed at several international web sites.

APPENDIX 'C'

GEORGE IVANOVICH GURDJIEFF

urdjieff lived from 1872-1949 and lived his early years in the Transcaucasia region which had rich ethnic mix comprised of Georgians, Armenians, Kurds, Greeks, Turks and Russians. At the age of fifteen he set out to wander the world, gleaning whatever ancient wisdom he could in scattered Sufi ashrams, Christian churches, Buddhist temples and assorted mystery schools across central Asia, Egypt, Rome, Iran, Russia and going as far as Tibet. He later established himself back home in Russia where he taught his esoterica under his own auspices, often in Moscow and St Petersburg.

Mo was a devoted reader of Gurdjieff while he was still on earth. I had heard very little about this mystic before my time with Eli and Mo, but became greatly inspired by these spiritual and sometimes esoteric ideas regarding human consciousness.

In the first half of the 20th century, Gurdjieff and Ouspensky brought many ancient esoteric traditions to the western world such as the Enneagram. They escaped the Bolshevik revolution by traveling on foot down through Georgia to Istanbul in 1920. Each established their own institute, Gurdjieff in Paris and Ouspensky in London, they taught and disseminated their ideas on the nature of consciousness and other arcane philosophies.

After returning to my Earth body, I've become very familiar with these teachings, primarily though the writings of his students, mainly his close associate Peter Ouspenky. I can hardly recount the many stimulating discussions we had about this *Forth Way* school of thought, including concepts such as *being present*, *self-remembering* and *non-identification*, to name just a few.

Unfortunately, concepts dealing with higher consciousness are hardly mentioned in most universities in the West, possibly because to few know anything about esoteric philosophy. (One notable exception is eminent Philosopher Jacob Needleman from San Francisco State University).

Anything written by Gurdjieff, Ouspensky or other students such as Orage, Nicoll, Nott and Bennett is recommended as significant, although, challenging at times.

The Gurdjieff Foundation has several affiliate organizations all over the world. (For more information refer to the Gurdjieff Foundation web site).